The Solitary Sparrow

The Solitary Sparrow

BOOK ONE OF THE MARGARET CHRONICLES

LORRAINE NORWOOD

atmosphere press

To my mother, who always believed

Contents

Hear my prayer, O Lord . . .
I am like a pelican in the wilderness;
I am like an owl in the wasteland,
I watch, and am become like a sparrow
All alone upon the house-top.
Mine enemies reproach me all the day;
They that are mad against me are sworn against me.

—Psalm 102

St. Michael's Mead
SCOTLAND
ENGLAND
WALES
Warwickshire
14th Century Warwickshire
Warwick
St Michael's Mead
Stratford-upon-Avon
ALICE'S COTTAGE
Acorn forest
Pigsty
Meg's cottage
Water meadows
Field #1
Field #2
Cottages
Caldecote Hall
Tithe barn
St Michael's church
RIVER AVON
Alehouse
Moat
Stream
Cottages
Fallow field
Bridge
Pond
Weir
Wasteland
Mill pond
Water mill
King's Wood
RIVER AVON

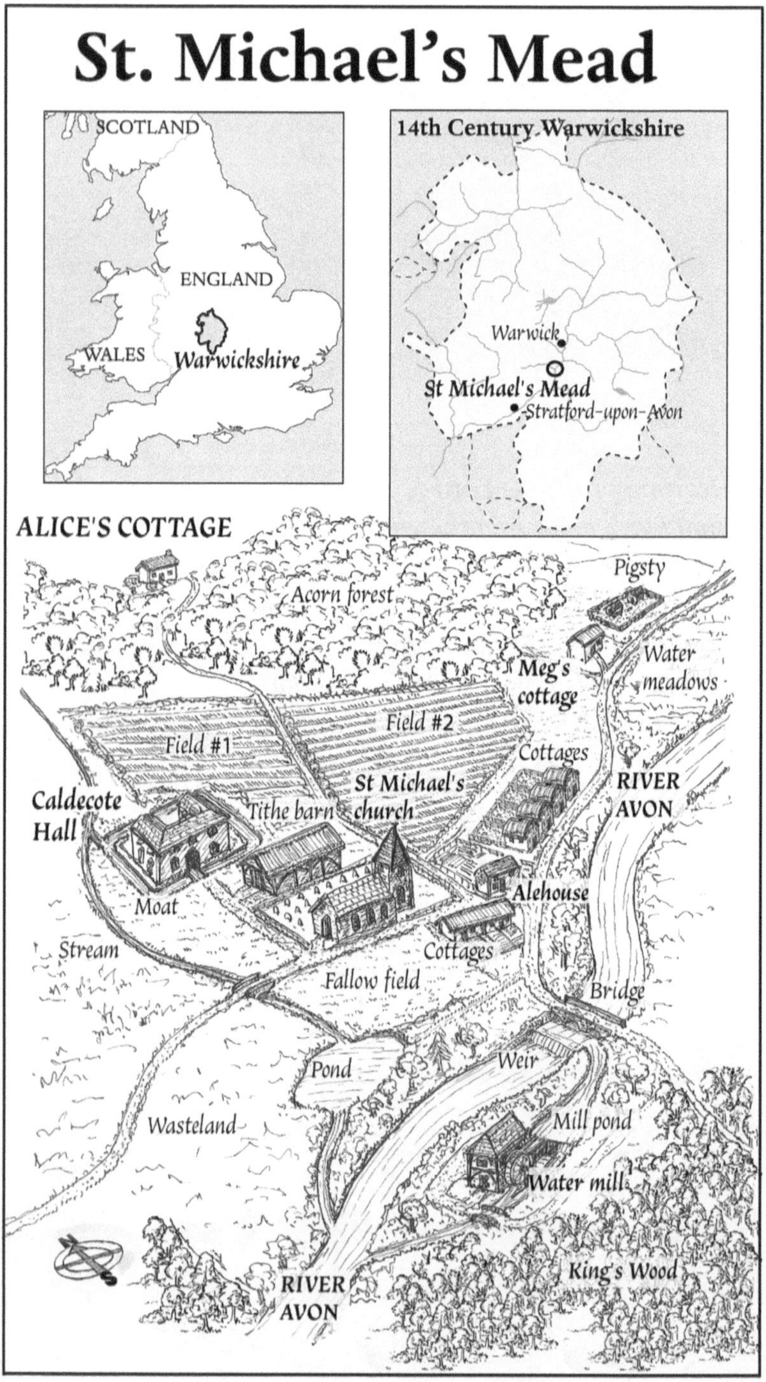

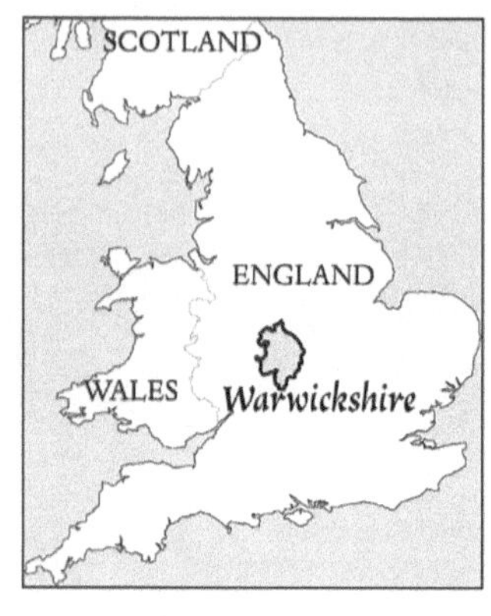

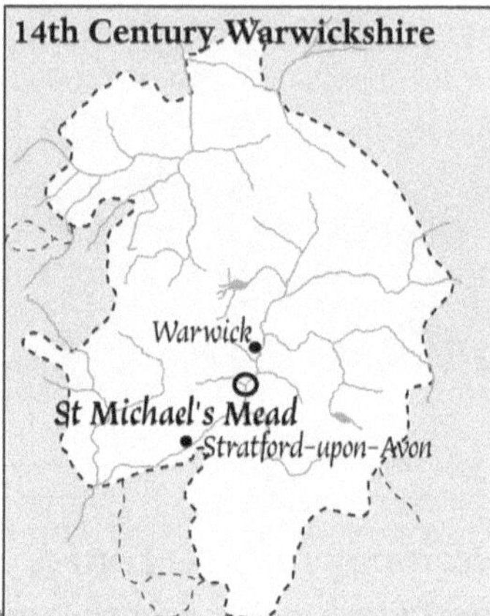

Chapter 1

THE FACE OF A BEAST

Warwickshire, England

Have mercy on me, O God.

All of Warwickshire knows the story of my birth, for it set in motion a shift in the wheel of Fate which I was powerless to stop.

I was born in the year 1308, during the reign of King Edward II in the village of St. Michael's Mead. My mother writhed in agony for three days and when finally my head appeared between her legs, even Mother Alice, the village healer and midwife, turned away in horror. My face was grotesquely misshapen, as if a giant hand had forced its way inside my mother's womb and pushed my countenance upwards until my chin was crushed into my cheekbones and my nose was simply no nose at all. No human nose. It was a snout.

Father Fitzhugh, the village priest, blamed my mother. She

had lain with the Devil as women are wont to do and was being punished for her lust. My face would serve as a reminder that sin marked a child forever. As I had the face of a beast, God commanded me to live among my kind. At the age of six years, I was to dwell among the village pigs from sunup to sundown. I was to care for them, feed them, drive them to the fallow fields and the forest at nut harvest. I was to love them as brothers and sisters. And I was to bring my brothers and sisters to slaughter at St. Martin's Holy Day each year.

Although my mother prayed a fatal sickness might kill me, I lived through fevers each winter and racking coughs each spring. I grew older, taller, and stronger, but my face never fully regained its shape. My nose, having taken on a human-like appearance, soon resumed its place upon my countenance in a manner wholly suitable, but one side of my face remained sunken and one eye drooped in perpetual sadness, as it does to this day.

Still, I was alive, and having reached the momentous occasion of my sixth year, I fulfilled God's destiny and joined my kind in the pigsty.

I sought comfort in my animal companions, prodding hairy beasts twice my size with a willow switch, driving them in snow and hail, sun and storm, and bringing them to slaughter. I thought the years would pass and I would become an old woman, bent forward with the pain of aching bones, mud caked forever beneath my fingernails, and the pigs no longer answering the sting of an old crone's switch. I might have lived and died in St. Michael's Mead not having seen beyond the next hill, but Fortune had other plans.

I am Margaret of St. Michael's Mead. In my youth, I was known as Meg the Devil's Daughter.

This is my story.

From the British Museum, MS 84269, folio recto 2,
1308-1349?? (date of Margaret's death not confirmed).
Also known as 'The Margaret Chronicles'

Chapter 2

OF BIRTH

Caldecote Hall, Warwickshire, England, April 1322

With shaking fingers, Meg of St. Michael's Mead arranged the contents of the birthing bag, a routine that usually calmed her. She picked up the virgin's nut, a smooth stone marked with a cross, and squeezed it, hoping to steady her hands. Next, she laid out the charms, and finally the jars of oils and salves to entice the baby to come forth.

She and Alice, the old healer, had midwifed village women from one end of the countryside to another, including the village of St. Michael's Mead. But the poor laboring woman suffering before them now was no ordinary villager. She was Lady Elisabeth Despenser, highborn wife to Sir Henry Despenser, in childbed again for the fourth time in as many years and with not a living child to show for her labors. Each babe had withered in her womb. This one was alive—so far.

Meg placed the virgin's nut in Lady Elisabeth's palm. "Hold this, milady, and don't let go," she said. "Squeeze when the pain is too much." Elisabeth dropped the stone and gripped Meg's hand instead. Meg gaped at the sight of Elisabeth's fingers, so swollen they resembled ten pale sausages bedecked with jewels.

As another pain increased, Elisabeth dug her heels into the feather mattress, arched her back, and stiffened as her huge belly rose into the air. Sweat rivulets rolled beneath her breasts, pendulous with the weight of milk. Finally, the pain subsided and Elisabeth collapsed.

Meg slipped her hand out of Elisabeth's grasp and stretched her numb fingers. No bones broken, thank the Virgin. *May God forgive me*, Meg thought, *but never, never will I have children.* A man gets all the pleasure while the woman gets the pain—or the death—that comes with the childbed. She knew she should confess her thoughts to Father Fitzhugh after evening chapel, but he was likely to lecture her about how she should go forth and multiply, which she had no intention of doing.

Meg jumped as Mother Alice shouted. "Stop your daydreamin' and pay attention to milady. Whatever was I thinking to pluck a foolish girl from the pigsty and think I could make something of her?"

"I'm sorry, Mother Alice."

Alice grumbled as she wiped a necklace of sweat from Elisabeth's neck. She moved from one side of the bed to the other, fussing with the bedcovers, her ample body shaking with each effort, her jowls fluttering.

Meg could have defended herself against Alice's fit of temper, but she had learned to stay silent. Indeed, she had learned a great deal since the old healer adopted her as an apprentice on Martinmas Day four years ago. She was a mere ten winters old then. How gawky and ignorant she must have seemed when she begged Alice to save her special pig, Robin. The reeve, Sir Henry's servant who oversaw the villagers and organized their duties, had ordered Meg to bring the pigs to slaughter.

"Meg, stop dawdling," Alice bellowed, "or we'll have Sir Henry breaking down the door!"

Tears slipped from the corner of Lady Elisabeth's eyes and disappeared into the tendrils of her disheveled hair as the next pain began. Alice smoothed a ringlet from Elisabeth's forehead and bent low, her cheek against Elisabeth's in a wet mingling of tears and sweat. "Our Father," she began. She whispered an entire *Pater Noster* and then began again. Five times she said the prayer until Elisabeth fell asleep.

The next pain roused her. She feebly gestured to a blonde lady-in-waiting. "Would you sing Maisie's Request? It would please me greatly."

The woman sang in pure, sweet tones while servants moved like apparitions to light tapers and bank the fire against the evening chill.

"Ye'll gie her a lady at her back, And a lady her beforn,

And a midwife at her two asides 'Til yon young son be born."

Just before sunset, Elisabeth's eyes rolled back and her mouth sagged. Meg feared milady had died, but the Alice said, "Exhausted, poor little one. The next pain will rouse her, but I fear she's getting weaker." She handed Meg a stoppered flask. "Rub her legs in oil of violets, then pat vinegar onto her chest and belly. The bitter smell of vinegar will drive the baby to the sweetness of the violets." She patted Elisabeth's swollen fingers. "I've heard there is a surgeon at Ambersley Abbey who is bleeding the nuns. I'll ask Sir Henry to send his man to fetch him here immediately. If he can bleed Elizabeth to relieve the congestion, I'm sure the babe will come forth."

Meg poured oil on the palms of her hands, then rubbed Lady Elisabeth's inner thighs in a circular motion, leaving oily tracks that shone pink in the last bit of light streaming through the windows. Under Meg's hands, Lady Elizabeth's skin felt taut, like a goatskin bag near to bursting. Even her dainty ankles and delicate toes were swollen, the result of stagnant blood pooling in her feet.

When Alice returned from speaking with Sir Henry, she ordered the cook to prepare a cauldron of boiled mallow, chickpeas, flaxseed, and barley. The steaming mixture was poured into a bathtub near the fireplace. Meg and Alice helped Elisabeth settle herself in the water.

When the next labor pain began, Alice placed grated pepper on her palm and held it under Elisabeth's nostrils.

"Achoo!" Elisabeth threw her head back and then forward as she sneezed violently. This remedy was repeated three more times. Water from the tub sloshed on the floor as Elisabeth shook her head with each sneeze. Still, the baby refused to leave the comfort of Elisabeth's womb.

"Bring St. Peter's tooth to me," Alice said to Meg. "It'll work for certain. It *must* work."

Meg reached into the birthing bag and pulled out the tooth of St. Peter, a valuable relic Alice bought after a great deal of haggling at the Michaelmas Fair.

While Alice held the charm above Elisabeth's head, she and Meg chanted three times.

"*Bizomie uteri, labium azerai,*

Benedictus vagini, Peter, Hugh, and Bart amen."

Nothing happened. Not even the power of St. Peter could entice Sir Henry's son into the world.

They pulled Elisabeth from the tub and slipped a clean linen shift over her head. Alice said to Elisabeth, "Milady, you have a stubborn child. But that's a good sign. Surely a strong heir for the Despensers. Or perhaps a brave warrior."

Elisabeth managed a lopsided grin, but her tears did not stop.

"We will have him born this night, never fear. But first, let's take a walk to shake him about. We'll show him what he is missing."

They struggled with Elizabeth's awkward body, but by

crossing their arms around her waist, they were able to carry her weight. Alternately teasing and scolding, Alice and Meg forced her to put one foot in front of the other. They walked from the lying-in chamber to the solar where servants slept two and three to a pallet. They walked through the adjoining chapel, across the minstrel gallery overlooking the great hall below, down the winding stairs where they moved sideways to accommodate Elisabeth's girth, through the east hall, into the buttery and pantry and the kitchen where the sleeping cook snored loudly from his pallet near the fire. Lady Elisabeth's attendants followed Meg and Alice like a bizarre processional, down another set of stairs to the cellarium where serving boys slept between the baskets of grain. Here, they turned around and retraced their steps.

In the great hall, banners emblazoned with the coat of arms of the Despensers hung above their heads. The thick rafters, richly carved and painted in yellow and red shields, so colorful in the daylight, were hidden in shadow. Sir Henry's men were sleeping noisily, sprawled amidst dice and chess pieces strewn about on the trestle tables. Dogs rummaged among the dirty rushes on the floor, searching for bones dropped during the evening meal.

Meg turned toward the main entrance, thinking the night air would refresh them after a day spent in a stuffy room. She asked Alice, "Should we go outside?"

"No. The cold air would surely cause the womb to close even further."

They stopped to rest and to scold Elisabeth as she tried to sit down. They climbed to the solar, halting only once for Alice to relieve herself in the night bucket. From there they began the circuit again. Thus, they traveled the length and breadth of Caldecote Hall, walking the halls and stairways until dawn broke and it became clear, as the mist lifted and vanished from the meadows and woods beyond the crenelated walls of Sir Henry's fortress, they were no nearer to birth than the morning before.

When they entered Lady Elisabeth's bedchamber at last, Meg cast a glance at the tapestries and multi-colored tiles. The bloom of color never failed to cheer her. Although she had been in milady's chamber numerous times, she was always astonished at the beauty of the room, awash in blue and yellow floor tiles, intricate white marble and limestone decorations around the mantel, glazed windows glowing red with the Despenser crest, and tapestries woven with red, blue and yellow millefleurs — "thousands of flowers,"—Elisabeth had told them on their first visit. "Made in France. Flowers that never fade, never die. I will always have a garden here. A beautiful garden no one can destroy."

Meg felt a deep sadness for the young woman who loved her millefleurs. It seemed during the night, the flowers had faded along with Elisabeth's spirit.

After she and Alice tucked Elisabeth into bed, Alice murmured to Meg, "We need to keep our strength up. We'll have something to eat. And then we'll begin again."

Meg, who wolfed down all the food the kitchen sent them, felt stronger physically, but her heart was empty. She watched as if in a trance as Alice rubbed weasel oil on her hand and thrust it into Elisabeth's womb. Alice twisted her fingers, pushing against the babe, forcing it out of the way while she opened the mouth of the womb, stretching and working the tissues. Just yesterday, Elisabeth had moaned as Alice twisted her hand up and down to get a feel for the baby's position. Today she was silent.

Alice wiped her hand on her apron and took a seat near the fire. Her shoulders sagged and she lowered her head. She sighed and said, "The babe is stuck fast inside the womb. He is too big and is buttocks first."

Meg took a seat on the bench and laid her head on Alice's plump shoulder. Alice's curly gray hair escaped in wet ringlets from beneath the stained wimple. Her face in repose appeared ageless, her skin, supple and white as blancmange. Dough-soft beneath the rough homespun of her tunic, she was neverthe-less strong of heart and mind.

Meg felt her eyelids grow heavy. She felt as if they had been in this dreadful castle for a hundred years or more. She sighed. She wanted to be anywhere on earth but at this poor woman's bedside. She wanted to be back in the pigsty at St. Michael's where the days were all the same, where the feeding and care of her pigs was a constant, where the worst possible thing that could happen was a beating from her mother or the taunting remarks of village children. Those days seemed so trifling now—nothing could compare with looking in a woman's face and seeing Death hover there.

Meg whispered, "Did you find Sir Henry, Mother Alice? What did he say? Is the surgeon coming?"

Alice sighed and waved her hand as if brushing away a fly—a fly named Sir Henry Despenser. "At first, he refused to pay for the surgeon to bleed her, but then I reminded him of his son waiting to be born. He changed his mind. The surgeon will be here this afternoon."

"What should we do until then, Mother Alice? If the bleed-ing does not work, could the surgeon cut the child out of the womb?"

"Yes, but that cut—through the stomach and into the womb—is deadly to the mother. I have never heard of a woman sur-viving it. Moreover, the Church forbids it unless the mother is dead and the babe is still alive. I have no desire to tangle with Church law. If Elisabeth were dead, we could cut through her to take out the babe. But she is alive. And her babe may be alive also. I just can't be sure."

"Then what are we to do until the surgeon arrives?"

"We wait."

Around them, another day dawned, and the house went about its usual duty. Meat was turned on the spit. Bread baked in the ovens. Laundry was washed and spread to dry. Knights practiced with lances and swords. Cows were milked. Butter churned. And upstairs in the room where a thousand flowers bloomed in French tapestries, women waited. And waited.

Chapter 3

HEAVEN AND HELL

Caldecote Hall, Warwickshire, England, April 1322

Alice wrapped a cover of lamb's wool around a sleeping Meg, who had curled up next to the fire. Meg twitched and mumbled, "Robin. Where's Robin?" Alice patted the girl's back and murmured softly until Meg fell asleep again. The poor little thing, Alice thought, after all these years she still had nightmares about her pig. The only reminder of Robin these days was the hogshair bracelet Meg wore constantly.

Alice decided to leave the room while Meg and Elisabeth were sleeping. Despite her outward composure, Alice was shaken. A feeling of crushing failure had replaced her initial excitement of two days ago. She needed some peace and time to think.

If Elisabeth died without an heir, Sir Henry wouldn't hesitate to blame her and Meg. He was a humorless overbearing man whose quest for a male heir would broach no excuses.

She knew in her heart that she had done all she could. Neither entreaties to the dear Lord nor special charms had helped Elisabeth. But Sir Henry would never believe her.

More than anything, Alice wanted to leave the lying-in chamber and never return. She wanted comfort and consolation. She wanted to see her beloved husband again, but he had died many years ago. She wanted the impossible: to feel Roger's embrace. Though she could no longer see or feel her Roger in the flesh, she could talk to him in a special place. She needed to go to the Despenser's private chapel located in the courtyard behind the east wing. There she would find Roger's spirit locked in stone.

She had first laid eyes on Roger when she was sixteen and a mere simpleton in the ways of love and courtship. They met at the village well one morning when he came over for a drink of water. He had been hired as a stonemason, he said, to carve the vaulted archway of the chapel at Caldecote Hall. She asked about the tools in his sack and his face glowed as he described his carvings, gesturing wildly, spilling water out of the gourd as he drew stone faces in the air. She loved him instantly.

For months she contrived to make deliveries to Caldecote Hall, to meet the stonemason on the path to the river quite by accident, or to be at the well each morning at the exact instant he needed a drink. Still he seemed to care more for his stones than for her. During the winter she took him hot drinks to warm his gullet as well as his frozen hands. While he drank they would talk of his dreams to see the great churches of England—Salisbury, Westminster, Canterbury, Winchester, and York.

"I will tell you this, Alice," he said to her one day as they sat under the arch, stone dust settling in the lines of his face, "it's as if the stones call to me in some strange way, as if I see things locked inside them that need to be free."

She had loved him even more.

Though he did not seem to return her affection, he appeared to welcome the sight of her each day. Once, when she was quite desperate and thought her heart would burst, she sneaked some of her mother's herbs and brewed her own love potion. Roger remained as unmoved as the stone he carved. Then finally the archway was finished and her heart sank in despair. He would pack up his tools and be off. She would never see him again. But instead, he appeared at the cottage gate to fetch her to Caldecote Hall, saying he wanted her to look at the finished carvings.

At the entrance to the chapel, she arched her neck and looked in the eyes of the baby Jesus and felt such a sweetness she thought she should die from the rapture of it. But where there was beauty in Roger's carvings, there was terror as well. To the left and right of the dimpled infant's face were the horrors of Hell: demons whose eyes bulged and tongues protruded from their snarling mouths. Others protected their heads with clawed hands. Roger was chewing his bottom lip, his face a copy of the torment he chiseled.

"Tis glorious work. You have God's gift in your fingers."

Roger smiled and clutched her hands. "I was hoping you would like it. I have something to show you, but you have to mount the ladder to see it."

He pulled the wooden ladder closer and Alice took a tentative step. The leather strips that lashed each rung to the frame creaked as she crawled upward. Roger held her hand at first, then moved behind her and steadied the ladder. When she got to the top, she stood still for a moment, trying to catch her breath.

"Now," Roger said, his voice shaking with excitement, "look there where the column meets the vaulted arch. Do you see it? To the right there . . . go farther. Now do you see it?"

Yes, she saw it. There at the very end away from the madness of Hell were the smiling faces of a man and woman. The woman was looking straight ahead, a saucy smile tugging at her lips, while the man's face was turned slightly toward her as if he whispered a secret.

The woman's face was her own. The man was Roger.

She realized then that Roger was a man whose speech was not fashioned with ease. The words he kept inside were rendered with his mallet and chisel.

They were married soon thereafter and had a happy life, happier than most she expected, so she had no reason to complain. Roger was a freeman, able to obtain a dispensation for land and two oxen in exchange for masonry services at the Hall. He and Alice settled in their cottage by the river. Four children followed, all of whom but one, Tim, died before the age of three, despite the desperate care of Alice and her mother.

Every time she came to Caldecote Hall, she contrived to go to the chapel to talk with Roger. She stood now at the entrance, seeing again the wondrous carvings. It was likely, after so many years, that no one in the Despenser household paid much attention to the stonework. It was something they saw every day. But Alice knew each curve, each grotesque face, each carved oak leaf and acorn, each echo of heaven, and each scream of hell. She had kissed the fingertips of the man who carved them. She had kissed more than that.

She craned her neck and gazed into the unseeing eyes of her husband. "Roger, what am I to do? I'm in a muddle. Yes, I know, 'tis a strange place for your stubborn Alice to be in." She leaned against the column holding up the vaulted arch. *I have tried everything, Roger. We are going to die.*

She thought of Meg, so young, so exuberant, so dedicated to healing. She would be an extraordinary healer one day. If she lived. And then she remembered why she was standing at the chapel door —Elisabeth's labor, a child presenting buttocks first, and the wrath of Sir Henry Despenser.

She thought of Elisabeth, also young, and so excited to give birth to a child who had managed to cling to her womb when the other babies had died. She feared Elisabeth would die as well, especially if this babe was already dead inside her. If she could save Elisabeth, there would be more chances at children, despite Sir Henry's anger.

Ah, Roger, my husband, my love, why did you have to die and leave me here on this cold grey earth to grow old alone?

One year after a journey to Winchester, Roger came home with a pain in his joints and a fever which soon turned to a corruption in the chest. Alice fed him linseed cakes with honey to ease the cough and spread warm linseed poultices across his chest, but he grew weaker. Around Eastertide, he coughed blood and she knew he would never recover. He died the following winter.

She looked at the stone figures huddled in the corner of the vault. She arched her neck, wishing she could always keep in her mind's eye a picture of the stone couple. *I love you, dear Roger.*

She felt a peace descend upon her shoulders and settle in her heart. No matter what happened to her, the stones in the archway at Caldecote Hall would endure long after she was gone. She and Roger would exchange their lovers' endearments, whisper secrets of the marriage bed, and share their blessings, as the chapel arch grew older and winter's frost and summer's heat slowly cracked the stone. Over time, moss would creep into the crevices, wrap them in a coverlet of green. Yet, they would be there still, Alice and Roger pledging their love, their smiles fixed forever.

She stretched her shoulders and straightened her spine. For two long days she had felt the burden of Elisabeth's labor as if it were her own. But no more. She knew what she must do.

She scurried across the courtyard to the back stairs. With each step she felt her resolve grow stronger. She had forgotten her purpose in the chaos and confusion of Elisabeth's labor. Her duty was to care for her patient, to keep her alive by whatever means necessary. By God, nobody, not even Sir Henry, would interfere without her permission.

As she entered Elisabeth's chamber, she felt a surge of confidence. She caught Meg's eye. "Find Sir Henry. Tell him we need the surgeon and we need him NOW."

Chapter 4

FATHER AND SON

Caldecote Hall, Warwickshire, England, April 1322

Meg searched the great hall, but it was empty except for a few servants setting bowls on the dais. She ran down the stone steps, striding across the inner courtyard, past the blacksmith shed, the sheepfold, the pigsty, and the kitchen garden.

She found Sir Henry leaning against the falconry shed, a small lean-to tucked in a corner between the bailey wall and the portcullis tower. A falcon nibbled tidbits from Sir Henry's gloved hand.

A tall older man leaned against the bailey wall. His face in repose appeared to be watchful, his eyes sharp and wary. Next to him stood a young boy about Meg's age.

"Sir Henry!" Meg called and then ran across the courtyard, through the horse droppings and remnants of food left there by the bailey guard. "Your Lordship!" Meg slowed her pace

19

but lost her balance on a clump of wet straw. She slid forward, regained her balance yet lost it again, and fell against Sir Henry, knocking the falcon from his wrist. The bird screeched, struggling against the tether, straining for the open sky.

"You stupid girl!" Sir Henry clouted her across the chin with his free hand and Meg went sprawling. The falcon's screeches echoed off the castle walls and the miniature silver bells tied to his legs tinkled viciously, as if he were tearing his prey apart in a frenzy.

For a moment Meg was too stunned to move. Bits of straw and dirt clung to her mouth. She spit them away and wiped her face. Feathers and fluff from the bird's soft underdown drifted onto her tunic and in her hair. God's balls, but her face hurt! She thought her jaw might be broken, and she moved it from side to side. Not broken, just sore. She'd have a black mark tomorrow to show for her trouble.

The tall stranger made no move to help Sir Henry who cursed and struggled with the bird. The stranger's skin was dark and weather-beaten as a shepherd, and yet his eyes were a remarkable deep blue, the color of a pond on a sunny day. His hair, what there was of it, had turned gray and the ends curled against the edge of his cape.

The boy stared solemnly, not even slightly amused, at seeing Meg slide like a headless chicken into the most irritable liege lord in all of Warwickshire.

Meg pushed herself to her feet. She squeezed her hands to keep from touching her aching face. Instead of looking at the ground in humiliation, as she should have, she stared at Sir Henry, fixing him in her sight as if he were a stag and she a bowman. She had a sudden image of him, naked and aloof, pumping away on top of a weeping Elisabeth. *You leprous good-for-nothing*, she thought, *may pustules cover your prick and women scream at the sight of it.*

"As I was saying, before this stupid girl interrupted me," Sir Henry said, "my cousin, Hugh Despenser, and his wife, Eleanor de Clare, will arrive soon. As my wife has decided to give birth at such an inopportune time, I must oversee arrangements."

"Hugh and his lady Eleanor hold a great deal of power in court, or so I've been told," the tall man said.

"Oh, most certainly."

"I've also heard Hugh is very close to the king."

"To be sure. He has the king's ear."

"It is even said the queen is no better than a prisoner in her own home, and Eleanor de Clare is the queen's keeper."

"The queen should be walled away in a convent," Henry said in disgust. A muscular man with an angular chin and sharp nose, he caressed the falcon's head, smoothing the bird's feathers from crest to tail in a long languid stroke. The bird pecked at the glove and then was still as if charmed by the man's touch. "Hugh the Younger and the King understand each other as few men can. Hugh and his father have much power in Parliament and the backing of many knights and earls, including myself. You would do well, William, to choose sides and let your choice be known at court."

"I care nothing for court politics, Sir Henry. I'll leave that to you and the other Despensers."

Meg had had enough of this foolish talk of the King's court and of royals who, unlike the good people of St. Michael's Mead, would never go hungry. "I beg your forgiveness, Sir Henry," she said, struggling to keep her voice calm, "but my mistress inquires after the surgeon. She has need of his services at Lady Elisabeth's bedside."

"Is that so?" he asked.

Meg raised her chin and set her jaw, determined to show him she was not afraid, though, in truth, her heart was beating so hard against her ribs it threatened to bounce from her chest. "Yes, she is having difficulty pushing out the child," she explained. "And Mother Alice says—"

Henry cut her off. "These are women's matters. I do not want to hear of them." He walked to the last cage and put the bird inside, giving it one last tidbit before he pulled off the hood and tether. "Do not bother me again until you have a babe to show me—a boy—not a girl. Drown the girl in the Avon." He threw back his head and laughed as if killing a girl child was outrageously funny. "What can a woman do but sit at home, turning her distaff and chattering with the other magpies about ribbons from Calais and lace from Flanders." He shifted his gaze to Meg who was growing increasingly frustrated with the man. "Women are only good for one thing. Especially little ones such as this." He grabbed Meg's right breast, a tender and painful spot just beginning to swell and he twisted the nipple, pinching it until her eyes watered.

It was all too much. She twisted away. She could not bear Sir Henry any longer, even if he did have the power to lop off her head. "This is not a game of hot cockles, Sir Henry. I am no longer a swineherd. I am apprentice healer to Mother Alice." She squared her shoulders. "And one day I shall be the greatest healer in all of Christendom. I need the surgeon and if it is not too much to ask, I need him NOW!"

"Why, you impudent . . ." Henry took a step toward her, his hand raised to strike and Meg backed up, but the stranger moved between them.

"Enough jest, Sir Henry," the stranger said quietly. He bowed to Meg as if she were a great lady.

"Mistress Meg, I am William of Oxford, the surgeon. How can I be of service to your dearest Alice?" He looked at her and winked. "And to the greatest healer in all of Christendom?"

Chapter 5

OF DEATH

Caldecote Hall, April 1322

"Well, Alice, how do you fare these days?" William asked.

"Quite well, Master William. And yourself?"

"Quite well, thank you."

"It has been a long time."

"Aye, it has."

There was an awkward silence. Meg glanced at the boy standing behind William. He was stone-faced. Did Alice and William know each other? And were Alice's cheeks red?

William cleared his throat. "Tell me everything, er, about Lady Elisabeth."

They were standing in the chilly hall outside the solar. Better to talk beyond the hearing of others, Alice had warned. She described the long two days of labor, and how Elisabeth was no closer to birthing her baby than a priest to keeping a vow of celibacy. "I fear she is getting weaker. When nothing helped, I sent Meg to find you."

"And is the babe alive?"

"I've seen no movement. I fear he wants to show us his buttocks first and not the crown of his head. And Lady Elisabeth's pains seem to have ceased."

William turned to the boy standing behind him and motioned him forward. "This is my son, Gerard." Gerard, dark-haired and thin with somber brown eyes, nodded but said nothing. "Gerard often helps me and hopes to become a doctor of phisik one day. What is your opinion, Gerard?"

"If the babe is dead, it will have to come out lest the good lady succumb to fever.

"Excellent," William said and smiled at his son. "Exactly what we will do."

Sir Henry surprised them by appearing at the top of the steps. "And what is this, then?" he shouted. "You dawdle here in the hallway instead of bringing my son into the world?"

"Sir Henry," William said. "I was discussing Lady Elisabeth with Alice.

"I care little what happens to my wife, only for the son she carries inside her."

William held up his hand as if to ward off Sir Henry's anger. "Sir, you speak in haste. Understandable with your wife in agony for so many days."

"I assure you, Sir Henry," Alice added, "I have done all I can to bring your son forth."

"Then why is he not born?"

William answered for her. "It is hard to say, sir. Some women have an easy time of it. Others do not."

"And some women, perhaps, have been bewitched by an old woman and her spawn of the Devil." Meg felt her face grow red and raised her hand to hide her drooping eye. She glanced at Gerard, but his face was a mask.

Alice drew herself up as tall as her short frame would allow. "I have done all I can to ensure you have an heir."

"Then, why, after all these years, do I not have a child?"

William placed his hand upon Henry's shoulder. "Sir Henry, Mother Alice is one of the best healers in England. She would never—"

Henry shook off William's touch. "She has attended my wife again and again and still there is no child. As I think on it, perhaps there is another reason." He glared at Alice and leaned close to her. "Perhaps you have poisoned her womb all these years to spite me."

"Sir Henry," William interrupted, "there is no reason—"

Henry dismissed Master William as if he were a mere serving wench. "You are here to bleed my wife, that is all. Do not entertain yourself with views of my wife's private parts. You will watch Alice and that filthy girl and report to me if they do anything to hurt my son."

"I assure you I want Lady Elisabeth to give birth as much as you do," Alice said.

Henry leaned close to her and snarled. "And I can assure *you* if anything happens to my son, you and your apprentice will beg for God's mercy before I finish with you."

✱✱✱

While Alice made light of Sir Henry's threat, her shaking hands gave her away. She and Meg lifted the covers from the sleeping Elisabeth. "I gave her a draught of belladonna while you went to find Master William," she explained as they pushed and pulled the poor woman's limp body to the foot of the bed.

William grew quiet as he passed his tools to Gerard, who laid them out on the bed, much as Meg had displayed the contents of Alice's birthing belt. But while Alice's tools were simple and suggested hope and compassion, William's were gruesome in their shape and hinted at something dreadful to come. Arrayed between Elisabeth's legs, the hooks and blades shone in the sunlight. The blades were long and thin, with red and blue striped handles curving into fanciful animal heads. William took the first instrument, a tool that reminded Meg of the yoke her father used on the plow oxen, and he widened each pole of the yoke by twisting the handle.

The ladies-in-waiting whimpered. For the first time, William noticed them. "Out," he said firmly. When they made no effort to move, he shouted, "Out, out!"

The blonde lady-in-waiting who had sung Maisie's Song to Elisabeth sputtered, "Send us away and Sir Henry will hear of it."

"I do not care what he thinks. Now go!" He scowled at them and they scurried out, their whimpers increasing to wails.

As soon as they were gone, William closed and locked the door. He examined Elisabeth, pressing against her belly with his large hands and laying his head sideways against her navel. "There is nothing. No heartbeat and no movement. And Lady Elisabeth is very weak," he pronounced.

"Aye," Alice said.

William then inserted his hand into Elisabeth's privates. Elisabeth roused and began to moan. William motioned for Meg and Gerard to come closer. "You are right, Alice. The baby is presenting buttocks first." He lowered his voice and glanced toward Elisabeth. "I fear the child is dead. We must remove it. As you said, Gerard, if we do not do this, Elisabeth herself will die." He fingered a knife. "This will not be easy," he looked at his son and then at Meg. "The child will not emerge entire. It will be quite shocking. You do not have to stay."

"Of course I will stay, Father," Gerard answered.

Meg, not to be outdone, but not at all sure of what she would face, said "I will stay as well. My mistress may need me."

Alice beamed at her.

"Then we will do what we must. Alice, you and Meg must

hold Elisabeth. Keep her from moving about. The sleeping draught will help, but nothing on earth will dull what she is about to experience. Gerard, hand me the instruments and keep the basin ready."

William spread Elisabeth's legs. He tied her swollen feet to the bedposts. Her moans grew louder.

"Shh, little one," Alice said and motioned Meg to the opposite side of the bed. "Keep your hands on her shoulder and do not let her break free."

William inserted both poles of the yoke into Elisabeth. Her eyes widened and she screamed. Elisabeth grabbed Alice's hand and struggled to look beyond her bulging stomach. "What is happening? Who is this? What is he doing? You promised me, no men. You promised!"

"Master William is trying to help you. We must —"

"My baby!"

"Quiet now and be still!" Alice commanded.

"Look in my bag," William ordered his son. "Bring me the knife with the bronze leaf at the tip. Be careful, the blade is sharp."

He kept his eyes upon Elisabeth but whispered to Alice and Meg. "I cannot get the child out—at least in one piece."

"I feared as much," Alice murmured and crossed herself. She gave Elisabeth a few more sips of the sleeping draught.

For Meg, the next hour passed as slowly as the longest night in midwinter. Time filled the room with a heavy silence, broken only by Alice's *Pater Nosters* and William's heavy breathing.

The knife blade, slender and beautiful in design, disappeared into Elisabeth's womb. Only the bronze leaf, the end of the handle, was visible.

Meg watched in horror as William, kneeling on the floor, carefully maneuvered the knife with one hand into Elisabeth as far as it would go. There was first a muffled crack, much as the sound of a chicken leg parted from its thigh bone, then pale soft limbs filled the basin along with bits of tissue and the birth cord.

"Meg," William said, "lean across Elizabeth and push against her abdomen as hard as you can."

Meg did as she was told.

"Single hook," William ordered Gerard.

Meg pushed against her with all her might. *Please, Blessed Mary, make me strong,* she prayed.

"Double hook."

Without warning, Elisabeth woke from her stupor and sat up. "Mary, Mother of God! Oh, my sweet Jesus, I cannot endure this!"

"Be strong, it is almost over!" Alice whispered.

Meg choked back a sob and, while pressing against Elisabeth, peeked at Gerard. He, too, was blinking tears from his eyes. Perhaps he wasn't made of stone after all.

William, stern-faced, set his mouth in a grimace against his efforts. "Alice, Meg! Keep her still!"

"Elisabeth," Alice implored, "do not move, I beg you."

Something landed in the basin with a soft *plop.*

William straightened. He wiped the sweat from his forehead with the back of his sleeve and looked briefly at Alice. They exchanged a glance whose meaning was hidden from Meg.

And then it was over. With a great gushing of water and blood, the limbless torso and pale head slipped down the birth canal and landed in the basin. Gerard gasped. His shaking hands threatened to slip, but he recovered and held the basin steady.

William stood and stretched his back. "Sir Henry got his wish. A boy." He cleaned his hands on his apron and then rubbed his eyes. "Alice, I leave the rest to you."

She motioned for Meg. "Prepare the pennyroyal in wine and honey and when Elisabeth rouses, force her to drink it. It will cause the secunda, the afterbirth, to bleed out. If the secunda tarries in the womb, she will die. In the meantime, I will wash her privates with wine and vinegar and pour it into her womb as well. We'll give her Melissa balm when she wakes."

William placed his hand on Alice's shoulder. "You did all you could, Alice. Do not let Sir Henry's choleric nature dampen your spirits."

"Bless you, William, but I never wanted this—" she nodded toward the basin.

"You could not have known. What is done is done." He reached for her hand and squeezed her fingers. Meg and Gerard exchanged quick glances and the questions on Gerard's face told her that he, too, wondered how well Alice and his father knew each other.

William removed his apron and gathered his tools. "I fear for you and Meg if we cannot produce a living son. Henry is not to be thwarted."

"I have been thinking on that," Alice said. "There may be a way. We will have to lie, but I fear if we do not . . ." She left the thought of their fate hanging in the stale air.

"At this point, we must do what we can to keep you alive," William said, and hastily added, "and Meg, of course."

"Then let us work quickly. I must persuade my son and his big lout of a wife to feed one less child."

When Alice and Meg finished at Elisabeth's bedside and the poor woman was sleeping deeply, Alice suggested Meg go outside. Meg did not need to be told twice. She was more than ready to stagger from that room of horrors.

St. Michael's Mead, April 1322

Alice found her son Tim working on the second plowing of the fallow field, his children following along behind, pulling weeds and thistles. His wife Emma was sitting under an old chestnut tree with the newest addition to the family, a baby boy, barely three weeks old and sucking like a piglet at Emma's teat. Emma spit out babies like she was competing in a game of cherry pits to see who could spit the farthest. A short labor, a couple of moans, and out slid the next baby. And wonder of wonders, the children were healthy. Even if they caught the pox or a winter ague, they were sick but a few days and were soon back on their feet.

"Good afternoon, Mother Alice," Emma said. Her twisted lips suggested, despite the greeting, there was nothing good about having her mother-in-law join them.

When Tim caught sight of Alice, he waved and called to the children to take a rest. "Here, Mother, sit with us please," Tim said, and made a place for her between himself and two of the children. "We were just about to have our meal. Would you have some ale? Something to eat?"

"No, thank you," Alice said as she lowered herself to the ground. She kissed and hugged her grandchildren who gathered around her. "I cannot stay long. I must get back to Lady Elisabeth's bedside."

"So she's in labor, then?" Emma brightened. She would be the first with news to tell the other women.

"Aye. And it doesn't fare well. In fact . . ." Alice was unsure how much to tell them. She had no doubts about Tim. She trusted him with her life. It was Emma who worried her. Emma was like the hen who ruled the henhouse, always cackling about something, always preening. She was vain and greedy. Tim, meanwhile, worked his fingers to the bone for her, taking odd jobs that needed doing in addition to plowing and planting. Having so many mouths to feed didn't make it easier.

Which was the reason Alice was here. Time to appeal to Emma's avarice.

"Lady Elisabeth has had a hard time of it and will probably need a wet-nurse. I thought of you, of course."

"Me? I have my own baby to nurse and my other children to take care of."

"Yes, I know. But hear me out. There may be a reward for you." Emma's eyes opened wider and Alice knew she had the fish on the hook. Time to let it wiggle and then haul it in. "Elisabeth's labor has been difficult and complicated." She paused, trying to decide how much to tell them. There was no way except to tell them everything, but not in front of everyone. "I, uh . . ." She nodded toward the older children and Tim finally understood.

"Boys, go tend the ox," he said. "I'll be there in a moment."

As the boys walked off, their sisters scrambled out of Alice's lap and toddled after their brothers.

Alice waited for the children to walk out of earshot and continued. "A baby boy was born today, but he is dead. Elisabeth is near death herself."

She told them of the long hours of labor and the grisly result when the surgeon was called in.

"Oh, Mary, and all the Blessed Virgins," Tim said when she described the scene in Elisabeth's room.

"I don't understand," Emma said hotly. "To cut up that poor child like a chicken. I cannot bear it. It's horrible. How could you?"

Alice felt her hackles rise and took a breath to calm down. It had been two long days and a night and she was as drained as a stuck pig. She could easily lose her temper and turn Emma against her. "Emma, you are most fortunate in your easy labors and healthy children. God has truly favored you. But Elisabeth is not as lucky. Her babe was too big to be born. He was buttocks first and with the size, he simply wouldn't come out. He died inside her. What could we do? Elisabeth was in agony. We thought it best to keep her alive to give birth to other children in the future. Perhaps the next one would be a boy and Henry would be happy."

"What is this reward you spoke of?" Emma asked.

Ahhh, Alice thought. Emma's display of pity was all pretense and all for show, a way to appear interested when she really wanted to come to the heart of the matter—money.

"I will come to that. First, you should know Sir Henry has accused me of using spells on Lady Elisabeth to prevent a son from being born."

"What? Ridiculous!" Tim said.

"He has threatened Meg and me with punishment if an heir is not born today. I have no desire to be tortured and then burnt alive or drowned in the pond. Nor do I want Meg to suffer. But that will happen unless Sir Henry holds a newborn baby boy in his arms tonight."

"What can we do?" Tim asked.

"If Henry thinks his son is alive and healthy, we will be saved."

"But how is that possible?"

"With another baby." Emma was one step ahead of Tim.

"Yes. *Your* baby."

Emma cupped her palm around the baby's head. "And why should I give up my baby—*our* baby?"

"Because you will be the baby's—your son's—wet nurse at Caldecote Hall. Because you will watch him grow. If you please Sir Henry, you may be asked to stay on as his nurse until your son is sent away to be trained as a knight. You will give him a chance none of your other children will have, a chance for fine things. A life of riches."

Emma was silent. Alice could see her working out the puzzle pieces in her mind. Finally, Emma said, "And in return?"

"In return, you will be rewarded with enough money—"

"And who has that kind of money in this village?"

"The surgeon has offered to pay you."

"How much?"

"Enough gold coins to keep you free from want for several years." Emma's eyes grew even wider.

While she let Emma mull over the proposition, Alice turned to Tim. "You've been silent. You're the husband and father here. What say you?"

"My son." Tim's face grew tender and his eyes filled with tears.

"You have enough mouths to feed, my dear Tim. And there will be other children, I am sure of it. Remember, he's my grandson as well. I will be sorry to lose him, but look at what he will gain. Look at what *all* the children will gain. In the meantime, you will be able to look after your son at the Hall and watch him grow into a fine young man."

"But he's *my* son, not Sir Henry's," Tim said. "Why can't

you just explain everything to Henry? Show him the body of his son? Surely he understands some infants die at birth."

"Would he understand the heir to the Despenser fortune in pieces in a bucket? Or would he see the working of a witch in league with the Devil?"

Tim lowered his eyes. His cheeks were mottled pink, so like his face when he was a child and angry with her. "But what about the other children?" he asked. "I can't look after them myself."

"Oh, don't be such a dolt," Emma scolded. "I'll ask my mother to come and help. We'll pay her from the surgeon's money. That will sweeten the pot."

Emma's excitement earned a caution. Alice observed her grandchildren, the girls picking wildflowers and the boys brushing the back of the ox. "You will never be able to tell your children the real story. You will never be able to tell the babe in the Hall that he is *your* son, not the son and heir to Sir Henry Despenser, that *you* are his mother, not Lady Elisabeth. Needless to say, you must not tell anyone. No one in the village. No one at the manor house. No one. Understood?"

They agreed, although Tim did so reluctantly.

Alice leaned toward them and repeated her words. She glared at Emma. "You must never tell anyone. Never. Our lives depend on it."

"Don't worry, Mother Alice." She clapped her hands. "Think of it, Tim, we'll finally have a chance to leave that hovel we're living in. Maybe even purchase a—"

"Discuss that later," Alice snapped. "Here is what we must do now."

Chapter 7

A Far Better Place

Caldecote Hall, April 1322

Despite the commands her body made upon her legs to walk with haste out of that accursed house, Meg moved like one still asleep.

She wandered into the courtyard, walking aimlessly, pondering what she should do next when she saw Gerard run toward the barn. Without so much as a backward glance, he disappeared into the gloom. It was odd that he should have business there. To satisfy her curiosity, and because she had nothing better to do, she followed him.

Inside the great vaulted structure, the air was cool. She shivered and pulled her cloak around her shoulders. Her nose tingled as the mix of pungent animal droppings and sweet hay wafted toward her. Gerard was nowhere to be seen, but a muffled sound above her suggested his whereabouts. She climbed the ladder to the hayloft. She found him on his hands and knees vomiting.

"What do you want?" he asked.

"Nothing." She inched toward him and sat down, fearing he would bolt like a frightened hare. "Are you unwell?"

"No. I mean, yes, perhaps." He wiped spittle from his lips. "I must have eaten something that disagreed with me."

"Your father is . . ." She tried to think of a word that meant "terrifying" in a nice way, so as not to insult Gerard on his father's behalf and yet all she managed was, "an important surgeon."

"Yes, well known all over the Christian world."

"Do you always help him?"

"When I can."

"Gerard," she said and slipped closer. "Have you ever seen what we just . . .?" She could not bring herself to describe it.

"No," he answered brusquely. He turned away from her and vomited once more into the hay.

She reached for his hand and felt his forehead. "No fever," she said.

"I am not ill. Leave me."

"I could fetch you some syrup of peppermint. 'Tis good for soothing stomachs."

"No! I told you, leave me alone!" His back trembled as he sought to hide his tears from her. "Do not talk to me."

She wondered if he was sick from the blood and gore, a terrible dilemma for a boy who aimed to spend his life as a doctor of phisik. "Do you sicken at the sight of blood?"

"Of course not." He turned to face her, his eyes bloodshot with the pressure of vomiting and the pain of salty tears. "How could you know what it is like to be the son of the great William of Oxford, to bear his hope for my future?"

"I do not know, Gerard."

"Did he falter at Lady Elisabeth's bedside? Did he heave his insides like a little girl? No, because he is stronger than I will ever be."

Meg could think of no reply. In truth, she often felt the same way about herself and Mother Alice.

She rose to her feet, but Gerard grabbed her hand. He wiped his face with his other sleeve and coughed. "Stay, please. I did not mean to shout at you. You saw the same horror I did, and yet I am the one to shed tears."

"It was a terrible, terrible thing to witness. I was frightened also, but I did not want to disappoint Mother Alice. I have never seen her so troubled."

They sat in silence, listening to the cooing of doves in the rafters. Below them, children ran through the barn, calling out to each other and laughing in reply. She heard a boy start counting and the sound of running feet as children searched for a hiding place.

Meg rested against a pile of hay and breathed in the comforting smell of hayfields on a hot summer day. Gerard lay beside her. He stared at the roof rafters and then asked her, "What happened to your face?"

An arrow pierced her heart. She had been so full of fear for Elisabeth that she had forgotten her disfigurement and how her drooping eye and the scooped bones of her cheek must look to Gerard and his father.

"I was born this way." She pressed the tips of her fingers against the drooping eyelid. "Some say it was my punishment. They say my mother must have committed a great sin which tainted me."

"Absurd," he hissed.

"You do not believe it then?"

"Why would I believe such a ridiculous thing? Like my father, I believe a child is born into the world blameless and innocent."

"No matter," she murmured. "I cannot change it."

He placed a cold, trembling fingertip against her drooping eye. Then he rolled on his side, away from her.

The doves called *you, you, you* to each other in the rafters.

Their songs reminded Meg of her mother's voice when she was angry, which was often. *"You. 'Tis always you,"* she would say as she hit Meg with a switch or spoon or her hand. When Meg was little, she didn't understand. Once she was older, she understood all too well. Her face reminded Agnes daily of the consequences of sin. Agnes had lain with the devil and her disfigured daughter was the result, Father Fitzhugh had said. The sin manifested in the flesh, Whatever went wrong would always be her fault. If the garden dried up, the pottage burned, the thread kinked, or the ox died, Meg was to blame. The storms that destroyed their crops, the mildew on the grain in the tithe barn, the child who died from pox after touching the Devil's Daughter—all her fault.

Fortunately, old Mother Alice had taken charge of her destiny. She was ten years old then—how different her life might have been had Alice not plucked her out of the pigsty, she thought. She chuckled, looking back now and realizing how witless she had been. On that Martinmas Day four years ago when the villagers slaughtered pigs and celebrated the feast of St. Martin, Mother Alice agreed to keep a strange bargain. She promised to hide Meg's beloved pig Robin to keep it safe from the Martinmas slaughter in exchange for Meg's service as an apprentice. Meg was astounded. Sir Henry would never allow her to leave her post as swineherd to apprentice to Mother Alice. Leave him to me, Alice said.

Usually, one or two pigs were chosen to die, but not that year. The villagers faced famine if all the pigs weren't killed and salted for overwintering, even Robin, the runt, and her favorite. Meg, in her ignorance, thought old Alice was a magician who could make the pig invisible, but she learned that Alice was a mere human like everyone else. She simply had an uncanny ability to look inside to see the reality of the soul hiding there.

For Meg, the reality was that Robin was the creature she loved most in the world and who loved her back. Unfortunately, as it turned out, not even Alice could save Robin from Theodoric, the miller's son. After years of throwing mudballs, spitting on her, and beating her as she got older, he had discovered Robin's hiding place in Mother Alice's old shed and brought him to the pigsticker to have his throat cut. She cried when she discovered Robin's head in the pigsticker's basket. So, she had beaten Theodoric in front of the village folk, but not before he had reduced her face to what resembled the ground sausage the village women were making. Fortunately, Alice treated her with herbs and willow bark tea and she recovered.

In ordinary times Meg's brother Walter would have intervened and beaten Theodoric for his trouble, but that very morning Walter had decided to run away to London. He had threatened to run away before, but Meg had always talked him out of such a foolish plan. On that particular Martinmas Day, with everyone busy at killing pigs, making sausages, and blood pudding, he could escape with ease. Meg had cried as he kissed her goodbye and fled by the old trackway across the Avon River.

She fingered the bracelet she always wore, a reminder of Robin. She had begged the pigsticker to bring her Robin's hair before he left the village. She and Alice soaked the hair, making it pliable, then they braided it with leather, twisting it into the bracelet she vowed to wear always.

And now after living with Alice in her cottage near the river, she knew which herbs could cure and which could kill, the difference in lungwort and mugwort, badger's offal and stoat's heart, and the various charms guaranteed to please the patient. Still, today, despite all the care they had given Elisabeth, death had won. Which was why she was laying in the hay with a somber boy who had witnessed death's victory and whose tears clutched at her heart.

Gerard raised on one elbow. "Do not tell my father you found me here crying like a baby." His voice was brusque. He had placed the mask upon his face again. The real Gerard, the boy she had observed so briefly, was now safely hidden behind a blank visage. One day perhaps she could coax him from his secret place and, like the children playing hide and seek in the great open space of the barn, discover him anew and bring him to light.

She said softly, "Do not fear, Gerard. Your father will never know."

✳✳✳

At dusk Alice's daughter-in-law Emma, wearing her most imperious expression, met Meg at the kitchen door at Caldecote Hall carrying a basket of small gifts for Lady Elisabeth. Meg led her up the back stairs to the solar, brushing past curious ladies-in-waiting gathered outside their mistress's room. Alice met Meg and Emma and quickly ushered them into Elisabeth's room, locking the door behind her. Emma lifted a layer of linens from the basket to reveal her sleeping baby. Alice picked him up and placed him with a dazed Elisabeth.

"Here is your beautiful baby boy, Lady Elisabeth," Alice said.

"My baby," Elisabeth murmured. "My sweet boy." She looked at Alice and frowned. "But, I thought I saw . . . I do not understand."

"A bad dream, milady. No need to fret now. Why don't we open the door and let your ladies in? They have been so worried about you." She nodded to Meg who ushered in the giggling women, oohing and aahing over the baby and mother.

"Lady Elisabeth is all right then?" asked the blonde lady-in-waiting who had argued with William and threatened to call Sir Henry.

"Yes. She had a difficult time, but she is alive and well, with her precious babe by her side, as you can see," Alice replied.

The woman frowned as if she didn't quite believe it. "There were screams..."

"As there always are during birth, milady." Alice gestured to mother and son, a picture of serenity. "And look here, Lady Elisabeth. Look who I have with me, my daughter-in-law, Emma. She will serve as a wet-nurse. Her baby died recently, and she has plenty of milk."

"Oh, God bless you. Thank you, Emma." Elisabeth's voice trembled, as if talking was too fatiguing. She reached for Emma's hand. "I'm so sorry you lost your baby."

Emma stroked the cheek of the baby asleep in the crook of Elisabeth's arm. "Oh, thank you, milady, but my son is in a far better place now than when he was alive." Emma grinned at Meg as if the two were boon companions, sharing a secret.

***

The next day, the inhabitants of St. Michael's Mead stood in the village graveyard to witness the burial of Tim and Emma's infant, taken during the night with a fever and bloody flux of his bowels. The distraught parents held hands at the edge of the grave and cried noisily as Father Fitzhugh threw dirt upon the tiny casket.

Alice told the story to anyone who would listen, how she fed the poor baby all the known remedies, how her son and his wife were beside themselves with grief, and how she was overcome with sadness when she could not save her own grandchild.

"Truly God's will was done," she said, dabbing at her wet cheeks, "for nothing seemed to work on the little fellow." Tim and Emma let loose a fresh torrent of tears.

Meg had to remind herself their grief was false, that the baby now sleeping forever in the black earth of St. Michael's graveyard did not belong to Tim and Emma, but to Sir Henry. An imposter lay swaddled in the cradle at Caldecote Hall. He would be raised as Sir Henry's rightful heir—unless Alice was exposed. It had been her idea to switch the infants. She had used her own grandchild. She would bear the brunt of the punishment.

Meg tried to swallow but only managed a guttural croaking sound. The truth was they would all be punished. Perhaps William and Gerard would be spared a harsher sentence. But she, as Alice's apprentice, would not. She looked at Alice and was amazed at the calm and unruffled woman accepting condolences from fellow villagers.

They returned to Lady Elisabeth's side after the funeral. While Emma nursed the baby, Meg stroked Elisabeth's arm to wake her. Something was wrong. Her arm was too warm. She placed her palm on Elisabeth's forehead.

"What is it?" Alice asked.

"She is burning with fever."

Alice called in Master William. Valerian, he said, the correct herb for female weakness. Alice argued for motherwort. William finally agreed. Fortunately, motherwort was growing in Alice's garden.

Meg was ordered to bring the blossoms to the manor kitchen.

She and Alice had used motherwort combined with mullein over the winter to cleanse the villagers who were coughing. It killed worms in the belly as well. There was no mistaking syrup of motherwort. It had a pungent odor and a very bitter taste.

"Should someone come to you complaining of melancholy, a syrup of motherwort mixed in wine will drive the vapors from them and make their minds cheerful and merry," Alice said. "'Tis powerful against wicked spirits."

Having tasted the bitter syrup, Meg decided it wasn't the syrup that cured melancholy, it was the threat of having to take it again.

Meg ran through an afternoon rain shower and was soaked from head to toe by the time she arrived at the cottage, but she was happy Alice had trained her to recognize the garden plants. She found the motherwort drooping under the heavy raindrops. She ran her fingers over the prickly teeth of the pinkish flowers, and satisfied she had chosen the right plant, pulled a knife from her belt and cut the flowers from the stalk.

Over the next few days, William and Alice tried desperately to keep Elisabeth alive, but her fever grew stronger and her breasts swelled to the hardness of stone. She shook with heat and chills and shrieked as the pains in her abdomen threatened to split her in two. She vomited until nothing but a thin green liquid came out of her mouth and then she vomited nothing.

Meanwhile, Emma offered Sir Henry's lusty infant her own leaking nipples every time he squawked with hunger.

By the fifth day, pus began to ooze from Elisabeth's womb and no matter how much Meg and Alice cleaned her, a rancid smell emanated from between her legs.

Three days later, she succumbed to the fever.

✳✳✳

After Elisabeth's death, Meg tossed and turned at night and must have moaned in her sleep, for Alice mentioned it and prepared a hot chamomile drink before bedtime.

Truth was, Meg had the same nightmare every time she closed her eyes. She saw Elisabeth's face appear before her, smiling and happy, but then Elisabeth spied William and Gerard coming to her bed. She begged Meg to send the men away, yet Meg could neither speak nor move. She stood rooted to the floor, powerless and weak against the two men who held double-bladed weapons against her. Weeping, Elisabeth reached for the basin holding her dead child. She handed the basin to Meg who stared at the bloody water. Instead of an infant in the basin, she saw . . . she saw . . . *herself*, sleeping peacefully, her head and limbs strewn about her. The eyes in Meg's head opened. The mouth spoke to her. "Do something," it said.

That was when Meg always woke with screams on her own lips. Quaking, she would turn over and spend the rest of the night playing Elisabeth's labor over and over in her mind's eye.

"No men," Elisabeth said in the dream.

After another sleepless night, Meg confided in Alice. Perhaps she would know what Elisabeth was trying to tell her. After thinking on it, Alice said, "Women are embarrassed to reveal themselves to strange men—in body as well as spirit. No woman wants a strange man looking at parts meant only for her husband's eyes. Would you want to be splay-legged and have a strange man poke around in your privates?

"No. But how sad that a woman should die of embarrassment," Meg said.

"The way of the world, but look on the bright side—it keeps me busy."

Truth was, the dream was right. She, Meg, was in pieces. There must have been something else she could have done to save Elisabeth, but what? She was a simple girl from the country, and more than that, a girl branded by the Devil himself. But women were dying, *dying* for lack of a woman who had the knowledge to help them.

The men of the world could call in surgeons or expensive doctors of phisik from London to look after their wounds or cure them of disease—but their wives and sisters, possessed of a womb and bearing its burdens, were confined to their own devices for the care of women's matters. Most, like Elisabeth, refused to confer with anyone but other women.

Meg wondered how many women had died because a learned man was not wanted at her bedside. How many lives could be saved if, instead of a man, a learned *woman* could help?

She had a gift. She was sure of it. She wanted to put her gift to use. It wasn't just a foolish wish to be the best healer in all of Christendom, as she had rashly bragged to William of Oxford. She wished to learn more. To *be* more. She wanted to be a surgeon and doctor of phisik like William. She wanted to go to university like Gerard.

But how would that come to pass? How could a country

girl with a face fit for pigs be licensed as a doctor of phisik? And what would Alice say about her improbable wishes?

She didn't have to ask. She knew the answer. It was one of Alice's favorite sayings.

If wishes were horses, we would all have a merry ride.

St. Michael's Mead, May 1322

After Lady Elisabeth Despenser's death, Meg vowed to concentrate on her lessons. She set to work with an intensity that surprised even Alice. She brewed a concoction for coughs without spilling a drop, ground coriander seed to the finest dust, stitched a garlic necklace without pricking her finger and made a salve for burns without asking Alice a thousand questions about the ingredients.

Alice said nothing, simply nodded approval. She tested the salve against the back of her hand and smiled at Meg. Both of them knew it was perfect, smooth in consistency with the right proportion of goose grease and lemon verbena.

Meg allowed herself to be pleased, but only for a moment. She had rashly bragged to Master William that she would be the most famous healer in all of Christendom and, truth was, she desired this with all of her being. She just wasn't sure how to get there.

A fortnight later, a delegation of men from the village stood at Alice's door. They jostled each other, one man waiting for the other to speak. Meg thought it amusing when grown men who strutted about the fields all day were reduced to yammering boys in the presence of Alice. Finally, the miller cleared his throat and begged Alice's pardon for disturbing her. He was asking, he said, for the blessing of the fields.

"I, uh, I mean we," he motioned to the men around him, "we've come to ask you to bless the Earth, Mother Alice. We've asked the reeve, and he's given his permission. We thought, well, there's been so much lost these past few years with the cold, all the rain, the crops."

Alice smiled. "And not as much business for the miller, eh?"

He reddened, adding a deeper crimson to his ruddy face. "Aye, 'tis true. That is why we thought you might help us."

"You want a blessing in the old way, then?"

The men agreed. "Would you say the proper words for us, Mother Alice?" the miller asked.

"On one condition. Meg assists me."

The men hesitated. There was an exchange of fearful glances. They stared at Meg. She dropped her head, her cheeks burning in shame, and hid her face against Alice's shoulder.

Following much muttering and swearing while Alice waited impassively, her hands folded calmly across her ample belly, they said Meg could come and assist Alice in whatever was necessary. In return for the blessing, they offered eggs, milk, and cheese.

"Hmmm," Alice said. "I'm not sure Mother Earth would consider that a fair return for the work Meg and I will need to do."

The miller started to object, but Alice raised her hand to stop him.

"We can always wait, see what the spring and summer will

bring. Perhaps it will rain. Perhaps not."

"All right then," the miller said. "I'll personally give you a silver penny. That should be enough."

"And a flitch of bacon."

"Done."

"And a loaf of bread. And a dozen eggs."

The miller frowned, but he relented. "Done."

They agreed the miller would prepare the plow needed for the service and Alice would bring the salt, herbs, and holy water. With luck, their magic would entice the earth to flourish.

"One other thing," Alice said as the men were about to leave. "The priest stays away. I do not want his interference. He'll ruin the magic for sure."

The miller promised to keep Father Fitzhugh out of sight.

"Well, girl," Alice said when the men were out of sight, "That was the most fun I've had in a very long time. Now let's get to work. Do you remember how the verse goes? Fairest . . ."

"*Erce, Erce, Erce,* fairest Mother Earth," Meg began and then recited the verses without missing a word or failing a gesture.

In the afternoon, they scrubbed and dusted until the cottage sparkled. It was necessary, Alice said, to have a clean home, body, and mind when beseeching help from Mother Earth who gave them so much.

Before the evening meal, they went to the river to strip off their clothes and bathe away months of grime. Meg ran into the water, but Alice hesitated. "Come in, Mother Alice," she called.

Slowly, the old woman walked until the water was up to her knees. She knelt and said, "This is far enough."

Meg laughed. "Surely not. How are you going to wash?"

"I confess I have a fear of water, especially of putting my head under," Alice said. "You'll think me acting like a child for sure."

"Here, give me your hands. I'll hold on to you," Meg said, and she walked backward until they were in chest-deep water.

They soaped their hair and bodies. Meg grasped Alice's hands again and squeezed as they ducked under the surface. Clean and rinsed, Meg raced ahead while Alice hobbled as quickly as she could, all the while cursing the pains in her knees and hips.

As they warmed themselves before the fire, Alice combed sweet rose oil through Meg's hair and then expertly twisted it into two long braids. Tired from the day's work and struggling to keep her eyes open, Meg lay down on her pallet. The sweet fragrance of straw and mint, which they had stuffed into the pallets earlier, rose to meet her.

Alice, her aches and pains forgotten, sat cross-legged in the firelight, looking as supple as a young woman. She swept her long white hair over one shoulder and combed rose oil through it until the tangles were gone. As she rubbed the oil across her pendulous breasts, stomach, and broad thighs, she sang to herself.

A worm came creeping and tore asunder a man . . .

Alice appeared to shimmer as she crooned. Meg blinked her eyes, knowing what she was seeing was impossible, but it appeared Alice was floating above the fire. The words she sang were strange and familiar all at once.

And Woden smote the serpent, and you, mother of herbs, you have power against the loathsome foe roving through the land . . .

She sang of mugwort and chamomile, of worm-blister and venom-loather, peculiar words that made no sense to Meg but gave her comfort nevertheless. She hoped she could banish the villagers' fears tomorrow with as much quiet calm. She sent a silent prayer to St. Anthony, the patron saint of pigs, and fingered the hogshair bracelet. *Please,* she whispered, *let it be so.*

Chapter 9

Of Worm-Blister and Venom-Loather

St. Michael's Mead, May 1322

Meg's feet were wet with dew, but she barely noticed. In her palm, she clutched a handful of dirt. The ground was cold, moistened by a thick morning fog, which skirted the field and hung in the wasteland near the river. She steadied herself and wished again for Alice. She could almost hear the old woman scold her . . . *wishing won't make it so, girl, do what you must based on your wits, not your wishes.*

The villagers' stares burrowed into her skin. *Oh, Alice, why, oh, why, did you have to be ill today of all days?*

"Must have been the night air and cold dip in the river," Alice grumbled. "My bones are too old for such foolishness. You will have to go on without me, girl."

Meg's legs went weak. "No, no, Mother Alice, I cannot. They'll be angry."

Alice groaned and pushed Meg away. "You know the ceremony as well as I. There's nothing to it. Just go up to the field at sunup, say the words, and come home. And don't forget to get payment from the miller."

"But why not just wait a day or two? I cannot do this by myself."

Alice had insisted. The time was right. There would be a full moon still visible at dawn. The first green shoots were just out of the ground. Another month and it would be too late. Besides, if a healer was having her monthly blood when she blessed the fields, the crops would be poisoned. Meg's last flow had just ended. The ceremony had to be conducted now.

So here she was, standing in the middle of the barley field at dawn, shivering, half-blinded by the morning sun, and asking herself just what in the name of all the saints she was supposed to do next.

Someone coughed. A baby cried. John and Agnes stood beside her, waiting for her to begin. She hoped they would be pleased the village was in her capable hands. Maud and Oswald leaned against each other and looked at Meg in anticipation. Maud lifted her head as if to say, well, little sister, get on with it. Oswald winked at her and wrapped his arms around Maud's waist.

What had Alice said? The time was right? Yes, right to call upon the mother who gave them food, right to say, what? Meg realized her arm was outstretched. Overhead, a crow wheeled and dipped, calling loudly in mockery of her feeble attempts to serve in Alice's place. She opened her hand and saw a clod of dirt in her palm. Her fingerprints scalloped the edges.

Earth. She held a piece of earth.

"*Erce, Erce, Erce,*" she began. Her voice was a husky whisper, soon rising to full strength, commanding the field and the people watching her. "Fairest Mother Earth, may the all-ruler grant you, eternal Lord, fields growing and flourishing, propagating and strengthening, hail to thee, Mother Earth!"

She broke the clod of earth with her fingers and spread the dirt around her. At her feet were four pouches of seeds. She reached for the barley. "Be growing and fertile, by the goodness of God, filled with fodder, our folk to feed." With a flourish, she threw barley seeds into the air. She did the same with the oats, wheat, and flax seeds. The wind scattered them across the field.

"We pray you Mother Earth, defend our crops from worms, from winged things, from demons, from lightning bolts, from all temptation of the devil, through the invocation of the most holy name, Jesus Christ."

As promised, the miller had prepared the plow by gouging a hole in the beam. Meg placed incense, fennel, hallowed soap, and salt in the hole and then accepted a loaf of bread no bigger than Meg's palm from the miller's wife. She put the bread in a bowl and poured milk and holy water over it. Then she poured the contents into a furrow beneath the plow.

With the miller standing ready, Meg held aloft Alice's gnarled hawthorn staff and waited for silence. Even the birds ceased chirping. She raised her arms aloft and then pounded the staff into the ground. "I force you, Mother, to grow and multiply!" she shouted. "*Crescite*, grow. *Multiplicamini*, multiply! Grow in the name of the Father!"

The miller pushed the plowboard forward, slicing the earth as easily as if the field were a sea parted by an old prophet. Meg fell to the ground and lay there prostrate, her nose buried in the loamy smell of birth and death, rot and flower. She was sinking, sinking into dark tunnels of hairy fibrous roots that wiggled and shimmied like serpents. She said a *Pater Noster* and pushed herself to her feet. "Be blessed. Amen," she whispered.

The villagers echoed her. "Amen."

Afterwards, as the crowd left the field and Meg wiped the last of the dirt from her hands, she saw the miller striding toward her. "Well done," he said. "Alice couldn't have done better herself." He pressed a silver penny into her palm. "My wife will bring the rest of the payment later."

Holding the penny tightly in her fist, she ran toward Alice's cottage. The old healer would be proud of her, she was sure. She turned west away from the river and into an area where the forest overtook the path, where low-hanging branches created a burrow of shifting shade and sunshine. The shadows scattered at her feet and made her uneasy. Even when she'd driven the pigs through here, she always hurried.

"Stop right there!"

Theodoric, the miller's son, blocked her way

He could often be found in the church whispering prayers with Father Fitzhugh instead of grinding grain with his own father. The priest was preparing him for studies at Oxford. The miller often boasted his son would one day be a bishop. If so, Meg thought, he would be the cruelest churchman these parts had ever seen.

Meg had no time for his foolishness. He had made her life a misery. "Move out of my way, Theodoric. I've work to do with Mother Alice."

"You," he said, "you're only fit to work with pigs."

"Don't be ridiculous," Meg sputtered. "I was merely help-ing—"

"Oh, I know. Father told me. You know you could be ex-communicated or worse. The old ways are forbidden."

"It was your own father who insisted we bless the earth in the old way," she spat at him. "Go talk with him and leave me be."

"Speaking of which . . ." He snatched her hand and twisted the penny from her grasp. "This belongs to my father."

Her humiliation brought tears to her eyes. She stifled a sob and felt her heart harden against him. She would take no more of his vicious ways. He had made her life miserable with his taunts and beatings. She had had enough of cruelty mas-querading as righteousness.

She forced her elbow into his chest. "Out of my way," she shouted and made a move to go by him. He stood his ground.

"What are the seven deadly sins?" he demanded.

"What?"

"Speak!"

Her mind raced. The seven deadly sins. Anger? No. Adultery? No, the Ten Commandments. "Covet, covet thy neighbor's . . ."

"No! Try again. In Latin."

"I do not know Latin! Are you mad?" Suddenly she was very scared. This felt serious. Deadly. He *must* be mad.

He grabbed her tunic and pulled her closer but she punched his chin with such force she felt the bones shuffle like a game of pigs knuckles. She tried to slide away from him, but she was caught in his grasp. Blood poured from his nose and lip.

"You whore!"

He pushed her and she fell backwards, hitting her head against a stone on the path. Pain radiated through her skull. She couldn't escape him.

Theodoric put his hands around her throat and squeezed. A gurgling noise came out of her mouth and the edges of her vision blurred.

"Wait," he said. "I've another idea before I kill you."

As he loosened his grip on her neck, she sucked in a deep breath, struggling to keep from fainting. She gasped as her sight cleared and realized he had taken off his tunic and was untying his braies.

Blessed St. Anthony, help me, she prayed. He means to force himself upon me. Please help me. For some reason, the words she had spoken earlier flooded her mind. *Erce, Erce, Erce.*

She felt a calmness spread through her. She felt light as if her body was rising higher and higher to blue sky, a safe place where she could fly above the village of St. Michael's Mead and the field she had blessed this morning, and most importantly fly above the boy who hated her. Her mind grew still. She felt as if she were made of sun and air, sky and earth. She could see Theodoric's rump moving rhythmically as he pumped away. She could see the Meg who lay on the ground, still, almost lifeless. A flood of sadness washed over her for the poor girl below, the child with the crooked face whose tears silently fled her body and wet the earth beneath her.

She slid away from the comforting bonds of heaven and slipped once again into herself. She felt the hard ground beneath her, a pebble pressing into her backbone, listened to a thrush singing in the wood. As Theodoric finished with his wickedness, he lay spent on the ground, exhausted by his labors. His eyes rolled back with pleasure and she felt his body slacken.

An arrow of rage shot through her at the sight of a smile on his contemptuous face. He began to snore.

She lay silent then wriggled onto her knees. She stood above him observing his unperturbed sleep, his rising and falling chest, his legs spread wide as if his wickedness had drained all his vigor, as if she was nothing but a lowly beast he could treat with contempt. She was disgusted by the look of him. One day he would pay for his wickedness. Until then . . .

She kicked him hard in the groin. He cursed in pain and sat up. She kicked him even harder.

He was rolling from side to side, writhing in pain, his knees pulled to his chest. She kicked his knees aside and reached into his money pouch. She grasped the penny.

And then she ran.

✳✳✳

Later, Theodoric's mother Betty delivered the rest of the payment. She handed the basket to Alice who found the flitch of bacon and loaf of bread, as well as extra eggs and cheese, and a special bonus—a jar of honey.

"Uh, Mother Alice," Betty said haltingly. "Um, it seems my dear Theodoric has come to some mischief."

So, Alice thought, the mystery is clear. The "mischief" as Betty put it no doubt involved Meg and explained the girl's current condition.

Seeing Alice's expression, Betty faltered and then said, "His lip is bleeding and a tooth is loose. He's in a fair bit of pain. If you could—"

"My knees and feet are crippled today." Alice shifted and grimaced as if to prove the point. "So, I could not help you if I wanted to. Nor could my apprentice, young Meg. It seems she has come to some mischief of her own. Perhaps the two events are related, then?"

"Oh, I think not, Mother Alice." Betty was backing up. "My Theodoric came home straight after the ceremony this morning, which I might add was done quite well by your Meg. We'll have good crops for sure. Everyone says so."

"I'm glad to hear it," Alice said. "Unfortunately, Meg lies in her bed with a draught of belladonna coursing through her body, hopefully taking away all memory of the 'mischief' as you call it."

The miller's wife blushed and waved an imaginary insect away from her face. "Theodoric is a devout boy who is faithful to Father Fitzhugh. Sometimes devotion gets the better of his reason."

"Then he needs to leave young girls alone and give what's left of his prick to the priests," Alice said sharply.

Betty gasped at the blasphemy.

"And I will tell you this," Alice added. "If he ever, *ever* touches Meg again, I can assure you he will regret it. Do you understand me?"

"Yes, yes, Mother Alice, I understand. Perhaps his father and I can set him to rights."

"You do that," Alice said.

Betty fled toward the village.

Watching her make haste, Alice remembered the horrible sight which had greeted her this morning when Meg returned from the ceremony. A mask of blood concealed Meg's face and her tunic was filthy. Her mouth was swollen, her lips a ghastly purple. Alice thought at first the villagers had beaten the girl.

But no. Meg handed her the penny and smiled, her swollen lips contorting into a grimace. "The miller gave me this. His son tried to take it, but I wouldn't let him." And she had fallen into Alice's arms.

When Alice laid her on the pallet, she noticed the blood running down the girl's legs. She lifted her tunic and cried out. She had been wrong to call it mischief. It was far worse than mischief. A rage and hatred had been thrust upon the child with a fiercesomeness that made Alice shudder.

Later in the evening, Alice watched Meg cry out in her sleep and jerk in spasms of fear, and she knew she must intervene in the course of Theodoric's life. Betty, fearful of a wise woman's power, would warn her son to stay away from Meg. But Theodoric's hatred surpassed any threats his mother or an old woman might make. It was never good to use magic to interfere with Fate, but if she did not intervene, Theodoric would accost Meg again, somewhere and sometime in the future, she was sure of it. Indeed, he would kill her if he could.

She assembled the ingredients of a spell she promised her mother she would never use. She reached for the special crocks hidden on the highest shelf. They were thick with dust.

Theodoric might hate Meg, but if he dared hurt her again, he would pay dearly.

Her magic would see to it.

Chapter 10

DEAD TO THE WORLD

St. Michael's Mead, May 1322

"Let's have a look at you. How long have you been bleeding, John?"

John ducked his head like a wood mouse skittering for safety.

"Soon after daybreak. It stopped for a time but started again. I thought only boys had nosebleeds. Here I am a grown man and bleeding like a gawky lad. I'm sure 'tis nothing." He wiped his bloody nose with the back of his sleeve. "But I thought perhaps you might help."

"Of course, John." Alice led him to the pallet, where she slipped a bolster under his head. She gingerly wiped his nostrils of excess blood.

He coughed again, and a bubble of mucus formed at the end of his nose.

Alice ordered Meg to fetch clean rags. Working together, they packed each nostril with a plug of cloth in an attempt to stop the bleeding, but to no avail. Meg watched in horror as each plug grew red.

"Lie still while we pack it again," Alice said.

"It'll be all right, Father," Meg said as she held his hand and stroked the rough skin of his palm. "We'll get you to rights in no time." She lowered her eyes, hoping her father was too distracted to see the look of shock on her face. Not only was he bleeding from the nostrils, but droplets of blood oozed from a misshapen lump at the end of his nose.

Alice had noticed, too. "You've had a sore here for quite a while, haven't you?" she asked. "I first looked at it, what was it? Four or five years ago?"

"Aye, but it's never bothered me much. Never paid much attention to it."

Alice gently squeezed the fleshy mass. "Hmm. It's changed shape over the past months. Perhaps it would be best if William the Surgeon looks at it. He is still at Caldecote Hall bleeding some of Sir Henry's men. Meg will fetch him."

"Oh, no! No surgeons with their bloody rags and knives! I like my nose just fine, thank you very much, even if it is a bit out of kilter."

"I promise you, Master William will leave your nose intact."

✳✳✳

It did not take much persuasion to coax William to Alice's cottage. On the contrary, he had bounded down the castle steps at the mere mention of Alice's name.

"Well, come on, girl," he had shouted and lifted Meg onto his horse's wide rump. "Let's go see what has stumped our fair Alice, eh?"

"It's my father, sir."

"No need to explain." William kicked his horse into a trot.

"I'll make up my own mind."

Which is exactly what he did. It had taken perhaps all of a *Pater Noster* for William to examine the swollen bleeding lump.

William and Alice exchanged looks, but said nothing.

"Are there any other lumps?" William asked.

"Some."

"Show me then."

John untied his hose and rolled the fabric to his ankles. His legs were a mass of nodules.

"Ah," William said. "And do you notice any tingling in your hands or feet, John?"

Meg marveled at William's quiet demeanor, so different from the man whose impatience she had witnessed at Caldecote Hall.

"My feet, sir. But it's often due to the cold."

"Let me see your feet, please."

John sat on a bench and removed his hose and shoes. Lumps of skin, like hillocks and valleys in a miniature land, spread from his toes to his knees.

William asked Alice for a sewing needle.

"Now John, close your eyes. Do not be afraid. I won't hurt you. Just shut your eyes and tell me when you feel the prick of the needle."

John complied and William lightly jabbed the needle into the fleshy pads of John's feet. He paused and began the examination again, this time jabbing with more vigor.

John kept his eyes shut. Finally, he said, "Have you started, sir?"

"I have finished, John," William replied.

John opened his eyes in panic and begged William to repeat the test. He looked at each of them as if to say, what sort of man cannot feel the sharp prick of a needle?

"Do you feel this?" William ran the edge of his fingernail down the sole of John's foot.

At first, nothing registered on John's face, then slowly he

understood. He felt nothing. The gravity of his condition spread across his countenance.

"'Tis the cold, surely, sir," he said, and rubbed his feet as if he could knead the sensation back into his skin. "I'm a plowman. I spend long days out of doors."

Finally, after what seemed to be hours of silence, William spoke. And true to his manner, he did not mince words.

"John, you are a good man and a good father to young Meg here, therefore I cannot lie to you. You have leprosy."

"Leprosy? No, no, it cannot be. You've made a mistake, sir. I work hard in the fields. I cut myself and it bleeds and scabs up and then heals. See here, look." John pointed to his left leg. A bruise covered his shin. "See here where the ox caught me with her hoof. Surely you're wrong, sir."

"I'm not wrong, John."

"Well, then give me one of Mother Alice's horrible tasting drinks or bleed me or cup me, or something."

Before John finished his entreaty, he dropped to his knees, his head in his hands. Meg choked back her tears and placed a hand on her father's shoulder.

"I am sorry, John," William said.

Meg knew almost nothing about leprosy, but she had seen lepers near the Warwick city walls. They were hideous creatures. Forbidden to touch anyone, they held their begging bowls for coins and shook their clappers to alert good folk to their presence.

"You must go before Father Fitzhugh," William said. "The church requires his confirmation, but I am sure the good father will agree."

"I must show him?"

"Yes. And not just him. You must stand before the entire village, stripped to nothing but your braies. The church must confirm. Then . . ." He paused, and when he spoke again his voice was softer, gentler, "you *must* be—"

"Cast out," John answered woodenly.

"Yes."

Meg's eyes filled with tears. First Walter ran off to London, then Maud got herself married and moved into her own cottage, and now her father was cast out, forced to move in with his kind. There was no one left but her mother, a soul bent nearly double by the shadow of misfortune.

Meg's heart skipped a beat. With her father gone, Agnes would force Meg to return home. To be sure, her duty was to her mother, but her heart was no longer content to spin and cook, tend to the cow, and listen to her mother's complaints and sharp words. And without her father's cheerful squeeze of her shoulders to take the sting out of her mother's arrows, there would be no contentment at all, just sad, lonely days caring for a woman who, in truth, hated her.

"I have a friend in York, Brother Adolphus, chaplain of St. Nicholas Lazar Hospital," William was saying. He stared at Meg. "He would be happy to take another leper."

"But couldn't Father stay here? Perhaps with Alice and me. Or, or, maybe there is an empty cottage nearby."

"Lepers must live only with other lepers. They are unclean, though I do not believe they have sinned and are therefore punished."

"Is there not a place in Warwick? Someplace closer where we might visit him?"

"There is a lazar hospital in Warwick. But I have been told the brothers there take alms for themselves and give none of it to the poor souls who suffer within their house. The lepers are ill-fed and clothed in rags. Do you want this for your father?"

"No."

"If John is to join the lepers at St. Nicholas, he must bequeath his worldly goods to the hospital. Brother Adolphus has no care whether he is rich or poor, even a small amount is enough to gain him entrance."

"Master William, I know you mean well, sir, and I am truly grateful. But you do not understand. We have nothing to bequeath. We have one old milk cow and a handful of coins. The oxen belong to Sir Henry. We have no land. Nothing."

For a few moments, no one spoke.

Finally, William said, "I have a plan which might suit us both. I shall discuss it with Alice and Gerard. And also talk to your mother." He put his finger to his lips as Meg asked yet another question. "Do not worry yourself. Gather your father's belongings. He will need them in York. I will make the journey with him and take him to St. Nicholas."

"I will go with him," Meg said.

William shook his head. "Not possible. It's a long journey to the north and it would do your father no good to reach St. Nicholas only to have his daughter wail and howl at the gates."

"I would not, sir!" Meg swallowed and stood tall. "At such a time he must have family with him. My sister cannot leave the village, my brother is nowhere to be found, and my mother is not strong enough in spirit. It is up to me, sir, and I *will* go."

She stared at Master William, daring him to disagree.

William appeared taken aback, as if no one ever opposed him. "Well, Alice, what do you say to that, eh? The girl seems to have made up her mind."

Alice scratched at the ripples of flesh under her chin. She brightened. "We'll all go. There's an apothecary in York who sells mandragora. Very hard to come by. I've been wanting to go for years. So this is what we will do. I will go to the apothecary, Meg will say good-bye to her father, and you, William, will visit with your old friend, Brother Adolphus. And along the way, we will teach Meg and Gerard about the sickness which afflicts poor John."

William grudgingly agreed, but only if Meg promised to say goodbye to her father at the hospital gates.

"And," he said brusquely, "lessons will be held every day without fail."

Meg accepted his bargain, but her stomach constricted at the thought of coming under his tutelage. Alice could be sharp as nails when Meg blundered, but William had even less patience for the slow-witted. Moreover, his son Gerard could read and speak Latin. She would pale by comparison.

"Gerard and I must go to Caldecote Hall. Once Sir Henry hears the word 'leprosy,' he'll be anxious to get John out of the village. I'll beg the use of his best messenger to ride immediately to York and deliver a letter to Brother Adolphus announcing our coming. In the meantime, John's wife needs to be told."

"Meg and I will go to Agnes," Alice said.

"Very well. Prepare for the trip to York. We will leave after Father Fitzhugh's pronouncement."

John, who had been staring at the floor, nodded at William and then at Meg as if he had known them from long ago but could not remember when. He said nothing and then turned his mind to the floor once again.

✳✳✳

Meg's mother had taken the news badly. When John, Meg, and Alice entered her cottage, she had been sitting alone spinning thread from her distaff. As soon as Alice said the word 'leprosy,' her head snapped up, then she fell to the floor, writhing and thrashing her legs and arms, and thrusting her tongue in and out like a snake testing the air.

Meg knelt beside her, but Alice called, "Let her be."

"Alice, help her, please." Meg tried to capture Agnes's flailing arms and legs. "We must do something!" Strange words poured from her mother's mouth, a secret language known only to those who entered a land of madness. A white phlegm coated Agnes's chin and dripped to the floor.

"No. When the fit is over, we'll help her, but not before." Alice pulled Meg away. "Never touch someone in a fit until the demon leaves. You're likely to get a black eye for your troubles."

Meg's sister Maud, who had joined them to hear the news about their father, was crouched in the corner, sobbing in loud gulps. Her father, too, was crying. Unlike Maud, he made no sound. His body was still, but his eyes, filled with overspilling tears, were locked on Agnes as if the fire of her anger could cure him.

They would dose Agnes with valerian and poppy juice over the next few days, Alice said. Agnes would know nothing of John's departure until he was well on his way north. When she awoke and was herself again, she would realize she was now alone in the world.

"Then I'm feared she'll lose her senses for good," Alice said.

Maud looked to Meg, one sister to another, each one thinking the same thoughts. John in York. Their brother Walter gone. Their mother alone.

Meg caught the slight shake of Maud's head as if she were saying, I have a husband and a home of my own now with crying babies and more to come. If anyone is to care for a madwoman, it is you, little sister.

You. 'Tis always you.

May 1322

They had been on the road for seven days, an interminable journey for someone who had never been beyond St. Michael's Mead and the occasional market day in Warwick. Meg shifted in the saddle. Her rump was sore to the bone from so much riding, and she was sure the skin of her backside would never be the same. She regretted the day she had ever wished to see the wider world, for it seemed the world was a great deal larger than she had imagined. And the lessons! Oh, how her head hurt from William's expectations.

On the first day, they left at cockcrow and rode until they found an inn near sunset. John, whose condition might bring stares and questions, gladly stayed in the stable with the horses. The inn was noisy and crowded, but their room on the second floor was clean, and the lamb stew and hard brown bread, which the innkeeper set before them filled their bellies. After they finished the meal, Meg brought a bowl of stew to her father and an extra blanket. He laid down on the straw, pulling the blanket over his head.

When she returned to the room, William said sharply, "Now. Lessons." Longing for sleep, she stole a glance at Gerard. He was aloof as usual.

They discussed cause and care. There was no cure. Leprosy started with pale spots on the skin which turned into red nodules. Eventually, the hands and feet lost feeling. The nose decayed. Blindness occurred.

William carried several books in his traveling bag and each night as Gerard read the Latin text and translated, Meg was filled with an all-consuming envy. Surely Gerard must have been born under a fortunate star to have such an easy life and so learned a father.

Remembering this now, she felt a pang of guilt and reached for her father's hand. He jerked away, as if ashamed to have her touch him. "We must catch up with the others," she said, as she pressed against her mare's sides until the horse grunted and picked up her trot. Her father followed slowly behind.

✳✳✳

As they approached York, they were joined by a variety of travelers. Families whose carts were filled with cheese, milk, and wool, and merchants transporting cloth and wine in wagons joined yeomen balancing crates of chickens or rabbits at the end of their yokes. Occasionally, they passed pilgrims traveling to the great cathedral or vagabonds going north.

When the sun was at midday, a thin man in a scarlet chaperon lined with squirrel fur rode beside them and raised his hand in greeting. "What, ho! Good day to you, travelers! On the road to York, are you? Have you been to York before?"

The man was dressed like an outlandish bird. His yellow

hose were crisscrossed with strips of blue silk and his tunic, a bright brocade of blue and green, sparkled in the sunshine. On his head was a jaunty felt hat of deep green encircled by a red and gold hatband. A peacock feather thrust into the crown of the hat bobbed as the man greeted them.

William opened his mouth to answer, but the stranger continued without notice, "Let me introduce myself ." He removed his hat, crushing the feather. "I am Robertus Medicamus. This is my traveling companion, Saracen." He stroked his horse's neck. The mare, a dapple gray with jutting hip bones, was so deep in the withers Medicamus's feet dragged the ground. He gave his bulky leather bag a pat. Out popped the head of a little baby, covered in hair and chattering loudly in a strange language. "And this is my helper, Pettipaw." The baby climbed Medicamus's arm and perched on his shoulder.

Meg had never seen such a child. It could climb with all four legs and at the end of his body, there was a long tail—a *tail!*—which he wrapped around Medicamus's neck. "I am a traveling healer. Saracen, Pettipaw, and I have lately come from exotic lands far to the east," Medicamus explained.

Meg wondered if people in those strange places were covered with hair and had long tails.

"But forgive me for going on and on. Who might you be, sir?" He looked at William. "I can see by your scarlet robe and cap you are a learned man, a doctor of phisik perhaps?"

"And I see, Medicamus, you have exchanged the legitimate scarlet of our profession for the costume of an imposter."

Medicamus stopped short and stared at William. "Ah, William of Oxford, forgive me. You have changed a great deal since our school days. Older. More wrinkles, less hair. But always the serious scholar, never the scoundrel. And ever the sharp tongue. A pleasure to meet you again after so many years." He tipped his hat and the baby chattered excitedly. Medicamus turned his attention to Alice. "And, madam, are you making the journey to York as well?"

"Yes, we all go to York. I am Alice of St. Michael's Mead. This is my apprentice Meg and William's son Gerard."

"A pleasure to meet you," Medicamus remarked while grinning at William who sat straight-backed in his saddle and looked ahead. "We knew each other many years ago, eh, William? And some of those years we were friends." He winked as if to say, more than friends, bosom companions, drinkers of fine ale, chasers of skirts.

"We were foolish students," William said, scowling. "Who could know one of us would *pretend* to practice medicine and make a fortune while the other would actually *practice* the profession and be none the richer for it."

"Ah, I believe someone suffers from the sin of envy. You are welcome to join me on the road, Master William. I will gladly share the stage with you."

"No, thank you. I do not fancy myself a thief and a cheat."

Medicamus put a hand on his chest. "William, it pains me to hear you speak so. I have only the finest medicaments made by my very own hands. Cures for everything from dropsy to falling sickness and . . ." He looked at Meg and smiled. "Love potions." Suddenly he sat upright. "Forgive me, I have forgotten to ask you of your plans. Where do you stay tonight?"

No one spoke.

Finally, William answered gruffly, "We stay with the kind brothers of St. Nicholas. Near Walmgate."

At the mention of the leper house, Medicamus jerked the reins but soon recovered, while eyeing each one of them curiously and settling on John, who was lagging far behind and whose face was disguised by a veil.

"I know them well, sir," he said. "The good brothers often buy medicine from me, as do the lepers. You'd be surprised what goes on inside a leper house. Not all prayers and gardening, if you get my meaning."

William sat taller in his saddle. "Sir, I do get your meaning and I assure you Brother Adolphus allows nothing but the best behavior in his hospital."

"Oh, I quite agree," said Medicamus. "Now, if you'll excuse me, I must make haste to York." He bowed again. "Do not forget the Minster grounds on the morrow," he called as he passed a carter and chatted with a young couple riding double on a swaybacked donkey. "Allow me to introduce myself."

"Father, who is that strange man?" Gerard asked.

"Ahhh, I knew him when we were young at the Schola Medica in Oxford. We were friends—more than friends, more like brothers—we did the usual things young students do. Chased women, drank far too much, brawled with our enemies. And studied. You would never know it, but he was a brilliant student. He could have gone so far."

William pulled his horse to the right to go around the couple astride the donkey and Meg and the others followed him in a single line. As Meg passed Medicamus talking to the young couple, he took out a vial and held it under the woman's nose. Meg smelled the sweet scents of lavender and rosewater, and something darker, earthier . . . mandrake root, perhaps. A love potion. Medicamus leaned down and whispered to the girl. She giggled and blushed.

Gerard twisted in his saddle to take a final look at Medicamus. "He doesn't look so brilliant now. He looks like a common phisik monger."

"Yes, exactly. As I say, he was like a brother to me, a younger, ill-mannered brother who took the easy path. When he discovered his skill at fleecing the public, he left Oxford. It was a painful leave-taking."

"Master William," Meg begged, "may we go to the Minster to see him? Please, sir?"

"Oh, most definitely." William's tone led Meg to fear he had something more in mind than buying medicine from the traveler. "But first we have a duty to your father."

"Of course." Meg, feeling properly chastised, pulled on the reins and dropped alongside John. "Father, are you well today?"

John grunted and eyed her morosely.

Last night William reminded her she had promised to behave at the hospital gate. She was not to shrink in fear of the lepers or call out in horror today at St. Nicholas. He meant no weak female displays of fainting or frenzy, she guessed. She lifted her chin and dared him to say more with her stare.

Now, as they rode closer to the city, Meg prayed for courage. She had to be strong for her father. She had to prove to Master William she could endure the cruel revelations of the disease. She pulled on her horse's reins and leaned closer to her father's arm, but he lurched away. Except for her father's outburst when William proclaimed he had leprosy, John had been strangely silent. Gone were his boisterous stories and ribald jokes, and his booming laughter. The old John was gone. Nothing she could say would change his destiny. Nothing would relieve his pain. Nothing would make him laugh again.

✳✳✳

"What ho, we meet again!" Medicamus greeted them loudly as they approached Micklegate Bar on the south side of the city walls. They had stopped at the entrance to York to rest before paying a fee to enter. "I have been thinking. You need a guide to steer you through this tempestuous pot of human flesh. With Parliament in session here, every baron, their wives, and retainers are swelling the city." He cocked his head toward Meg, waggling his peacock feather.

Meg agreed with Medicamus. A cacophony of voices rose above the gray stone walls towering above her head. She had never seen so many people. And they were in such a hurry! They jostled past with no apology for bumping against them and some even shouted in strong northern accents for the newcomers to get out of the way or go back where they came from.

Atop the walls, the heads of murderers and thieves rotted

upon pikes and served as a warning to ne'er-do-wells they would face swift justice in York if they transgressed. Meg could not imagine what horrors were contained behind those walls, but the ever-cheerful Medicamus seemed undaunted by the thought of selling his wares to the townspeople.

"I'll take you to St. Nicholas if you like," Medicamus continued. "I thought I would go there myself as I have a special ointment which may give the poor creatures relief. It's made from the horn of a unicorn recently kissed by a virgin."

Medicamus looked Meg up and down, and she felt her face grow hot.

"The hospital is outside the city walls and I can get you there," he continued, "but if you choose to go through the gates and into the city, you'll have a long walk in this crowd—down Micklegate, across the Ouse Bridge and then past the Minster where Walmgate leads out the east wall. And the multitudes—"

William interrupted impatiently. "I do not need your help, sir. I have been to York many times."

"When Parliament is in session? Look at this crowd!"

So it was they found themselves following Medicamus outside the great stone wall rather than entering the city. Medicamus led them down Baggergate keeping the moat and wall on their left, and occasionally pointing out special sights as if he were the Lord Mayor himself.

"And how do you know so much about the king and York?" William asked. "In the king's pocket, are you?"

"Oh no, certainly not," Medicamus sputtered. "If I were in the king's pocket, would I roam the land selling elixirs?" Medicamus pointed to the opposite shore where a smaller river, the Foss, emptied into the wide fast-flowing Ouse. "The ferry is just ahead. Let us move on."

Across the Ouse, church spires soared heavenward, their sturdy stone buildings anchoring each parish like ships at sea. The farthest church on top of the hill was their destination, William said. Meg hoped St. Nicholas was as close as it looked.

She was exhausted from the trip and felt faint from hunger. Also, her poor horse was beginning to stumble and could do with hay and a rest.

Within a short distance, they arrived at the ferry post. With calm assurance, the stocky wherryman loaded their horses and helped each passenger on board, even a shaking Alice. Meg remembered a time when she and Alice washed themselves in the river before the blessing of the fields. Alice refused to enter the deep water and admitted she had a fear of drowning.

"How can I trust when I cannot see the bottom?" Alice fumed. "Look how deep this is, how fast. If I fall in, I'll float to the sea and never be found."

The wherryman gently held her hand as she crossed from the bank to the rocking ferry. She sat down immediately and kept her eyes shut until the ferry bumped against the opposite bank.

Once they were all unloaded, they walked along a footpath on steadily rising farm fields until they came to the gates of the hospital. When William rang the bell, a stout man wearing a russet robe opened the gates and bade them enter.

"Welcome, William, welcome." The man embraced William and kissed him on both cheeks. "Your messenger arrived several days ago. We've been expecting you." He turned to Meg's father. "And you must be John. I am Brother Adolphus, the chaplain here. Our Master, Robert de Grymston, is in Parliament today at the Minster. You will meet him later." He turned to the traveling healer. "And Medicamus? How are you, sir? You came with these travelers as well?"

"Only briefly, but I enjoyed their charming company."

He described to Brother Adolphus his new ointment for the lepers and was told to come back tomorrow to show it to the sisters and brothers within the gates. "I will leave you here then," Medicamus said to the group. "Don't forget, tomorrow at the Minster."

Adolphus gestured to the group as if to speak, but William

interrupted. "Adolphus, I have known you for a long time, yes?"

"Why, yes, William," Adolphus said.

"And you know I have nothing but praise for your care of lepers and the infirmed."

"Yes, William. What is it? What troubles you?"

"Why do you allow that imposter . . ." He gestured toward a retreating Medicamus. "How could you let him within your gates? You know he has nothing of value."

"On the contrary, William," Adolphus said, "he has hope for these poor unfortunates. Yes, they may waste their money, but what else have they to do? Had you the bodies of these poor souls, perhaps you, too, would grasp at any possibility, even one as slim as powdered unicorn horn."

William's face flushed. "Not just any unicorn horn, mind you, but one kissed by a virgin."

"Well, then, given these times, it's rare indeed! Now, let us stop standing about like beggars at the city gates. We have a stable for the horses and nice accommodations for everyone here."

Adolphus pushed open the great wooden door and waved them into the grounds. Meg made no attempt to move, and the chaplain motioned to her. "Come on then," he said. Meg glanced at William, asking his permission to enter. "Yes, come in," he said, but he gave her a look meaning "no fainting fits."

Adolphus continued to wave, "And come in, madam," he motioned to Alice, "and, of course, Gerard. How are you, my lad? You were but the size of a turnip when I saw you last."

Gerard turned several shades of red and mumbled a greeting. Adolphus dropped the great iron bar on the gate, and the resounding finality of the noise seemed to shrink John into a shadow. He stared at the church and the small lodgings nestled across the cloister and then at Adolphus who put an arm around him and firmly led him into the hospital grounds.

"You would not care for life among the living, John," Adolphus said. "Just last week we buried a poor leper who was beaten to death outside the gates near St. Mary's Abbey. Oh, yes," he said as Meg and Alice gasped, "a young maiden reached from her horse to give alms to the poor leper and the man must have tripped, for he had no feet left to speak of, and he fell against the horse and without thinking grabbed the young woman's hand. She screamed and the leper was set upon instantly."

Adolphus made the sign of the cross. "Here, there is no such worry. Your clothing is provided and there is daily bread and drink, not to mention good care. Our grounds are large enough for growing our own food, and the Lord favors us with good vegetables and fat pigs and sheep."

John looked as if he understood, but Meg knew he was walking inside a dream, still in St. Michael's Mead and soon to be wakened by the cock crowing in the rafters.

"Father," Meg said and clutched at his sleeve, "you will grow to like it. And I'm sure they could use a plowman with your skills."

"Oh, most certainly," said Adolphus. "Although you may not feel up to it as your sickness progresses, but you may certainly supervise."

Trailing behind Adolphus, they followed a footpath which put them in front of low stone lodgings comprised of leper cells, each room with a door and window on the front wall. The rooms were joined to each other under a long thatched roof and faced a courtyard blooming with flowers and herbs.

"Decent and ample houses," Adolphus explained. "For men only." Women were housed inside the hospital in separate cells to eliminate temptation, he added.

He stopped and gestured toward another building. "You've had a long journey. If you like, we can stop for refreshments."

When everyone agreed with enthusiasm, Adolphus directed them to the refectory where meals were served. After Meg gobbled up her sesame cake and sucked down the last drop of ale, she folded her arms on the table and rested her head against them, hoping for a brief nap. She was exhausted, but her stomach fluttered at the thought of what would come later. Her father was drinking but not eating, still in a state of bewilderment, as if he had been dropped in a foreign land.

William leaned into Adolphus and whispered, "So Parliament is meeting here."

Adolphus nodded. "At the Minster, in the Chapter House."

Meg opened her eyes and caught William staring at her. She turned her head and pretended not to listen.

"Why York? And where is the king?" William asked.

"The king has been fighting the Scots in the north. York is as good a place as any to raise men and bully the barons."

"What does he want?"

"Besides his way?"

"With a king, that is a given, is it not?"

"Oh, certainly. But with famine these last years and flooding, not to mention the failure of every harvest and cattle murrain, we're lucky to have any morsel of food left in Yorkshire," Adolphus said. "And now the news has gone from bad to worse. Rumor has it the king has something up his sleeve regarding the Despensers, both Hugh the Younger and the Elder."

"Those two scoundrels? I thought they were banished."

"Banished no more, it seems. The king called them back. The Despensers are here in York. And ready to stand by Edward."

"The most evil father and son in Christendom. In England again. Unbelievable," William hissed.

Meg inhaled—the Despensers, kinsmen to Sir Henry—greedy, grasping men according to William. If they ran to Caldecote Hall to take refuge with Sir Henry, their enemies would follow. St. Michael's Mead could be destroyed in the process.

"I don't understand it," Adolphus said. "Before the Despensers, it was Piers Gaveston, another greedy sodomite. I thought the king would return to Isabella when the barons killed Gaveston, but it was not to be. Despenser. A man even worse than Gaveston." Adolphus drank his ale and belched. "The

King must not care for women."

"In London, it is said he cares for at least one woman ."

"Who?"

"His niece, Eleanor de Clare."

"His *niece*?"

"Worse. She is the wife of Hugh Despenser the Younger."

"An abomination!"

"I care not a whit whether Edward's prick tilts for male or female," William said. "It is his inability to govern that frightens me. Hugh the Younger is cruel and ambitious, yet the King is blind to his faults. Worse, Hugh has humiliated Queen Isabella publicly and privately. She hates him."

"I have seen her. She is a formidable woman. I do not think she will sit quietly at her embroidery."

"Nor do I," William replied. "She will not stand for it. Perhaps the barons will rally to her side."

"If they do, you know what will happen."

"Civil war."

"Exactly."

Meg sat up and watched as Adolphus tipped his head and stretched his neck to receive the last of the ale. "Ah, well, what can we mere mortals do but hide under our beds when the arrows start to fly?"

All this talk of a king and queen who hated each other, barons and evil men, war, and arrows flying had given Meg a headache. She didn't understand most of it, but she grasped the essence. If the Despensers were involved, there would be war. People would die. She wanted to ask William about Isabella, but Adolphus rose and invited his guests to continue their tour. When they reached the chapel steps, Adolphus turned to Meg's father.

"We have eight services a day, John, and you are expected to attend every one of them. Strict rules, but necessary for the orderly running of our special place. I would put us against Burton Lazars, the largest leper hospital in England, and we would not be found wanting," he said proudly.

Adolphus glanced at the sky. "It's getting late and I'm sure you are tired. I will say Mass and welcome John officially to our community, then the rest of you may sleep in the hospitium, away from our brothers and sisters who suffer God's punishment."

Meg saw William open his mouth as if to rebuke the priest for his notion of a God who would strike down innocents with so foul a disease, but apparently he thought better of it. He caught Meg's eye and shrugged.

Adolphus motioned toward a heavy oak door surrounded by a stone archway carved with four rows of astrological figures and strange beasts, sneering devils, and frightful dragons. Meg hurried past, thinking the stonemason must have carved his nightmares into the portal.

Alice stopped, her mouth agape at the strange beasts above her head. "Oh, how my Roger would have loved these stones," she murmured to Meg.

The priest lifted the heavy iron latch and pushed against the door, then hesitated. "When you arrived, I sent word to our brothers and sisters so they might welcome you to our little family. They are waiting for you inside." He looked at Meg, then at Gerard. "Their afflictions have affected them greatly. Please do them the honor of not crying out."

The door opened.

The denizens of hell manifested themselves in the flesh before them. Meg knew the creatures standing in the nave were human, but had she not been told she would have mistaken them for beasts. Their bodies and faces were twisted in a grotesque mockery of God's image. She felt Gerard flinch, but to his credit, his face did not reflect his fear.

A girl of about Meg's age greeted them. "Come in. Welcome." Her voice was low and husky, as if it belonged to an old crone near death. *Nodules in the throat will cause the voice to grow hoarse,* Meg remembered William saying. The girl bade them enter with a contorted grin — *a stroke caused by the leprosy pulls the face into a grimace* — and waved them into the church. Her fingers were now mere stumps. *The fingers and toes will lose feeling, then the flesh will rot until only the stubs remain.*

The girl motioned for them to approach the altar. Meg and Gerard stood to the left of John, with William and Alice flanking him on the right. Two lepers shuffled forward. In their fingers they held a long white linen cloth which they wrapped around John, enfolding him in layers, winding from head to foot, foot to head. They helped him lie down upon the cold stone floor, with his feet toward the altar, and bade him close his eyes. He was now covered in a shroud. He was a living corpse.

A deep-voiced bell tolled in rhythmic sorrow. Brother Adolphus, clad in a brightly embroidered cope, sprinkled John with holy water and then recited the story of Lazarus, who rose from the grave and was cured of leprosy by Jesus.

The gravity of her father's disease settled on Meg's shoulders like the gloom of a winter storm. She trembled, and Gerard reached for her hand, entwining his fingers around hers. The warmth of his hand stilled her and gave her strength to endure the priest's chanting.

Finally, the lepers removed John's shroud, and all walked in a mournful processional to the burial grounds between the church and the river. Meg stumbled along the path, and Gerard, who had not left her side, reached for her arm to steady her through the falling dusk. The bells of the city rang out, bidding farewell to the day, a day Meg wanted to forget.

Adolphus pointed to a rectangular hole in the ground the size of a coffin. A wooden cross stood at one end. "We will finish here," he said.

He ordered John to step into the grave. Two lepers helped John put one foot forward and then the other. "When your soul has left this mortal land," Adolphus said, "you will be buried here. Your flesh will return to the earth." He picked up a handful of dirt and threw it on John's feet. "As of this moment, John of St. Michael's Mead, you have departed the world of the living." He threw a second handful of dirt. "Dust to dust, ashes to ashes."

John was officially dead, as dead as if he had caught the pox and perished in its fevered grasp. His shoulders sagged and tears ran down his face, running past the landscape of nodules, and dropping like rain onto the dark soil at his feet.

Meg squeezed Gerard's hand. Alice stepped beside her and wrapped an arm over her shoulder, giving her a little pat.

"John of St. Michael's Mead, you are hereby commanded to reside at St. Nicholas Hospital for the remainder of your days. You may leave only to beg alms, but you must cry out 'Unclean, unclean!' wherever you go. You are forbidden to enter the city of York. You will carry a begging bowl and clapper. You will stand downwind of good folk. You are forbidden to touch anything except with your staff. Do you understand?" John nodded. "John of St. Michael's Mead you are now a brother of St. Nicholas. Enter into our family with blessings."

The lepers clapped with hands muffled by rags and bandages and shouted welcome.

In nomine Patris et Filii et Spiritus Sancti. Amen. Adolphus made the sign of the cross and reached for John. "Give me your hand, my son, and I will help you out. The grave is a cold place to stand."

Chapter 12

ROBERTUS MEDICAMUS

York, England, May 1322

York's crowded market was alive with the flesh of shoppers, hawkers of wares, entertainers, and bewildered countryfolk—Meg among them. Indeed, it appeared all the world had journeyed to York, and they were now jostling her for a look at Robertus Medicamus and his hairy baby. The crowd swelled as she walked with Gerard and William over the Foss Bridge past the fishmongers with their morning's catch laid head to tail, and up Walmgate toward the Minster. Along the way, the smell of human and animal waste, butcher's offal, and wood smoke mingling with the odors of cooking threatened to overwhelm her. The way people swarmed about her without a thought to her feet or their elbows and shoulders bumping against her made her feel as if she needed some ginger root to settle her stomach.

The great pointed arches and turrets of York Minster soared heavenward behind Medicamus. A passel of boys, aiming for a better view, clambered up the scaffolding around an enormous round window at the top of the building. Craftsmen laying orange tiles on the roof yelled at them to get down, but the boys ignored them.

Medicamus was standing on a table holding aloft a flask of liquid. He whistled the crowd into silence. "My good people," he said, "the female body is an unknown land."

"Speak for yourself, healer!" someone shouted from the back of the crowd and everyone laughed.

"Well, then, let us say the *pains* of the female body are a mystery and yet with every moon the pains return. How can you spin or bake or help your husband when your womb troubles you so? Well, I will tell you how." His voice grew stronger, and he raised the flask even higher. "With this elixir, all pain will vanish. You will have the energy to spin a thousand distaffs, bake a thousand loaves of bread, and outrun your husbands should they decide a tumble in the hay will cure what ails you."

He smiled and stood still. The crowd settled down. "We mere men can never know a woman's suffering. To bear our children, to feed us, to keep us clothed, and all the while suffering." Medicamus held the elixir close to his heart. "Oh, it makes me weep to think of it."

A woman somewhere in the crowd sobbed loudly. Medicamus sought her out and pointed in her direction.

"You, madam," he shouted. "Come here."

The woman hid her face in the folds of her tunic, but she made her way forward and was helped onto the table by Medicamus who then bowed and kissed her hand. He examined a swelling on her neck, pressing his fingers against it and peering at it closely.

"Ah-ha, I have just the medicine for you." He pulled a flask from an inside pocket and opened it. "I will give you the entire contents to take home with you. The swelling should reduce in a fortnight."

The woman clasped the bottle to her chest and disappeared into the crowd. Medicamus asked the audience if there were any other afflictions in need of a cure. A man standing near Meg raised his hand.

"And you sir, what is your affliction?" Medicamus called to him.

"My wife."

The crowd roared with laughter.

"Well, I can cure many things, but I cannot rid you of your wife, sir! That's against the law!"

Meg sneaked a sideways glance at William. He was stone-faced, though Gerard next to him was smiling.

"Go on, then, do not be afraid to tell us," Medicamus urged. "We're all friends here." The crowd murmured in agreement and strained to hear the poor man's confession.

The man hung his head.

"Come up here. Stand by me."

The man jumped onto the table and Medicamus put his arm around him.

"Tell us. What is it? Besides the nagging wife?"

The crowd hooted and called for the man to tell all.

"I'm ashamed, sir, to have my affliction known."

"Not to worry. We understand. Do we not?" The crowd murmured in assent.

The man took a deep breath. "Well, sir, my wife nags me that I cannot service her properly."

Medicamus smiled like a cat that drained the milk pail. "Well, you have come to the right place. Yours is an easy affliction to remedy. It's a misfortune, which troubles most men at one time or another, especially after a night of too much drink."

Medicamus uncorked a flagon and gave the bottle to the man. "Now, sir, drink my Elixir of Venus and watch what happens."

The man threw back his head and gulped the entire contents of the bottle. He and the crowd waited. "I feel nothing, sir. Nothing stirs."

"Oh, but it will, be patient."

The crowd grew silent as they waited for the elixir to take effect.

A low moan erupted from the man's lips. He moaned again, louder this time, and grasped at his crotch. A bulge appearing beneath his tunic grew in size, and the man danced on the table. "Oh, thank you, sir," he exclaimed. "Thank you! I must hurry to my wife!" And he jumped into the crowd and danced toward Stonegate, his privy member bouncing like a sausage with each step.

The crowd clapped and called for more and many of the men in the audience stepped forward to purchase some of the extraordinary Elixir of Venus. The hairy baby, chattering excitedly, took their coins and dropped them into a basket behind Medicamus.

Suddenly, a voice boomed from the crowd.

"Sir!"

Meg realized with a start the voice was coming from next to her. Oh, dear Lord above, it was Master William. He called again to Medicamus, louder this time.

The crowd grew quiet and Medicamus pointed to William. "Ah," he said, "we have a learned doctor of phisik in the crowd who, I venture to guess, is going to enlighten us on the qualities of urine, astrology, and the virtues of bleeding and cupping."

Meg groaned. She wished the earth would open up and swallow her. She sneaked a peak at Gerard. He rolled his eyes as if to say, Father is at it again.

"You, sir," William shouted, "are a thief. You spread your wares with no care for the results. The woman who will die of a tumor in her abdomen is no better after she leaves you and is likely to be worse because of the false hope you have given her."

"But I give no false hope. She takes my remedy and feels no pain for the first time in years. Are you there to witness that? No, sir, you are not."

There was a murmur of agreement from the crowd, and some even called out, blaming a doctor of phisik or a surgeon for killing a wife, a husband, or a cousin.

The hairy baby, who had been sitting on the table, jumped down, threaded his way through the feet of onlookers, and hopped on William's shoulder. Meg laughed and reached for the little thing, but William, uttering oaths and spitting in fury, struck at the baby who held onto William's tunic with sharp claws.

"Master William," Meg cried, "please be careful."

"Stand still, Father," Gerard said. Quickly, the wiry thing snatched William's cap and jumped through the crowd, climbing up Medicamus's robe and handing him the prize with excited shrieks.

"Thank you, my good Pettipaw," Medicamus said.

Donning the cap and prancing around the crowd, strutting and preening as if he were a peacock with all his feathers displayed, Medicamus called out, "I am the learned doctor of phisik, Monsieur Moneybags. I charge you five pence to smell your urine and tell you with great authority you have pissed in the pot." The crowd roared in laughter and Meg felt William tense beside her.

"We were friends once, Medicamus, but you have taken a different path," William shouted. "You take from those in need and feel no shame."

"Leave us alone," someone called out. Soon the crowd was pressing against them, gesturing for William to move on. Meg, fearing she would be crushed, reached for William's cloak. He held her close and enfolded Gerard, who was begging his father to say no more, but William aimed a parting shot.

"Do not come to me begging for a cure when your legs turn black or you vomit blood," he yelled to the crowd. "Go back to Monsieur Medicamus, that is, if you can find him, for he'll be in another city peddling his wares to another gullible crowd!"

"Father, go." Gerard pushed desperately against his father's chest until William, finally understanding the wisdom in a quick retreat, hurried past the surly crowd with Meg and Gerard in tow.

He ran to the west until he reached the corner of York Minster, and then turned right, taking the steps of the great church two at a time, and heaving himself against the heavy oak doors of the entrance. A stumbling Meg and Gerard followed. William, bending double and out of breath from their escape, panted no one would have the temerity to follow them into the minster.

"Father, one of these days you will push someone too far," Gerard said. "You cannot rid the countryside of every imposter who sells wine and calls it Christ's blood."

"It's the least I can do to rid the streets of men such as Medicamus."

Meg, whose heart still thundered from their narrow escape, was rooted to the floor of the minster, stunned by the beauty before her. She raised her face. The cathedral was massive in length and height, with a ceiling so high it must have skimmed the clouds. Never in all her days had she beheld something so extraordinary. The church in St. Michael's Mead would have fit handily in a corner of the vast building.

Clambering around her were masons, carpenters, glaziers, and painters, all as busy as ants following a honey trail. Like the tilers on the rooftop outside, the men scrambled on ladders and scaffolding, chiseling marble or painting bright colors onto the gray stone. Some of the workers appeared to be demolishing part of the cathedral, while others were raising it up.

The ceiling, webbed in white and gold, was dazzling as were the red, blue, and gold colors on the walls and sculptures, but it was the glass that captured her. Sparkling colors trans-ported on each beam of sunlight swept down from the mighty windows, transporting her to a magical place. Chanting filled her ears, incense her nose, and colorful lights her eyes. That there should be such a place on earth—had mere men built it? Surely not. Surely angels flew to its lofty beams and whispered holy words there.

"Meg, are you deaf?"

She realized William had been talking to her. Reluctantly, she pulled her eyes away from the splendor before her. "Yes, sir?"

Rather than scolding her, he smiled. "It *is* splendid, isn't it?"

"Yes. Could we not stay?"

"I have a powerful thirst," he said. "If we're to meet Alice at the Black Swan, we need to hurry. We'll have something to eat and then walk to St. Nicholas and spend one last night with Brother Adolphus."

Gerard pointed to the top of William's head. "Medicamus may have gotten the better of you, Father, for he still has your cap."

"Well, he can let his little Pettipaw wear it," William an-swered. "A monkey has as much right to be a doctor of phisik as Medicamus himself. Now follow me."

Chapter 13

A Potion for the Future

York, England, May 1322

A juggler in a velvet tri-color surcoat deftly picked his way past Alice while walking on stilts and tossing three golden balls in the air. Someone bumped against her and she looked down at a wiry young lad whose hands were exploring the folds of her surcoat.

"Look out there," she shouted, and the boy begged her pardon as he pushed further into the crowd, ducking in and out of the onlookers, snipping baubles and purses from the belts of unsuspecting bystanders.

A fat gentleman laughing at the juggler's antics took no notice as the little cutpurse made a quick snip and retreat. Alice pressed against her own purse hanging under her surcoat and tut-tutted as the scoundrel ran toward the Minster. The fat gentleman would leave the shops on Fossgate a little lighter in his step today.

She turned right, hurried down two lanes and through a dark passage into a small alleyway no wider than two people shoulder to shoulder, and came out into another street. The yeasty odor of bread told her she was on the bakers' street, but no closer to the apothecary shop. After asking directions of a bakester whose pink face was speckled with flour, she followed another alleyway and finally found herself ducking out of the raucous street into the quiet calm of the apothecary shop on Low Petergate.

Tools of the trade lined the shelves: weights and scales, a mortar and pestle, and small pottery jars and bowls in which buyers could carry home their medicaments. A higher shelf contained lancets, crucibles, gallipots, and clyster pipes. Baskets of roots and flowers, leaves and seeds were stacked against the inner wall. Her pulse quickened as she inhaled the aroma of faraway lands. She frowned, attempting to decipher the pungent earthiness of foreign spices. She forgot her list of wares and stood, instead, as if in a daze until the apothecary interrupted her.

"Excuse me, madam?"

Feeling like a foolish country cousin come to town, she straightened and introduced herself. "I have need of quite a few wares today, sir." She recited the list of herbs and spices. She would buy anise and fennel for Meg's monthly cramping, and a small amount of saffron (so costly!) to cure labor pains, and caraway seeds to brew in a tea to aid digestion, especially in colicky infants. And, of course, the most important item and the reason for her visit—mandragora.

"As to mandragora, I need the real root, mind you," she warned. "Not some false root you bring me as trickery."

The apothecary disappeared into his back room and soon returned with a root the size of Alice's forearm.

"Will this do, madam?"

Alice examined the brown root, which was shaped like an

armless man sprouting legs akimbo, and at the top, just the hint of a round head, with a wisp of hair upon his noggin.

"And you can vouch this is true mandragora, not bryony root you pulled up and carved into the shape of a man, so you can cheat your customers?"

"Madam, you hurt me," the apothecary whined and placed his hand over his heart. "I sell only the best here and none of it false. The root is genuine. I assure you, I am an honest man."

"I'll be the judge of that." Alice slit the root with her fingernail and sniffed the exposed flesh. She turned the root over and over in her hands, searching for carving marks which would expose the root as a fake.

"Take care," the apothecary warned. "This is a potent drug. Too much renders a man speechless . . . perhaps for the rest of his life."

Alice placed the root upon the table and met the apothecary's eye. "Sir, I have tended the sick for more years than you have been on this earth. Indeed, I was a healer while you were still pissing in your swaddling clothes."

The apothecary apologized, saying he didn't mean to insult madam. The warning was merely necessary for his own protection. "My customers do not have your many years of experience, madam, and some wish to use my lovely plants and roots for evil uses."

"Well, I'll take the root," Alice said at last, "But I want to look at your other wares first."

Much later, after she handled and sniffed as much as possible, and haggled with the apothecary over the price of saffron, which she declined, and the mandragora root, which she bought, she reluctantly left the shop. She could have spent far more than she did, had she the money, but even so the mandragora had cost her dearly. It would be worth it, though, to induce sleep in someone suffering great pain.

The bells of a nearby church began to ring. Alice glanced at the sun. If she hurried, she had time to complete her next bit of business and then meet Meg, Gerard, and William at the Black Swan.

She was looking for a house on Gropecuntgate, almost cheek by jowl to St. Egbert's Church, a house with a red door on the outside, and on the inside, women who earned a living by the flat of their backs. The owner of the house was named Madame Aurora. Her real name was Joan. She was an old acquaintance of Alice's, a widow from Warwick whose thrifty husband, a freeman, managed to put aside some money before he died, leaving Joan a widow with no children. Joan had thought of setting up a weaving business, but confided to Alice that sitting at a loom all day would drive her to madness.

No, Joan said, there's more than one way to earn a treasure. Keep the treasure locked up, out of sight, and tell everyone how amazing it is. "Men will pay a fortune for the right kind of jewels and when those jewels have tits and a quinny and can suck a man's eyeballs out his cock, they'll pay even more."

When Madame Aurora opened the red door of the house on Gropecuntgate, Alice barely recognized the woman she had known as Joan. Aurora was plump, with a heavy coating of white lead on her face, two purple splotches of color on her cheeks and hair the vivid red of a rooster's comb. A heavy odor of myrrh and rose oil announced her presence. After a kiss and brief greetings, Alice remarked on the color of Aurora's hair. The color of dawn, the color of love, the color of money, Aurora laughed. "Whatever it is, 'tis a color to be remembered. And what brings you to York?"

Alice told her about Meg, John's leprosy, and his confinement in St. Nicholas.

"And you came by yourselves?" Aurora asked.

"No, we were blessed to have William of Oxford and his son, Gerard, accompany us."

"Ah, it seems you spoke of him many times in the old days. And it seems you always had a smile on your lips at the mention of his name."

"Pah, no such thing. Besides, I am an old woman. What would a handsome man like him want with an old crone like me?"

"For the likes of you? You're a good strong woman, all your teeth, thick hair, though too much gray for my liking. You should try my special dye. I'll give you the recipe if you want. Give a shake of those hips and he'll beg for it."

Alice laughed at the thought of William on all fours whining like a dog for a bone. "Enough about me," she said. "You appear to be faring well in York."

Aurora smiled. "Faring well, as long as a piece of my proceeds go to the mayor, the bailiff, the priest at St. Egbert's, and to everybody and his brother. Still, I make a profit. And my girls are clean, well behaved, and clever. In fact, since you're here, perhaps you could do me the favor of looking at Rosalinde. She's a favorite. I would hate for anything to happen to her. I could keep her busy day and night."

Alice consented and then asked a favor of her own. "I must confess I visit you with false pretensions."

"Yes?" Aurora said warily.

"Of course, I mean to renew an old acquaintance, but also to ask if you have on hand something I need for the women in the village."

"And what is it?"

"There are stories of women who, well, like the women you employ here, who have a secret to keep them from carrying a child."

"I've heard those stories, though to do such a thing would be a sin."

"So says the Church. But Church law doesn't keep the priests from sampling your wares, does it?" She paused. "If you have it, I will pay for it."

"Surely Alice, you know the recipe for such a secret. You have been a healer for many years and your mother before you."

"Sadly, I find old age brings more than gray hair. I can no

longer remember the recipe." She frowned now to think on it, annoyed she was forced to purchase something she once could have made at home, but in truth, she was more annoyed at old age, at the pains in her joints, at the failing eyesight, and the holes in her recollection which put the knowledge of so many generations of healers in jeopardy. Getting old was irksome, Alice thought. How fortunate that she had Meg to help her. And then, with a wrench of her heart, she remembered. Meg would be leaving.

"I have the best whores in the north of England," Aurora was saying.

"Then perhaps you have learned the best remedy?"

Indeed, she had. She promised to divulge it once Alice examined Rosalinde. The bargain sealed, Alice climbed the stairs to the girl's room.

Rosalinde was perhaps a year older than Meg. Her face was drawn and pinched, as if the light of her spirit had been extinguished by the weight of too many customers pumping their seed into her thin body.

"The girl won't eat half the time," Aurora complained, "though I've tried all sorts of sweetmeats and tonics. But then, the thinner they are, the more angelic they look, the more the men like them. She could look like a wraith and they'd beat the door down for a taste of her sweet little quinny."

Aurora patted the girl's head as if she were a docile lap dog. Rosalinde looked at Alice and, in that glance, the difference between her and Meg gave Alice a shock to her breast. There was no liveliness, no curiosity, no joy to be living upon the earth. There was instead a despair so deep Alice feared no amount of tonic would cure it.

She motioned for the girl to lie down.

"Her customers complained of it just yesterday." Aurora stuck her head between the girl's legs and pointed to the sore. "So perhaps we have caught it before the worst of it comes. No man will lay with a girl whose quinny is oozing blood and pus.

But you can see why they love her so." She lifted a small tuft of blonde hair curling above the girl's privy parts.

Alice gingerly touched the red and swollen wound.

It was not the pox—Alice breathed a sigh of relief—only a blister of Venus. The skin of her privy had been worn away, Alice explained, due to too much use on one so tender. Alice warned it could worsen if the girl wasn't given some rest. Pus, fever, and death could be her fate if the sore did not heal.

"But, she's our prize whore," Aurora protested.

Aye, Alice thought wryly, and your best moneymaker.

"They love her," Aurora added with a whine.

"Ride her till she's lame and she's no good to you," Alice advised. "Give her a rest for a week."

"A week? Do you know how much money I'll lose?"

"And after a week, no more than four men per day for a month."

After some additional persuading in which Alice suggested keeping her away from the men would make her even more desirable, Aurora agreed and hugged the girl to her breast, with a promise to take good care of her. "Such a treasure," Aurora said.

At the mention of a week's rest, there had been a flicker of life in the girl's eyes, but the moment Aurora touched her, it was gone.

"Now you've fulfilled your part of the bargain," Aurora said to Alice. "I'll fetch what you asked for."

As soon as Aurora left the room, Alice said, "My name is Alice of St. Michael's Mead in Warwickshire. Should you ever need me again, send someone and I'll come instantly. For now, stay in bed with your legs spread to the open air. The sore will scab over and heal, and you'll be to rights again." Without a word, the girl rolled away from Alice and pulled the covers over her ears. Alice sighed and left the room with a heavy heart, sure in the knowledge the girl would be ridden to a young death.

Downstairs, Aurora placed a jar carefully in Alice's hands, holding it as if it contained the blood of the dear Christ himself.

"And do you know its ingredients?" Alice asked.

She did not, she said with an apology. "One of the girls bought it from an old healer in Durham, but did not ask what was in it."

"No matter, I can sort it out." Alice reached inside her surcoat and produced a leather pouch attached to her belt. She placed the jar carefully within the pouch and pulled the drawstring tight. She then bid Aurora adieu. "Remember, give Rosalinda beef broth three times a day, no customers for a week, and air to the wound—no bandage or salve."

"God bless you, Alice,"

"She'll toughen up. Unfortunately, in more ways than one."

Aurora took no notice of the jibe. She kissed Alice's cheek and the heavy odor of Aurora's perfume washed over Alice and left her nostrils quivering.

"When next you're in York, perhaps I could dye your hair with my special color," Aurora called as Alice walked away. "Sulphur, quicklime, and walnut dye, and your hair will be as gorgeous as mine."

As Alice carefully stepped through the dark lane, she tried to rid her mind's-eye of the vision of bare buttocks pumping away at Rosalinde while Aurora grew richer. She had no intention of returning to Aurora's unless Rosalinde grew worse. And she certainly wasn't going to let Aurora come within a furrow's length of her hair, regardless of the gray.

She turned east on Low Petergate walking as quickly as possible through the crowds and toward the river. She patted the purse bouncing from her belt with each step. Her trip to York had been successful indeed. When they returned to St. Michael's Mead, she and Meg could untangle the puzzle of Aurora's ointment and determine its ingredients. And then she remembered.

Meg, whose lively, inquisitive heart cheered her days and

filled the cottage with questions and laughter, was going to leave with William and Gerard to start her life anew. Meg had not been told the news—Alice and William thought it better to deliver Meg's father to St. Nicholas before revealing their decision, and though it was a decision to which Alice's head could agree, her heart could not.

At first, when William divulged his plan Alice had argued against it. Loneliness stretched before her and caused her to be stubborn. But William's argument was powerful and soon won her over. Sir Henry, they knew, would be the stumbling block, but when William broached the subject, Henry was not difficult to persuade and William, for once, had not lost his temper but cajoled with an oiled tongue and a bagful of coins.

"I need a servant," William told Henry. "I need more than a stupid serving wench who spills my ale and steals my money or washes my clothes but leaves them dirty. I need someone who can pound my medicines, feed my patients, change their bedding, and also feed Gerard and me."

William jiggled the bag of coins and Sir Henry's jaw dropped at the sound of so much money. He had taken it, but not without chiding William for buying a girl more suited to a pigsty than serving a notable surgeon. "You value your servants too highly," he said. "Mark this well, William, with servants they must know their place and not be elevated above their station."

William promised to beat Meg soundly if she made any trouble.

✻✻✻

At the Black Swan, William ordered ale and a hot meal all 'round and then recounted his adventure to Alice, sharing his frustration at the gullibility of folks eager to part with their money.

Meg leaned to Gerard and whispered, "What is a monkey?"

"What do you mean?"

"When Master William said the monkey could keep his hat."

"The monkey?" He looked at her as if she were an onion just pulled out of the ground and with as much sense. "The creature on Medicamus's shoulder. The one that stole Father's hat. That's a monkey."

"Oh. Not a hairy baby then."

Gerard burst into laughter. "No, it's a creature from far away in the east. It's an animal, Meg, not a human baby."

Gerard pulled at his father's sleeve. "Father, you will never guess what Meg thought." He told them about her notion and they laughed, even Alice, until Meg's ears burned. She slumped against the back of the bench and finished her ale. Gerard had been so kind during the Mass for the Dead and yet here he was, taunting her, shaming her in front of the others.

"Hail, travelers!"

Robertus Medicamus landed a hearty slap on William's back.

William glowered. "How did you find us?"

"My spies are everywhere. I have taken the liberty of joining you in order to return your cap to its rightful place." Medicamus placed the cap on William's head and gave him a playful pat.

William was not amused. "I see you've finished fleecing the good citizens of York."

"Oh, Master William, you have such little faith in humanity."

"I know what I see—a phisik monger. You play on people's worst fears and their last hopes."

"Nay, on the contrary, I give them hope just as you do. And I sell nothing to hurt them." He slid next to Alice. "More ale? My gift to you for making this day one of the best in sales ever."

William stood. "I think not."

"As you wish," Medicamus said, and helped himself to their supper.

They left the city crowds as they ambled along, walking unhurriedly in deference to Alice's aching feet. They passed occasional cottages, lonely outliers beyond the safety of the city walls, and churches where a whiff of incense roused their tired spirits. When the walls of York were far behind them Meg asked William why he was so angry with Medicamus. "Sir, I mean no offense in asking this. Everyone at the Minster seemed to have a good time. And some may even be cured."

William told her the men and women Medicamus picked out of the crowd were actually in his employ and not really sick.

"But they complained of real ailments," she said.

"Part of the deception. It's all a ruse to sell Medicamus's 'medicine,' most of which I'd venture to guess is a combination of herbs and verjuice. If it tastes bad, people will think it works."

"So even the man with the, um, the problem in his nether region? Even he was in Medicamus's employ?"

William laughed. "Yes, even him." Medicamus, he said, would send his players ahead to the next town so they wouldn't be seen together. By magic, they would appear in his little play, moaning with pain or sobbing with lost hope.

"But his . . . it . . . grew."

William smiled ruefully. "I'd venture to guess it was a well-placed cow's horn held in place with a piece of leather. When the man grabbed his crotch, he unloosed the binding and, like a miracle, his prick grew before our very eyes. It's an old trick, Meg, one which plays upon a man's weakness."

"And the monkey? Why the monkey?"

"For entertainment and to make fools of good people." William's face turned a dusky shade of red.

"Like silly girls who think a monkey is a hairy baby," Gerard said and smiled in her direction.

Meg stopped in her tracks and glared at him. Had she daggers for looks, Gerard would have been dead from a thousand wounds.

✳✳✳

The next morning as they stood in the outer courtyard preparing to leave St. Nicholas, Adolphus ran to them, his cowl and belt flapping with each step, his cheeks red with exertion.

"It has been a delight to chance upon you again, William, and to have met your fellow travelers. Strangers no more, eh? You have a place here when next in York."

"And the same to you if ever you find yourself in St. Michael's Mead," Alice said.

As Gerard and Alice watched while a servant tied their leather bags to the saddles, Adolphus put his arm around William and they walked a few steps away. Meg, pretending to look for something in her bag of medicines, contrived to move closer.

Adolphus whispered, "I have just heard from a baker who delivered bread to the Chapter House this morning. The King has crushed all opposition in Parliament. The barons have lost."

William stopped in his tracks and pursed his lips. "So, Edward and the Despensers are masters of England. Queen Isabella will never stand for it. She'll muster troops—quietly, of course. And that means—"

"Civil war." Adolphus led William back to the horses and gave him a hearty embrace. "These are troublesome times, my old friend. Let us remember England in our prayers."

Later as the great walls of York receded behind her, Meg remembered their conversation and shivered. She had waved a last goodbye to her father, her head high and shoulders back, not a tear in her eye or a weakness to her countenance. But now she apprehended the truth, as if someone had punched her in the chest. She would never see her father again or feel his protective arms around her. If civil war broke out, St. Michael's Mead would be at the mercy of whoever invaded the village, the king's men one week, the queen's men the next. She dropped her head and shoulders. Her chin quivered. With William and Gerard riding ahead, she had no reason to pretend a bravery she no longer felt.

Sniffling, she remembered the conversation in the hospital courtyard and amended Adolphus's last words: *Let us remember England in our prayers. And let us remember St Michael's Mead, my father, my mother, my sister, Alice, William, Gerard—nay, everyone, and may God keep us safe. May the king's hate and the queen's revenge never reach us.*

Chapter 14

A Lamb in a Wolf's Lair

London, England, June 1322

Two weeks later, after saying good-bye to Alice in St. Michael's Mead, William, Gerard, and a nervous Meg passed through the London city walls by way of Ludgate Hill. They rode towards West Cheap through masses of people swirling around them and pressing against the horses. They had just turned alongside St. Paul's Cathedral when the great bells rang out. Shaken by the noise and horrified lest others look upon her, Meg pulled at her hood in a vain attempt to conceal her face.

"My dear Meg," William roared above the din, "Londoners care not a whit about your deformity. They care for one thing only—money! If you have it, you're their best friend. If you don't have it, a pox on you!"

Meg thought, *I'm poxed, for I haven't so much as a farthing.*

As they rode down Cheapside, cooks stood in the door-way of their shops shouting, "Hot pies, hot pies!" Brewsters tempted the thirsty with descriptions of their fine ale, and shopkeepers of all kinds held up their goods and offered a special price. Bustlers danced or sang for money or occasionally sold cheap baubles to passersby. On each side of the street red-tiled half-timbered buildings, running cheek by jowl and twice as tall as those at home, hung over the street so close a man could jump from his second-story window into the house on the other side. She was astonished at the size of the city, even larger and busier than York, and at the deafening noise of animals and shouting shopkeepers, and grimy children who pulled at her legs and her horse's mane.

"Stay out of the ditch there," William warned and pointed to the rivulets of debris and animal waste running on both sides of the street. "Poor footing for the horses."

As they wearily dismounted at William's front door, he spread his arms and announced, "Welcome to London, my dear girl. A city of pimps, actors, magicians, beggars, pederasts, dancing girls, and the occasional honest gentleman." He laughed at the sight of Meg's stunned face and assured her she would come to know and love the city soon enough. "You'll find everything you need here. There's bread on Bread Street, milk on Milk Street, rushes in Candlewick Street, sable from Russia, and gold from Arabia, and best of all, French wines."

In a daze she reached for William's bags. She had assured William and Sir Henry that she would be a dutiful servant. William had paid a fine to Sir Henry for taking Meg out of the village. He had also paid for her father's entry to St. Nicholas in York. In return, she had promised to serve William as a means of repayment. Now, having seen London in the teeming flesh, she wasn't sure she could fulfill that promise. So much to do. So much to learn.

"Meg, listen!" Meg shook off the haze of confusion and dropped William's bags as he shouted at her. Fearful lest she had made her master angry on her first day in London, she asked, "Should I make your meal, sir? I confess I'm not a good cook, but you won't starve. I'll run to the poulterer."

"No. Stay where you are."

Was she a failure before she had begun? Her heart pounded at the possibility she would be thrown on the streets of London on her first day in the city.

"You are not my servant," William said.

She looked in confusion to William and then Gerard.

"Gerard," William said. "Our Meg has grown deaf since leaving the village. Perhaps you can talk sense to her."

"What my father is saying . . ." Something in Meg's expression must have caused Gerard pity, for he put both hands on her shoulders and said, "Welcome to our home, Meg. You are not a servant in this household. We already have servants who cook and clean for us. You are his apprentice, not his serving girl."

"I do not understand. You told Sir Henry—"

"Yes," said William. "A ruse, I'm afraid. I was not sure he would let you go. You are to train as my assistant, *not* my servant. I am especially in need of a female who can tend to other females."

Meg sank to the bench opposite.

"You will clean women patients, change their bedclothing, feed them, take care of their children if necessary, and give them medicine on my orders."

"And Gerard, sir?"

"Gerard will be preparing for university. He also assists me with patients."

"I see," Meg said.

"What is the matter? Would you rather be a servant as I promised Sir Henry?

"No, sir." She sighed and picked at splinters on the bench.

"Then what? Do you want to go home?"

"No, sir. I mean, of course I want to stay here but I want to be more than a serving girl to your female patients."

"Well, what do you want? Out with it."

Meg had observed William's temper at Caldecote Hall but this was worse. He was purple with anger. If she told him what she truly wanted, he would kick her out of the house. If she stayed silent, her dreams would come to naught.

William threw up his hands. "I paid Brother Adolphus for your father's care at St. Nicholas. You will apprentice to me in exchange for that payment. I've paid a fine to Sir Henry for taking you out of the village. Alice has given her blessings. You'll be clothed and fed. What more do you want?"

"I want to be your student, sir. I want to learn everything, to help you with women patients, of course, but also to do everything you and Gerard do."

"What?" he sputtered.

"Father, she is certainly capable," Gerard said. "Look how well she studied on the journey to York. And think of Lady Elisabeth's birth. Is there another girl in Christendom who could have endured that?"

"I know I am a mere girl, sir," Meg said, "and right now I haven't the skill, the knowledge, or the—"

"I don't understand," William said. "Do you want to be an apothecary? A midwife?"

Meg took a breath and crossed her arms to hide her shaking hands. "I want to be a doctor of phisik, sir. Like Gerard. Like you."

"Impossible. You are woefully behind. You've had no rhetoric, geometry, astronomy, dialectic, or grammar. Moreover, you're a—"

"A simple country girl?"

"Women cannot be doctors of phisik. Not in England. Italy perhaps, but not here."

"Then I will move to Italy."

"Young woman," William shouted, "have lost your wits?"

She hung her head. "No, sir."

"Well, if you continue with this nonsense, you will make me lose mine. Right now, I am tired and hungry. I'm going to eat and go to my bed. Perhaps Gerard will set you straight."

After his pounding feet indicated he had climbed the stairs to his room, Gerard said, "You will learn when—and how—to argue with my father. You must feed him tidbits, much like the bear-baiter feeds his prize animal. Give him one nugget at a time and then when he is finished, he will lay down and let you rub his belly."

Meg doubled over in laughter. The vision of Master William with all four appendages in the air and a grin on his face as she tickled his belly was too comical.

"And you?" she asked as she wiped her tears. "Do you wish me to be a household servant? A servant to sick women? Or a doctor of phisik?"

Gerard's grin disappeared and he grew serious. "As I have said, I believe you can learn to be a doctor of phisik. I greet you as a sister and as an equal, not as a servant. You are too able-bodied a healer to waste in the kitchen." His lopsided grin lit up his face again. "Besides, I have tasted your cooking."

Chapter 15

SECRETS

London, England, October 1326

Elias the Blacksmith, having taken to his sickbed for two months past, knocked on Death's door for the last time. He sat up, reached for the ceiling, smiling as if Death bade him enter, then fell backward and was no more.

"I am deeply sorry, Agneta," William said to the blacksmith's wife, who was hovering near his shoulder.

The woman gazed blankly, as if William's words made no sense, and then she looked at Elias's lifeless body. "No, it cannot be. It cannot be!" A wail of deep longing and grief escaped her throat. She kissed his face, begged him to wake and when he did not, she slapped him, as if she would bring him back from the dead. Her children, too, were weeping. The older ones clawed at their father while the younger ones howled into their mother's skirts.

Meg gently closed the blacksmith's eyes. She trembled, knowing what this calamity would mean to the family. Their living quarters, a warren of small rooms above the butcher shop and next to the tumbledown shed holding her husband's business, were rented from the butcher, who would probably evict her as soon as word spread of her husband's death. Agneta and the children would face a cruel life begging for food on the streets.

Elias, always a somber man tending toward melancholy, according to Agneta, had sickened when their youngest son died three years ago. The boy was badly burned while playing with his father's tools near the fire. His wounds soon filled with pus and he died within a fortnight. Elias had never recovered from his grief.

"Sometimes I would take the back stairs and enter my husband's shop, expecting to see him hammering at the anvil, only to find him in the corner, sitting as if in a drunken stupor," Agneta said.

When her husband took to his bed complaining of severe stomach pains, she had sent her eldest child to fetch William.

"We aren't rich folk," she explained to William when he first arrived at Elias's bedside. She reddened and twisted her hands. "We cannot pay you in coin, Master William, but my husband's apprentice will make whatever you want, sir. He's skilled at the forge. Let him know what you need."

William waved her off impatiently, more eager to examine her husband than discuss payment. He promised to visit the blacksmith's apprentice later and have a new lock made for his chest of valuables. "For now, do not worry about my fee."

After William completed his examination of Elias, he ordered Meg and Gerard to consult their astrological and urine charts, tables of humors, and their notes on melancholy. They were to develop a treatment for Elias before morning.

Gerard suggested the cause of the blacksmith's deep sorrow was an overabundance of melancholic black bile. He should be given hot baths followed by hot moist towels placed upon his body. And, Meg added, as she consulted the book of tables and charts attached to her belt, he should be bled to void the imbalanced humor if the hot treatments failed to work.

"He is a Scorpio," Meg said. "Best not to cut him near his anus or testicles. We should recommend a longitudinal cut in the basilica vein above the elbow."

In the morning, their theory of out-of-balance humors was confirmed when William examined the man's feces and urine. He showed Gerard and Meg the black bile present in the man's stool. He collected the man's first voiding in a Jordan, then sniffed, and offered the flask to Gerard and Meg, "Think of the bile of rage, fury, wrath—that is the true nature of Elias's pain. His melancholy is not based on sorrow, but rage. Rage that his child has died as a result of his own livelihood."

Several weeks later, when Elias had shown no improvement, William approved Meg's recommendation to open his veins to draw out the noxious humors and bring the man into balance. As the blood flowed from the crook of Elias's elbow into a bowl, William drew Gerard and Meg closer.

"Look there. The blood is thin and dark." William sighed. "I fear melancholy has a firm grasp on our patient."

Since then, despite repeated bloodlettings, the blacksmith had grown weaker. William wondered aloud if perhaps his stubborn attachment to melancholy had been more powerful than any medicine. Near the end, Elias had burned with fever, his insides boiling from the heat. Now the blacksmith would make acquaintance with the soft earth of a pauper's cemetery.

"What am I to do?" Agneta was crying. "I've no money to bury him."

William patted the woman's shoulder and promised he would take care of the burial. "Not to fear, madam. All is handled. You must look after your children."

He handed Meg a few coins and asked her to buy two oxtails in the butcher shop below. At least the children would have full bellies on the occasion of their father's death. Meg descended the stairs and went out to the street level where the butcher's open-air stall was located. She asked for the oxtails and watched carefully to make sure he hacked the tails off the fresh carcasses hanging on the back wall rather than handing her the decaying meat he kept under the counter.

The butcher dropped the oxtails in a basket and jerked his head at the sound of shouting in the street. A crowd was gathering.

"I fear the rifflers and roarers have taken the street again," he said. "They've left my shop alone but with such rumbustiousness in the air, no one is safe."

Indeed. It was more than rumbustion, thought Meg as she took the oxtails and gave the butcher her coins. It was Civil War. Queen against King. Baron against Baron. And the common folk left to suffer.

The matter had come to a head last month. But it had been building for years. William had told her Queen Isabella played the patient wife to a husband who preferred the company of other men, but now the queen had had enough. From the first days of their marriage Edward had belittled her, even on their wedding day when he had given all her dowry jewels to his favorite courtier, Piers Gaveston, who wore the jewels in public as if they were his own. When Piers was executed by the barons, another favorite, Hugh Despenser the Younger, took his place.

Isabella became a captive in her own palace, having to ask permission for every move from her custodian, Hugh Despenser's wife, Eleanor de Clare. Her lands were confiscated. Her youngest children were taken from her and placed in the Despenser's custody. Her servants and ladies-in-waiting were placed in prison.

King Edward, however, made a fatal mistake. He allowed the queen to journey to France to visit her brother King Charles IV. Her son, Edward, a lad of thirteen, joined her. And having her son by her side meant she could safeguard his life and future. Over the summer nobles who opposed Edward gathered around Isabella. One of the nobles, Roger Mortimer, became her lover.

All summer there were rumors of an invasion. It was all anyone in London could talk about—at the shops, in the street, as the families gathered for supper, although William counseled Meg and Gerard against the madness. Barons were sending word of their support to the queen. Then last month, word flashed through the city like lightning: Isabella, Mortimer, and Prince Edward had landed at Orton in Suffolk. They meant to depose the king.

"There is nothing to fear. The Royals will do as they wish," William said. "We work-a-day folks will continue to work."

Everyone expected Isabella to march into London and take up residence in the White Tower with its moat and double walls, but Isabella's nose was on the hunt. When the King fled to the West Country with money from the treasury, she and her army turned west, hounding Edward and the Despensers, father and son.

With the hated king and the Despensers out of the city, Londoners declared for Queen Isabella and cheered their freedom.

Their cheers were short-lived. Gangs of youth now roamed the city. Robberies and even murder were on the rise. All of London was drooling with anticipation, expecting the bodies of both Despensers to be displayed on Tower Bridge. Meanwhile, anyone who had been in the king's employ and who was foolish enough to stay in London was a dead man.

The mob now building outside the butcher's stall was not a good sign. Meg hurried upstairs again, handed the oxtails to Agneta, and reported the news to William.

He opened the shutters slightly and peered into the street. "Meg, you and Gerard must take yourselves out of harm's way," he warned. "The lords of misrule are at it again."

Suddenly a woman's shriek pierced the air. "Murder! Murder! God help us."

"What is it, Father?" Gerard asked.

"Evil."

Gerard and Meg ran to the window.

"The Bishop of Exeter, Walter de Stapledon."

"What has happened?" Meg asked, standing on her tiptoes and peering around William. The scene below was madness. One of the men, having stabbed Bishop Stapledon, was now cutting off the bishop's head. Blood puddled at the stump of the Stapledon's neck, the garish red color out of place for a civilized street in London in the broad light of day. The crowd roared as the man held Stapledon's head aloft. It frightened Meg that ordinary citizens had within themselves such a lust for bloodshed.

"Not many of the king's confidantes are left in the city," William said. "Stapledon was probably arrogant enough to think he would never be harmed. He had the ear of the king as Lord High Treasurer. But no more."

"Take his head to the queen," someone in the street shouted. "A present from her loyal subjects."

Meg's eyes widened.

"Go home," William said. "And stay away from crowds." He reached into his bag and pulled out a double-bladed knife. "Take this," he said, handing it to Gerard. "And don't be afraid to use it."

"Aren't you coming with us?" Gerard asked.

William didn't answer. Instead, he pressed a coin into the palm of the blacksmith's oldest son and gave him directions to a house near the river. "You'll find the carters there," he said. "Tell them we'll need two of their strongest men to carry your father down the stairs and deliver him to St. Saviour's graveyard in Southwark."

He opened the door and motioned for Gerard and Meg. Lowering his voice, he spoke only to them. "You know what to do. Make haste."

***

The burly carters rolled the body of Elias the Blacksmith onto the table. The strongest of the fellows, a man with a deeply pockmarked face and pugnacious nose, held out his hand. Looking around at the strange room, he let his gaze land on Meg before he said, "Master William's at his usual work, I see."

Meg did not take the bait. Instead, she asked the man if he had been followed.

"No miss," he said. "No one followed us."

"Come back at the end of the day when the bells ring for Vespers," Gerard said sharply. "You know what to do."

Once the carters left, they began their preparations. The first task was to wash the body. The corpse must be a clean slate on which to read Death's messages: no *vomitus* or bloody flux to confuse or distract William from deciphering the cause of death. They rolled the blacksmith onto his chest, grunting with the strain of the man's limp weight. They washed his back, buttocks, and legs, then turned him again and washed his front.

Meg lifted the blacksmith's arm and marveled at how quickly life could be extinguished. Once a muscular man capable of hammering at the forge for hours, Elias was wasted, his arms no longer sinewy but thin sticks.

Meg was an old hand at helping Gerard and William conduct their scientific experimentations as William described it, but she had been terrified at first.

One night after a late supper, William said to Meg, "Gerard and I have been engaged in a special undertaking of scientific learning. I hope you will join us."

"Of course, Master William. I am here to learn," she said.

"In that case, follow me." He opened a small door recessed under the stairs. He held a candle before him and stepped into the darkness. Meg and Gerard followed.

William held his candle to the rush lights. The room they were standing in was located in the cellar, barely visible from the street above and accessible through a door leading to the back alley. The room was devoid of wall hangings and furnishings save for a cupboard and a long table on which a sheet-covered bundle lay. Buckets of water lined the wall. William was pulling pots and knives out of the cupboard.

As William unwrapped the strips of cloth, Meg glimpsed toes, then a foot, calf, knee, and then the thin torso of a man. She felt the blood drain from her head as William threw the rags on the floor. The naked form of a man lay before her on the table. The man was a patient they had seen earlier. A poor poet, the man had no relatives to mourn for him and no money for burial. William told his servants he would arrange the man's burial in a pauper's cemetery in Southwark. Instead, the poet was splayed out on a table surrounded by knives. Meg backed up against the wall and questioned whether she could creep out and run for her life. Perhaps she could flee, but she had no place to go. She couldn't remember how to get back to St. Michael's Mead.

William caught her staring at the body. She must have looked horrified, for he said to her, "Of course you recognize this man. He's the poet we saw this afternoon. An impoverished man in life, he presents us a rich opportunity." William picked up a long thin knife and held it while Gerard scrubbed the man's chest.

Meg felt sick. They were going to cut open his body.

"Many of my dissections are performed on those who cannot afford a burial," William said. "Fortunately for us, their bodies provide great knowledge."

"B. . . but," Meg's tongue refused to form the proper words. She caught sight of the knife in his hands and shuddered.

"The Church forbids dissections," William said as he made a long incision. "It's a desecration, apparently. On the other hand, I believe it to be invaluable. And since the patient is dead and can't object, why not?" When Meg didn't answer, he motioned to Gerard. "I believe our new apprentice is horror-struck. Go to her, please."

Gerard approached Meg gently as if she were a lamb trapped in a wolf's lair. "There is no need to be afraid, Meg. The human body is a machine with many moving parts. To fix those parts, we must know how they work. That is what we do here. It is a necessary part of science."

"Well said, my boy," William bellowed.

Meg winced but allowed Gerard to put his arm around her and lead her to the table.

"The physician must lift his head from his books and look at the patient," William said as he searched through his knives. "Surgeons—*they* are the practitioners who truly understand medicine. The barber-surgeons, with their bloody cloths drying in the sun, can pull a tooth or stitch a man's ear back together after a fight in the alehouse, but they have no knowledge of the human body. As useless as a surgeon who does not know anatomy. Might as well be a blind man operating on a log!"

Gerard smiled at her and squeezed her shoulder. "You'll find Father is rather passionate about his calling." He leaned toward her and whispered, "And loud. Do not let him scare you."

"This is how I teach, Meg. If it makes you sick or you feel faint, I do not believe you are meant for medicine. If you can bear it, you will learn and your patients will be the better for it."

Part of her wanted to run to St. Michael's Mead, where she would take over from Alice and cure coughs, cuts, broken bones, and deliver babies. Part of her wanted to learn as much as she could. Alice had said she was ready to go into the wider world and learn more. Indeed, Alice had called her gifted.

She took a deep breath and exhaled. "Do it, sir. I am ready."

She had clutched the table for support and ordered the whirring in her head to go away, focusing instead on the tip of the knife as it cleanly removed organ after organ from the body of the man who had so lately penned his poetry not giv-ing a thought to the humming of his innards.

Since that day four years ago, Meg had participated in many

of William's scientific investigations. The dissections had become, if not routine, not quite as shocking.

Now, as Meg washed the blacksmith's privy parts, so filthy and encrusted after weeks of sickness, she worried about the danger should the barber-surgeons, the Oxford Masters, or the Church learn of their clandestine dissections.

William had many enemies among the grand physicians of England. It was only through the grace of old friends at Oxford that Gerard was considered for schooling there. If William were to be caught, Gerard's prospects for an education were over.

William would say it was worth a chance. Meg was not so sure. She wasn't sure about the punishment either. Excommunication. Public flogging. Or worse. William and Gerard might be condemned to prison or hung from the tower gibbet.

She glanced at Gerard, hoping he could not read her thoughts. No, she decided, nothing would happen. They were too careful. And the knowledge they gained was worth the danger. When the carters returned and received their coins for payment, they would carry the blacksmith's body across London Bridge to the pauper's field. Elias would be buried in a mass grave, no one the wiser and no one to speculate at the long row of stitches running from the dead man's pubic bone to his chin.

To loosen the knot in her stomach, she forced her thoughts to turn to dear Alice and St. Michael's Mead. She had to admit she missed Alice desperately. Unbelievable to think four years had passed since she rode away from the little cottage.

On their last day together, she and Alice had embraced several times, holding onto each other as if they would never see each other again.

"You have a gift," Alice said as they embraced for the last time. "Do not let anyone tell you otherwise. Remember, you are destined to be a doctor of phisik. Do not let anyone stand in your way." Alice embraced Gerard and William, who held on to her as if he, too, regretted leaving. Gerard boosted Meg onto her horse and as she reached for the reins Alice grabbed her hand. "I will miss you, my dearest girl."

"I will miss you, too, Mother Alice," Meg said.

Remembering those days, Meg smiled but fought back tears.

"He's clean enough," Gerard said. "Now we wait for Father to return."

Chapter 16

LET THE DEAD TEACH THE LIVING

London, England, October 1326

William struggled to hold the door against a blustery wind forcing cold air and rain into the dissection room. Apparently, his libations hadn't washed away all thoughts of Agneta and her wailing brood for he was still muttering about them. "Poor woman. It's never a good time to be homeless and destitute in London, but now is worse than ever."

Meg could hardly believe the boisterous city she had grown to love had sunk to lawlessness. Things could turn ugly very rapidly as they had witnessed just this afternoon. Perhaps when the Queen returned, London would be at peace again. And maybe, Meg thought, she could catch a glimpse of the queen's lover Roger Mortimer, as well as the young Prince Edward who people said was very handsome.

William rubbed his hands and tucked them beneath his

armpits to thaw his fingers. "So, are we ready then?"

"Yes," Gerard said. "We've washed front and back."

"Good. Let us begin. *Mortui vivos docent*—which is?"

"Let the dead teach the living," Gerard and Meg answered in unison.

William made a long incision in the blacksmith's chest. He reached under the sternum and removed the heart, the muscular center of being and the conductor of all feeling. Next, he withdrew the lungs, creamy with a tinge of blue, and then the stomach. He examined all the organs carefully and found no abnormalities. He pulled out the ropy mass of entrails and carefully checked all sides. He was about to dump it in the bucket when he spotted a section of interest.

"What is this, then?" William muttered. He lifted the creamy rope and rotated it. "Look here. See the swelling? This is the site of putrefaction." Gerard and Meg moved closer. "This—" William pointed to a gray lump in a ruptured intestine. "This explains why the poor bastard suffered so. No chance at all with such a thing growing in his gut. No wonder he succumbed to melancholy. That and the death of his son."

He wiped his hands on his apron and sighed. "Well, we can do no more. Let's get him sewn up and into the ground."

Gerard replaced the heart and other organs, then took a length of silk, threaded the long needle, and stitched up the man's torso.

"Watch there," said William, pointing to a pucker below Elias's navel. "A good place for problems later on. Remember, both of you, give the patient as much chance for improvement as possible. Let him suffer not, let us do no harm."

"Yes, Father," said Gerard.

"Yes, Master William," said Meg.

"Now, take the stitch out and try again. *Usus magister est optimus.* Meg?"

"Practice is the best teacher, Master William."

Gerard glanced at Meg and chanced a grin.

This time the stitch was straight without the offending pucker. Meg pondered, not for the first time, how Gerard might explain his excellent surgery skills to the Masters at Oxford. She doubted whether the learned gentlemen would believe he had practiced on the family cat. He could always say he learned by watching his father, which was true, but that alone would not explain his talent for stitchery.

When Gerard was finished, they wrapped Elias in a shroud. The carters appeared as the bells rang for Vespers and William paid them for their service, slipping them extra coins for the gravediggers.

"Tell them Master William has lost another patient. They are to find him a suitable plot of dirt. No trickery," he warned. "No hunting in the shroud for treasure. The man died poor. He has nothing to take to the grave except the cloth he's wrapped in."

The carters hurried to take the body, their eyes sliding toward the bloody floor and the bowls of fluid still on the table.

Gerard waited for the sound of cart wheels to fade and then whispered, "Father, I fear one day the carters will report you to the authorities."

"Not likely. They know which side of the coin they receive."

"True, but if threatened with excommunication or the rack, will they keep quiet?"

"Not to worry. My enemies may bluster and threaten, but in the end they'll ask for money, as everyone does, and look the other way."

Meg could tell by the irritated look on Gerard's face he didn't believe William but wouldn't chance an argument. Master William's stubbornness was fierce, his diatribe about the learned physicians of London and Oxford unchanging. Those arrogant men in their long red gowns would have thrown up their hands and attributed the blacksmith's death to fate. It was a combination of the wrong stars, they would say, or an inauspicious date and time of birth, the movement of the planets, or any number of unfortunate events which killed the blacksmith. They never dirtied their hands with the patient's fluids other than urine. Indeed, they never even got close enough to a patient to smell his breath. They never deigned to palpate an abdomen or inspect a patient's nails for anemia, preferring instead to work their astrological chart and consult their volvelle to determine the position of the sun and moon.

William's experience, first as a doctor of phisik, then as a surgeon, taught him much about the body's intricate workings. The human body could not be reduced to a chart showing the position of the stars. He would always end this denunciation with a question to Meg and Gerard. "Do you not agree with this?"

"Yes, Father, I do agree," Gerard would answer.

And Meg would echo, "Yes, Master William, I do agree."

✳✳✳

In the days following the blacksmith's death, William stayed in his room writing notes on Elias's illness. William had written in his *Chirurgia* following each visit to his patient and he read and re-read each entry, straining for a clue as to the man's condition and the link to the growth in his intestines. As usual, he wrote in Latin enhanced by a private code. Anyone trying to decipher the book would be repulsed by the difficulty of translating gibberish. Even his drawings of the human body were coded.

At the end of the week, he had come to one conclusion: the growth in the man's intestines must have choked the body's ability to feed itself. Without the proper nourishment, Elias grew weak and eventually died. If William had known of the growth earlier, perhaps he could have cured Elias. He could have pulled the toxins from his abdomen and perhaps cut out the malicious aposteme. That is, if Elias survived the surgery.

William groaned and buried his head in his hands. He

was in danger himself of catching the man's morose temperament, though he knew melancholy was not contagious—it just seemed so. There were some days when his normally confident (some would say overbearing) air disappeared and in its place was a deep despair, a black fog in which he could see the faces of those who had joined their Saviour in heaven because he, William of Oxford, was powerless to save them.

Mortui vivos docent. Indeed. The dead did teach the living, but sometimes the lesson appeared too late.

There were some, like the blacksmith, who defied their place in the book of phisik. Questions. Too many questions. William closed his *Chirurgia* and locked it in a cabinet. He was young once like Meg and Gerard. Young and foolhardy, skeptical of his teachers, eager to take on the world. He had fallen in love—several times—and lived to tell the tale. He had even married once. Now he was old. Gruff. Disillusioned. The world hadn't changed. He had.

He reached under his bed and pulled out a large rectangular box decorated with ornate ivory carvings of Biblical heroes. He placed a key in the lock, waited for a clicking sound, and gently opened the lid. He knelt over the box, one hand against the bed to steady himself, and observed the treasure below, over one hundred silver coins. The real treasure, however, couldn't be counted in coins. It was priceless. He reached around the side of the box and pressed a hidden knob at the end of a carved leaf. A secret drawer slid out from the bottom.

He pulled out a white shawl, a book, and a rectangular piece of yellow cloth.

With a sigh of pleasure, he rocked back on his heels. He pressed the yellow cloth to his cheek and inhaled a faint scent of cardamom and orange—his mother's perfume, exotic and foreign, hinting of strange customs and mysterious people. The cloth, about the size of his palm, marked the wearer as Jewish, an outsider in the Christian world.

For several hours, William sat quietly in his room as the

shadows deepened. Candlelight flickered on the book and on the yellow felt. He placed the white shawl, the tallit, on his head. Caressing the fringe of the tallit, he read aloud, haltingly at first as he struggled to decipher each word and then with more skill as the old language came back to him.

Now these are the names of the sons of Israel, who came into Egypt with Jacob, every man with his household . . .

William read throughout the night, pausing only to light a new candle, to drink a cup of water or to relieve himself in the pisspot. In the morning as he heard Gerard's muffled footsteps outside his door, he closed the book and tenderly kissed its cover. He sighed, realizing he should destroy the ivory box, but he could not. It was the only remaining link to his mother.

Returning his attention to the secret drawer, he folded the tallit over the yellow badge and the book and pushed the drawer until it clicked. Safe again.

He walked to the window, his heart heavy with guilt and deceit. As he pushed open the shutter and greeted another raucous day in London, he asked his mother's forgiveness for turning his back on her people—*their* people.

He turned once again to the box of treasures. He closed the ivory lid, locked it, and slipped the box beneath the bed. He would lock away the truth as well. Gerard must never know.

Jewish blood was a dangerous legacy.

Chapter 17

THE TOWER

London, England, December 1326

A waxing gibbous moon cast shadows of pale silver upon the city's alleyways. It was well past curfew. All lights had been covered and all fires banked for the night. The streets of London were deserted save for three people—-William, Meg, and a man-at-arms—-riding through the moonlight, shifting their horses in and out of narrow lanes, making their way to their destination.

Meg sat straight in the saddle, the very model of comportment, save for an occasional shiver in the chilly damp. Only her chattering teeth and wide eyes hinted at the fear beneath. The beefy soldier whose violent knocks on the door had roused them, rode ahead, the royal coat of arms shining prominently on the sleeves of his quilted gambeson.

William leaned to her and whispered, "Gerard will be sorry to miss this adventure." Gerard was visiting Bernard of Stratford, William's old friend, the newly appointed Master of Phisik at Oxford, who, at William's request, was determining Gerard's suitability for admission. Gerard was brilliant and well-prepared, Meg thought. Stratford would be foolish not to accept him as a student.

Meg smiled wanly and nodded. Her clothes were disheveled and her shoes mismatched, the result of being rousted from bed, but when a soldier of the Queen demanded your presence in the middle of the night, you did not tell him to go away if you wanted to keep your head on your shoulders.

The soldier who pounded on the door was adamant: Meg, and only Meg, was to come with him. He would not tell them who was ill. Meg could only deduce someone in the royal household, a female most likely, required her care and wanted their meeting kept secret.

William had begged the soldier to take him instead, but the soldier pulled a dagger from its scabbard. "I have my orders to escort only the girl," he warned.

"I need to accompany her," William pleaded. "She's young and a mere apprentice. She may have need of me." To entice the soldier further, William promised, "There will be no interference from me. I give you my word."

The man-at-arms thrust the dagger under William's chin. "You may come then, but stay out of the way."

"At least tell me where we are going," William implored. "Westminster? Windsor? And to King Edward or Isabella? We need to know how many days' worth of supplies to take."

"You do not need supplies," the soldier said. "We are going to Tower Hill."

Meg was puzzled. While King Edward and Queen Isabella had apartments in the heavily fortified building known as the White Tower, they were at war with each other and no longer in London. The royal court had scattered. She wasn't even sure who was living in the White Tower or the sturdy towers surrounding it. Nor was she sure why the man-at-arms was leading them on a route that circled and backtracked, following hidden lanes, instead of the direct path through East Cheap and thence to the tower entrance.

Meg shifted in the saddle. They would know soon enough. William had taught her it wasn't politically prudent these days to ask too many questions. She glanced upward at the shuttered windows lining the street, blind eyes behind which Londoners tossed in troubled dreams. These were indeed un-easy days. The affairs of the rich and powerful endangered everyone, even lowly commoners sleeping fitfully on a moon-lit night.

The man-at-arms raised a hand, motioning them to stop. They were on the northern edge of the tower moat with the tower postern straight ahead. Once through the postern gate, they would be outside the city walls. The sentry waved them on and they kicked their horses up the narrow wooden ramp and passed through the opening. The man-at-arms turned to the right. William and Meg followed.

As best Meg could tell, they were riding toward the south-east in the vicinity of St. Katherine's Church and Hospital. The stench of mud and salt blowing on a breeze from the south meant they were closer to the Thames.

"Leave your horses here," the soldier said. "We will walk over." He motioned to a causeway leading to the base of the outer curtain wall. "Hold your tongues until we're inside."

Clutching each other, Meg and William followed the murky figure of the soldier. Once on the other side of the moat, the man-at-arms waved to a guard atop the tower in the outer curtain wall who descended the stairs and opened a small door adjacent to the portcullis. The guard pocketed the coins he was given, then waved them on, glancing curiously at Wil-liam and Meg as they passed.

At the end of a tunnel, they straightened and found them-selves in the Inner Ward, inside the tower grounds. Just before they stepped onto a spiral staircase leading to the southeast tower, Meg caught a glimpse of the whitewashed walls of the royal residence, the White Tower, standing stark in the moonlight, its four turrets piercing the night sky.

***

"My name is Eleanor de Clare. Do you know who I am?"

"Yes, Your Ladyship." Meg bowed, unsure of whether she should fall to her knees, kiss the lady's hand, or simply stand with head lowered. What did a country girl know of courtly rituals?

In the center of the room was a chair and table at which Lady Despenser sat, straight-backed and impassive. She was dressed in a close-fitting tunic and surcoat of deep green with an ermine trim around the shoulders and cuffs. A necklace of gold filigree and amber adorned her throat. She appeared to be past her thirtieth year, but not by much. She was the most beautiful woman Meg had ever seen.

Eleanor beckoned the man-at-arms and placed several coins in his palm. "Stay near. I may have need of you in the future." The man bowed and left.

Meg stood at attention, wishing she could edge closer to the warmth of the hooded fireplace near Eleanor, but she dared not move without permission. The first-floor chamber of the tower was larger and brighter than she expected. Light from the wall torches and blazing fire bounced off the whitewashed walls and threw shadows on the high ceiling. Near the fireplace was a tall chest covered by a linen cloth. A few furnishings were pushed against the far wall: a small bed fit for one person and a low chest bearing a red, black, and white coat of arms. Next to the bed was an empty cradle.

Eleanor examined Meg from head to toe. She stared at Meg's face with a grimace. "So, you are the little apprentice. My husband's cousin speaks highly of you though he did not tell me of your deformity."

Meg asked with caution, "May I inquire as to the identity of your husband's cousin?"

"Sir Henry Despenser at Caldecote Hall. You and the wise woman from the village cared for his wife, Elisabeth. Sir Henry told me how you saved his infant son from a certain death and tended Elisabeth until she died."

"Yes, milady." Meg remembered too well the horror of Elisabeth's birth, how they had switched infant boys, secretly spiriting Alice's infant grandson into the castle, removing Sir Henry's dead child, and burying him in a grave at St. Michael's. Sir Henry had no idea his son was the child of ordinary villagers.

"I understand you have apprenticed to William the Surgeon and are living in London," Eleanor said.

"Yes, milady."

Eleanor tapped the amber necklace, then folded her hands on her lap. "You are probably wondering why I ordered you here."

"I supposed you were ill."

"I am in a way." Eleanor rose and looked out a narrow window into the depths of night. "Sick at heart, most assuredly."

Eleanor's movement caused something in the room to flutter. Meg jumped, startled by the beating of unseen wings. Eleanor smiled and walked to the covered chest near the fireplace. She pulled away the cloth revealing a tall wicker birdcage. Goldfinches, in a flurry of yellow agitation and crashing bodies, flew from one perch to another, chirping in terror until Eleanor's calm voice settled them.

"Beautiful, aren't they?" Eleanor asked. "A gift from King Edward. Forty-seven of them in honor of . . ." She smiled at Meg as if she had a secret to tell. "Well, in honor of a private matter. Edward gave them to me before he left London. The constable kindly allowed me to bring them here. I didn't expect to have finches as my final companions, but they keep me company."

"Your final companions? But surely Queen Isabella will spare you."

Eleanor threw back her head and laughed, a sound filled with more poison than mirth. "Not too long ago, I counted His Royal Highness, the King of England, as my companion. His wife, Queen Isabella, was *my* prisoner. Now *she* is free and *I* am in prison." She gestured toward the empty cradle. "And the she-devil got her revenge. My youngest child, barely a year old was torn from my arms and placed in the Queen's custody. My husband and father-in-law are dead. My three young daughters are shut away in convents."

Meg stood silent, feeling sympathy for the lady, but questioning why she had been disturbed from her sleep to hear this tale of woe and to gaze at goldfinches in the tower. Eleanor did not appear to be in pain, nor was she flushed with fever, rather the spots of color on her cheeks grew darker with the vehemence of her speech. Could she simply need someone on which to vent her hatred of the Queen in the middle of the night, or was she truly ill?

Eleanor carefully recovered the birdcage, then she turned to Meg. Her voice was steady, but bitter. "Do you know what the Queen did to my husband?"

Meg had heard rumors—rumors were flying through London—of horrible deeds. Rumors that pieces of Despenser's body now adorned the gates of York, Newcastle, Dover, and Bristol.

"My loving husband was roped to four horses," Eleanor was saying, "and dragged through Hereford to his own castle walls. There he was stripped naked and hoisted above the slavering crowd where he was hanged. But then . . ." Her tongue darted from her lips as if to unlock the words burdened by her misery. "Then just before he died, he was revived. The Queen was not finished with him. She would have her revenge for Hugh's love of the King, and so she took vengeance upon the part of Hugh which gave the King his greatest pleasure."

"Please, your Ladyship," Meg pleaded, "calm yourself. Maladies of the heart and mind are—"

Eleanor paced from wall to wall, from door to bed, and back again. "The executioner cut off his member and testicles and threw them into the fire below."

Eleanor ceased her pacing, her eyes wild and unfocused, seeing only what her imagination called forth: the scene of her husband's humiliation and gruesome death. "His intestines and his heart were cut from his body and thrown into the fire. Finally, his head was cut from his neck." Eleanor slumped into the chair, her aloofness giving way, her mask of reserve crumbling.

Meg was not sure what to say. The Despensers, father and son, once so powerful, had been executed like common thieves. Lady Eleanor was left alone in the tower to mourn the loss of her husband and children. And to contemplate her own fate, whatever that might be.

"Your Ladyship," Meg ventured. "I have something in my bag which might be soothing to you." She moved toward the door. "Master William is holding it for me."

"What?" Eleanor hissed. "My orders were to bring you and no one else."

"He came only for my protection. He will be discreet, milady, as he is with all his patients." Meg moved to open the door, but Eleanor caught her arm.

"No! I do not need your numbing herbs. I need a powerful medicine, one strong enough to remove something clinging inside me, something that must be banished." She placed both hands upon her abdomen.

"I do not understand. If milady has a stomach ailment—"

Eleanor whispered harshly, "I am with child and it must be gone."

Meg stiffened.

"I need pennyroyal. Queen Isabella used it, as well as others at court. The whores in Cock Lane are known to consume it in wine. You will fetch it, prepare the right dose, and give it to me."

Meg knew it well. On one of their last trips to the watery meadows, Meg and Alice had harvested pennyroyal on Midsummer's Eve and dried it in the shade, as was the proper method. When Meg left for London and a new life with William and Gerard, Alice shared the herb with her. It would be useful for certain women in the city whose monthly flow was dammed within the womb and would not come forth. It could also be used to expel a stillborn child, but only when used in small doses.

Unfortunately, Meg had long ago used up her supply of pennyroyal so great was the demand for it in London.

Using pennyroyal on a woman with a living child in her womb was risky, Alice had warned. The consequences could be deadly for both mother and child. Alice's words of warning rang in Meg's mind as she stood before the powerful Eleanor de Clare. "Your Ladyship, many women do not want their baby at first."

Eleanor's eyes glittered in the firelight. She spoke carefully, her words as piercing as an arrow shot. "I have given birth to nine children. I have quite enough experience in motherhood. I need your medicine, not your platitudes. If this child is born, I will die."

"A robust woman like yourself?"

Eleanor walked to the fire, her hands outstretched for warmth, her back to Meg. "You do not understand. I do not speak of childbirth. Once this child is born, it will not take long for someone to count backwards and realize the truth. I will be executed. And the child will die as well."

"Why would anyone care when you and your husband, when his seed—"

"My husband was away in Wales, tending to personal business for several months when this child was conceived. I was close to only one other man. We met often in his Hall at Sheen. We dined privately, away from those who troubled him or fawning courtiers begging a favor. He would bring me sweets, sometimes money, but occasionally he surprised me with a special gift." She nodded toward the birdcage where the finches were sleeping.

Meg struggled to keep her face expressionless, yet shock threatened to undo her best efforts. Was Eleanor implying that the King, her uncle, was her lover? To be certain, Meg had overheard William discussing the possibility, but to hear it from Eleanor's own lips was disturbing. And could it be? No, not a child from . . . no, it was too foul to think upon.

Eleanor whirled to face Meg. The woman's face was flushed from the fire or perhaps memories of forbidden trysts. "Do not look so shocked, apprentice. My husband and I loved the King. Sometimes my husband would join us and the three of us would share in each other's company all night. Is it unthinkable our love should have many facets?"

"And what of Queen Isabella?" Meg asked.

Eleanor's face hardened at the mention of the Queen. "That *whore?*" Eleanor spat. "If Isabella discovers this child is her husband's, she will kill me and the child. She would never allow her son's rival to live. Only *her* son is to be king, not some bastard out of the king's niece." She turned once again to the fire. "If I live, I will remarry and have more children. At least I will still have my head on my shoulders."

A wave of nausea overtook Meg, and she swallowed to keep from gagging. The room, so cold when she first entered, now felt hot and close. She felt surrounded and crushed by Eleanor's birds, the empty cradle, and the woman's hatred.

"How far along are you?"

"I know what you are asking. Have I felt the child quicken? Yes. He kicks day and night."

Meg felt a gust of panic and confusion, like a sudden gale blowing off the North Sea and into her thoughts. Quickening. That was the dividing line. *Foetus erat formatus et animatus.* A child who has quickened is formed and animated. He has a soul. A soul belonging to God and the Church. If she aborted a quickened child, she would break Church law. Even worse, a late abortion was against English common law. It was considered homicide. Murder. The punishment was death.

William advised against a late abortion, but with one caveat: "The great Arab physician Avicenna teaches sometimes abortion is necessary where birth endangers the life of the mother. When you are a *magistra of phisik* and practicing on your own, you will sometimes have to make hard choices. Abortion may be one of those. Do you want to save your own skin or kill the mother?"

But Eleanor de Clare did not appear to be in mortal danger. She appeared healthy and perfectly capable of having a child. If Meg performed an abortion, she would commit a mortal sin. Worse, she would be guilty of homicide.

"Well?" Eleanor demanded.

"I, uh, I am afraid, milady, I am unable to do as you ask."

"Why?"

"I was never taught how to expel a child from the womb. Besides, pennyroyal is dangerous. You could bleed to death and—"

"And what?"

"The Church forbids it."

Eleanor seized a cup from the table and threw it hard against the wall. Rivulets of wine left a stain on the whitewash as if the room were bleeding. "I do not care if the Pope himself stands before me and threatens me with the Last Judgment. This child cannot live!"

"Milady, English law considers abortion a homicide after quickening."

"There is only one English law and that is *my* law! I am the king's niece. I come from a long line of earls, barons, and kings. Men who made the law you speak of. Do you not think they would look the other way if one of their own needed to flout the law?"

Oh, Meg understood all right. In some machination or

sleight of hand at court, Eleanor would be excused and forgiven—punished in a small way, a penance perhaps or a donation to St. Bartholomew Hospital, but she would still go about life with a head on her shoulders. Meg would bear the blame, all of it. She would be tried— if she were to have a trial at all—and put to death. She would be a warning to all women not to interfere in the ways of God and nature. And English law.

"Please let me fetch Master William," Meg pleaded. "I am sure he is just outside the door and would be glad to be of service to your Ladyship."

"No," Eleanor answered, her voice cold. "This is between you and me. Two women who understand what it is to bear the burden of the womb. I will tell the Constable of the Tower I am in need of women's things. Men always look askance at the mention of a woman's monthly necessities. I will tell him you must come and go as I wish."

She turned to Meg once more, but this time her lips were thin against her teeth, like a feral dog fighting to the death over a bit of bone.

"I will give you money. There is a man on Camomile Street near Bishopsgate who has the necessary herbs. You will make a pessary and give it to me."

"But milady, surely you would prefer to drink it in wine."

"Yes, I do. But I also want it where it needs to be—at the mouth of my womb so the child may drink of it and die."

Meg's horror stifled any reply.

"Until you return, William will stay here in the tower."

At this, Meg roused herself. "But—"

"If you do not return, apprentice, I will gladly slit his throat."

Chapter 18

THE RAYKER

London, England, December 1326

As soon as the sun rose, Meg and a servant girl left William's house and headed northeast on Threadneedle in their quest to find Camomile Street near the city wall. The servant, a young girl of Meg's age who slept in the kitchen, was new to William's employ but Meg suspected she had suffered a hard life. The girl skittered from one chore to another as if she were a frightened mouse. When Meg told her their destination, the girl cowered against the kitchen wall, saying she had never been far away from Cheapside. Meg told her that was no excuse.

"I must go this morning even if I have to roust the owner of the herb shop out of bed," Meg fumed. "Gerard is in Oxford and Master William is, well, he is not here." She snatched the cowering girl by the scruff of her neck and hauled her to a standing position. "I cannot go by myself. Master William would skin my hide if he found I was running about the city unaccompanied. Now get up."

With a whimper the girl set off beside her.

***

The herbalist's shop was in serious danger of falling on its owner's head. But then so were the other shops to the left and right. Across the row of tumbledown buildings was an empty plot of land full of wild plants and rubbish running to Bishopsgate. The herbalist, a man whose long nails were caked with grime and whose face bore the unmistakable deep valleys of a pox in his childhood, looked at her with curiosity when she asked for the pennyroyal.

"I've never seen you before," he said.

Meg said nothing.

"You're here early. I was barely out of bed."

"I have many errands today. I'm in a hurry."

"Pennyroyal, eh?" He perused the bottles and jars behind him until he found one in particular. He scooped the contents into a clay jar and tied a piece of linen around the top. "You know," he said as he placed the jar in her basket, "most young girls your age . . ."

Meg handed him the payment and without another word fled the shop while the servant girl called in fright for her to slow down.

As Meg approached Bishopsgate, the figure of a waste rayker caught her eye. The man was short and stocky, muscular, but stooped by his labors. Later, as she was telling Gerard about the incident, she couldn't explain what had caused her to stop and stare. There was something about the way he lifted the handles of his cart that caused Meg to follow him as if in a trance. The servant girl cried out, "No, miss, home is there," and pointed behind them, and yet there was nothing Meg could do to stop herself. She followed the rayker until he paused at the broad ditch on the other side of the city wall. He tipped the cart and dumped the load of rubbish, stretched his back, and with a grunt lifted the cart again.

It was the grunt that finally brought her to her senses, a grunt she had heard many times, a singular sound—a musical "oomph"—so unlike the other men in St. Michael's Mead.

As the rayker walked by her, she stared at his face. Beneath the dirt caked in the wrinkles of his eyes, there was no mistake. He had his father's bristled brows, long ginger hairs sprouting in all directions. His wide shoulders were used to hard work, first with a plow, and now with a cart.

"Walter!" she called.

Her brother turned as if a ghost had called his name.

Chapter 19

Free Man

London, England, December 1326

"Walter, I can hardly believe it is you!" Joy bubbled through Meg, along with astonishment and disbelief. "Here you are in London after all. Why have I not seen you? Where have you been?"

They were sitting with their backs against the city wall just inside the gate. A patch of blue in the clouds brought unexpected sunshine and a brief feeling of warmth. The servant girl sat next to Meg, fashioning wildflowers into a necklace.

"I've been here, mostly. We work at night or in the early morning hours so as not to bother good folk. From Camomile Street down to Fenchurch, from Bishopsgate in the west to St. Mary Axe."

"Oh, Walter, look at you." She placed a hand on his face, on the layers of dirt and muck dried on his skin. It was hard to believe the stocky boy who ran away on Martinmas so many years ago was now a grown man. "Why did you not come home? We would have taken care of you, and you know there is plenty of work in the village."

"Come back with my tail between my legs? Never. Besides, Sir Henry would have had his revenge. I'm a free man here. I'm paid for my work."

She wanted to say "a free man but a rayker of dung, rubbish, offal—all gathered and tipped into the ditch and nothing like your dreams when you ran away," but said nothing instead.

Walter watched the crowds teeming through the gate. "I cannot stay long. How are Mother and Father and Maud? And how did you come to live in London?"

Meg described the last eight years, beginning with her apprenticeship with Alice and the bargain struck by Master William—payment of John's confinement at the leper hospital in return for Meg's education and assistance with his patients.

"God's blood." Walter's look of shock and horror reflected the pain in Meg's heart. "Father in a lazar hospital. Hard to think on it."

"Yes. And Mother took it badly. When I left, she was barely herself. But Maud will help her. Maud is married to Oswald and they have a passel of children."

"I cannot imagine our Maud with a babe at her tit and a snot-nosed child on her lap. Poor Oswald. He's got the ass-end of that bargain." Walter grinned, the dirt on his face splitting into laugh lines. It was the face Meg remembered from her childhood and she couldn't help smiling herself.

"And this William?" Walter asked brusquely. "Is he a good man? Kind?"

"Oh yes, the best of teachers, though he can be gruff some days, but most kind. He has a son named Gerard. He wants to be a doctor of phisik as well. He is planning to visit Oxford to speak with the new master of medicine. He has a brilliant mind."

"And you have feelings for this Gerard?"

Meg felt heat rising from her chest. "I, uh, I feel for him as a brother, as befits my—"

"Never mind. Your face tells me otherwise. You always were a poor liar. Between your yammering and the redness of your cheeks, you'll always be caught."

She reached for his hand. "Oh, Walter, I do not want to go now that I have found you, but Master William is in danger." She touched the red skin around a cut on his arm. The wound looked suspiciously like a slash mark from a knife. "I'll return and bring you food and medicine. Where do you live?"

He shook off her hand. "I need for nothing." He fingered the bracelet on her wrist. "What is this?"

She told him about her pig Robin and his death on St. Martin's Day, and how Alice helped her to fashion the bracelet from the pig's hair and hide. It had begun to fray shortly after she arrived in London, but William, recalling a silversmith he had once cured of a nasty stye in his eyelid, asked the man to refurbish the bracelet, which was now wrapped in a silver coil.

"I wear it always, as a reminder of my life in the village."

She paused, loathe to leave her newly-found brother, loathe to know Walter spent each day in rubbish, rayking the detritus of other people's lives.

"At least agree to dine with us, Walter. We're on Lickpenny Lane. Everyone knows Master William. Please say yes."

"Perhaps."

They stood and embraced, holding to each other as if the years could be erased.

"I must go. I need to get this to the Tower." She picked up the basket. "I'll be back soon. Where do you live?"

"Go, little sister. See to your William. I'll join you for dinner one day, if you'll have me."

"Yes, yes, of course." Walking backward, she waved and then turned forward to take a few steps, but turned again, afraid he had disappeared in a puff of smoke, afraid he would be gone forever. "I love you, Walter. Remember, Lickpenny Lane off West Cheap."

He waved. She and the servant girl crossed Bishopsgate, weaving between throngs of people coming into the city. When she turned again, he was gone.

Chapter 20

RIFFLERS AND ROARERS

London, England, December 1326

Eleanor de Clare shuddered as Meg pushed a tightly-wound tube of cotton into the woman's most secret place. Meg, aware that her fingers were cold and shaking, apologized but Eleanor snapped, "Get on with it."

With the boiled remains of the mint-like pennyroyal in a pot on the fire, the room smelled fresh and sweet. But Meg knew there was no sweetness in Eleanor's heart, only hatred and terror.

If Meg had measured correctly, the cup of pennyroyal-laced wine and pennyroyal-infused cotton should successfully end Eleanor's pregnancy. However, if she had measured incorrectly, it would end Eleanor's life. She had used only enough pennyroyal to fill a chestnut as Alice had taught her, but the herb was not to be trusted. Had she been in St. Michael's Mead, Meg could have prepared it properly.

For the next few hours, Eleanor slept. When the finches stirred, she motioned for Meg to remove the cover from the birdcage. As the birds chirped and flitted from perch to perch, Meg wondered if Master William was still waiting for her. She hadn't seen him on her return from Camomile Street. She feared the man-at-arms had locked him in a dark hole.

Eleanor used the pisspot and crawled into bed again without even glancing Meg's way. Grimacing, she pulled her knees to her chest.

The back of her shift was stained with blood.

And so it begins, Meg thought.

✳✳✳

Later that afternoon, Meg convinced Eleanor she needed William's help. Eleanor hastily agreed, for she was in no condition to argue. She was doubled over in pain with severe cramping. There was no crying out, only the occasional muttered curse word. William said nothing when he came into the room. He looked at Meg and raised his eyebrows. She nodded, signaling that she was safe. They waited. When it was over, William gathered the sheet and rolled its contents into a bundle, carefully hiding any trace of blood.

Eleanor ordered him to dispose of it.

"I would be happy to do so, milady," William said. "But I'm sure you have a loyal servant—"

Eleanor's voice showed no sign of gratitude. Each word was uttered as if it were an icy dagger. "Do it or I shall have you both locked away forever."

Now as Meg and William walked swiftly toward home, still convinced that Eleanor would send someone to kill them, they stumbled onto a crowd gathering near St. Mary le Bow Church and the great Cheapside Cross. William shifted the sheet, rolled it tightly to cover the bloody evidence, and grabbed Meg's hand.

"Let's turn on Milk Street," William said.

"There's riots at Westminster!" a woman shouted. "They've broken into a great house."

The energy of the crowd shifted as if it were a living thing and all the people in it attached by an invisible will. They started running ragtag, whooping with glee, heading in a westerly direction.

Suddenly a grubby man in the crowd snatched at William's hands and pulled on the sheet. "What have you got there, your highness? Been doing your own rumbustion?" He tugged at the sheet. "Silver? Candlesticks?"

"Get away!" William shouted. "There is nothing here for you."

"I'll be the judge of that," the man said as he pulled on the sheet.

A bloody spot appeared.

"Eh, what's this then?" The man stepped closer, grinning through toothless gums.

Others stopped to have a look as well, sensing a possible gain.

"Meg, run," William said sharply.

"Not without you, Master William."

The man reached past Meg for the sheet. She grabbed his hand and bit the fleshy underside of his thumb and palm until she tasted blood. She kicked the man in the kneecap for good measure. The man howled with anger, hopping on one foot and holding his knee, then shaking his bloody hand. He dove for Meg. "Why, you ugly whore!"

"*Now* it is time to run," she yelled to an astonished William.

They turned for Lickpenny Lane as someone called to the crowd to leave them and run for Westminster. The man peeled away and Meg and William dashed for the safety of William's house. Only when William bolted the door and they collapsed at the kitchen table, did Meg finally feel secure.

"Well, he got more than he bargained for," William said.

"How did you—?"

"I had good training from birth." She fingered her bracelet. "You might have made me into a silk purse, Master William, but on the inside I'm still a sow's ear."

"Well, thank heavens for it." William stood and glanced toward the back garden, the bundle of linen still held against his chest. "I must bury this," he said. "You stay here. And don't let anyone come inside."

"Yes, sir."

Eleanor de Clare had promised their lives would be safe. Meg shivered. People like Eleanor used others strictly for her own purposes and when she was finished with them, she tossed them out like tatters to the rag-and-bone man.

Meg heard the sound of a spade breaking earth behind the house. William was burying the sheet.

Trust Eleanor de Clare? Never.

Chapter 21

GERARD THE SPY

London, England, December 1326

A dog barked. Gerard ducked into the arched doorway of the Saddler's Hall and flattened himself against the stones. He had been playing a cat-and-mouse game with a beggar for the better part of the morning, keeping the man in sight but staying behind at a safe distance. Occasionally, as now with the barking dog, the beggar would pause and glance around.

The beggar had led him from Lickpenny Lane to west on Watling, passing the bakers on Bread Street and the fishmongers on Friday Street before taking an abrupt right that led into St. Paul's Churchyard. At that point, the man backtracked through the cathedral grounds where Gerard almost lost him among black-robed Benedictines and gray Franciscans, and shoppers who haggled and gossiped at the market stalls.

The beggar stopped to buy an apple from a costermonger,

polished the fruit on his ragged sleeves, and stood studying the crowds in the churchyard. When he finished the apple, he threw the core to a dog and turned northeast, making his way to West Cheap before turning north.

For weeks Gerard had been suspicious of the beggar's behavior. The man sat in the same place each day, always in view of William's house, not caring whether passersby filled his cup with coins or not. He certainly didn't act like any beggar Gerard had ever seen. He confided his suspicions to William, but his father was dismissive.

"These are anxious times," William said. "You're perceiving things that aren't there."

It was true. Rumors ran through the city like sparks from a house fire. Riots and murders, pillaging, and mobs roaming the streets put everyone on edge.

One morning last week Gerard had mustered the courage to approach the beggar seated cross-legged on the street. The man's face was grimy, his ginger hair ragged and his beard matted and dirty. His clothes were so tattered that only the air held the threads together. When Gerard said "good morning," the man pointed to his throat and ear, signaling he was a deaf mute. As Gerard dropped a coin in the man's cup and bid the beggar good day, he noticed the man's feet. Gerard had observed hundreds of beggars on the streets of London, but never one wearing expensive red leather shoes.

Since then, he had been waiting for an opportunity to follow the mysterious beggar. Today was the day. He was supposed to be in Oxford to meet with a committee of masters, including Bernard of Stratford, the new master in charge of medicine, but he had slipped his servant's care as soon as they approached Ludgate, the western gate in the city walls. He returned to Lickpenny Lane and took up his post near the deaf mute. Within a short time, the man gathered his cup and walking stick and hobbled away with Gerard in pursuit.

Gerard's instincts were correct. The man was not a beggar.

Nor was he a cripple—he walked far too quickly to be infirmed. In fact, come to think on it, he wasn't a deaf mute either. When buying his apple, he had talked to the costermonger.

To get his bearings, Gerard stopped and stared in all directions. Cripplegate, the northern entrance to the city, was straight ahead. They were in the vicinity of rich merchants and special craftsmen—goldsmiths, curriers, saddlers, and bowyers. What business could a beggar have with the likes of them?

When the man turned to the left, Gerard knew his destination: the Company of Barber-Surgeons. Red and white flags hung above the entrance to the building and waved smartly in the breeze as barbers who had business within the hall hurried up the steps. Built snug against the city wall, the Worshipful Company of Barber-Surgeons was home to some of William's most outspoken enemies. From the number of men being admitted, Gerard assumed a meeting was about to start.

Gerard spied the beggar hiding behind the trunk of a stout elm tree. The beggar glanced about, then abandoned his stick and stood upright. As the man peeled off the rags wrapped around his body, multi-colored hose appeared, followed by a brightly embroidered tunic. He uncovered his head. Then he tugged at his beard. Gerard was stunned as the ginger beard peeled away from the man's face. Next, the beggar placed a hand on his scalp and pulled off his hair. The man rubbed his clean-shaven face and scratched his real hair, which was short and brown. He stashed his costume, false hair, and beard against the city wall and then turned to enter the hall, brushing the dust from his shoulders. He climbed the steps and stood facing the street as if waiting for someone. Finally, a man coming from the opposite direction raised his hands in greeting and both men entered the building.

Gerard let out a long breath. The man who met the beggar at the top of the steps was Bernard of Stratford, the new Master of Phisik at Oxford, William's old friend and the same man Gerard was supposed to be meeting to discuss his qualifications for entry to the university. Gerard thought the master would have a hard time explaining to William how he could be in two places at once.

While seeing Bernard in the flesh was a shock, it was the beggar's transformation that was most remarkable—almost magical. Indeed, no one but a magician—or a phisik-monger who spent a lifetime fooling a gullible public—could have managed such a disguise.

The man who revealed himself was no beggar at all. He was the noisy hawker of elixirs they had met in York.

Robertus Medicamus.

✻✻✻

The next morning Gerard rose early, even before the servants. The house was silent except for his footsteps. He was determined to confront Medicamus and to, well, he didn't know what he would do, but he would think of something. Like everyone he carried a knife on his girdle, but its use was limited to slicing meat, peeling apples, and occasionally cutting leather or rope. He had never used it as a weapon but would if he must.

He stepped into the kitchen and jumped, startled by the sight of Meg sitting at the table with a book open before her.

She jumped as well, letting out a little squeak of surprise. "Oh, God's breath but you frightened me! What are you doing?"

He grinned. "I'm sorry. I didn't expect anyone to be up at this early."

"And why aren't you in Oxford? Your servant suffered William's wrath when he returned without you. We supposed you continued to Oxford on your own. Foolhardy, to be sure."

"I sneaked into the house last night after everyone was in bed. I never went to Oxford." Glancing at the book on the table, he asked, "Haven't you read that several times?"

She ducked her head in embarrassment. "Yes, but I learn

something new each time I read it. Look here, where Mondeville defies the concept of laudable pus: 'It is not necessary that pus be generated in wounds. No error can be greater than this.' And yet, does not Guy de Chauliac support the generation of pus within three days?"

Gerard stifled his laughter lest he wake the household. "Meg, it's far too early in the morning for a discussion of pus."

The light from the tallow candle cast a glow against Meg's skin as she leaned in to look at the book. She was dressed in a nightshift with a coverlet around her shoulders. Her hair, mouse-like and thin when she left St. Michael's Mead, was now a thick auburn brushed with shades of red that caught and held the candlelight. She swept a strand of hair away from her face and then traced the drawing on the page with gentle fingers. The rough red skin and grubby cracked nails were gone, replaced with hands that were soft, but capable of stitching a wound without a pucker. As always, she wore the leather bracelet wrapped in a silver coil. She removed it only when working in the dissection room.

Gerard smiled, remembering how he had teased her when she first came to live with them, telling her that hogs hair wasn't exactly the fashion in London, but she lashed back at him, saying she would *never* wear another bracelet, even if she were the richest woman in Christendom.

It was true that many who met her for the first time recoiled at the sight of her disfigurement, but Gerard no longer noticed it. Instead, he saw a beautiful young woman of unearthly demeanor. Where other women would have flinched at dissections, fainting dead away or not deigning to get their hands dirty, she stood in rapt attention untroubled by the blood and fluids, which later she cleaned without complaint. Though they were of the same age, he often felt younger than she. And while he knew a great deal of Latin, he had to admit that now, after four years of tutoring, she could speak and read it better than he — she who knew nothing but garbled Church

Latin and the guttural tongue of her native village when she rode with them to London.

She had devoured William's medical books, pouring over drawings of the human body, listening good-naturedly to his father's lectures, and showing a remarkable attention to each patient, showing no sign of weariness as they rambled on. Many times she would hold a patient's hand and sit in silence.

In August, William allowed her to prepare the dissection of an elderly woman. After Meg examined the organs and stitched the deceased back together again, declaring that the woman had died of a diseased heart, William praised her work and presented her a gift to mark her progress, a *vade mecum* to hang on her girdle.

She flipped through the pages of the leather-bound book, exclaiming at the beautifully painted tables of phlebotomy, the Zodiac charts, the illustrations of urine flasks with their variations in color to indicate disease and cause, and finally on the last page, the venous man whose body bore the sites for bleeding and cupping. Seeing her flushed face and wide smile as she hung the book on her belt, Gerard had to admit that he was happy for her. He was also riddled with envy.

Meg pulled the coverlet tighter around her neck. "What?"

"What? What do you mean?"

"You were staring at me."

Gerard felt the blood rise from his neck to his cheeks. "My apologies. I did not mean to be rude."

Now it was her turn to laugh. "No need for apologies. If you had truly meant to be rude, I would have known it. Like your father, you say what you think. Sometimes I fear that Master William's temper will get the better of him."

"It already has."

"What do you mean?"

"If I'm right, you'll know soon enough. I must go."

"What are you—?"

"I must go."

Meg reached for his hand. "The streets are fearful these days. Take care, Gerard."

He squeezed her fingers and then grinned. "I leave you to your examination of pus." He departed the house and took up his post around the corner from the beggar's usual position.

✳✳✳

As the gray light of dawn broke over the city and church bells called Londoners to the day's work, Gerard caught sight of Medicamus approaching the rear of Lickpenny Lane. But instead of taking up his usual post, Medicamus, no longer in disguise and dressed in somber shades of brown, walked past a shocked Gerard and lifted his hat in greeting.

"Good morning, Gerard," he said. He looked Gerard full in the face as he strode with deliberate intent to William's house. When he stopped at the rear entrance, Gerard ran to him and put the knife to his throat.

"Put that down, boy," Medicamus growled. "That poor excuse for a knife will barely cut butter."

"Butter or your neck, it makes no difference to me," Gerard responded. He held the knife steady against the phisik-monger's throat while he kicked at the kitchen door and shouted, "Meg, open up! Meg!" The latch shifted. He saw a frightened Meg, still in her nightclothes, peeping from behind the door. "Go fetch Father," he ordered, "and tell the servants to stay in their rooms."

Once inside the kitchen, Gerard pushed Medicamus away, knocking the table and Meg's medical book to the floor. "How did you know it was me behind you?" Gerard asked.

"I've known it was you from the first, you artless pup. Why do you think I took you on such a wander yesterday? I was trying to lose you, you fool. But there you were, always behind me, always ducking in and out of doorways like a dog taking a piss. Finally, when I saw you lurking at the Guild Hall, I gave up trying to shake you off my tail." Medicamus picked himself up off the floor and wagged his finger under Gerard's nose. "Take my advice, young man. Do the sick of this wretched world a favor and continue your medical studies. You know nothing of the street."

Medicamus, Gerard thought, was playing him for a fool, thinking him naïve and easily outwitted. He scoffed, "I know enough. I know that you're in league with the barber-surgeons and you plot against my father."

"You know nothing. And you'd better latch that door. We haven't much time."

"What do you mean?" Gerard asked as he pulled the latch into place.

"I have eyes on the street. They'll alert us before it's too late. We'll have time to flee, but not much."

A voice boomed behind them. "Robertus, I do not gladly entertain thieves in my kitchen. And you, Gerard, what is the meaning of this?" William bellowed. "Since when do you roam the streets of London with a knife in your hands? And why aren't you in Oxford?"

"Father, this man—the man you call your brother, your friend from the days of your youth, Medicamus—has been watching the house. *He* is the beggar I described to you and yesterday I saw him enter the Barber-Surgeons Hall in the company of Bernard of Stratford. They are plotting against you."

"Bernard? I don't understand. He was to meet with you in Oxford."

Medicamus interrupted. "We do not have much time. Let me explain it and then we must make preparations to flee." He held up his hand as Meg, William, and Gerard exploded with questions. "First, I am not in league with your enemies, William. The carters you employ to carry dead bodies to your dissecting room—"

William sputtered in protest.

"Do not play innocent, William," Medicamus continued. "The carters were foolish enough to steal goods from Smithfield Market. When they were caught, they decided to sacrifice you, Meg, and Gerard to save their own skins. Torture has an amazing ability to open mouths. Your activities were reported to the guild and then to the sheriff. The sheriff reported you to the Church and to Bernard of Stratford. I was brought in to gather further information."

"So, you *are* a part of the plot!" Gerard shouted.

"I admit that I was at first. I was simply doing the guild a favor and in return, well, let us just say that London is a city ripe for the picking if only guild members look the other way. Four years ago the guild asked me to follow you to York and to spy on your activities there and in London. I confess I thought the guild wanted only to censure you and force you to join, but when Bernard was brought in, things grew more serious. He talked of excommunication and then yesterday, he changed his mind. He is pressing the guild to take further action. He and the Archbishop are talking of torture followed by excommunication—for all of you."

Gerard glanced at Meg, who had gone quite pale.

William exploded. "That is ridiculous! Bernard is an old friend. He would never—"

"And there is more," Medicamus added. "Last night I learned that Queen Isabella has discovered a plot against her. It involves Eleanor de Clare and a young woman, an apprentice to a surgeon, who has been coming and going from Eleanor's quarters in the Tower. The young woman is to be brought up on charges of treason for trying to help Eleanor escape." He looked directly at Meg. "*You* are the woman."

Meg took a step toward Gerard and crumpled to the floor. Gerard caught her and cradled her, as William grabbed a vial of *sal ammoniac* from the cupboard. He held it under Meg's nose. She choked and sputtered, gasping for breath, and tried to sit up but fell back into Gerard's arms.

"You are right, Medicamus. We must flee immediately," William said.

"No," Meg protested. "They want me. I will go to the Queen and explain."

"Do not be an idiot," Gerard said. "The Queen cares not a whit whether you are innocent or guilty. She will murder you without a second thought simply to show her strength."

"If I may suggest." Medicamus peered out the window and then turned to the others. "The Queen's men will be watching every gate in the city. They will be expecting us to flee to Dover or one of the other Cinque Ports and thence to Calais. If we flee to the northeast through Bishopsgate—"

"But," William interrupted.

"There is no time for arguments. We'll divide into two parties—you and Meg, and Gerard and me—we'll meet my players at the Ram's Head Inn just beyond Bishopsgate. I have a friend with a boat in Southampton. He trades with ports in France and could be persuaded, with enough money, to embark immediately."

"Why *us*?" William asked. "Why are you coming?"

"I'm afraid that my players and I have worn out our welcome with the guild. Now that the Queen is involved, there is a high level of danger that does not bode well for my neck. Besides, I have traveled many times in France. It's a good place to make a fortune. I think we will start in Paris and work our way to the countryside."

"And why should we even trust you? Perhaps you're in the sheriff's employ. How do we know that you aren't walking us into a trap?" William asked.

"You do *not* know." Medicamus peered into the courtyard behind the house and then motioned to someone outside the window. "Except that once, many years ago, we were friends, William. More than friends—brothers. You may consider me an imposter and a fraud, but I am not a murderer and I will not have your deaths on my hands."

Medicamus summed up their choices. "Take a chance on Southampton and the possibility of freedom, or stay here and face certain death. If you want my advice: *Vir prudens non contra ventum mingit.* A wise man does not piss against the wind."

"Very well then. This is what we must do," William said. "Meg, you must dress as a boy. We don't have time to cut your hair, perhaps you can stuff it into a hat. Gerard, bring her some clothes immediately. Tell the servants to leave and not return. Do not pack anything. You will need only the clothes on your back." He turned to Robertus. "I would be grateful if several of your players, as you call them, could bring my chest down the stairs. It is under my bed, the box with the ivory top."

Meg and Gerard protested that he must leave the heavy box behind, but he cut them off. "The chest goes with me. No arguments."

Robertus opened the back door and whistled. Four "beggars" appeared out of nowhere. Robertus ordered two to go upstairs with William and fetch the chest. The other two were to hire pack horses and cart from the nearest stable. "Once you've loaded the chest, wait for us at Bishopsgate."

Within an hour the servants had fled, and the chest was loaded onto a four-wheeled cart led by a team of stout sumpter horses. Meg was in tears, having attempted to stuff medical books in a bag to take with her, only to be reprimanded by William. "Yes, they are valuable and beautiful," he said. "But they will slow us down. You must be able to run if you have to." Seeing her misery and her unspoken accusation as she stared at his large box of valuables, he picked a book and stowed it in the chest. That done, the beggars shook the reins and the team of packhorses headed toward the northern opening in the city wall.

Chapter 22

ESCAPE

London, England, December 1326

Bishopsgate teemed with England's masses: common folk looking for a new way of life and a path to luxury, the self-important rich trailing insistent beggars, crippled men and women on their knees, madmen calling out in gibberish, marketers and patrons, and men hauling carts of food, cloth, animals, and goods from the countryside. Strolling through the gates were foreign travelers dressed in exotic costumes and hats. The scene was a riot of colors, noises, and smells.

Meg, walking on shaky legs next to William, knew the crowd could work to their advantage. They could blend among the populace until they found themselves at the Ram's Head. But just as she was about to shake off her fear, the crowd parted and Meg recognized the colors and livery of the Queen's men.

Four of them stood in front of the gate and scanned the approaching crowd. They were obviously looking for someone.

"Do not be afraid," William murmured, sensing her fear. "They're looking for a young woman, not a boy with a dirty face."

That was true, but it was no comfort. As a precaution, William had rubbed soot on her drooping eye and cheek. Meg's stomach churned as one of the guards stared at her. He took in her face, her clothing, her feet, and then turned his head away.

She let out a short breath.

"Stop here," William said.

They were standing in front of a cart piled high with crates of chickens. William tossed a coin to the vendor and grabbed a crate. He handed it to Meg. "Carry this on your shoulder. It will hide your deformity."

She hoisted the unwieldy crate with its two squawking hens and struggled to put it on her shoulder as the hens hopped about and feathers flew. The guard who had stared at her moved closer. When he was within a stride of her, William gave her a clout on her back.

"Look lively, you lazy boy!" he shouted. He spotted the guard and said, "Boys today. Lazy and good for nothing. All they want to do is play."

The guard grunted, but didn't move. *He's not convinced,* Meg thought. He called and motioned to the other guards who sauntered closer, nearly surrounding Meg and William.

Just at that moment a hunchback, seemingly oblivious to the crowd, wheeled his cart over one guard's foot. The guard roared and reached for the hunchback, but the man had stopped and was bending down to examine a rickety wheel. Meg gagged. The cart was loaded with dead dogs and cats and animal parts in varying stages of decay. The smell of putrid flesh and organs was overpowering. William's hand flew to his mouth and he and the guards motioned the carter to move on, but the man appeared to be a deaf mute as well as hunchback.

The guards were shouting at him now, pointing him to move the cart, but he in turn pointed to the cart wheel and shrugged.

The crowds were giving them wide berth as a freshening breeze wafted the smell in all directions. Some stepped hastily away, holding their sleeves to their faces.

Meg, her hand covering her nose, eyed the hunchback closely. There was something about him that was . . . *oh dear Jesus, Mary, Joseph, and all the saints in heaven . . .* it was Walter.

Walter lifted his eyes from the wheel and grinned at her. He stood, stretched as much as his falsely hunched body would allow, and turned his back on the guards who were threatening him with torture.

He straightened the crate of hens on Meg's shoulder and murmured, "I hear a lot of gossip working the streets of London. You and your friends are in grave danger."

The guards moved closer to roust the hunchback and rid the street of his cart.

Walter whispered, "Take care, little sister. I love you. Now stand back."

Meg reached for William, who for once was looking confused.

Just as they took a step backward, Walter grabbed the bottom rail of the cart and jumping to his full height, flipped the cart onto the guards. All four men tumbled to the ground, covered by the blood and bowels of decaying creatures, and pinned by the upside-down cart.

"Get this off of me!" shouted one of the guards, while his compatriots scrambled against the ghastly pile of refuse and the wagon. Two of the men were vomiting while the other two cursed. "I'll kill you, I swear. Come here, let me get my hands on you." He reached for Walter who slipped out of his grasp and ran into the gawking and gagging crowd.

"Run," William hissed. Meg threw the crate of hens to the ground and sprinted through the gate, threading her way through the crowds who fussed at her to watch where she was going.

"I'm behind you," William shouted. "Keep going."

Meg ran, compelling her feet to go forward long after she was exhausted. Finally, a sharp pain in her side forced her to stop. William grabbed her arm, and they ducked into a side alley between a stable and leather shop.

They waited in the alley for a few minutes until Meg could breathe again and then cautiously peeked into the street. As far as they could tell, no one was following them. The street was filled with people who had a purpose and that purpose did not include chasing after an older man and his lazy servant boy.

"I'm not at all sure of what just happened," William said, "but we owe our lives to that hunchback. Or whatever he was."

"He is . . . my brother," she gasped.

William stared at her in disbelief.

Meg wished she could somehow capture his expression forever. She was sure she would never take the wind out of the cocksure William of Oxford again.

She laughed. "It is a long story."

As the bells of London signaled noontime, Meg and William entered the Ram's Head Inn. They spotted Gerard among the others, all of whom were sitting at a table in the corner and looking as serious as a wake. When Gerard caught sight of Meg and William, he jumped up to embrace them.

William hugged his son as if he never wanted to be parted from him again. "If we're to leave England with our heads on our necks, we must go now. Meg and I escaped by the skin of our teeth."

Medicamus stood. "We're ready."

William regarded Medicamus's players. He recognized a few of them from York. "Is everyone here?"

"All who wish to join us," Medicamus answered.

"Then let us go before our luck runs out."

Chapter 23

PROMISE TO RETURN

December 23, 1326

As it happened, Medicamus' friend in Southampton was readying his little ship, *Godisgrace*, to deliver a cargo of wool to Marseille. He planned to return to England with casks of wine and spices. Medicamus persuaded him, with the additional incentive of silver coins, to sail immediately.

Meg stood at the stern of the ship holding onto the railing as the cog slid down the face of another steep swell. The ship's master stood behind her pointing the bow into each breaking wave and fighting the tiller as the cog pitched and rolled. A single square sail billowed to its full capacity, catching every breath of wind and sending them full speed across the English Sea. Spray from the crest of a wave blew against her shoulders like thudding raindrops. Fighting back tears, she watched the coast of England, a misty line on the horizon, gradually recede in the distance as sunset gilded the sails.

Seated on the deck near the mast, William and Medicamus were engaged in deep conversation. Around them Medicamus's companions played cards or lounged in a drunken stupor. As the cog changed course, tacking into the wind, Meg was glad that William had bought powdered ginger root at the apothecary shop in Southampton. The nausea would have been unbearable without it. Her vomiting had ceased for now, but she was not yet prepared to go below decks. If she had to spend the entire journey standing right here on the stern she would do so, for feeling wet and miserable on the open deck was preferable to the stuffy dank air below. The ship's master had promised them easier sailing once they headed south and hugged the coastline of France.

"Feeling better?" Gerard asked.

She nodded.

A roll to the stern caused him to lurch against her and he apologized. She shook her head signaling no harm done, and he stepped behind her, encircling her waist with his arms. The warmth of his body comforted her, the strength of his stance making her feel more secure on the slippery deck.

William had discussed plans for their future after they fled London. When they landed in Marseille and disembarked, they would ride to Montpellier where Gerard would enter the university. Many of the great names in medicine had studied there: Ricardus Anglicus, John of Gaddesden, Bernard de Gordoun, and, of course, William's young friend Guy de Chauliac. Meg and William would travel onto Paris and Bologna where William could renew old friendships.

Meg's heart cleaved in two each time she thought of leaving Gerard, but what could she do? She would never be allowed to stay with him at Montpellier and she couldn't survive on her own. She was dependent on William's care.

One night on their anxious journey to Southampton, Meg had thought to lighten the mood of the evening by teasing

Gerard about his capture of Medicamus. They were seated in front of a fireplace in a dilapidated inn where it appeared the horses in the stable fared better than the people.

"I was impressed with your capture of Medicamus," she said, adopting the tone of mockery that was always present in their conversations. "You were very brave."

"He was threatening the two people I love the most," he said.

She glanced at him, shocked at his honesty and surprised that for once sarcasm was lacking.

He continued, looking squarely at her with no hint of anything other than concern. "When Medicamus told us of Queen Isabella's accusations against you, I thought we had lost you forever."

"We? Would you have been so devastated to see me in the Tower?" she teased.

"Do not even jest about such a thing, Meg. I would have moved heaven and earth to save you."

She was unable to stop the tears that threatened to topple her bluster. Fortunately, William had called Gerard to join him at a game of chess and the conversation ended.

Now, as England's shores vanished altogether, she felt anchorless, as if she were flying like some nameless sea creature through a country where sea and sky merged, where there was no place to fold her wings and land. It was as if her old life had never existed. She had neither the energy nor the inclination to cloak her words in playful wit. She would say what she felt.

"England is gone," she said.

"Yes," Gerard answered. "But we will see it again."

"I am not so sure. Perhaps it is gone forever." She turned slightly so that her words would not be lost to the wind. "I cannot bear the thought of losing you."

He bent low, his face against hers. "Never fear, we will never be parted. And one day we will return. And then you and I—"

William walked up behind them and slapped Gerard on the

shoulder. "Medicamus and I have been discussing our journey. He thinks Meg and I should travel with his group for safety and I am inclined to agree."

"Father, I have my own thoughts about that," Gerard said.

"Is that so?"

"Yes. I have a better proposal."

"Go on."

A wave crashing against the stern castle sent spray in their direction. Gerard wiped sea water from his cheek and continued, "This is perhaps not the best place and time, but let me say this while I have the courage." His solemn face worried Meg. It meant that whatever he planned, William was not going to like it.

"Well, go on then," William said impatiently.

"Father, you know women cannot attend university in England."

"That is correct," William said. "They do not have the proper—"

"Anatomy?" Meg said with a sly smile.

Gerard laughed.

William did not. He continued, "The masters do not think women have the aptitude for such a level of study."

"With respect, Father, there are schools that have a more enlightened view. You have said so yourself."

"So?"

"We are going to Montpellier, are we not?"

"What are you getting at? My cloak is drenched. Make your point."

"Well, why not place Meg in school with me. She has the aptitude, Father. You have seen it yourself. You know she can do the work. And I will look after her. Surely, with your good word, the masters would not turn her away."

"A waste of money and time," William countered. "The university does not accept women. I can teach her all that she needs to know."

"Can you, Father? You certainly know surgery and the care of wounds. You can stitch a man up after battle, but can you really say that you understand why a woman is too modest to discuss her monthly flow? And if she were pregnant you would call in a midwife and be done with it. There is more that can be done and Meg is the person to do it."

William turned to Meg and asked, "And what is your say on this matter?"

Meg looked across the stern to a place on the horizon where hours earlier the shores of her homeland sparkled in the mist. Gerard had surprised her with his understanding and passion. He was right. She had witnessed the need herself, the need for someone with more training than the village wisewoman—*no offense, dearest Alice,* she thought—who could talk to women about women's matters. Painfully clear at the bedside of Elisabeth Despenser who had refused to allow a man at her bedside until it was too late. And Elisabeth, in wont of a woman doctor, died as a result.

She turned to face William, steadying herself by grasping a line that ran from the stern to the top of the sail. She placed her other hand on Gerard's forearm.

"The graveyards of England are full of sisters, daughters, and wives who lie dead because a man must not be in attendance or because women are too modest to tell men the truth," she said. "They may not tell *you,* but they will tell *me.* I wish to be a doctor of phisik and I will do anything to make it so."

✳✳✳

An inky darkness swallowed the last vestige of sea and sky. Meg and Gerard huddled together on deck, sitting inside the forecastle to escape the biting wind and the rolling of the ship. Medicamus and William, having emptied four bottles of wine, were lolling at their feet, oblivious to icy sea spray or stomach-lurching swells, and wallowing instead in gloom and melancholy.

"Ah, Medicamus," William sighed. "Children. What can you do?" He gazed at Meg and Gerard with rheumy eyes.

Medicamus wiped the lips of a wine bottle and took a deep drink. "Never having any children of my own— any that I know of— I cannot answer that question."

"What will I do without them?" William murmured.

William expelled a dramatic sigh and poked Medicamus who was cradling the last wine bottle in his arm. A muffled snore indicated his drinking companion was finished for the night. William lifted the bottle and offered a toast. "To the gods of young love." He downed the last of the wine and curled up on the deck, asleep before the ship reached the bottom of the next swell.

✳✳✳

Meg and Gerard, sitting hunched against the cold, glanced at each other and rolled their eyes. "I believe Father had one bottle too many," Gerard chuckled. "Don't worry about Montpellier. Father won't go back on his word."

"I hope not. But what if he does?"

"We won't think of that. You will be accepted to the Schola Medica. In fact, you'll probably do better than any man in the classroom, including me."

She laughed and huddled closer. "Not likely. But we'll help each other, won't we?" She lifted her face.

"Of course." Gerard smiled and kissed her on the forehead.

Despite the cold wind, Meg felt her face grow hot with embarrassment. She snuggled against Gerard's warm chest and thought of her own father praying with the other lepers at St. Nicholas Hospital, of her sister and Oswald feeding their little ones, of her mother—so frail of spirit, and of Alice banking the fire for the night and rubbing her stiff bones.

She hoped she would see them again one day. But in truth she suspected that many years would pass before her feet touched English soil again.

Now there was only the darkness and depth of an ocean of no horizons lifting her, carrying her from billowing swell to crashing wave. Between the surface on which they skimmed and the solid bottom below them, was an impenetrable mystery. Fathoms of unknown terrain, murky, with phantoms lurking in dark shadows. Given the whims of Fate and a storm, a leak, or a wave of vast proportions, their voyage could end in catastrophe. The ship was, after all, no more than a cork bobbing on a vast sea.

She pulled her cloak tighter. Gerard was snoring. William and Medicamus were asleep as well, along with Medicamus's players. What a strange group of people she had ended up with. So different from St. Michael's Mead.

She was starting anew in a foreign land. She was frightened. She was hopeful. Perhaps now she could fulfill the destiny Alice had predicted.

One day she would return to England. Like some great bird that spanned sea and sky, she would spread her wings and float down, down past this impenetrable sea until she finally landed on firm ground again. On that day, she would fold her wings and cease to fly. She would find her feet and stride across the land of her birth.

I will return, she vowed. *And when I do, no one will ever cause me to leave my homeland again.*

Chapter 24

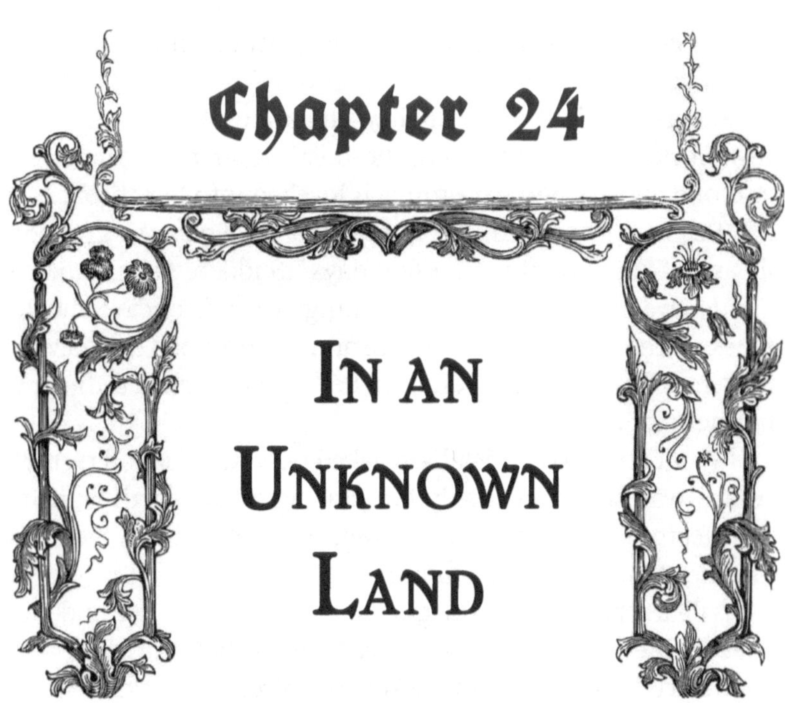

In an Unknown Land

Marseilles, February 1327

Meg's legs wobbled as she stepped onto dry land after five weeks aboard the *Godisgrace*. Their voyage from England had been smooth until an intolerable winter storm forced them below decks for three days. When the storm ended, Meg vowed never to leave the upper deck and enter the rolling, dark, stifling hell below. Aloft or below, it made no difference. She was miserable. Just when she could not endure a single day more at sea, the cog passed through the Strait of Gibraltar into the calmer Inland Sea and a few days later sailed through a dawn mist to the busy docks of Marseilles.

Despite the early hour, dozens of foreign merchant ships, tied bow to stern at the wharf, were offloading bales of furs, leather, and from the *Godisgrace*, English wool. Sailors and traders, shouting in strange languages, jostled for room on the quayside.

She had to fight to steady herself as she, William, and Gerard worked their way along the busy waterfront. She felt a bout of dizziness and her stomach lurched into her throat.

"Sea legs, it's called," William chuckled when she grabbed his arm. "You'll be fine in a few days." Suddenly she remembered her disfigurement, the drooping eye and concave cheekbones on the right side of her face and she dropped her gaze to her feet. She pulled her veil over her face and tucked the end into her tunic.

"What about you?" William asked Gerard. "Legs all right?" Gerard was standing steady but staring at the earth as if he could command it to stop moving. He grabbed his stomach and shoved a fist into his mouth.

William handed him a ginger confit to suck on and the three of them threaded their way through bales of cloth and wool, barrels of wine, and baskets of spices that tickled Meg's nose. Robertus Medicamus, the hawker of goods they had met in York and who had saved their lives in London, stepped in front of them and blocked their path. As usual, the little creature Pettipaw perched on his shoulder.

During the voyage, Robertus decided he and his troupe of players would stay in cheap lodgings near the waterfront while they replenished their elixirs and made new costumes. Afterward, they would travel to Paris. Meg sighed. It would be a sad leave-taking as Robertus could always be counted on for merriment.

"Good morning, Robertus," William said. "We cannot thank you enough for your help in London. Were it not for you, we would be sitting in the Tower now or worse—our heads would be rotting on London Bridge. Alas, we'll say goodbye as we leave today for Montpellier."

"I thank you, William," Robertus said, "but there's no need to say farewell. I have decided to guide you to your destination."

William's smile disappeared. "No need to put yourself out, Medicamus. I will hire a local guide."

"You forget that I've traveled to these parts many times. I know the roads. I know the rivers where we can safely cross. And most importantly, I know the inns where you can sleep without getting your throats cut."

"And why would you go out of your way when you could be fleecing the gullible in Paris?"

Robertus pressed a hand to his parti-colored surcoat. "I am hurt by the insult, sir. Even after saving your pompous skin in London, you still doubt me."

"I don't doubt you, I *know* you," William was saying to Robertus. "There's a difference."

"All right, then. You force me to admit to an ulterior motive."

"I'm shocked."

Robertus ignored the jibe. "The truth is Montpellier is a lucrative city for my profession. People travel there because the weather is warm and pleasant. It is also a stopping point for pilgrims who walk the Way of St. James to the shrine at Santiago de Compostela. Those who seek the grace of St. James are often infirmed and looking for a cure. They are more than willing to part with their money."

"Aha!" William snorted. "At last, the motive. Why not help them? Why cheat them when they are desperate?"

"Listen, my old friend, there is one immutable fact in this world. No matter how much we argue, we will never agree. I say we call a truce. You practice your brand of phisik and I will practice mine."

William's back stiffened as Medicamus gave him a hearty slap on the shoulder. Gerard leaned over to Meg and whispered, "Perhaps the journey to Montpellier will be interesting after all."

She grinned at the thought of the two men jousting with words from sunup to sundown.

Yes, Robertus was a mountebank as William insisted, but he was also a jester, troubadour, a teller of romantic tales, and a voyager to every country in the known world. He had hawked his wares from Cordova to Cathay, from the land of the Vikings to the dark tribes of the Sudan. One night on the *Godisgrace*, he told of his narrow escape from the magnificent harem of the Sultan of Istanbul. "I was hiding in the harem, for what crime I dare not say, when a beautiful slave girl with white skin and golden hair and a pair of luscious apples ripe for the plucking approached me."

At this point William cut him off, suggesting the tale was not appropriate for the ears of a virtuous young woman. A disappointed Meg decided virtue sometimes had its disadvantages.

Because of William's heavy strongbox and Robertus's supplies, they bought a horse and wagon for the four-day journey. The players would walk behind— the better to get to know the pilgrims, Robertus said.

"Humph, the better to fleece them," William responded.

"We will travel west from Marseilles," Robertus announced, "to Arles to Nimes to Montpellier, and if fortune smiles upon us, we will gather the sick and infirmed along the way like little chicks needing care and tending,"

Once they got underway, they fell into the routine of taking to the road just after sunup, then stopping three to four times a day to water the horse and exercise their legs.

From her vantage point on the back of the wagon, Meg was able to spy on the players in Robertus's troupe. There was a dwarf named Halybutte and two jongleurs who juggled anything they could find along the path—including Halybutte. Then there was Serafina, a young woman not much older than Meg with red hair and a slender body, and an older man and wife who lagged behind. Meg recognized the older man as the "customer" in York who needed help servicing his wife. She blushed, remembering how she had been taken in by the man's performance, and had asked Master William about it later. It was embarrassing, too, when Gerard ridiculed her in front of William and Alice for thinking Pettipaw was a hairy baby instead of a monkey. The worst memory of that trip, however, was leaving her father in the leper hospital. She prayed a quick *Pater Noster* for her father and then added two more for her mother and Alice.

At night Robertus shepherded everyone into an inn.

"Sir," Meg said shyly to Robertus as they brushed away the dust from the road and prepared to eat on the first day, "what became of your horse Saracen?"

"Ah, poor Saracen. She fell to her knees, unable to stand. Shortly after we parted in York. It broke my heart, for she was a good companion. I sat with her while she died."

William snorted. "A horse is a means to get from here to there," he said. "They are neither human nor companion."

"No, Master William," Meg said. "With all respect, sir, I disagree. As you well know, I had a pig once who was as human as you are." She fingered the bracelet around her wrist, its tightly woven pig's hair and leather bound in the silver coil. The bracelet contained the last vestige of Robin her beloved pig and friend of her youth. "He was my dearest—–and for many years my only—companion."

"Well then you understand my heart, dear Meg," Robertus replied as he kissed Pettipaw on the lips.

As Robertus had predicted, men and women on their way to Santiago de Compostela joined them in Arles. Many of the pilgrims, young and old, used a walking staff for support. Some wore a scallop shell on their cloaks while others carried a shell in their hands or hung it from the crooks of their staffs. At night, the pilgrims took refuge in nearby churches or monasteries where they were given donations of water and food.

As the caravan passed through Nimes and drew closer to Montpellier, Meg noticed scallop shells painted on the trunks of trees or on signposts.

"What do the shells mean?" she asked William.

"What shells?"

"The scallop shells." She pointed to a signpost. "Why are they painted everywhere? And why do some of the pilgrims wear them?"

"It is a symbol of St. James."

"But what does it mean?"

Robertus turned in his seat, still holding the reins. "It harkens back to the time of James the Apostle," he said. "He preached the gospel in Galicia. Then he was beheaded in Jerusalem. His body was sent back to Galicia—"

"Where is that?" Meg asked.

"Far to the west at—"

William interrupted. "Where James's body was sent but then his body was lost at sea. When it washed up on shore, it was intact—or so it was said. Miraculously scallop shells had covered it and protected it."

"So James was buried in Santiago de Compostela, in Galicia along with the scallops, and soon his grave became a shrine," Robertus said.

William added, "The scallop became his symbol." He paused, then grabbed the side of the wagon as it lurched forward. "The pilgrims who wear the scallop do so as a badge of completion. They've been before and now they're returning."

Meg regarded the dozens of pilgrims who formed a ragged line, voyagers suffering afflictions of the body, cripples, those who were sick at heart, diseased, and despondent, all walking beside the happy sinners who chattered like magpies. Some of the pilgrims wore one or more scallop shell badges.

"They must have great faith to make such long journeys," she said.

"Either that or they believe anything they are told." Gerard rolled his eyes in the direction of the travelers.

William laughed. "Well said, young man. You sound more and more like your blasphemous father every day."

The dwarf Halybutte, who had been riding in the wagon since the second day and who had listened to the endless theological and philosophical discussions bouncing like juggler's balls between William, Gerard, and Meg—and occasionally Robertus—sat up and pointed his finger at William. "You are a learned man, but your mockery is not wanted here."

"What? Am I not able to speak my mind? Or is that forbidden on this journey?"

"You mock the beliefs of these people and you belittle the miracles of Our Savior. God's judgment will be on your head."

"So," William barked, "I receive theology lessons from a scheming dwarf who tricks people out of their money and sells them false cures? You dare to lecture me about God's judgment?"

"I have already received God's judgment, have I not?" Halybutte punched his crooked legs and winced at the pain. "I have lived with my affliction, faced the mockery of many, yet I dance on the stage so that others might laugh. This is the body God gave me, just as that is the face God gave *her*." He swung to Meg and pointed at her hollow cheek, at the place where bones had refused to grow, despite Alice's best ministrations.

Meg's face grew hot, and she sucked in her lower lip to keep the tears at bay.

"Leave Meg out of this," Gerard shouted.

Halybutte sat in silence and then sighed. "Pardon, mistress, I did not mean to pain you. I suspect you have received many hurts in your life, but with a face such as yours you have a lifetime of hurts before you." He turned to look at the pilgrims. "Master William, I simply meant to say that those people, even the ones who make the journey in gaiety and frivolity, do not deserve your scorn. They have faith. Something which is obviously foreign to you."

"Oh, I have faith," William said. "I have faith that the sun will come up in the morning and go down in the evening."

"I can only hope that God sees fit to lift your black humor

before your death. Perhaps then you will enjoy life among the living."

"And I hope, little man, that you will keep your sermons to yourself for the remainder of the journey."

"Gentlemen, gentlemen," Robertus interrupted, "let us not quarrel among ourselves. We are all tired and anxious for this journey to end. We want to sleep in a comfortable bed, have a warm bath, and be rid of our fleas and lice." He clicked to the horse to pick up her trot. "But look here, see the road ahead of us?" He pointed toward a section of cobbles, which rose out of the dirt path. "That is the old Roman road. The Romans who built it have been moldering for hundreds of years, their disagreements long since forgotten. A lesson for us all."

"Robertus, you should have been a philosopher," William said. "Or a bard. You have a silver tongue in your mouth."

"Ha!" Robertus laughed. "Why do you think Fortune smiles upon me?"

Chapter 25

SISTER EUPHEMIA

February 1327

On the fourth day of their journey, Meg scrambled into the wagon and, shivering in the dawn air, took her usual seat between William and Gerard where she could be protected from wind and cold.

"You shiver now," Robertus said as he straightened the reins on the horse, "but were it August you would be parched from the heat. It's oppressive some days in summer—far different from what you are used to."

Oppressive heat. What kind of a strange place were they coming to? So far, in comparison to her beloved England, she was not impressed. A part of her had begun to regret all those childhood wishes to see the greater world.

Robertus climbed into the wagon and lifted the reins.

Just as the wagon lurched forward, a voice called out, "Kind sirs, stop!" A pilgrim ran to them waving his staff to get their attention. "I, uh, I am told that you are doctors of phisik on your way to Montpellier. I implore you, please, help me. Some of my pilgrims . . ." The man bent over, trying to catch his breath. He was more bones than flesh, so thin he resembled a living cadaver. On his chest, he wore six pilgrim badges from Compostela.

"What is the problem?" William asked.

"An internal flux. Fever, cramps. Some can no longer sit up. We are staying at the L'Abbaye St. Just, only a short distance from here."

"Doesn't the abbey have an infirmarer?" William asked.

"Yes, but this is beyond his skill. Please, sir."

William looked to Robertus who, much to Meg's surprise, agreed to make a detour to the abbey even though it meant arriving in Montpellier later and thus delaying his profits. Robertus handed food and water to his players who had gathered around the wagon and were listening intently to the pilgrim. He told them to stay where they were, there was no need to tire themselves walking to the monastery.

"Entertain anyone who comes this way," he ordered, "and be sure to give me *all* the money you collect."

"Come along then," Robertus said, motioning the pilgrim to sit next to him.

"Bless you, sirs," the pilgrim said. "I am Godwin of St. Albans, now living in Marseilles. I lead pilgrims to Compostela." He took a seat next to Robertus. "It will be bad for my business if all my travelers die."

William nodded to the pilgrim. "I am William of Oxford a doctor of phisik and surgeon, and this is Gerard and Meg, my students."

Godwin gave Robertus directions to the abbey, indicating where they should turn at a wooden post carved in the shape of a crucifix. "Stay on the dirt track until you cross a small stream. You'll see the abbey gates from there." Robertus flicked the horse's rump lightly, and the wagon rolled forward. As soon as they were underway, Godwin the Pilgrim fell asleep, snoring lightly, his head lolling on his chest.

A short ride later they came to a fast-flowing stream shallow enough to allow a safe crossing. The Abbey of St. Just, surrounded by a stone wall, sat on a small rise above the stream, Adjacent to the abbey's protective wall was a vineyard and beyond that, fields lying fallow for the winter. Surrounding the fields were trees whose limbs were twisted into grotesque shapes—the result, William told Meg, of storms blowing in from the sea.

After they announced themselves to the porter at the gatehouse, they made their way into the abbey grounds where the church, cloisters, and outbuildings, built of gray stone blocks, provided a sober anchor of prayer against the wind. A bell tower pierced the blue sky, softened by woolly clouds sailing in from the north. Doves flew to the tower, carefully walking the ledges and bowing their heads to their neighbors before diving into the small dome-roofed dovecotes nestled against the church. In the outer precinct between the gatehouse and the abbey, wood turners, potters, and other lay craftsmen worked at their trades, looking up in curiosity as the wagonload of visitors passed by.

As they approached the second enclosure, the monastery bells rang, their pealing notes calling monks to prayer. One by one the brothers who had been pruning trees, or tending to the rows of lavender plants in the herbal garden, or replacing tile on the roof, brushed off their hands and filed into the church. Clad in the black surplice and cowl of Benedictines, the monks looked like crows reluctantly leaving breadcrumbs behind.

Godwin jumped from the wagon and pointed to a low building beyond the open cloister. "Brother Peter will be so pleased that you have come. He is quite young, trying to do his best." He was walking backwards as he spoke, waving them on with cadaverous fingers towards the infirmary and the sick pilgrims. "I must join the brothers at service. May the Lord bless you." He turned and disappeared into the church as the last bell rang.

The infirmary sat at the end of the cloistered walkway but was separated from the main buildings by a walkway of its own, and enclosed by a low wall surrounding a well-kept herb garden. The door to the infirmary was closed and the windows shuttered, as if the young infirmarer was trying to keep the sickness away from his brothers.

William knocked once at the door and they entered, but not before the smell of human waste overwhelmed them. Meg gagged and forcibly swallowed the bile that rose from her gullet. Although Godwin the Pilgrim had not exaggerated the extent of the flux or its serious effect, he had not warned them of what they might find inside the infirmary. The men and women lying on the straw mattresses were near death, looking more like pale rotting corpses than the excited travelers they must have been only a week ago.

Meg glanced at Gerard who was barely containing his revulsion. His jawline was set and his lips were thin, but his face had a decidedly green tinge to it. Meg suspected his expression mirrored her own.

A slender monk broke away from tending a patient and rushed to them, his hands outstretched. "You must be the traveling doctors of phisik," he said, looking them over with an obvious hope that his days and nights of struggling with the bloody flux were over. "I am Brother Peter." He rubbed his hands over his eyes and chin and explained that the old and experienced infirmarer had died recently. "I was his assistant, but his sudden death has left me here alone."

He was young indeed, thought Meg, as she watched the infirmarer look away, but not before tears filled his eyes. The stubble of his whiskers was so sparse the cat's tongue could have shaved his chin. His blonde hair, baby-fine, curled in wisps around his tonsure.

"Our tasks are usually light," Peter continued. "Small cuts or bruises or a runny nose. But mostly I take care of the older brothers, rheumy and phlegmy, who need rest and a warm fire—in fact, the old brothers usually stay here in this room, but the sick have taken their beds, so I have moved them to the warming room behind the refectory." He looked to William as if needing approval for his decisions. Peter gazed at the room, as if incredulous that such a catastrophe had landed at his front door. "I have never encountered the likes of this."

While they walked among the pilgrims, trying not to breathe through their noses lest they be overcome by the smell, Brother Peter described his troubles. "I barely get one clean, then someone else is struck with a flux of the bowels. I tried to feed them, but most are too weak to swallow. There were seventeen at first. Two are already dead." Panic rose in his voice.

"What are their symptoms?" Robertus asked.

"Watery bloody stools and terrible cramps. Some have fever. All are weak. They strain mightily with a need to pass a stool, and yet all that comes out is slime and blood."

William put a hand on Brother Peter's shoulder. "You have done the best you could under the circumstances. We're here to help you now, but we will need some things which you can fetch for us."

William, Meg noticed, was speaking to the monk in a low calm voice, uttering each word carefully as if Peter were about four years old. "First, open the shutters and doors. We will need clean rags, as many as you can spare. And buckets of water. Are there other brothers who could help us?"

"I believe so," Peter said. "The novices might help if the abbot agrees." He was opening all the shutters and Meg gulped in the sharp cold air. "After the service, I will ask him."

"Tell him we need as many hands as possible," Robertus added.

"Yes, sir. And I will ask the rest of the brothers to pray."

"Good. In the meantime, let us assess each patient." William clasped Peter's shoulder. "I have always found that hard work keeps fear at bay." He motioned to Gerard and Meg who were hanging back. "This will be an excellent opportunity for our young would-be university students here. Gerard, Meg, come closer and tell me what you see."

They walked among the pilgrims, checking heartbeats, observing breathing and pallor, and surveying the general hardiness of spirit. The ten men and seven women were unable to stop vomiting and suffered agonizing stomach cramps. Most were barely conscious, although a few were able to grunt answers to questions. The pain had started several days before with vomiting coming on later.

After their assessments, Meg and Gerard pronounced five near death. William and Robertus agreed and William suggested they be given last rites.

"Yes, we did that yesterday," said Peter. "We feared all would die."

"Where are the dead buried?" asked William.

"In consecrated ground east of the nave."

"Tell the abbot you will need five more graves. Perhaps more."

"Yes, sir."

As the ringing of bells signaled the end of the service and the monks returned to work, Brother Peter raced to find the abbot to beg for more help. William returned to the last patient they had examined, an elderly woman dressed in a nun's habit who was deathly pale. He lifted her upper lip to observe the color of her gums—pale as well. Her eyes were sunken and her breathing labored. She was holding on to life by the faintest of strings.

William leaned into her. "What is your name?"

"Sister Euphemia," she whispered. Her eyelids fluttered but remained shut.

"Sister Euphemia, my assistant Meg will help you. We must wash you. We are washing everyone."

"No," she said weakly, though her eyes stayed closed against the daylight.

"Should you wish, we will move you to a separate room for privacy."

"Yes."

William spied an antechamber, which he explored. "This will be suitable for her," he called to Meg and the others. "We'll move her here."

The four of them gripped a corner of the woman's pallet and brought her—with ease, for she weighed next to nothing—into the small room which held Brother Peter's supply of herbs and flowers.

"The pleasant smell alone will make her feel better," William said.

Brother Peter soon returned with a basket of clean and folded rags, as well as old woolen garments. Following like ducklings behind him were four young novices carrying buckets of water from the well. The novices caught sight of Meg and each blushed and looked away, as if having a female to gaze upon was too much excitement. Godwin, leader of the pilgrims, brought up the rear.

William clasped his hands in a way that brought everyone to attention. "Here is what we must do. First, you must follow my instructions carefully. You must stop feeding them solid food. For the next three days, we will alternate astringent herbs with mucilaginous herbs. We will start with witch hazel. After an hour they will drink barley water followed by marsh mallow tea."

"Sir, we have no marsh mallow roots," Peter said, "but there is a patch of mallow near the stream. These young men will dig it for you."

"Do you have vervain or rose hips?"

"Yes, sir, I have both as well as witch hazel."

"Good. Until you can steep the mallow roots, we'll treat them with vervain and rose hips, followed by witch hazel and then the mallow. We will follow that routine until their bowels are better. Afterwards, you may give them mutton broth."

"You are not planning to leave us, are you?" Brother Peter asked, his brow furrowed at the prospect of losing his help.

"We can stay for a few days but must then be on our way. Never fear, we will not leave if your patients are worse." He looked to Robertus for agreement and Robertus nodded.

"We mustn't stay here forever, Father, if Meg and I are to enroll," Gerard said.

William scowled.

Gerard added, "The university—"

"Can wait," William said sharply.

Gerard hung his head and murmured, "Yes, sir." He rolled his eyes, but Meg knew the gesture was a defiant shield against humiliation.

"As I was saying," William continued, "after a few days of mutton broth, you may introduce solid food but slowly and carefully. This can be followed by small portions of meat. Avoid chills. Dress them in woolen clothing. Above all, they need to be kept clean lest sores fester from the expulsion of waste."

Meg looked at the ghastly pale men and woman, most of whom had curled into a fetal position, and wondered how many of them would live to taste mutton broth, let alone mutton. And even if they survived, would they be well enough to journey on to Compostela? Or were their hopes of obtaining the scallop shell of St. James doomed by this dreadful wasting sickness?

"Meg, your duty is to Sister Euphemia," William said, interrupting her thoughts,

"But, sir, I can help with the others as well," she said, wanting him to know she could handle many patients at once, not just an elderly nun who was sure to die during the night.

"No. I want you to concentrate on Euphemia. She is a member of the Order of St. Clare. The world needs her and more of her like."

Examining the nun's habit, Meg thought no one could accuse the woman of being haughty given the state of her clothing. Euphemia was dressed in a ragged habit of unbleached wool and a veil of black wool lined with linen that had once been white but was now yellow with age. Encircling her waist was a cord tied in four knots. Around her shoulders, she wore a cloak of coarse wool russet. The habit, veil, and cloak were faded and patched. And she was barefoot. The soles of her feet were calloused from the journey. Dried blood stained her heels and toes where blisters had broken open.

Meg removed the woman's veil, baring a head of short gray hair, uneven and ragged with bald patches exposing a white scalp. She lifted Euphemia's cloak away from her shoulders and deposited it in a pile to be washed. Then she eased the skirts of her habit over the woman's abdomen. As she tugged at the fabric, bunching it around Euphemia's neck and holding the woman's shoulders in an effort to raise her, something caught her eye—something wrapped around the woman's chest. Something alive and moving.

With a start and a shriek of surprise, Meg pushed herself away from the sickbed.

"Master William!" Meg shouted. She struggled backwards, catching her heel on her tunic and falling against a basket of dried lavender. Whatever covered Sister Euphemia's chest was hairy like a wolf's hide and had a mind of its own, almost as if it sheltered against the woman's pale wrinkled skin.

William poked his head in the room, his eyebrows raised in surprise.

"Look," she said and pointed to the thing that covered the upper half of the nun's body.

Meg backed up as far as the baskets would permit. "What, what is it?"

"A cilice—a hairshirt—filthy with fleas and vermin by the look of it and studded with twigs and wire to prick the skin beneath."

"But why?"

"To mortify the flesh. Remind her of her sins."

Meg couldn't believe that this shriveled nun would have

that many sins to repent. "What should I do?"

"Take if off and we'll ask the monks to wash it with the other clothing."

Meg grimaced, her sour expression a mirror of her thoughts. She made no move to help the nun.

"You are not the only person working at an unpleasant task. We *all* have our duties," William scolded.

Stinging from his rebuke, Meg attempted to untie the filthy vest. Bony fingers gripped Meg's hand and Sister Euphemia whispered fiercely, "No!" Though her eyes were still closed, her lips were pursed and her jaw set.

"But Sister this must be washed."

Euphemia rolled her head from side to side and pulled at Meg's fingers, fumbling with the ribbons of the cilice, although she was too weak to undo them. "No, no," she hissed.

To calm her, Meg patted the back of her hand and smoothed the woman's hair, which though ragged was as silky as a newborn's. "Never mind then," Meg said. "We'll leave it on for now."

Turning away, Meg examined Euphemia's lower body which was covered in blood and feces. As Meg washed away the waste, the old woman's skin shone translucent, her veins rolling worm-like beneath the surface. Her bones felt as fragile as a baby bird's. Carefully, Meg rubbed balm of Gilead over Euphemia's red and raw bottom and did the same for the nun's bleeding feet. Then she dressed the woman in an old Benedictine habit, pulling it over Euphemia's head and tugging it to her ankles, praying as she did so that the creatures living inside the cilice would stay there and not jump off.

When the nun was clean and dressed, Meg slipped a hand under the woolen tunic and, lifting the old woman's bony hips, placed a clean rag under her bottom. She pulled a coverlet up to Euphemia's chin. Although the nun had kept her eyes shut during Meg's ministrations, the fierce expression of her set jaw and clamped lips had been replaced by a look of relaxed calm, as if her mind was finally at ease.

As Euphemia slept, Meg consulted William about the hair-shirt. "It is alive with all manner of creatures. We must take it and wash it, but she won't allow it."

"Then leave it on her," he said, adding as he saw Meg's horrified face, "It must be important for her to protest so vigorously."

"But—"

"Indeed," said Godwin, who had come up behind them. "Of all the pilgrims walking the Way, she is the most devout. And the most important—not that they aren't all important in the eyes of God—but she comes from a noble family, though she has asked me not to speak of it lest others think she is haughty."

"The Poor Clares take their vows seriously. See there on her girdle"—William pointed to the cord with its four knots lying on a pile of filthy clothes—"the knots remind them of their vows of poverty, silence, obedience, and enclosure. And unlike some nuns, they keep those vows. Unfortunately, their vows also call for abstinence from meat," William added. "And many days they abstain from food altogether. That is why Sister Euphemia has no reserves left."

As concern settled in the wrinkles on his forehead, his glance at Meg carried a warning. "You must be vigilant tonight. She is on the knife edge."

William's caution only increased Meg's worry. They had been invited to join the abbot for supper in his lodgings. To decline the invitation would be an insult, William said. As a precaution, William ordered a novice to stand watch and fetch them if Euphemia or another patient took a turn for the worse.

As they walked from the infirmary through the graceful arches of the cloister and into the abbot's private lodgings, Meg hoped Sister Euphemia, indeed all the pilgrims, would continue to sleep and would wake in the morning.

❋❋❋

185

Bernard de Marcy, Abbot of St. Just, greeted them warmly as they entered his living quarters, rooms that were white-washed and clean but sparsely furnished. A makeshift altar and kneeling stool, a crucifix, and beeswax candles were the only items in the front room. Beyond, in the dining room there was a long table covered with a white tablecloth and flanked by benches. An open shelf at the end of the room held simple pottery dishes washed with a green and brown glaze.

Bernard was a thin man, stooped, but spry as he moved among them, apologizing for delaying their journey to Mont-pellier. Curiously, for a man of Christ, especially one of his standing, a long scar traveled the length of his face, from a point at the top of his tonsure across his cheek to the intersec-tion of his lips.

"I cannot tell you how glad I am to see you," Bernard was saying. "Poor Godwin was desperate for his pilgrims. He al-ways stops here on his way to Compostela." He took his place at the head of the table and motioned for everyone else to sit. "Well, let me just say you were an answer to his prayer."

"We are glad to be of help," William said.

"Your lodgings by the way are just above me on the second floor. I'll have my servant show you where to go after supper." He held his hand up as William argued that they would stay in the infirmary instead. "Surely not all of you are needed in the infirmary at once. Some will need to rest. As to eating, I've instructed my cook and servant to provide for you. Whatever you want."

"You are very kind," William murmured.

Bernard laughed, but it was the short bark of a feisty ter-rier. "I must confess it is a pleasure to converse with you. My usual supper consists of eating in the refectory in silence with my brothers while someone reads a lesson. Meals are frugal and we are forbidden the meat of four-legged animals. While I believe wholeheartedly in the teachings of our beloved Ben-edict, it is good to have a change. So tell me, what news of the world outside?"

For the rest of supper—a large roast surrounded by carrots and turnips, accompanied by dried apricots, and bread pudding— Robertus and William described the latest events in England and France, the news only secondhand and at least a month late but of interest nonetheless to Abbot Bernard who by his own admission lived in an island of silence punctuated by prayer and work. "Our founder was fond of saying, *'Orare est laborare, laborare est orare'* and that is what we attempt to do," Bernard said.

William looked at Gerard. "Which is to say?"

"To pray is to work and to work is to pray," translated Gerard. William beamed.

"Oh, forgive me," Bernard interrupted. "I, ah, I should have mentioned before . . . I must ask that Mistress Meg stay in the infirmary from now on. Our abbey is for men only. Women are not allowed in cloisters or in the church." Meg and William stared at each other. Something in William's look told her to comply. They were, after all, many miles from the nearest tavern or inn and dependent on the hospitality of the abbey.

"No insult taken, sir," Meg said. "I had already determined to stay in the infirmary. I would be too anxious if I slept away from my patient."

"One of us will be in later," William said. "We'll take turns tonight so that you may rest."

"I do not mind helping," Gerard said. "Perhaps I might go first?"

William nodded in agreement.

"At the next bells, I'll join you," Gerard said to Meg, who smiled in return.

"Very well," said the abbot and rose to his feet

Meg noticed that he stumbled and leaned against the table for support. Bernard took Meg's arm and guided her to the door. "I'll lead you to the infirmary gate."

Cresset lanterns hanging between stone colonnades lit their way as they walked the cloister alley. A light evening breeze carrying a chill danced through the colonnades and caused Meg to shiver. The abbot patted her hand.

"Before I was a monk, I was a soldier and a man of the world," Bernard mused, "eager to follow any baron or king into battle and bed down with any bit of skirt who would have me. But I put that life behind me many years ago." He grimaced and held on to a stone column. He squeezed his right thigh. "Let me stop. I have a bad leg. The pain reminds me of how I once fought for God with a sword."

"Would you indulge my curiosity, sir?"

"You want to know how I got this scar." He pointed to the line that ran down his face.

Meg dropped her head and grinned. "Yes, sir."

"I was at Acre during the last Crusade. What was it? Thirty-five, thirty-six years ago. Hard to believe. Suffice it to say I was there during the siege and when Acre fell, when the Saracens overran us. They were crazed, beheading the Christian fighters, calling us infidels, shouting God is great in their tongue. I fought my way out and got this—he pointed to the scar—from a scimitar. I was one of the lucky ones. Many more were massacred." He stopped and once again squeezed his thigh. "There are other scars. On my body. On my soul. I vowed from that day forth that I would never pick up another weapon, that in gratitude to God I would serve him with my hands, with my prayers, my celibacy, my silence, and my loyalty to the Benedictine cause. And I have done that." He gazed at the stars shining through the vestiges of sunset. "But some days my old wound aches and the scar itches. I consider it God's message to me—a reminder if you will—to stay on the path."

They were at the door to the infirmary. "Good night, my dear," the abbot said. "The sick are fortunate indeed to have you come to their aid."

"Thank you, sir."

She watched him leave and turned her thoughts to Sister Euphemia. Perhaps the old nun needed the horrific cilice as a reminder to stay on her path, but to overcome what yearning, what earthly desire, Meg couldn't say. The burdens of temptation are so great, she thought. Her own burdens were freely accepted, and her duties freely administered. But sometimes—Gerard's face swam in her mind's eye—she wished for all the money, all the beauty, and all the freedom in the world.

She shook her head so savagely it threatened to tumble off her shoulders. Foolish thinking. Stay on the path! She wanted the license to practice as a doctor of phisik. A Medica of the Long Robe. That was her Temple of Jerusalem. That was her fight against the barbarians. That was the war in which she must suffer wounds and survive.

***

During the night, despite the ministrations of William, Gerard, and Robertus, who took turns in the infirmary, two more pilgrims died and joined their fellow travelers in the graveyard of St. Just.

Sister Euphemia was not among them.

As the bells tolled throughout the long darkness, Meg roused the old nun and forced her to drink witch hazel or marsh mallow tea. Each time the woman purged her body of the poisons gripping her, but as the night wore on, there was less blood and slime and finally near dawn, though her abdomen cramped, nothing was expelled.

Gerard joined her on the floor beside Euphemia's bed. "Do you remember many years ago when we hid together in the barn at Caldecote Hall? When I was a weeping fool?"

"You had reason to weep. The birth was horrible."

"I treated you badly. I'm sorry."

"Gerard, you have never treated me badly." *Except as a foolish love-stung boy besotted by a wanton dancer with flowing red hair and wearing little tinkling bells that advertise her wares,* she thought.

They took turns sleeping while the other remained awake and watchful. Sometime in the early morning, Gerard left to return to his chamber.

When Sister Euphemia awoke, she greeted the daylight with a wan smile. "I am alive," she said with amazement.

"Yes," Meg answered.

Euphemia pulled at the borrowed Benedictine habit. "This is not . . ." She patted her chest. "You didn't . . .?"

"Do not worry," Meg said. "I left the cilice on you. Against my better wishes."

"Thank you." Euphemia dropped her head against the bolster and sighed.

She slept again, awakening only for a cup of tea and, later in the afternoon, mutton broth for the first time, which she managed to keep within her bowels, a sign that she was on the mend.

That evening, after another cup of mutton broth, Sister Euphemia asked to sit up. Meg reached behind her, lifting her at the armpits, and slid her to an upright position. The woman's color was much better, even a bit of pink in her cheeks.

"I am grateful that you respected my wishes," Euphemia said between sips of broth.

Meg, not knowing what to say settled for a polite, "Thank you."

"What I am trying to explain is that I wear it for a reason," Euphemia continued. "Rough wool is supposed to remind us of our vows, but when it does not, when I yearn too much for silk and velvet, I wear the cilice."

"Like the abbot's wound," Meg murmured.

"Pardon?"

"Oh, nothing. I think I understand, Sister Euphemia. But won't you at least let me wash it?"

Sister Euphemia seemed transfixed by a nubby spot of wool on the black tunic. She twisted it beneath her fingertips. "Because I am a lay sister, I am allowed to come and go more than the others. My sisters depend upon me to go out in the world and obtain special items for the convent, but in doing so I am tempted by those things which I gave up. This time even the hairshirt was not enough to break my yearning. I vowed to walk barefoot by myself to Compostela to remind me of why I joined the Poor Clares."

"And then you became ill."

"Yes."

"Perhaps you could try again next year."

"Perhaps." She closed her eyes and then opened them. "Promise me that you will not remove the cilice. Not even to wash it. And do not put salve on my sores. If they fester and cause me to die, it is the Lord's will."

Meg opened her mouth to say that she had *already* put salve on Euphemia, but thought better of it. "Consider this, Sister Euphemia, perhaps the Lord has sent the bloody flux to test you. He has not found you lacking in faith. You are alive and well. I believe He wants you to use the salve to show you trust his judgment. To save yourself for his further will."

Euphemia looked at Meg sharply, the fog of her illness momentarily driven away by Meg's reasoning.

"Perhaps you are right," she said. "But I am too tired to think on it now. Give me your promise."

"I promise."

Euphemia rested her head on the bolster and pulled the covers to her neck. She closed her eyes and slept.

That night three more pilgrims died, making the gruesome prediction of their first day at St. Just come true. Five bodies were to fill the newly dug graves east of the church.

✳✳✳

In the morning, after a quick breakfast and a walk in the phisik garden, Meg returned to the infirmary to find laughter coming from Euphemia's room. She peeked inside and found Robertus entertaining the old nun.

"Oh my," Euphemia tittered and covered her mouth, "you have had your share of adventures, Robertus."

"That I have. And more to come, I am sure."

"Robertus, are you bothering my patient?" Meg interrupted.

"On the contrary," Euphemia said, "his lively stories have made me feel much better. Not that I believe a word, mind you."

Meg was struck by how different Sister Euphemia appeared now that she was no longer in the throes of the flux. Her face, once stern with sickness, was soft and gentle. Her voice was no longer shaky but calm.

"Remember your promise," Robertus said and left to tend to his own patients.

Meg raised her eyebrows and Euphemia smiled. "I promised him I would tell the abbess about his cure for women's ailments which come each month. The cramping, the crying, the ill nature. With twenty-three women in the abbey, you can imagine how they mope about. I did not have the heart to tell him that the abbess believes the best cure is more prayer."

Meg, who swore by Mother Alice's remedy of comfrey, nettle, and blackberry tea for her own painful flow, was not so sure prayer was the answer.

"He's certainly a charmer," Euphemia said. "I can imagine he would do well in a busy marketplace. Now as to you, my dear, you leave me today?"

"Yes, we are taking to the road again. We must pick up Robertus's players and then travel to Montpellier."

"Well, perhaps I will see you there in a week or so. I have decided to recuperate at my brother's home near the Herbaria Market. Perhaps when I feel better we might meet for a small supper together."

"That would be very nice. Thank you."

"In the meantime, perhaps you would do me the favor of thinking about joining the Poor Clares. We need more young women of your strength and clarity of thought."

"I am flattered, Sister Euphemia, but I am hoping to attend the university in Montpellier. I wish to be a medica, a doctor of phisik tending to women."

"An ambitious plan to be sure," She raised on one elbow. "Before you go, I want to thank you for helping me regain my own faith."

Meg couldn't imagine how treating Euphemia with broth and kindness could possibly produce so monumental a result. "Why thank *me*?"

"I was deeply troubled before I grew ill. My pilgrimage was meant to solve my crisis of faith. But now, now that I have nearly died, I realize God allowed me to live for a reason."

"What reason is that?"

"I must return to the convent. Our sisters must be confident in their vows. There must be no gossip, no jealousy, for that is how the Evil One enters our place of worship. Above all, they must show a love of God through deep meditation and hands to work."

"But, Sister, you must take care. You have been near death."

Euphemia smiled as if she were explaining the mysteries of God to a small child. "You, my dear, see the proper working of the body as if it were a wagon wheel that needs sanding and oiling. Install the proper bolts and then the wagon will move forward to its destination. On the other hand, I see the hand of the Maker. You provide the broth, the kind words, and I respond by getting better. But I could have easily died, joined my fellow pilgrims in the cemetery." She motioned to the infirmary door and beyond to the graveyard. "There are many mysteries in the universe. Mysteries that oil and bolts will not answer."

"You sound like Mother Alice, a healer in my village."

"And where is that?"

"In Warwickshire, England. Saint Michael's Mead."

Euphemia smiled. "Perhaps one day I could visit there. And meet your Alice. There is a sister abbey in London I would love to visit. The Abbey of the Minoresses of St. Clare outside Aldgate. It was founded about 30 years ago. The Pope speaks highly of it. And there are two or three others scattered about the country."

Meg kissed the thin cheeks, which were soft as lambskin. "I wish you well, Sister Euphemia," she said, as William motioned for all to depart.

"If ever I can do anything for you, my dear, please let me know. And you are welcome at the convent anytime."

Meg lifted her hand and waved farewell.

Chapter 26

On the Road to Montpellier

February 1327

When they returned to the main road, Robertus's troupe was waiting for him, eager to show the bag of coins they had earned on his behalf.

"Well done," Robertus exclaimed, calling them the best players in Christendom. Sarafina, the red-haired girl, beckoned to him before he could pick up the reins and whip.

"Robertus, our feet are sore. We've had enough of the road. If Halybutte is allowed to ride, why can we not join him? Let us ride. Please?"

He sighed. "Get in then. We'll be in Montpellier by nightfall. The horse can take the extra weight for one day."

Sarafina and the others whooped and hollered and were soon climbing over Meg and Gerard and stepping on William's feet in an attempt to find a comfortable seat. It seemed

195

to Meg that Sarafina insisted on a place next to Gerard. The girl shoved Halybutte aside and said to Gerard, as she pressed against him, her thigh touching his, "May I sit next to you, fine sir?"

Gerard smiled at her. "Certainly."

William, deep in conversation with the dwarf once again, did not notice his son had a new admirer.

Meg was mindful of how plain she must appear to Gerard. Sarafina's hair, unlike Meg's, was loose, her red curls flowing wantonly, brilliantly against her blue velvet surcoat, decorated with slashes to reveal a red tunic underneath. Bits of metal and bells, sewn to the surcoat, glinted like sunbeams and jingled as she walked. Meg, as was her usual, was dressed in gray wool, her hair plaited and covered by a coif.

"My name is Sarafina," the girl said to Gerard. She tossed her curls, releasing a tinkle of music from her costume. "They tell me that you are traveling with your father and sister."

"Father, yes. Sister, no. She is my father's student, but we are like brother and sister."

A sister. So that's how he sees me, Meg thought with a sinking heart. *A mere sibling. Someone I might fight with over scraps of food or a toy. What happened to the feelings he revealed on the Godisgrace? He was so tender.*

"Do you mind if I put my head upon your shoulder?" Sarafina asked. "I am so exhausted from walking. Oh, yes, how lovely. But wait, I had no idea that you were a man of such power." She ran her hand up and down Gerard's arm. "So much better. I won't be a bother to someone so strong."

Meg snorted. Strong? Muscular? Powerful? Gerard was thin as a fence post. He could pick up a feather quill and a book, but no more. Gerard scowled at her and she turned away, drifting off into a semi-sleep, the clip-clop of the horse beating a rhythm she could not dismiss: *sis-ter, sis-ter.*

Later, as the light faded, and the afternoon grew chill, Meg woke to find they were crossing a bridge. "Where are we, Robertus?" she asked.

"Crossing the Lez River. There is Montpellier. The city is built on two hills and is surrounded by walls. Inside there are steep narrow streets. And crowds of people."

Meg looked ahead to a mountain of stone, the city walls stretching far to the right and left, topped by towers whose cone-shaped roofs provided shelter for the guards walking the parapet.

"Who governs the city?" William asked.

"The lords of Montpellier and the bishop of Maguelone. Occasionally they piss on each other's territory and then there's a crisis. Above them are the kings of Majorca and Aragon who keep tossing possession of Montpellier back and forth like a ball." He pulled back on the reins to calm the excited mare. "Whoa, girl. Whoa there." He pointed to the crowds of people heading for the city gate like rats funneling into a hole in the wall. "So who knows who these people will belong to tomorrow? They keep their heads down, do their work, take care of their families, and try not to cause too much trouble. A little enjoyment isn't too much to offer them, is it?"

"Humph," William grunted.

"We'll go through the gate and—"

"And find food and shelter," William shifted his weight, careful not to wake the dwarf whose head lolled in William's lap. Meg stifled a laugh and William grinned, shaking his head as if to say, *What could I do? Halybutte was sleepy.*

"I know just the place," Robertus said. "The Herbaria Market."

Following their entrance through the Gate of St. Giles, where the female players waved and flirted with the guards, they rode through a labyrinth of narrow winding streets. Merchants called to them offering sugar and spices, the finest leather, embroidered textiles, cloth from Bruges. Their going was slow owing to the many passersby, some of whom cursed at the wagon. Several times, a street ended as a building loomed ahead and what appeared to be alleys to the right and left turned into dead ends. When that happened, the entire party had to scramble out of the wagon while Robertus backed the horse. Fortunately, the creature was exhausted and not inclined to protest.

"I thought you said you had been here before. Do you know where you are going?" William grumbled.

"Have faith," Robertus answered and cast a sideways glance at Meg, muttering to her, "Not an easy thing for him to do."

Finally, the narrow street on which they rode emptied into an open-air square. "Herbaria," Robertus announced. "Montpellier was once a rustic backwater but is now at the center of spice trading. So, it's actually the merchants who yield the power here. I'll stay with the wagon. Find what you need but do it soon. The light is going."

William, Meg, and Gerard threaded their way through the many fruit and vegetable stalls, picking items to stave off hunger until they could get a full meal. At each stall, they asked if there was a place to stay near the university. Their words appeared to fall on deaf ears, or more correctly, neither ears that understood English nor tongues that spoke it. Instead, their language bore no resemblance to the French that William had taught Meg and Gerard. As a consequence, they were reduced to hand signals.

"Sleep, monsieur? *Dormir*? Home?" Gerard asked a butcher. The man gestured to his stall, which was nearly empty. "No. Home. Sleep." Gerard walked away in exasperation.

They tried four more stalls until an old woman selling flowers pointed them across the aisle where another woman packed up pieces of woven cloth. Through assorted gestures they understood that she had a house near the university where she rented rooms.

"Excellent," William said. "We'll take you home. Follow me, *allez*." He filled her barrow with the lengths of fabric she hadn't sold and motioned for Gerard to do the same.

Once they had the woman and her wares safely in the

wagon, which was now full of the waiting players, they asked for her address. Her answer made no sense, but she pointed to the right.

"Robertus, can you understand this woman or anyone else in this god-forsaken town?" William fumed. "I thought I knew French, but this is not the French spoken in Paris."

"They are speaking a dialect of French, Spanish, some Arabic, and whatever else was spoken by races who settled here. This is the Langue D'Oc, remember? It is not France. Languedocians don't particularly like the French." He flicked the horse lightly with the whip and pulled on the reins to change their direction.

By way of pointing, grunting, and frantic gestures when Robertus took a wrong turn, the woman from the market guided them through the streets to her home. As night fell, they finally stopped in front of a small stone building on the Rue de l'Ecole de Medicine. The woman pressed a hand to her chest and said, "Madame Tisserand." When she opened the door, she motioned everyone inside, even the players. They entered a small front room filled to bursting with pieces of woven cloth, spools of thread, and a loom. While Madame lit candles and started a fire in the fireplace, Robertus and the players stretched out on the floor. Serafina gave Gerard a kiss on the cheek and whispered, "Sleep well" before she curled up in front of the fire. Meg, disgusted, followed Madame up two flights of stairs to a tiny attic room furnished with a small bed. She dropped onto the straw mattress and was asleep before her head hit the bolster.

Chapter 27

SATAN'S WARTS

Montpellier, March 1327

The next day William met with the Regent Master of the medical school to discuss admitting both Meg and Gerard while his two young pupils explored the city streets near Madame Tisserand's. At the evening meal, William announced the results of his meeting. Gerard had been given leave to enter the school, provided he pass his examinations.

"And what of Meg?" Gerard asked.

Meg, who had opened her mouth to ask the same question, said, "Master William, I am anxious to attend."

William placed a hand on her shoulder. "There is a problem, I'm afraid."

He described his conversation with the Regent as heated. The Regent stood firm. The university had rules and those rules must be obeyed. No women were to be admitted to the *studium generale*, much less to the school of medicine. Women would disrupt a class. Women would faint at the sight of blood. Women would distract the male students causing them to think only lustful thoughts. Women would poison the air with their monthly flow. Women would do this, women would do that.

"*Ad nauseum*," William scoffed. "His arguments have nothing to do with you, Meg. You are more than capable of doing the work."

"Isn't there a way to convince him?" Gerard asked.

"Leave it to me. As you both know, I can be very persuasive."

Gerard and Meg looked at each other and laughed, though, in truth, Meg felt all mirth had left her world. Her heart had stopped at the litany of excuses the Regent offered to keep her from entering the school.

If William failed to convince the Regent Master to accept her, she would have to leave Montpellier and continue as William's apprentice until she married or died. Her dreams of practicing as a doctor of phisik would vanish. Worse, Gerard would forget about her. Instead, he would meet a young woman of virtue and marry, leaving Meg's dreams of a life with him to vanish as well.

For a week William left the house early in the morning, coming back glumly in the evening, his black humor furling around him like the clouds of a winter storm, warning all in his presence to neither banter nor jape. Each day his scowling face meant that he had failed in his quest to open the university doors to Meg.

To keep their minds occupied, Meg and Gerard studied for Gerard's examinations. Because Gerard had not attended university but had been taught by his father, the Regent wanted to assess his knowledge of the trivium and quadrivium, both of which Gerard had passed under William's tutelage. Having left their books at William's house in London in their panic to escape the Queen's men, Meg and Gerard were forced to discuss the subjects of grammar, logic, and rhetoric by memory. By week's end, they moved on to arithmetic, geometry, music, and astronomy. On Friday afternoon they were seated near the fire in Madame Tisserand's overcrowded front room, the click-clack of Madame's loom accompanying their discussion of the movement of heavenly bodies. A loaf of bread and two cups of wine on the table had enhanced their studies.

"This is your last question of the day," Meg said, as Gerard complained that his head was far too woolly to continue. "But it will be your hardest."

Gerard groaned and pressed his hands to his eyes.

"In what way are spherical harmonies related to the position of the planets? Please explain in geometric terms. How do the harmonies affect cosmology and vice versa?"

"You have asked me two questions, not one!" Gerard sputtered.

"Never mind. You are not to doubt the logic of the examiner," she scolded.

Gerard was deep in thought when the door burst open and Master William strode in, a wide grin hinting at the good news he carried.

"What is it? What has happened?" Gerard asked. William looked at Meg and smiled like a cat in the milk pail. "After a week of accosting every faculty member at the university, I believe we have made progress."

"Tell us, Father."

"Yes, please, sir," Meg begged. "I am at my wit's end after waiting for word day after day."

William pulled a hunk of bread from the loaf on the table and stuffed it in his mouth. "God's truth, I'm famished," he sighed.

"Father! Tell us!" Gerard shouted.

William laughed, swallowed the bread, took a great gulp of wine from Gerard's cup, and said, "Meg must go before the faculty of the school of medicine as well as the bishop. They will examine her knowledge. If she suits them, she may have a chance." He held up his hand as Gerard and Meg stood and moved to embrace him. "May, I said. Do not get your hopes up, but it is promising news."

William's choleric nature and profound lack of patience had, in this instance, served Meg well. He had badgered everyone he knew—and some he did not know—to obtain an interview for her. He was sure that once they met her and evaluated her knowledge, they would have no objection to her entry into the school.

"A month from today, the faculty and the Bishop of Maguelone will meet at the Regent's home. Both of you will be tested. A decision will be made at that time."

The blood drained from Meg's face. Now that the moment was here, she was shocked. One month! One month to prepare for her future. One month to dredge up everything she had learned from William in the last four years. She pictured the faculty, sour-faced, resolute men, prejudiced against her sex, determined to toss her fate to the winds in an effort to keep Montpellier an all-male bastion.

She dropped to her chair. By Satan's warts, she had no hope whatsoever.

Montpellier, April 1327

In the morning William announced their schedule. They would begin their studies at first light, after which they would take a break for a mid-day meal followed by a brisk walk to exercise the limbs and shake the cobwebs from their minds. After that, they would start anew. To make sure they covered every possibility, William found a stationer in Montpellier who sold him pieces of manuscripts covering the lessons they needed. They would begin with the *Ars Grammatica* and end with the *Tractatus de sphaera*, the most important book on astronomy. In their last lesson, they would review the astrolabe.

At this announcement, Meg groaned inwardly. Knowledge of the astrolabe was necessary for a practicing phisik. Without an understanding of the patient's astrological history, a doctor of phisik could not determine when to administer the correct medicines, bleed or purge, and prognosticate life or death. William had taught Meg how to hold the astrolabe, to move the various pieces, and sight through the alidade, but every time she attempted to use the instrument, her mind went blank, a *tabula rasa* that failed to tell her fingers what to do.

William announced that their lessons would begin immediately. "*Repetitio est mater studiorum*," he said. "Meaning?"

"Repetition is the mother of learning," Meg answered.

"And we will repeat and repeat until you have it." He promised to interrogate them to the limits of their endurance. And so he did. He pounded the table and ranted about their appalling use of Latin and paced the room when both Meg and Gerard attempted to give a demonstration of logical proof, real or apparent.

One night, Meg's lackluster answer to his question—"What is an example of *logos* as one of three kinds of artistic proofs in Aristotle's rhetorical theory?"—sent him marching to the door, which he slammed with such vigor that Madame Tisserand squeaked in surprise.

Gerard sighed and announced he was going to bed. "I must gird my loins for another day in the lion's den," he joked. Seeing Meg's crestfallen face, he added, "Father's temper is foul, but he cares for us. Otherwise, he wouldn't prod us so."

Madame Tisserand tut-tutted under her breath as she rose from her loom. She dabbed at Meg's tears with a rag and murmured something in her dialect about a "little lamb." Her muttering, which had begun when William stormed out, rose to a vituperative torrent accompanied by hand gestures toward the door and the occasional use of "Monsieur Guillaume." This was followed by phrases, which Meg thought rebuked William for his temper—she recognized "beast" and "ogre"—until Madame's torrent sputtered to a halt. She asked a lengthy question, something about Monsieur Guillaume and medicine, which Meg was at a loss to understand.

Meg looked at Gerard who raised his eyebrows and mumbled, "Do not look to me for guidance. I cannot understand a word she says." Meg giggled. Then Gerard giggled. And soon they were holding their sides and howling with laughter.

"I think 'Guillaume' had better stay out of the house for a while. Madame is likely to break a bottle over his head on our behalf," Gerard cried.

Meg shrieked and stomped her feet as tears rolled down her cheeks. Madame Tisserand stared in amazement and grumbled under her breath. They caught the words *"fole"* and *"Anglaise"* which started another round of hysterical laughter.

"Ah," Meg said, when she had caught her breath. "So, Madame thinks we English are fools, eh?" In her best imitation of Master William's deep voice, Meg asked Gerard, "Are the English foolish? How do you know? Use a syllogism to illustrate your answer."

Gerard crossed his arms and sat in thought. Then he grinned. "The English are human. All humans are fools. Therefore, an Englishman is a human fool."

"Excellent, Monsieur Gerard. You may now enter the school of medicine." She placed the tear-stained rag on his head. "And here is your cap to prove it."

Gerard swiped the cap from his head and threw it at her. Meg shrieked and, lifting her arm for a hard return of the cap to Gerard's mid-section, stopped when William stormed in, his scowl provoking them to silence. He glared at them and stomped upstairs.

Meg left to find Madame, who stood at the kitchen door throwing scraps from dinner into the back alley. "Madame, *ici*," she said. She handed her the wet rag with a *"merci."*

Madame rolled her eyes, threw the last bits to a pack of scavenging dogs, and grunted, "Humph."

✳✳✳

William's temper did not improve the following morning. He lectured without remorse, reminding them that the examination would be held in two days until Madame Tisserand announced the mid-day meal. Meg was famished and happy to find bowls of dates, cheese, olives, eels, freshly baked bread, and candied lemon set before them. Feeling guilty for her treatment of Madame the night before, Meg rubbed her belly and pantomimed eating a good meal. "Mmmm, Madame," she said, *"c'est tres bon."*

Gerard also joined in the play-acting. "Ohhhhh. Eat. Gooood," he said, pretending to bring food to his lips.

Madame smiled and dished out more olives.

"I suppose I shouldn't ask why the two of you are treating Madame Tisserand like a deaf-mute," William said.

Meg and Gerard studied their food intently but said nothing.

At the end of the meal, William announced that Meg was to explain the philosophy behind Plato's statement, "Art has no end but its own perfection." She redeemed herself from the previous night's poor performance by lecturing Gerard and William on the Idea of the Good, art in the City of Perfection, and art as an enemy of Reason.

William held up his hand. "Very good. That will do for now."

"Thank you, sir," Meg said. Her voice was cool, but inwardly she was ecstatic. She permitted herself a slight smile. *Very good*, he said. Considering the source, high praise indeed.

Unfortunately, her ecstasy turned to misery within an hour as she missed all of William's questions about the astrolabe. She could name its parts, point to the degrees, months, and days, but if asked to determine the time or to find the position of certain stars and planets in order to cast a horoscope, her thoughts became a jumble. She could only hope that the instrument would not be her downfall.

She had no time to dwell on the miseries of the astrolabe, however, for William turned to the *Almagest* and harangued them on astronomy. Just when Meg hoped he would suggest a respite, he began a discussion—one-sided as only William was allowed to talk—on the allegory of Plato's cave.

"Remember," he said, as he finished his lecture, "Look beyond the shadows, look to the truth." He stretched and to Meg's relief announced a brief walk.

Setting a swift pace, William strode up the steep Rue St. Pierre, Gerard and Meg trotting behind him, then turned left through the streets of leather workers and drapers and, side-stepping the tables of cloth and leather goods, walked uphill to the Herbaria Market. A huge crowd had gathered at the market square and blocked their way.

"What the devil?" William asked and peered over the heads of gawkers to see what drew their attention. "Ah, speak of the devil. I might have known."

"What is it?" Meg asked and stood on tiptoe.

"Robertus and his players."

"Oh, may we stop, Master William? Please?"

"We have work to do. You both are woefully lacking in—"

"Please, Father," Gerard joined in. "Sera . . . I mean, the players, what I mean is Meg is surely exhausted after this morning's lecture."

Meg, stony-faced, said nothing. *He cares no more about my "exhaustion" than a mouse cares for shoes,* she thought. *He cares only for that dancing fool, Serafina.*

"A few minutes only then," William said. "I'll lead us to the front, but do not ask to see Robertus again. I'll not waste any more time on that scalawag."

Halybutte and the jugglers were performing as they pushed their way to the front. Serafina was dancing. She then sang a love song while cutting her eyes at a blushing Gerard.

Suddenly, Meg heard a woman calling her name. Scanning the crowd, she was astonished to see Sister Euphemia waving to them. Euphemia said something to her servant who then pushed onlookers aside with a *pardon*. After they elbowed her way through, Euphemia embraced first Meg, then Gerard, and finally, William, kissing them on both cheeks and jabbering like a happy child.

"I am dumbfounded, Madame," William said. "You look like an entirely different person."

"I am indebted to the three of you and Robertus, of course."

Robertus, who acknowledged Euphemia with a nod of his head, chided them from the stage for talking loudly and they dropped their voices. In a half-whisper, Euphemia explained that she was recuperating at her brother's house near the market. "Perhaps you'd like to dine with me."

With a grand sweep of his fist, Robertus threw a fine powder above the crowd, which then exploded with an ear-splitting *Bang!* followed by a flash of light. Women in the audience yelped and clutched their chests, Euphemia and Meg among them.

"Now that I have your attention," Robertus yelled above the gaping crowd, "I will perform a miracle." He paused and waiting for complete silence. "I will turn ordinary water into wine."

"And if you believe that you're an imbecile," William sneered.

With great ceremony, Robertus waved his hands over a clear goblet containing only water. Nothing happened. He planted his feet on the stage and furrowed his brows, murmuring something beyond the crowd's hearing. Ever so slowly, the water changed color from clear to pink to red. Everyone except William gasped.

Even Euphemia was stunned and mystified. "I have seen this thrice now and still I cannot understand how he does it."

Halybutte danced with Pettipaw in celebration as Medicamus beckoned two members of the audience to approach the stage and drink from the goblet.

"How?" Meg gasped as the water in the goblet deepened to burgundy and the crowd broke into applause.

"Deceit," said William. He put his hands on her back and gave her a gentle push. "Back to studying." To Euphemia, he said, "Meg and Gerard face the Schola Medica examiners in two days."

"Good luck, my dears," she called.

Two days, Meg thought with dread. Two days. Not nearly enough time.

Chapter 29

BEWARE THE BISHOP

Montpellier, April 1327

On the day of their oral examination, Meg and Gerard attended Mass at Notre-Dame-des-Tables, where Meg prayed fervently the Blessed Virgin would guide her answers. She was glad William did not scoff, as he normally would, at her prayers for divine intercession. She would ask Zeus himself to intervene if necessary.

After the service, William led them through the tables of moneychangers, dyed fabrics, and spice merchants until he reached a table heaped with tiny black balls about the size of a pea. "Here," he said, as he paid the vendor. "A treat for today. It's a sweet made of honey and licorice. Called grisettes." He offered one to Gerard who waved it away. William put two in Meg's hand. "A second one for good luck and to keep your mouth moist while you answer questions."

As they walked up the steep slope of the Rue de l'Aiguillerie and over the crest of the hill, Meg sucked on the honey ball, savoring the tang of licorice. The street, barely big enough for four people abreast, narrowed to a mere lane between houses and shops jammed together tightly on both sides. They followed a steep walkway down to the Regent's home on the Rue de la Tour near the city walls. Meg's legs were shaking so violently she had to clutch Gerard's sleeve to stay upright. Gerard, as usual, seemed no worse the wear for the ordeal about to overtake them. While they walked in silence, Meg sang to herself the verse that helped her remember the meaning of the Seven Liberal Arts: *Gram loquitur. Dia vera docet. Rhe verba colorat. Mus canit. Ar numerat. Geo ponderat. As docet astra.* Grammar speaks. Dialectic teaches truth. Rhetoric adorns words. Music sings. Arithmetic counts. Geometry measures. Astronomy studies stars.

Wishing she could tuck one grisette in each cheek to call on its soothing properties during the interrogation, she had a sudden vision of meeting the bishop, both cheeks full like a squirrel gathering nuts before the snows of winter. A nervous titter escaped her mouth, and she covered her lips in embarrassment. Then she giggled. She caught the glance between Gerard and William, the look of concern that said, *perhaps she is losing her mind.*

The arched entranceway of the Regent's house was surrounded by Roman gods and goddesses carved in stone. Tucked into the eaves on the second floor were grotesque figures of monstrous fish, their mouths open wide to serve as downspouts when it rained. As she stared at the carvings, Meg no longer thought of grisettes or giggles. She was more than serious.

She was terrified.

✱✱✱

The hush in the great hall seemed ominous. The air felt thick and heavy as if a storm gathered. Petrus Muller, Regent Master of the Montpellier School of Medicine, sat at the end of the hall near a massive marble fireplace carved in rotund cherubs. Muller, who had placed himself in the center of a semi-circle of men, watched as Meg and Gerard drew closer, his eyes lidded like a reptile sunning on a rock.

Muller's house, with its cut-stone façade and carved doorway, could have belonged to a modestly successful cloth merchant or jeweler. Inside, the house told a different story. The interior was lavish with thick Turkey rugs, tapestries embroidered in gold thread, and paneled walls rubbed to a sheen. In the fireplace, logs as thick as a man crackled and popped, sending sparks to hiss and die on the floor. The tile floor, designed in a chevron pattern of black and white, made Meg feel lightheaded and unsteady on her feet.

Like Muller, the men to his left and right were dressed in the long red robes and the red velvet caps of their profession as doctors of phisik. They remained silent as Muller introduced them. Only one, a master named Sorianus, smiled in greeting. The master named Horlogus scowled as if he had eaten a rotten turnip.

"And this is the Bishop of Maguelone," Muller said, gesturing to the man at the far right.

The bishop, whose white tunic and cape glittered with gold embroidery, lifted two fingers in greeting. He sat aloof from the others, his gaze upon Meg.

Muller reminded his colleagues they had met Master William previously. "Most certainly a man of persistence."

"I take that as a compliment, sir," William responded. "These young people have studied diligently. We are honored that you would consider them."

"Their knowledge is due to your teaching, no doubt," said Muller, "Although I wonder that an ordinary surgeon would have the skills to instruct anything beyond bloodletting and barbering."

William looked as if he had been struck a blow. "Sir, you dishonor me. I am a graduate of Oxford as you know, Regent Master. I studied among learned men. I am a surgeon, it is true, but I am a licensed doctor of phisik first, not a common barber-surgeon. In fact, I know nothing of being a barber." William's face was red with the exertion of holding back his temper. The veins were standing out on his neck. The next step, as Meg had witnessed many times, was a full-fledged fit.

Muller was not convinced. "Better to have studied at the University of Paris or Salerno or even here for that matter. I have heard few students study medicine in that godforsaken northern city. In fact, I hear only of drunken brawls with unfortunate townspeople."

"I will not stand here . . ." William took a breath and paused. He looked at Meg and Gerard in turn. "These young people have served me well for years. They are ready to follow in my footsteps at your great university."

Muller waved toward the door. "Very well. If you and Meg would wait in the library, we will question Gerard first."

William shook hands with his son and clasped his shoulder. "*Bona fortuna*, young man."

"Thank you, Father."

A servant ushered Meg and William into a large octagonal room lined with books. Two chairs flanked a fireplace where a cheerful blaze promised to warm them. Meg took one of the chairs and stretched her legs toward the fire, hoping it would break the chill crawling into her bones. William, however, chose to stand, or rather, pace. Clasping his hands behind his back, he walked from one end of the room to the other.

"Master William, do not worry. Gerard is clever. He will do well," Meg said.

"Yes, yes." He strode from wall to wall, scarcely noticing the leather-bound volumes filling the bookshelves from floor to ceiling.

Meg folded her hands and waited. She was so lost in thought, concerned about Gerard despite her affirmations to William, that she forgot she was the next candidate until a flushed Gerard entered the room barely an hour later, his wide smile indicating a successful examination. Muller, who stood behind him, said, "May I introduce to you the newest member of the Montpellier Schola Medica. Gerard did well on his examination, just as you predicted."

William, who had ceased his pacing and stood frozen until the regent finished his congratulations, hugged his son. Meg, too, threw her arms around Gerard and held him in a tight embrace. "I knew you would do well. Didn't I say as much, Master William?"

Gerard placed his mouth against her ear and whispered, "Beware of the bishop."

Muller interrupted them. "Your turn, Mistress Meg."

William put a hand on Muller's forearm. "I would just remind you, sir, that the Schola Medica in Salerno admitted women two hundred years ago. Surely Montpellier, a school of even greater renown, would admit one female without the world coming to an end?"

"And we know what happened to Salerno, do we not? Barely able to call itself a university today. Eclipsed by Bologna, Paris, *and* Montpellier." He glanced at Meg. "Come along."

William squeezed Meg's hand. "*Crede quod habes, et habes,*" he whispered.

She straightened her shoulders and followed the regent to the great hall. She took a deep breath and slipped the second grisette into her mouth.

William is right, she thought, as she sucked on the sticky treat. *Crede quod habes, et habes. Believe that you have it, and you <u>will</u> have it.* She lifted her head and met each man's stare.

Muller took a seat beside his colleagues. Although their faces were unreadable, Sorianus, the master at the far end of the semi-circle, smiled and she sensed that he might have sympathy for her. Horlogus glared. He was thin, with hollow cheekbones and only a few strands of hair, which he repeatedly combed forward with his fingers.

Horlogus leaned to Muller and in a coarse whisper said, "Her face, once seen, not soon forgotten."

"True," Muller replied. "At least she won't drive the young men to lust."

Meg felt the blood rise to her cheeks, but she stood her ground.

Muller chuckled and promised Horlogus they would discuss the issue later. He then turned to Meg. "Let me begin by expressing our gratitude that a young woman with your skills would be interested in our school of medicine. William thinks your knowledge far surpasses any beginning student and you should enter at the master's level. We need to ascertain this for ourselves."

"Yes, sir."

"You apprenticed to a village healer and then to William, is that correct?"

"Yes, sir."

"And you learned the trivium and quadrivium?"

Horlogus pursed his lips and said, "Not from a cunning-woman in a backward village. Cures of bat wings and stoat spleens—*that* she learned, not rhetoric."

The other masters, including Sorianus, snickered.

Meg flushed and took a deep breath. "With all respect, the village healer, Alice, taught me much that was useful and practical. She is greatly respected by many, including Master William."

"Oh, we mean no disrespect," Muller said. He tilted his head toward the thin man sitting next to him. "No disrespect at all, eh, Master Horlogus?"

Horlogus tugged his hair toward his forehead and shrugged.

"Let us begin with the trivium and quadrivium," Muller said. "They are the best paths to philosophic truth. Masters, you may ask your questions."

Horlogus spoke first. "What is an example of *logos* as one of three kinds of artistic proofs in Aristotle's rhetorical theory?" Meg, remembering William's tantrum the night she answered that question poorly, covered her smile with her hand.

"Are we boring you, Mistress?" Horlogus asked.

"Oh, no, sir. I was not yawning. Just a tickle in my throat." She pretended to cough and then proceeded to answer his question. Although she knew her answer was perfect, Horlogus looked more sour than ever.

After Horlogus, each master took his turn. Thanks to William's incessant lecturing, Meg's answers were clear, logical, and instructive. She also remembered not to fidget, resisting the urge to wave her arms about or to shift from one foot to another as she talked. Instead, she stood quite still, hands clasped, looking each questioner in the eye, answering without faltering or wavering. She was the very image of a virtuous demure young woman.

Several hours later when the questions dribbled to a halt, Muller said, "Mistress Meg, you have done your work, that is for certain. Your knowledge of the ancients is exemplary."

"Thank you, sir."

"Do you have anything to ask, bishop?"

The bishop smoothed the cincture tied around his waist, caressing the ruby and diamond studded belt as he might a lover's cheek. He cleared his throat. And then he caught Meg in a stare so bold she felt as if she were a fly in the center of his web. He pressed his hands together and let his chin rest on the steeple of his jeweled index fingers.

"Tell me, why do you persist in this foolishness?"

"Excuse me, Your Excellency, I do not understand."

"The Holy Writ speaks to us, does it not?"

"Yes, Your Excellency."

"It gives us directions for living. It is the source of truth in all things. It is the method of all teaching."

"Yes, well, that is—"

"A doctor of phisik is not your profession. Your profession is spinning and sewing. Your profession is housewife to your husband. It is written in Holy Scripture."

Master Horlogus leaned forward and gestured to the bishop. "So true, Your Excellency. A young woman should serve her husband in the bedchamber behind the bedcurtains, not roam the world as a single woman, dirtying herself in the muck of bodily fluids, wallowing in the stink of urine—"

"Yes, yes, Horlogus, you make your point." He pursed his lips and continued. "Now, Mistress Meg, I am speaking of the Holy Writ for, as you have agreed, it guides us in all things. Therefore, is it not God's will that a young woman should marry, bear children, guide the house, and not speak reproachfully to an adversary?"

"Yes, however," she continued swiftly to prevent the bishop's interruption, "does it not seem logical that if God gave me intelligence, he would want me to use it rather than squander it? And given my obvious skills in healing, would not medicine be a logical profession in which to use my intelligence?"

The bishop and Horlogus frowned. Master Sorianus smiled, but when she caught his eye, he looked away.

The regent stood and gestured to the others. "Shall we take a brief respite? I believe refreshments are ready." He motioned to the servant standing near a door at the far end of the room. "And you, Mistress Meg, may sit while we confer." He pointed to a chair in the corner.

Meg was glad for the rest. Her legs wobbled as she took a seat. Shadows from the fire leapt to the walls and textiles and collapsed as one flame extinguished another. Ceiling arches painted in red, gold, and blue stripes dazzled above the firelight. It was indeed beautiful—and richly appointed—but even its beauty could not overcome the stultifying atmosphere of the room.

While the men ate and talked *sotto voce*, Meg reviewed the examination. She had responded with persuasive arguments on the rhetoric and dialectic questions. At least two of the masters, Sorianus and the gentleman sitting next to him, seemed to favor her. Horlogus abhorred her, of that she was sure. She wasn't certain about Muller. But clearly, the bishop, the man who held the most power in the room, thought her foolish—or mad—to even consider a profession in medicine. Well, she thought, I've been called mad before.

A vision of St. Michael's Mead flashed into her minds-eye: the villagers going about their daily duties, the women gathered at the well, Alice wrapping red flannel around a child with fever so as to draw out the heat, Meg's sister Maud offering her breast to the latest suckling babe, her father John urging the ox forward through the unplowed field, her mother Agnes spinning thread onto the spindle whorl. Suddenly a surge of doubt rolled over her. *Maybe the bishop is right. Maybe I should give up, return to Warwickshire, find a husband, and live out my days according to Holy Writ.* She pictured herself in the small thatched cottage, stirring the pot hanging above the fire, spinning thread, giving birth to baby after baby, tending to the villagers as Alice's successor, all the while absolutely certain in her heart that she could have ministered to the sick the wide world over.

These were prideful notions for certain, but as she looked at the men eating and drinking at the regent's table, a thought struck her so forcefully she felt as if she had been set upon and slapped. Those men who interrogated her, those men who were puffed up like cardinals in their red robes—they were prideful, were they not? Even the bishop appeared proud of his jewels and embroidered cope. And her beloved Master William? Oh, most certainly prideful.

Perhaps she could not place herself within the boundaries of the Holy Writ, but weren't her skills at healing as necessary as the spindle whorl? If her God-given intellect could help her save a woman's life or cure a child, why would God spite her for being prideful?

She decided to take a different approach to the examination. When they began again, *she* would take the lead.

Muller motioned to his servant, gesturing toward the fire-place. The servant stoked the fire, which roared to life, and then added another log to the flames. "Join us, mistress," the regent said.

Meg assumed her previous place, her back to the fire. "Glad-ly, sir, for I have something to say." She gripped her fingers so that she might look composed. "Women the world over are ashamed, nay afraid, to discuss private ailments with men. They trust only their midwives—and yes, there are midwives whose experience does not go beyond watching the milk cow drop a calf—but how much better would it be for women to see a female doctor of phisik, trained at the most respected medical school in the world, educated to the highest stan-dards, taught from the relevant books of the ancients? If you accept me . . ."

The masters were muttering, twisting in their chairs, and glancing at Muller as if waiting for him to interrupt. The bishop cleared his throat. Meg glanced nervously at each, but willed her voice to continue.

"If you accept me, I vow to you that I will study hard, fin-ish well, and practice to the exalted standards of Montpellier's graduates. Your daughters, your wives, your mothers will thank you for providing them with care they trust."

Muller turned to Meg. "A fine speech. Very passionate, as I would expect from a member of your sex. Since you bring up the subject of care to women, perhaps we should discuss the care you would offer a patient. Uh, Master Sorianus, you wish to speak?"

Sorianus had raised his hand. Pushing his red biretta away from his forehead, as if the cap were a bother, he leaned back in his chair and wrapped his hands around his voluminous belly, "I have told you, Petrus, how much I disagree with ques-tioning the applicant on medical matters which are foreign to her. She has not learned how to care for patients in the Mont-pellier way. She has no patients because she has not finished her studies. And she has not finished her studies because *we* will not allow it."

"Sorianus, your opposition is duly noted." Muller turned to Meg. "Now, mistress, were you to encounter a female patient suffering from a wasting disease, what would you do?"

Master Sorianus was right. It wasn't fair to ask a medical question. Still, she had to answer or look a fool. "First, I would meet with the woman, feel her head for fever, and examine her countenance. I would talk with her family to determine how the disease began. I would examine her breasts and press upon her abdomen in order to find lumps and other apostemes, for these are the primary reasons for wasting disease in women. Then I would examine her urine."

Meg thought about Elias the blacksmith, the man they treated before being chased out of London. He also suffered from a wasting disease. No matter what cure they attempted, they were not able to save him. He blamed himself for the death of his son and would not hear otherwise. "Above all, I would talk with the patient," she added. "Sometimes talking will reveal mitigating circumstances for a sickness in the mind."

"Wrong. Wrong. Wrong," Muller scolded. "Talking to the patient is not necessary. First, you should consult the astrolabe to determine the patient's horoscope. This would provide information for treatment such as bloodletting. Then you should ask the woman's servant to bring you a bottle of the woman's urine. You do have a urine table in your *vade mecum*, do you not?"

Meg patted the small book of medical drawings and advice hanging from her girdle. William had given her the book as a gift in London. "Yes, sir, I do."

"And do you know the astrolabe?"

"Master William has tutored me in the use of it."

Muller motioned to Horlogus who reached into a pocket inside his robe and pulled out a small brass instrument. Speaking precisely, giving each word its full pronunciation and letting the vowels and consonants roll off his tongue as if he were delivering a sermon—or a lecture—he said, "God placed the sun and moon, planets and stars in the immutable heaven so that man could know the signs and times for treatment of disease." He handed her the astrolabe. "There is a sign and time for everything under heaven. Without the astrolabe, you cannot interpret those signs."

"Thank you, Horlogus," Muller said. He then commanded Meg to dismantle the astrolabe, put it back together, and explain the function of each part.

The brass disk in Meg's hands was a beautiful piece of work, engraved with the names of the twelve signs of the zodiac, the circle of days with 365 divisions, and the circle of months. The back was embossed with scales and a calendar. Its filigreed parts pointing to the placement of stars, glinted in the firelight, as did the spiderweb of incised circles on its face.

Meg fumbled with the center pin holding in place the tympans or flat plates, which rested on top of each other. With trembling hands, she finally loosened the sections, then described the functions of each part as well as the various points of engraving. She stuttered only once when she attempted to replace the pin.

As she finished her explanations, Muller muttered, "Correct." Abruptly, he stood and gestured to his colleagues to follow. "Let us go outside and ask our applicant to execute mathematical calculations."

Meg groaned inwardly. This was the crux of her examination. Once they saw how inept she was with the astrolabe, they would point her toward England and say, "Do not come back."

As they stepped into the Muller's courtyard, she was shocked to see the sun dropping in a late-afternoon sky. She had been in the great hall since morning. Her stomach gnawed at her insides as a reminder that she had only eaten two tiny grisettes hours ago.

"Using the astrolabe, determine the correct time," Muller instructed.

Meg flipped the astrolabe and consulted the calendar. She raised the astrolabe, hooking her thumb through the circle at the top of the disk, and sighted down the alidade. Her hands trembled and she struggled to steady them. She made her calculations and then announced, "It is 4:30 in the afternoon."

Master Horlogus raised his eyebrows and whispered to Muller, who said, "Determine the height of the cypress tree there."

Meg stared at the cypress planted in the center of the courtyard until movement above it caught her eye. A great white pelican, taking advantage of currents blowing from the sea, stretched to its full wingspan and floated like a dreamer on endless ocean swells, until a sudden surge of wind broke its reverie. The bird tucked its wings and dropped its head, diving toward the oncoming dark and restful sleep from the labors of the day.

Meg wondered for the second time why indeed, as the bishop had asked, she pursued a dream so outlandish as the one she defended before these intractable men. And yet, she knew she must doggedly pursue the path set before her. At this moment in the regent's courtyard holding the hated astrolabe, she was as certain as she had ever been in her life: her flight must be straight and true. She would feast on knowledge and one day wear the scarlet robe and biretta of a doctor of phisik.

Meg focused on the instrument, moved a ring, and then made her calculations. "The cypress tree is twenty-one feet tall."

Horlogus snatched the astrolabe from her hands. "Give me that. And move out of the way." He glowered at the tree, turned the tympans, sighted, and then thrust the astrolabe into her hands again.

"Find the four quarters of the world, east, west, north, and south."

The bishop yawned and patted Horlogus's arm, urging him to put away the astrolabe, but Horlogus ignored him.

"Find the four—" he repeated, his voice rising.

"Enough, Horlogus," Master Sorianus interrupted. "The young woman knows the instrument. She knows the Greek masters. She knows the trivium and quadrivium. And she even answered well enough for me regarding the wasting disease. As far as I am concerned, she would make an excellent addition to the Schola Medica."

The masters erupted into shouts and insults. The words tradition, honor, alumni, money were thrown like rocks hurled at thieves. Horlogus pressed his index finger into Sorianus's chest. The master next to Sorianus stepped between the two and begged them to remember their place as learned men before they resorted to blows. Muller shouted, "Enough!"

No one heeded him.

"Petrus," Horlogus shouted to the regent, "Petrus, tell this Philistine that I will die before I see us sullied by the womb of Eve!"

"And I will be happy to make your wish come true," shouted Sorianus in return, just as he swung his right fist and barely missed Horlogus's chin.

Meg, who was rooted to the ground, caught the air from Sorianus's swing and stepped back, knuckles against her mouth to keep from crying out.

The bishop shouted, "Gentlemen! Gentlemen! For the love of Our Savior, stop it at once!" Silence prevailed. Horlogus and Sorianus straightened their robes and caps while casting their eyes anywhere but on each other. The bishop gestured toward the great hall. "Let us return to the fire now that the sun is setting. I have one last question for our applicant."

After they returned to the great hall and the men were once again seated, Meg stood before the fire, praying her shaking legs would not give way. She was exhausted. What could they possibly want with her now?

She took a deep breath and steadied herself, attempting to put the scene in the courtyard out of her mind. She stepped to her place in front of the fire, which had been refreshed with two logs as thick as a man's waist, enough to burn the house down.

"Now Mistress Meg," the bishop said, "we will address the subject which has been on our minds, but which we were too polite to mention."

"Yes, Your Excellency?" she asked.

"Your disfigurement."

What? After hours of exhausting interrogation, they were addressing her face? She felt a wave of embarrassment wash over her and yet what followed in the next wave was a red-hot fury so deep it had no bottom. *Careful. Remember Gerard's warning: Be wary of the bishop. He intends to goad me into losing my temper.*

She clasped her hands and sugar-coated her words. "I am not sure, Your Excellency, how my disfigurement pertains to my intellect."

"God has given us Beauty in the world to show Order, Proportion, Grace, and Symmetry."

Meg said nothing. The bishop had not asked a question, but she knew where he was headed: the teachings of St. Thomas Aquinas.

"There are three requirements for Beauty," he said. "First, integrity. Second, proportion. Third, clarity."

Master Sorianus stood and addressed the bishop. "Your Excellency, I respect your knowledge of Aquinas, but how is this—"

The bishop raised his hand, palm outward. "Patience and you will see."

Meg wiped her forehead. Sweat dripped from her hairline and soaked her coif. The fire blazed, the wood split with harsh *pops*, and the shadows on the paneled wall danced like crazed men who had lost their senses. The back side of her tunic was hot against her legs. She smelled an odor of burning hair and realized the wool had scorched.

"If something is impaired," the bishop continued, "it lacks integrity. It lacks symmetry. It is ugly. And on account of your disfigurement, you are impaired. You lack symmetry therefore you are ugly."

Meg had had enough. She was hungry, weary, homesick for England, and tired of these arrogant men who meant for her to cook and clean, weave and spin, bed her man, and birth his child instead of practicing medicine. If that's what they wanted, so be it then.

She was also hot. If she stood here one minute longer, she would catch fire. Without a word she pushed her way through the seated masters, moving into the shadows on the other side of the room, forcing the men to stand and rearrange their chairs. "What are you doing?" Muller gasped, while the others objected and seated themselves again. She noticed that they were sweating also. Apparently, the ruse to upset her composure had failed, for they were as uncomfortable as she.

With relief, she breathed in the cooler air of the shadows. She held up her hand to stop any further objections from the sputtering men. "I am going to answer the bishop and then I will leave you here as it seems to me you have no interest in accepting me. Indeed, I suspect you have already voted among yourselves to deny me a place in the medical school and today was no more than an exercise in your own entertainment." She faced the bishop. "You are correct in your summation of Aquinas's philosophy."

The bishop spat, "My knowledge will not be judged by—"

"There are those who believe beauty exists only in the mind which contemplates it, but that is subjective. Each mind perceives a different beauty. Indeed, one person may even perceive beauty in a deformity such as mine."

Horlogus chuckled. "Not likely."

"It is true that by St. Thomas's definition of Beauty, I lack proportion or symmetry. I lack perfect unity. Therefore, I am ugly. And yet let me ask you to contemplate an example of disunity which may persuade you." She closed her eyes, remembering an ethereal vision, a vision not of saints or angels, but of heaven on earth. "When I journeyed to the city of York several years ago, I slipped into the great cathedral. I was stunned to see such loveliness. Light spilled through the colored windows and I felt I had been transported to some strange position in the universe where only beauty filled each moment of time. It was a sublime place, far from the impurities of the world, indeed it seemed to me that what I witnessed was the purity of Heaven."

She opened her eyes and looked first at the bishop and then at each master, one after the other, holding each in her stare before moving on to the next face. "And yet let us suppose for the sake of argument that one of the beautiful gem-colored windows cracked from top to bottom, would that make the cathedral less pure, less beautiful? Do we not contemplate the overall beauty of York Cathedral and say, 'This was truly guided by the hand of God?'"

"Surely you do not compare yourself to a church building," the bishop said. He laughed, and Muller and Horlogus joined in, exchanging glances.

"I do not. I compare myself to the cracked window. I have a fault, but I am made of many pieces. I have a strong intellect. I have a good and generous heart—"

"But surely you understand that patients will be frightened by your deformity. They will turn away—"

"Patients fear what they cannot understand. They understand suffering. One look at me and they know I understand it too." She stared hard at the bishop. "Even more than St. Thomas Aquinas."

The bishop shot from his chair as if he chased the Devil himself. "How dare you ridicule the Great Philosopher, you . . . you . . . blasphemer!" he shouted.

So be it, she thought.

She squared her shoulders and strode out the door.

Chapter 30

THE CAUSE OF FEAR

Montpellier, April 1327

"A travesty!" William shouted to no one in particular. He marched up the Rue de la Blanquerie with an exhausted Meg and Gerard trotting behind. They were on their way to the Cygnet Tavern where Robertus had planned an evening of feasting to celebrate their successful examinations. Instead, Meg thought ruefully, they would raise their cups to only one future doctor of phisik since the masters clearly did not support her. Still, she could hardly wish ill for Gerard. He would make a brilliant practitioner one day, but her long-held dream of practicing with him was fading with each step she took.

William now threatened to kidnap the masters and the bishop and keep them hostage until Meg was allowed into the medical school.

"You've done enough, Master William," Meg said.

Indeed, William had left the bishop and masters in an uproar. Upon seeing Meg's dejected face as she entered the regent's library, William barged into the great hall and accused the regent and his colleagues of gross ill-treatment of Meg, of wasting his time and causing grave harm to medicine until Meg and Gerard managed to drag him out the front door, ahead of two burly servants who threatened him with their fists.

William's rage propelled his legs up the hill toward the city gate with a speed Meg could not hope to match. With the last ragged edges of sunlight disappearing behind them, Meg feared losing William in the dark. She had only been to the Cygnet once before. She shouted to William to slow down, but he paid her no heed. "Master William, sir . . . Sir!" She held her aching side and bent double, trying to catch her breath.

"What? What is it?" When he caught sight of Meg panting in the street, his sheepish grin was as close to an apology as she would get. William reached Meg sputtering, "All of them cowards. Ignorant cowards." He shouted to the empty street and the shuttered buildings and to Gerard who had joined them. "*Timendi causa est nescire!* Ignorance is the cause of fear!" He turned again to Meg. "And that's what they are. Afraid and ignorant. Afraid of the rich hands that feed them. Afraid of *you* . . . a slip of a girl who could beat them at their own profession any day."

Meg took his arm and patted it. "As I said, sir, you've done enough. Let us not forget that this is Gerard's important day. We shall celebrate for him, if not for me."

William stopped and looked at them like he was waking from a bad dream. "Yes, yes, of course, you are right." He draped his arm across his son's shoulders. "You have made me proud this day."

"Thank you, Father," Gerard said.

With his free arm, William embraced Meg and pulled her to his side. "Come along then. Fury makes me thirsty."

The Cygnet was located outside the northern wall past the stalls of the laundresses, women with ruddy cheeks and chapped hands whose clamorous voices carried above the beating of wet washing. On the other side of the tavern were the tanners, men whose craft was so malodorous due to the urine used in the tanning process that they were placed outside the city walls—and thus outside the quivering nostrils of most townsfolk. Most of the washerwomen and tanners had closed up shop and were now drinking in the tavern, as were Montpellier's loudest and rowdiest citizens.

The noise assaulted her as soon as she stepped over the threshold. The tavernkeeper, greeting William with a hearty slap on the back, gestured to a table where Robertus and Serafina sat waiting. When Serafina spotted Gerard, she called out, arms extended. He walked to her, a little more lightly in his step Meg thought, and Serafina crushed him to her chest. "Oh, I have missed you, Gerard," she squealed in her lilting accent. "Why do you not come to see me at the market? And now we are traveling again, and I shall think of you forever." Her thick red hair, twisted in a yellow silk chignon held every color of autumn, but her eyes, a startling shade of green, promised not the cool of an autumn morning but the sultry heat of a summer afternoon. Serafina caught sight of Meg and her lips twisted into a sneer.

Gerard, cheeks red, apologized for missing her performances. "I'll come soon," he promised.

Robertus, who made room for William and Meg at the table, raised his eyebrows. "Well?" he asked.

"Gerard, yes. Meg, no," William said.

Meg's body flared hot with humiliation and then anger—anger toward the whim of fate that caused her to be born a girl. Through the fault of her gender, the masters had denied her a place in the medical school. She was ready for the examination and performed well, of that she was sure, but there was nothing she could do about being born a girl.

Robertus took her hand. "Do not lose heart. You did your best." He kissed her fingers. "The Schola Medica has lost a brilliant student. It is *their* loss, my dear, not yours."

Meg said nothing. She struggled to keep tears from sliding down her cheeks.

"Think of the sunshine and not the shadow. William has gained a brilliant assistant."

Shouts and laughter turned her attention to one corner of the tavern where the dwarf Halybutte was leaning over a table, moving three upside-down cups at dizzying speed, as two young men tried to follow the nut hidden in one cup. Meg had watched Halybutte play cups before and knew the young men were soon to be shorn of their riches.

The tavernkeeper brought lamb stew and a hunk of brown bread with fresh butter. The grisettes from Notre Dame des Tables had long ago departed Meg's stomach, and she was ravenous. She ate greedily knowing that in the Cygnet, no one put much stock in manners and wouldn't care if her face was smeared with butter or if lamb stew dribbled across her chest. She was nearly finished with her meal, leaving just one piece of lamb and a shriveled carrot swimming in the broth, when she noticed Serafina, arms lolling across Gerard's chest and shoulders, lips nibbling on his ear lobe. Gerard had been transformed. He was no longer a human being. More like a slobbering wolfhound enjoying a belly rub.

Meg took her knife and speared the lamb with such force that the point went through the trencher bread and stuck to the table. She jerked the knife loose and with the piece of lamb balancing precariously on the tip, threw the meat into Serafina's trencher, causing the broth to splash onto the girl's dark green surcoat.

"Oh, *Mon Dieu*," Serafina yelped, "I bought this only yesterday at the market."

"Meg," Gerard shouted, "you've ruined Serafina's fine dress."

"I thought she should nibble on something more flavorful

than your ear," Meg spit in return.

Gerard borrowed a cloth from the tavernkeeper and wiped at the wet spot, which blossomed in the valley between Serafina's legs. She smiled and murmured something about his kindness.

Disgusted, Meg looked away and marveled—not for the first time—how easily men could be swayed by the attentions of a pretty girl and the inevitable response of the *membrum virile*.

"Meg," William said.

"Yes, sir." There was something about his voice that worried Meg. His look was profoundly serious, as if she was in trouble.

"Yes, sir," she said again.

He reached into the leather bag hanging from his belt. He handed her a small book. She recognized it as the one he had snatched from his chamber at the last minute when they fled London. "I want you to have this. It was meant to be my gift after you passed your examinations." He caught sight of her downcast face. "It is no fault of yours. Those bastards planned to deny you entry from the beginning. Nevertheless, this book is yours. My gift."

She opened the book. *The Trotula Medica from Salerno.* "Oh, Master William, you shouldn't. This is very rare." She looked at him, surprised he would part with it.

"It is yours. You say you want to minister to women. You should have a book by a woman. I do not agree with those who say it was written by a man. I have been to Salerno. I have friends there. They revere Trota in that city and honor her name."

Meg's eyes filled with tears.

"I am sorry for what happened today. Perhaps this will make you feel better."

She threw her arms around his neck and buried her face in his chest. "Thank you, sir."

She glanced at Gerard and Serafina.

Love was fleeting.

A book was forever.

***

By the time they returned to Madame Tisserand's, William was enjoying the mellowing effects of the local wine, and his furious rantings had turned to hopeful reasoning once again. He had a brilliant idea, he told Meg and Gerard. He would approach the regent and apologize for his outburst, then propose that Meg be tutored as an "unofficial" student of the university, perhaps attending medical lectures but not as a legitimate member of the Schola Medica.

"I know you are filled with regret and disappointment and are beyond consoling," he said, "but at the risk of losing a brilliant assistant . . ." She raised her head in surprise. "Oh, yes, Robertus is right, you *are* brilliant, although you shouldn't let it go to your head. At the risk of losing you, I will do all that I can to get you into the school."

Over the next few days, William made numerous attempts to meet with Petrus Muller, but according to a servant who answered the door, the Regent Master had been called to Paris and wouldn't return for several weeks. William found the regent's disappearance too coincidental to be trusted.

Meanwhile, Meg staggered through each day unable to eat or drink and unwilling to pack her things, for it meant giving in to the inevitable. She believed William would not be successful in changing the regent's mind. She struggled like a woman thrown overboard who swims against the current to reach the surface. She could see the light of the sun cutting through the water, but with each kick of her feet and stroke of her arms, she slipped deeper and deeper.

Soon she would join William on the road to Paris and then

Bologna. She felt a stabbing pain in her heart each time she thought about leaving Gerard, but there was no remedy, no potion, and no herbal concoction that would make the pain disappear. In time, perhaps, it would dissipate but it would remain tucked under her heart like a sleeping creature, awakened by a sound, a smell, or a thought that augured a memory.

Four days after her examination at the regent's house, she sat next to Madame Tisserand as the woman wove a piece of linen bordered in pink and blue. Meg, who was twisting wool onto a spindle, sighed deeply and Madame made a motion with her index finger that Meg interpreted as tears falling from her eyes and then placed a palm over Meg's heart.

"Gerard?" Madame asked.

Meg wondered how she would explain in gestures what she could barely put into words. Instead, she attached another section of wool to the thread that took shape as she spun the whorl. They sat in silence, aware only of the *thwack*! of the batten and foot treadles. Suddenly there was a banging on the door. Both Madame and Meg jumped in fright.

"Let me in," William shouted. "Open up!"

Madame unbolted the latch and was swept aside by a breathless William who knelt before Meg and took her hands. "I believe we have found a resolution. Find Gerard and make yourselves presentable. We go to the Regent Master's home in one hour."

Chapter 31

Njata Keita

Montpellier, April 1327

The Regent Master of the Montpellier Schola Medica sat in the open-air courtyard, resplendent in his robe of scarlet velvet lined with gray silk. A salt-laden breeze from the sea ruffled the cypress tree behind him and Meg shivered as she remembered her interrogation on the intricacies of the astrolabe. The smell of salt reminded her of the long voyage from England. England, a green and glorious land, soft, mist-covered, so different from this place with its never-ending sunshine and cacophony of languages: Languedocienne, French, Greek, Arabic, Catalonian, and Aragonese.

The regent pointed to the sweetmeats, stuffed dates, and marzipan swans arranged on the table. "Please, take some refreshment." A servant poured spiced wine into four silver goblets, then glided quietly through the courtyard lighting candles.

While they ate, the regent regaled them with stories of past students who found fame and fortune as doctors of phisik to the rich and well-connected kings of Aragon and Castile. "Perhaps our newest student will someday serve the kings of England," he said, smiling at Gerard. After dabbing his lips with a serviette, he declared with a sniff that some graduates found their calling in helping the poor. "I do not disapprove of ministering to the poor," he said, "but when the poor are cured of their sickness they do not send money to the university in gratitude."

William brought a sweetmeat to his mouth and countered between bites, "That is true, sir, but I have found in my practice that the poor endeavor to pay by whatever means they can, even if the patient has died. The rich, however, endeavor to run away as soon as they are cured. And if the patient dies, they refuse to pay altogether."

The regent laughed. "That is why you must demand payment first, before you even see the patient—yes, yes, your scowl tells me that you disagree—but it's simply good business." He gestured to the well-manicured courtyard around them. "Look around you. The poor did not provide this home, these beautiful flowers, or the food you eat. The rich—the *sick* rich—did that."

He motioned for the servant to refill the goblets. "Speaking of the sick," he said to Gerard, "you will begin this summer in Master Sorianus's anatomy class."

"Thank you, sir," Gerard said. "I appreciate the master's vote of confidence. However, I had hoped to attend with Meg, as you know—"

"None of that," the regent said, pursing his lips as if his wine had turned to verjuice. "I believe we made the right decision as far as the university is concerned. However, we are not without sympathy. We understand your disappointment, and so we have an offer that might make up for our decision."

Meg, who could barely stand to look at the regent and only

half-listened to the conversation, snapped to attention.

"Heed his words, Meg," William said. "He and the masters mean well."

Meg looked at William in confusion. Was he on their side now?

The regent raised his hand, palm toward her. "I understand you are distressed, but if you will listen, you will see that our plan provides an opportunity for you."

"Yes?" Meg asked. It was all she could bear to say to the man.

"There is a midwife in the city who is aged and infirmed. She needs help."

Ah, their great plan is to pawn me off on a decrepit midwife. Meg said nothing leaving the regent to swing on the end of his own words.

"I have taken the liberty of inviting her here so that you might meet her." The regent clapped his hands, and a servant brought in a small hunched woman so ancient she must have birthed thousands of babies, if not more. The old woman attempted a crumpled curtsey toward Meg. "This is Madame Petronilla," the regent said and smiled. "The fruits of her labors are many."

"I do thank this . . ." Meg couldn't think of the proper word. Frail? Feeble? Crippled? Her first description of 'decrepit' seemed apt, but as angry as she was, she couldn't bear to hurt the old woman. "I do thank this generous woman for offering to take me on, but I am afraid I cannot work with her. Master William needs my help as he travels and—"

"Think on it, Meg," William interrupted. "You will remain in Montpellier with Gerard. You will further your skills, perhaps learning new techniques from Madame Petronilla. You said yourself that your dream was to minister to women in need."

"Master William," Meg said, "I do not even speak the language. How am I to learn new skills? The skills I want to learn come from the Schola Medica, not an old healer with a virgin's nut in one hand and a potion in the other." Immediately, she felt her heart constrict with the traitorous words. Old Mother Alice had pressed the virgin's nut into the hands of many panicked mothers and soothed them with oil of violets, among other calming herbs.

William read her expression and frowned, no doubt remembering his old friend.

"What I mean, that is," she stuttered, "there is still the language problem."

"Ah, but we have a solution to your predicament," the regent said.

My predicament? Meg thought, feeling the heat rise to the top of her head. *I do not have a predicament. I have ambitions and desires that you have crushed.*

Muller crooked his finger toward a servant and whispered in the man's ear. The servant left the courtyard, ducking into the house through an arched doorway hidden by espaliered wisteria, its thick trunk winding snake-like over the entrance.

"We have agreed that you need an escort who speaks the local tongue, someone who could accompany you at all times and offer you protection. And someone who does not shrink from medical matters. I think we have found the man."

"Sir?"

"Master William and I were discussing your future and we believe you need a tutor in the art of phisik, an adviser to the best medical practices, and an overseer to your comings and goings, especially when William is gone. Someone must be in authority over you."

Meg relaxed. Finding the right person who fit those descriptions would be impossible.

"Fortunately, there is a scholar within my employ," Muller continued. "His name is Njata Keita. He joined me several years ago as a scribe and copyist."

"What? How can a mere scribe offer advice on medical matters?"

"He has a medical degree from Songare University in Timbuktu. He is not licensed in Montpellier but he most certainly can give advice. He reads in three languages, Arabic, Latin, and Hebrew, and he speaks Italian, English, and Occitan."

"And," William added, "he was the curator of the library of the Caliph of Grenada."

What a stroke of fortune, she thought. *Out of thousands of people in Montpellier, they have found a genius.* She looked toward Gerard hoping he could intercede for her.

Reading her thoughts the regent said, "Gerard will have his own duties. He cannot be expected to tag along with you like a schoolgirl, especially to women's matters."

"But, I do not need a guard. I am more than capable of taking care of myself."

William's hand signal warned her to silence. "Njata is not your guard. He is not your companion. He is your tutor. He is a man of extraordinary scholarship and we are fortunate he has agreed to help you. You will give him the respect he deserves. Yes, he will accompany you when you visit patients but as a translator and escort. If you cannot accept this, you must come with me. In fact, I am making plans to leave for Bologna in the coming weeks."

"Please, Meg, take heed of their offer," Gerard pleaded. "It will not be the same without you."

It? What did "it" mean?

"Then you want me to stay?"

"Think of it," Gerard said. "This is an opportunity for you. And who knows? Perhaps the faculty will see how well you put your words into practice and vote to accept you."

The regent motioned toward the archway. "If you stay, you will offer your skills to Madame Petronilla who will teach you all she knows about midwifery. You will be accompanied by Njata Keita who will also tutor you in advanced medical knowledge."

Coming her way was a tall black man, carrying himself rigidly erect, walking with silent footsteps as if he were floating above the earth. He was dressed in a yellow robe, a matching yellow turban, and pointed red leather shoes that curled above his toes. A necklace of small white shells adorned his throat and clicked softly as he walked.

He bowed. "Mistress Meg," he said.

She cast a sideways glance at the man. No doubt he had his orders to report back to the regent, bishop, and masters. If she stirred up trouble, they would know about it in an instant.

"One would think you'd be grateful to have a benefactor as generous as William," the regent was saying. "He is willing to pay Njata to function as your tutor. He is paying me for the loss of Njata's services. And he will pay Madame Petronilla to teach you the ways of midwives."

And then she understood.

The regent had thrown a sop to William, a concession to stop his complaining and causing trouble, to make sure William kept Gerard at the university and more importantly to keep William's money forthcoming. The regent's plan to foist her off on Madame Petronilla meant William would be happy, Gerard would be happy, and presumably *she* would be happy. Meanwhile William's son would become a doctor of phisik, the regent and masters would be paid, the school wouldn't be vexed by the notion of a female asking to join the male students, and she would do what they expected of her.

Her dreams meant nothing to anyone, not William or Gerard despite their love for her, and least of all the masters. Nothing to anyone but herself.

To stay or go? To leave Gerard or stay with Njata?

"I will stay," she said.

Muller nodded to William. Meg had the uncomfortable feeling that the nod was more of a private handshake. "In truth, you have no choice," the Regent Master added. "The arrangements have been made."

Chapter 32

MISTRAL

Montpellier, April 1327

The wind had been blowing for days. It roared from the north-west like a beast driven to madness, sucking at Meg's breath and clawing at her clothes. Its constancy made her irritable.

"Mistral," muttered Njata as a gust of wind made her stagger. He seized her elbow and steadied her. "Winter and spring."

Meg grunted, instantly irritated by his voice. A man of few words, Njata never spoke unless addressed and even then in short sentences. But in truth, his silence unnerved her more than his few words of speech. He kept to himself, but when she left Madame Tisserand's, and ventured into the city, he was her constant shadow, as if sewn to her side. In the evening he ate alone and retired early.

Struggling ahead of them, twisting against each gust, was a scruffy boy whose ragged clothes were held together only by dirt. He was guiding them to his mother, in labor with her tenth child. He shouted at Meg to hurry, but a blast of wind hit them hard causing them to stumble backwards, as if the mistral warned them to keep away.

"Where is the street?" she shouted. Njata translated for the boy, who pointed ahead, his words lost to the wind.

She hunched her shoulders, head down, until Njata said, "Here it is." He pointed around the corner. "Rue de Bon Astre."

She raised her head. They were in a section of the city near the tanneries where the houses were old and crumbling. The messenger boy had disappeared—swallowed, Meg imagined, by the blustering beast that engulfed the city.

They entered the building and climbed rickety stairs to the second floor, where the number five painted above the door signaled their destination, a fact she would have known regardless, as the groans of a laboring mother reached her before the top step. She sighed, dreading what she would find behind the door.

Her meeting with Madame Petronilla—the meeting Petrus Muller, the regent master, insisted upon—had been a disaster. Muller demanded she learn the old woman's procedures and meet her patients, but Meg learned that madame's "procedures" consisted of letting Nature take its course with patients she barely knew. As the old woman talked—Njata translating Meg's questions and the midwife's answers—it became clear that her senses had been lost to old age. Njata offered no comment when Meg slammed madame's door on the way out, grumbling, "An idiot! God help anyone in her care!"

Now they were attending the first labor under madame's charge. According to the midwife, the labor would be quick with no complications.

"A couple of grunts and that will be that," she had predicted.

Meg knocked and entered a disheveled room, grimy with dirt and soot, and gloomy despite the morning sunshine which shone feebly through a narrow, unshuttered window. The single room was home to the laboring woman, her husband, and their four children. The other seven children had died of pox or fevers or were stillborn.

A straw pallet covered with dirty linen homespun lay on the floor. On it, Meg's patient thrashed from side to side, knees up, heels dug in. Her eyes were clenched shut against the pain.

Sleeping next to the woman was Madame Petronilla.

"Madame Petronilla!" Meg shouted at the midwife. "Do your duty to your patient!" But the midwife would not be roused. Despite the mother's flailing arms and legs, Madame Petronilla slept on, as if enchanted. "God's balls," Meg muttered.

Njata jerked his head toward her and scowled. "It is unseemly for a young woman to swear. Remember your place."

Meg felt flames shoot out of her ears. *What right did he have to chastise her*? And then she remembered William's admonishment: You are to respect him.

"Yes, Master Njata," she said.

The laboring woman, startled to hear a strange voice, opened her eyes. Meg reached for her hand and squeezed it. "My name is Meg. I am here to help you."

The women sucked in her breath and exhaled an "Oh." Meg, aware her sunken cheek, raw from the morning cold, and her sloping eye weeping tears from the wind would be a shock, paid her no heed. She was used to stares and comments, and could usually ignore the gawpers. What she couldn't ignore were the intentional malicious comments such as those the bishop made during her examination. He had used her deformity as an excuse to deny her a place in medical school, saying she would scare the patients. Well, here was her first patient in Montpellier. Her first test.

Meg dropped her birthing bag of tools, dry rags and swaddling blankets, potions, and oils onto the straw pallet.

Master Njata explained to the woman that Meg would serve as her midwife. The woman nodded, instantly trusting Meg to do what she needed. She pointed to the sleeping Petronilla and said something to Njata who translated the words: "She says

Madame Petronilla arrived early this morning and—"

"Tell that good-for-nothing midwife to wake up."

Sweating as if it were the height of summer, Njata wiped his face with the end of his turban and called out to Madame Petronilla. Meg wanted to ask him if he was repulsed by pain, blood, and sickness. Maybe that's why he wasn't a practicing doctor of phisik. *May the Virgin help me*, she thought, *the regent master has burdened me with a tutor who has a weak stomach and a midwife who is an idiot.*

Still, Madame Petronilla refused to move. Meg looked closer. There was something odd about her, her unnatural stillness despite the kicks and punches of the woman lying next to her, her deafness to Njata's entreaties, her white pallor, as if the blood had drained . . . Njata must have had the same thought for he felt the woman's neck and quickly looked at Meg.

"Mort," he said.

The laboring woman shrieked and tried to crawl out of bed, but her huge abdomen forced her backwards against Madame Petronilla's body. The more the woman tried to push herself away, the more entangled she became in Madame's arms and legs.

"Njata, move Madame Petronilla," Meg ordered. "Take her away, I don't care where, just get her out of here.

Njata raised himself to his full height and scowled. "It is *Master* Njata to you, young woman. I am your tutor and translator, not your servant. It is not my job to hoist a dead woman to my shoulders and carry her around like a sack of dead cats. I do not take orders from you. On the contrary, *you* are to take orders from me."

"What? I don't remember hearing those words come out of Muller's mouth or from Master William."

The woman screamed as the next pain overtook her. She pushed at Petronilla, trying to move the dead weight off the bed.

"Do you expect this poor laboring woman to give birth

next to a dead person?" Meg put her fists against her hips.

"I will this once and only this once remove a dead person. But if any of your teachers or patients die in the future, I will not touch them." He hoisted the old midwife to his shoulders and walked down the stairs. Meg heard him grumbling to himself and calling out something in a foreign language. Cursing her no doubt.

She seized her patient by the shoulders and helped her to lie flat, talking to her in a quiet voice, as if lying next to a dead woman while giving birth was the most natural event in the world. When the woman settled down, Meg pushed against her knees and spread her legs, opening the entry to her womb. She was stunned to see the baby's head crowning. Two minutes later, with a great push and a gush of blood and water, the baby arrived.

Nature had indeed taken its course.

Once the afterbirth was expelled and the mother wiped clean, Meg wrapped the howling newborn in swaddling clothes and changed the linen on the bed, finishing just as the husband and children returned from a neighbor's house. With the baby successfully latched onto the mother's nipple and vigorously tugging at the breast, Meg packed her medicine bag, feeling that she had done all she could. She promised she would return in a few days but the woman merely mumbled something which Meg took to mean 'thank you.' Her husband pressed two coins into Meg's hand as she slipped out the door. Meg wished the bishop had been present to see the satisfied looks from the husband and wife. Obviously, she had passed the test despite her shocking face. Her deformity was of no consequence to a mother in the throes of labor. Indeed, a laboring mother would have the hounds of hell deliver her as long as the deed was done.

Njata stood outside, his back to the wind. Next to him lay Madame Petronilla who was propped against the building, head slumped to one side as if in a drunken stupor. Njata was ashen, his face awash with sweat, his eyes sunken and glazed.

"Master Njata, what is the meaning of this?" she asked. "Why have you left her here on the street like a piece of rubbish? Take her somewhere. Find someone to help us. You can't—"

"I am not a complete idiot. I have done that," he gasped. "The boy who showed us the way here is fetching the parish priest. And I would remind you I am not your lap dog to be kicked when you . . ." He gasped and held his side.

Meg frowned, thinking there was nothing else to do but wait. She certainly couldn't leave Madame Petronilla's body to rot on the street like a beggar. She had been angry after meeting with the midwife, but now her anger was as strong as the wind blowing around them. How dare Madame Petronilla accept her as an apprentice and then die!

In a few minutes, the priest ran toward them, followed by a stout man at the handles of a two-wheeled cart. As the men lifted the corpse, Njata gripped the wheel of the handcart and fell forward.

"Master Njata! What are you doing? What is wrong?" Meg asked.

Raising his head, Njata stood, faced her, took a small step, and tumbled to the ground.

"Njata!" she shouted. As she knelt by him, he attempted to sit up but fell back to the street, senseless and mute. She felt his forehead and the skin of his cheeks and pulled her hand away as if she had been scalded.

Njata burned with fever.

The priest and his helper, horrified at the sight of the sick African, dashed toward the church with Madame Petronilla's body bouncing in the cart. The boy who had guided them to his mother's bedside and who had run for the priest still stood in the street, his mouth agape. With hand gestures and the rudiments of the boy's native tongue, Meg coaxed him to her side. She told him to hurry to Madame Tisserand's and fetch William and Gerard along with a horse and wagon. She put a coin in one palm and held up her other hand indicating that he would get a second coin when he returned.

"Quickly, *vite, vite,*" she said, shooing him onward.

The wind pounded her again and blew dust into Njata's face. His turban tumbled off his head and bits of dirt and sand caught in his black curly hair. He looked vulnerable, not at all like the formidable tutor who irritated her. She reached for the turban as another gust overtook them and gently slipped it on his head. He groaned and his eyes rolled back until only the whites could be seen.

Njata was ill—seriously ill—by the looks of it. That explained the sweating. He wasn't queasy or weak of stomach near the sickbed— he was actually sick.

"Stay still," she cautioned. He lifted his head, tried to focus on her, but collapsed again. She reached to touch his shoulder but stopped herself. She had found that reaching the sick, perhaps stroking the forehead, the hair, or holding hands, had many uses—calming patients, alleviating pain, and sometimes in a mysterious way, travelling across an unseen bridge to meet them in a place where their senses had flown. She often brought them back from that place within themselves, back across the bridge to enter the land of the living once more. She wouldn't have hesitated to touch most patients, but Njata was different. Rigid and proud, he would have been embarrassed to know that she had stroked his forehead or held his hand.

After what seemed like a lifetime of waiting, the messenger boy came running to her, his hand outstretched for the other coin. Behind him, struggling breathlessly against the wind were Gerard and William, pushing a barrow.

"A barrow?" she asked. "Couldn't you have brought a cart?"

"No, this was all we could find," William said. "Madame uses it to carry her cloth to the market stall. She let us borrow it."

"It will have to do then."

She and Gerard lifted Njata by his arms as William grabbed his feet. The African looked absurd in the barrow, his legs flopping over the sides, head lolling to and fro as if he were drunk.

William and Gerard took turns pushing him through the city as passersby stared or laughed at the spectacle.

Meg shouted at them, "Go about your business! Go on now!"

When they arrived at Madame Tisserand's, William and Gerard lifted Njata by his armpits with Meg grasping his ankles, and somehow, they managed to maneuver his dead weight up to the tiny room at the top of the stair. He roused and began babbling in his native tongue. The strange words sounded like water flowing over stones, but then he cried out as if he were in pain.

"Shhhh, Master Njata, it is all right. You are safe now," Meg said. "We've brought you home."

Chapter 33

A Plea to Bembaa

Montpellier, April 1327

Meg tended to Njata for several hours, struggling in vain to bring down his fever with wet cloths and comfrey tea mixed with honey and mint. Occasionally, William or Gerard would knock on the door and inquire as to his progress; she would shake her head, perplexed by the tenacity of the disease. In late afternoon, Gerard entered the room and announced that William would bleed Njata.

"He is waiting for the most efficacious time to bleed since we know nothing of Njata's birth," said Gerard.

Njata, who had roused from his stupor when Meg put the tea to his lips, whispered in a rasping voice, "No bleeding."

"It is for the best. Master William has great knowledge of such things," Meg said and patted his face with a wet cloth.

"No! I do not want to be bled."

Gerard glanced at Meg, then left to fetch William.

Meg put another pot of water on the fire for tea. She carried a bucket of cool water upstairs and changed the cloth on Njata's forehead. The fever showed no signs of abating. Njata was sweating again. He threw off the covers and groaned.

"Njata, you need the cover to sweat out the fever," she said, trying to spread the blanket around him.

His glassy eyes searched for her and he shouted, "Ah-eee! My head is a *djembo*. Beating. Beating." Beads of sweat dotted his forehead and his upper lip. He held his palm against his temples and pressed. Twisting in the bed, he arched his back and dug his heels into the pallet. "*Fafalo*, it hurts. My head. My body."

"That's the fever. You'll be better once the drink takes effect," Meg said.

As he lay down, squirming to find a restful position on the pallet, she wiped away the sweat from his face and pulled the covers to his chest. He slapped her hand and snarled at her—

"Stay away, *bwa*, witch"—then he stared at the wall opposite, cocking his head as if listening to commands from an invisible spirit. "The evil wind brings her, my mother. She and the *jinnoo*, they steal me to the place of death." He waved his hands as if swatting at flies, then turned his head and staring at the ceiling, said in a normal voice, "And how are you today, great Mansa? Are you well? No evil spirits in the night?"

A knock interrupted him. William peeked around the door and said, "I have more tea. Meadowsweet I bought from the market and willow bark. It should help with the fever."

"Thank you, sir," Meg said. "He is delirious as well."

Njata sat upright, his arms crossed as if protecting his body, and looked with wild unfocused eyes at William. "Bastard! Get away, *nbula bila*. Leave me alone." He reached for Meg. "Oh, my mother."

Meg leaned to him and put her arms round his shoulders. "William will not hurt you. He wants to give you a hot drink to make you better." Njata collapsed as if the last outburst had sapped all will from his body. Meg hugged him gently and said, "Do not be afraid. We are all your friends here."

When Njata grew steady and was breathing regularly, she pulled him to a half-sitting position, took the cup from William, and brought the drink to Njata's lips. A trickle of the liquid ran down his chin and, following a rivulet of wrinkle in his neck, pooled on his chest. Meg blotted it with a cloth and then braced his back as he lay back down.

"*Nbati, mamamusuo*," Njata whimpered. "Help me, my mother, my grandmother." He brought his knees to his chest and cried as if he were a frail infant left to die on the street.

Meg put a hand on his shoulder and pressed gently. "Sleep now. We will not hurt you. You must trust us, Njata, for we will do everything we can to cure you."

Soon, his breathing became rhythmic and his lips parted as the pain eased. Finally resting, he fell into a deep sleep.

While Njata slept, William and Meg ate a small meal and then walked in the sunshine. The mistral had died down, blowing now only in fits and starts, as if the beast had exhausted itself.

They rested for an hour until Njata began to stir upstairs. Meg found him awake and sitting up. "How are you feeling?" she asked and felt his forehead.

Njata frowned. "Better, but arrows are in my mouth."

"What arrows?" William asked.

Njata pointed to the back of his throat. "The ones here. They hurt. I cannot swallow."

William paused as a commotion downstairs—two women shouting at each other—grew louder. One voice belonged to Madame Tisserand, who was shouting "non, non, non"; the other voice, taut with panic, was Serafina's.

"Meg," William barked, "Go see what is happening."

Meg raced downstairs and then ran back, taking the steps two at a time, with Sarafina following behind, her hair flying in all directions like Medusa.

"Well, what is it?" William said, as Meg and Serafina entered the room. He pulled the covers to Njata's chest. "This man is ill. I've no time for trifles."

"They've taken Robertus," Serafina said.

"What? Who?"

Serafina was wringing her hands, looking first at Njata and then Gerard. "The bishop's men, sir. They took him to the bishop's palace. He is to stand trial."

"For what?" scoffed William. "Fleecing the gullible? Surely that is a matter for the city, not the bishop."

"No, he pays the city fathers from each day's profits," explained Serafina. "The bishop says he has committed a crime against the church for turning water into wine, a sacrilege." She burst into tears. "Please sir, you must help us. The bishop said his dungeons are so deep Master Robertus will never see the light of day."

"Ridiculous," William sneered. "I'll speak to the bishop. It won't take much to convince him that magic tricks are harmless. Meg, stay here. We won't be long."

Meg sat beside Njata throughout the afternoon. He twisted and turned, calling out in a drunken half-sleep to *bembaa* to help him. Finally, as he fell into a deep sleep, she slipped downstairs and ate a bowl of hot fish broth with Madame Tiserrand.

In the middle of the night, when the church bells of the nearby Franciscan monastery signaled the monks to prayer, Meg woke and stole quietly downstairs expecting to see William and Gerard talking over the day's events, but the front room was dark and empty. She prowled around the house and could find no one but Madame Tisserand snoring on her pallet in the kitchen.

Fearing Njata would wake and need her, she brought two more tallow candles upstairs along with another cup of wine, but when she tiptoed into the room, she could see that he was deep in sleep. He hadn't moved in hours and his expression, usually so serious, had softened in rest.

In the morning, his breathing was regular, but his forehead and cheeks still felt warm. The fever held on tight. She must have roused him when she placed her hands on his face, for he kicked and pulled at the covers.

She grabbed his hand and whispered, "No. Njata, you must stay still."

He groaned and rolled from side to side, as if trying to escape an unseen enemy.

"The arrows," he groaned. He pulled at his neck. His voice was rough. "Hurt. My throat."

"Let me see, Njata." She pulled a candle closer and held it near his head. "Open your mouth."

She pulled the candle near, careful not to spill hot wax on him, and peered down his throat. Her heart skipped a beat. "Stick your tongue out." She looked again. No mistake. "Close your mouth," she said.

She must get William and Gerard immediately. Her safety and theirs—indeed the whole city's welfare—was at stake.

There were no arrows stuck in Njata's throat. It was worse than arrows. Arrows killed one at a time. This sickness could kill hundreds.

Chapter 34

THE SPOTTED DEATH

Montpellier, April 1327

"Small pox."

"Are you sure?" William asked her as he climbed the steps two at a time.

"I believe so, sir. I had it myself when I was four years. Alice cured me, but I have this pox scar as a reminder." Meg pulled her braid away from her neck and pointed to a scar where a pustule scab once formed. "I was fortunate to live through it."

She was returning to Njata's sickbed, her arms laden with expensive red silk cloth. Fortunately, when she asked Madame Tisserand where she might find the special red cloth at the market, madame had led her to a cupboard where she had it hidden in a locked drawer. The cloth was crucial to the cure.

Now as William knelt by Njata and examined him, it was

clear that pustules had multiplied over night. They were ev-erywhere. On his face, his legs and arms, his stomach, inside his ears and nose, on the soles of his feet. Not an inch of skin was spared.

"Yes. You're right, Meg," William declared. "Small pox. There is nothing we can do except make him comfortable. Treat the fever and hope for the best."

"Mother Alice favored the like-to-like cure. That is why I asked Madame Tisserand if she had any red cloth. Fortunately, she had this locked away." Meg patted the folded silk she laid at the end of Njata's bed. "Thank you for purchasing this, Master William."

The red silk, Montpellier's most expensive fabric, used in the courts of kings, had cost William a king's ransom which he paid to Madame Tisserand. She had locked the money in the drawer immediately.

"Alice used to say 'Red cloth for red bumps. Red to red from window to bed.' And red food and drink. If you'll help me, sir, we can hang it from the window."

"Gerard will help you. I must leave for a while."

Gerard had stepped in and was unwrapping the silk. "Should he have red wine?"

"If he is Muslim, he doesn't drink wine," William said.

"I am *not* Muslim," Njata snarled, startling them. Meg jumped. She had thought him asleep. "I am Malinke. I will drink your wine. But what is this?" He pulled at the red cloth which Meg had draped over him. Gerard was tucking the edges under the pallet. "What is this?"

Meg explained the cure of like-for-like. "It must stay on your bed, Master Njata. We'll hang some on the window as well. The room and your bedding must be red."

"You English, you have lost your heads with your ridicu-lous red cloth." Njata scoffed.

"Master Njata, it is a good cure. Please." she pulled the cloth out of his fingers and spread it from his neck to his feet.

"Bah! You should be thinking about yourselves. Who of you has had this sickness, what you call the small pox?"

"I have," Meg answered.

"And I," William said. "But Gerard has not."

"Then I must help you, Gerard," Njata said.

"What can you do? You are a sick man, Njata," Gerard said.

"In my homeland, we call this The Spotted Death. It is *finyabana*, a wind illness. The mistral must have brought it to me. Before the Arabs invaded, many of my people died of this *finyabana*, but the Arabs have a cure and they taught it to us."

"What are you talking about Njata?" William asked.

He collapsed on his bed and waved his hand, "I must rest. My back hurts, so painful. And my head. Later. I will explain later. But you must do exactly as I say or Gerard could die."

Meg's heart stopped. "Yes, of course."

"And for now, Gerard, you must stay indoors, out of the wind."

"But I have to see Sera—"

"Do as he says," William ordered. "You are at risk. In the meantime, we foolish English will give you a red room, Njata,"

"And red wine. And pomegranates," Meg said. "The redder the better."

"Yes. It can't hurt and it might help. Now I must go to Maguelone and try to get our friend Robertus out of the bishop's jail. I'll be back in two days."

✳✳✳

The next morning, Master Njata asked Meg to go outside and pick a thorn off Madame Tisserand's rose bush. "A large thorn," he said. "Strong, with the sharpest point."

When she brought the thorn to him, he asked her to fetch Gerard and to find a quill, unused if possible.

She found Gerard sulking by the fire. "Master Njata is ready for you," she said. "And bring a fresh quill."

"This is ridiculous," Gerard said as found the quill and stomped up the stairs. "Everyone knows there is no cure for small pox. What does he want with a quill?"

"I don't know. Humor him. It will help him get better."

Njata sat with his back against the wall. He held the thorn in one hand and reached for the quill. "Hand me your arm, please, Gerard. Palm up." Njata gripped Gerard's wrist hard. "Gerard, I will be gentle, but it may hurt."

"What are you going to do?" Gerard asked, his voice shaking.

"This is a cure long known to my people. You will be sick for only a day or two and it will be mild compared to what I have."

Meg dropped to her knees. "What? Are you going to give him small pox on purpose? No, no, no, Njata."

Gerard tried to pull his arm from Njata's grip, but the African held steady. He reached for the flesh of Gerard's forearm, thorn ready and scratched the skin, barely breaking the surface. "My hands are shaking. I am too weak. You will have to help me, Meg."

"No. What if it doesn't work? What if he dies?"

Gerard looked like a rabbit caught in a snare, shivering, wide-eyed.

"Do you love this man?" Njata asked.

"What?"

"Answer me."

"Yes, I do," she said.

"Then you must do as I say. If you do not, he has a higher chance of dying."

Meg sniffled and wiped away tears. He put the thorn in her hand and with his finger drew three imaginary parallel marks across Gerard's forearm. "Follow that. You do not have to go deep, but there must be blood."

"Meg," Gerard was begging, "for the love of God, please don't." He pushed against Njata's chest and pulled at his grip.

"Stay still!" Njata barked. "The children in my village be-have better than you. Do it, Meg."

Quickly she scored three lines and watched as droplets of blood oozed out of the scratches.

"Now, take the quill and open one of my pustules."

"No."

"Do it."

She watched as the tip of the quill pierced a pustule near his shoulder blade. A thick yellow viscous liquid seeped out.

"Put the tip of the quill onto the scratch and let the pus run into it."

She looked at Gerard and shook her head, as if her mind could send the words.

"Mother of God, I cannot believe you are doing this," Ge-rard breathed.

When she ran out of pus, she opened another pustule, and repeated the action until all three scratches were covered. Gerard was crying silently. So was she.

"Very good," Njata said. "Now we wait."

Meg and Gerard pulled an extra pallet into Njata's red room so Meg could care for both men. She pulled a piece of red silk off the wall and wrapped it around Gerard's shoulders.

"I will never trust you again," Gerard hissed.

***

The fever started in the middle of the night. Shivering fol-lowed. Swelling and redness surrounded the three scratches on Gerard's forearm. Meg wiped him with cool wet cloths as sweat poured down his face. The shivering began again. She covered him and then turned him on his side with his back to her. She lay down next to him and put her arms around him, holding him tightly as he shivered with each spasm.

"I love you, Gerard," she whispered. "Please don't die. I will never forgive myself."

The shivering stopped. She thought he had fallen asleep. Then he whispered, "I love you, too." The room was silent except for Njata's snuffle. Meg held her breath, but Gerard said nothing else. She fell into a worried, anxious sleep until the morning sun streamed through the red curtain and turned the room the color of dawn.

***

"You did *what?*"

Meg trembled. She was trying to tell William why his son was upstairs suffering from small pox, but only a little bit of small pox, certainly not enough to kill him, and Njata knows what he is doing, sir, so please don't be mad.

"I can understand that Gerard might get small pox naturally, but you are telling me that you actually *gave* it to him? Are you mad?" He bounded up the stairs, driven by his fury at Meg and Njata.

"Do not blame Meg, sir," Njata said. "She was only following my orders. I had to act quickly before Gerard got small pox from the wind. It is better to control the disease—"

"I'm sorry, Master William," Meg sobbed. "You know I would never hurt Gerard."

"But you could have killed him. He may still die."

Her crying started afresh. She tried to control her sobs, but, in the light of William's rage, she was horrified at what she had done.

"Father, I am feeling better," Gerard called from his pallet on the floor. "Meg has taken good care of me. The fever seems to have diminished and the chills have stopped. For the love of all the saints in heaven, Meg, stop crying. You haven't done anything wrong."

Meg gulped and wiped her eyes. "You know I would never hurt you."

"I know that," he said gently. "But if you don't bring me some food, I will surely starve to death. And no pomegranates or red wine. I want beef broth. Brown beef broth."

As Njata described the method and reasoning behind the Arab treatment, William settled down. When Njata explained that Gerard would never catch the small pox again, William's curiosity got the better of him. He examined Gerard's forearm and the dozen pustules on his son's body.

He looked at Meg. "And you did this?"

"Yes, sir." She started crying again.

"Meg, stop," William said. "I'm not mad. I'm impressed at your bravery."

"Thank you, sir." She brought Gerard a bowl of broth and Njata bread with butter. "Master William, I was thinking about, well, everything last night, this horrible sickness, and how the wind brings it, and I wondered about the other people in Montpellier."

"What about them?" William asked.

"Well, sir, what if Njata's treatment worked for everyone?"

"Are you suggesting we should give everyone in Montpellier this treatment?" Gerard asked. "How would that even be possible?"

"Not everyone, but maybe your friends, Gerard. Maybe others who need it, like families whose children are in danger of catching it . . ."

"First, Meg, no one is going to believe us," William said. "How do we explain that we make people better by actually giving them small pox? And second, how do we know Njata's treatment is going to work with Gerard—no offense to you, Master Njata."

Njata nodded. "You are right, sir. Sometimes there are deaths from the scarification, poisons get into the wound, or there is too much or too little small pox rubbed into the scratches. Not everyone survives the treatment."

Gerard and Meg stared at each other in horror. "You're

telling this to me now, Njata?" Gerard asked. "I thought you were sure."

"There is no surety in life, my son," Njata said. "We do what we can to help and then we hope."

"Well, that's a good enough reason why we stay here until the small pox blows over," William said. "There is no way we can help everyone in the city. And even if we wanted to help your friends, Gerard, or anyone else, we cannot take the risk. If we gave someone the treatment and they died, the consequences are too great—an inquest, court, and worse. In addition, Gerard's future is at stake. Not to mention Njata or Meg being found guilty of murder. I'm sorry, Meg, but we must take care of each other and leave the rest of the city to chance."

"I understand, sir," Meg said. She had no desire to be hauled into court for trying to save people. She would concentrate on saving Gerard and Njata.

✳✳✳

Three weeks later, when Njata's scabs had fallen off and the fever had vanished, Meg coaxed him outdoors where he could soak up the afternoon sunshine. Gerard helped him navigate the stairs and lowered him onto the bench beside the rose bush.

Once Njata was resting, Gerard thanked him and Meg for their excellent care. Gerard's fever lasted only twelve hours and he was back on his feet within three days, with only a handful of scabs and three impressive striations on his forearm.

"To have such a dangerous sickness for only a short time and to get well so fast, well, it was astounding," Gerard said. "I'm so fortunate that you were living with us, Master Njata, and could share your amazing treatment."

"Thank you," Njata mumbled.

Gerard waved farewell and started to walk away.

"Wait, Gerard," Meg called. "I, uh, I have something to ask you."

261

"Yes?"

"The first night you were sick, do you remember when I spoke to you? When I was holding you to keep you warm?"

"I was feverish, I don't know."

"Do you remember saying something to me?"

"No. I don't remember anything. Why?"

"Oh." Meg swallowed. "It was nothing. Nothing at all. So, where might you be going now?"

His blush was answer enough. He waved and was gone. *Serafina*, she thought. He had been spending every free moment with the girl, lately sneaking home long after the night watchman called curfew. Meg hadn't any idea what he saw in her. The girl was silly, flighty, and flirtatious. She couldn't possibly cook a meal or use a spindle whorl. Her only virtue was her beauty. She watched Gerard walk up the street, no, *skip* up the street, and she knew that she would never be the cause of such joyfulness in his steps. She wasn't silly or flighty, and the good Lord was certainly aware that, try as she might, flirting was beyond her ken. She could stitch up a man's belly, but let that same man banter with her, and she grew as dumb as a stone.

Well, never mind then, she told herself. *Your patient sits beside you. He is the one who matters. Let Gerard sow his oats in Serafina's field. He would rue the day—of that she was sure— pray for crop failure more like.*

As Njata rested his head against the warm stone wall of the house, he let out a sigh. "A beautiful day," he said. "I am happy to be here among good people."

Meg stretched and lifted her face to the sky, eyes closed against the brilliant sunshine. Master Njata was right about one thing—it *was* a beautiful day. The punishing winds of the mistral had disappeared as mysteriously as they arrived and in their place was an unnatural calm and a dazzling blue sky. At the end of the street, climbing roses unfolded against the city wall and every so often a gentle breeze brought the sweet scent of musk.

Njata shifted on the bench and she asked, "Are you all right?"

"I still itch in places." He examined his arms and hands. He would have scars from the pustules, he said, including at least four on his face, but it was a small price to pay for living through such a terrible sickness. "You have given me good care. Without your help—and William and Gerard's—I would not be sitting here today." He tilted his head toward the sun and closed his eyes, a sudden frown dampening his good mood.

"I have a confession to make, Mistress Meg. I'm afraid I cannot keep this secret any longer. It hurts my heart and makes me ashamed of my deceit."

"What is it, Master Njata?"

"I lied."

"About what?"

"About the small pox."

"But your small pox was real. I saw the pustules. I see the scars on your face. There is nothing deceitful in that."

"Not about *my* small pox, but Gerard's."

Meg's heart stopped mid-beat. "Gerard had small pox too. I saw his pustules and his scars."

"Yes, I was glad that it went well. I was worried."

"But you said the treatment was used by your people. I assumed that you had ministered to the sick, that you had scarred them with the pox."

"No. That is my deceit. I have never seen it done. Small pox has not been in my village for many, many years. I've only heard the old people talking about it. And I read about it in the Arab medical texts at Songare University."

"You mean you have never seen that treatment used?"

"No. I have never seen it."

"You yourself have never used it on anyone."

"No. I have never used it on anyone."

"God's balls."

"Yes."

She stood and walked away, rubbing her forehead, trying to absorb what she had been told.

"Why, Njata?" she asked. "Why take that chance?"

"Because I knew Gerard had a good chance at living if we treated him, but a poor chance if we left it to the wind. I am sorry."

"Good afternoon," William shouted from across the street. "It is wonderful indeed to see you up and about, Njata. Do you mind if I join you?"

Meg and Njata moved over on the bench before William collapsed and exhaled as if he had run a footrace. "These trips to Maguelone are beginning to wear thin. And to wear upon my usual self-assurance. I have yet to see the bishop or Medicamus. The guards refuse me entrance." He rubbed his elbow. "Today they were rougher than usual."

They talked about several ways to free Medicamus, all of which were doomed to failure given the bishop's stubborn belief that he mocked the sacrament when he turned water into wine.

"There isn't a plan in the world that will work with that intractable, pompous . . ."

Meg peered at William curiously. If anyone was hatching a plan—in secret—it was William. She had no idea what it might be, but something mysterious was going on. One of Robertus's players had been coming to the house every night for a week now, just as it got dark. He would knock, William would answer, and they would have a short discussion outside. One night she asked William what the man wanted, but he just smiled enigmatically and said, "Nothing."

They sat in companionable silence for a few minutes, faces upturned to the balminess of the day until Meg remembered the question she was going to ask before William joined them.

"I have a question, Master Njata," she said, "if you feel like talking."

"Yes, what is it?"

"When you were delirious, you spoke of your homeland, your mother, and your grandmother."

"It was a dream—"

"Where did you come from?"

"My people are the Malinke."

"Where do they live? Is it where you were born?"

"Meg," William chided, "perhaps these are things Njata is too sick to discuss."

"No, no," Njata said. "I will be happy to tell you my story, but I must warn you, it is long and windy. Perhaps you have more important duties."

"No, Master Njata." She would sit by his side for hours to assuage the guilt she felt for her treatment of him—she could hardly believe she had made the poor sick man lift a dead woman and carry her to the street.

He coughed once and sat straighter on the bench, as if gathering the courage to speak. He cleared his throat. "Well, then, I will begin. I was born in the village of Lawalo, a place many, many months to the south of here between the Great Sand Sea and the Djoliba River, a river wider and longer than any I have ever seen."

He stared ahead, as if searching for a river in his memory, as if in his mind's eye he floated on the massive waters of the Djoliba. He roused himself, coming back to shore as his memory sharpened.

"Eight days after my birth the holy man held my name-giving ceremony, the *kaliyoo*. He shaved my head. He prayed. And then he held me in his hands and raised me above his head. He shouted my name, Njata Keita, the name he had seen in his vision." Njata dropped his voice to a low timbre, allowing the words to roll off his tongue, mimicking the holy man's prediction: "Henceforth this child will be called Njata Keita. He will be a giver of languages, a writer of words, and the redeemer and protector of a special book."

"A book?" Meg asked. "What kind of book?"

Njata lifted his head as if the holy man's words still swirled within his mind. "He said the book would be written by a woman and it would be read for generations to come."

"Who was the woman?"

"He did not say. The villagers scoffed at this, for no woman has the sense to write, but the holy man became angry and said his visions were sent by the gods who knew the future. My mother was pleased, but I had no wish to be a scholar. I wanted to be a warrior like my father."

He smiled ruefully. "As you can see, that boyish desire did not come to pass. But the holy man was right about the languages and words. I still do not know what he meant about the special book. And I do not know a woman who can write." He turned to Meg as if struck by a thought. "No woman that is, except you."

"Yes, thanks to Master William."

William stirred from a sun-drenched torpor. "My pleasure. You are an easy pupil."

Njata took a deep breath. "My father tried to teach me the ways of warriors, but he could tell I was hopeless." He smiled at the memory. "He was a great man. Strong. Tall. Much respected. He was the *dugu tigi*, the village master, and a skilled archer. He had one-hundred quiver masters at his beck and call." He paused and then sighed heavily. "Still, we were no match for the army that invaded our land."

"Who were they? The invaders, I mean," Meg asked.

"Powerful men from the East. They spoke Arabic and made us change our religion to Islam. To please the Mansa, the great ruler, my father sent me to Niani when I was seven years to live at the Mansa's court and to learn his ways. I studied hard and learned to read and write Arabic. I traveled with the Mansa and saw many amazing sites in the land of the Arabs. When I was fifteen years, the Mansa sent me to Sonkare University in the great city of Timbuktu."

William raised his eyebrows. "Ah, I've heard of it. A place

of brilliant scholars. And great wealth."

Njata nodded. "Many rich men. Merchants especially. And yes, brilliant scholars. Eminent teachers from Cairo, Baghdad, and other great cities. And about ten thousand students."

"Ten thousand!" exclaimed Meg.

"Oh, yes. My teachers discovered I had a natural skill for writing and drawing. And I seemed to have an easy time with languages. You would be overjoyed, Master William, to see the thousands of books in the library there. Distinguished works of astronomy and mathematics, medicine, and law. And, of course, sacred Muslim texts from the far corners of the empire."

William's expression reminded Meg of a hungry child drooling over hot buns at a baker's stall. "I would love to get my hands on those medical books."

"Later, I entered the Schola Medica at Songare, although I found out soon enough that I did not like to touch sick people nor be in their presence." He laughed at the shocked looks on William and Meg's faces. "Yes," he chuckled. "As long as I found medicine in books, I was a most successful student until I stepped into the sickroom and had to face a living patient."

"Nevertheless, I graduated as a doctor of phisik. With the Mansa's help, I obtained an important position in the Caliph's library in Grenada. I was paid very well. I copied and sold many books. Then several years later the Caliph fell on hard times—he spent all his money fighting the Christians—and he could no longer afford me. By chance, one of the Caliph's best customers, Abraham the Jew from Montpellier, was visiting and offered me a position in his bookshop. I made copies of Abraham's books which he sold to the masters and students at Montpellier University. His books were worth a lot of money."

"Where is his bookshop?" William asked.

Njata sighed. "Gone. All the Jews were driven out of the city. It wasn't the first time they'd been banished from Montpellier. This time the king allowed the Jews to take their possessions with them. One day I was helping him pack his books when soldiers wearing the uniform of the Bishop of Maguelone appeared out of nowhere. They forced Abraham to leave immediately with nothing but the clothes on his back. He was barely able to say goodbye. He begged me to protect his books, but I failed him."

"What happened to him? And to his books?" William asked.

"I do not know. He probably died of a broken heart. His books were his children. As to the whereabouts of the books, I used to see them every day."

"What do you mean?" asked William.

"At the home of the Regent Master."

"Petrus Muller?"

"Yes, in his library. By coincidence he was at Abraham's shop when the bishop's men came. He took all of Abraham's books and personal possessions. And then he offered me a position as copyist and translator. I sat in on his lectures, took notes, and translated the notes to Arabic and Hebrew. He sells the copies to students."

Meg remembered the round room with the cozy fireplace at Muller's home and the hundreds of books shelved from floor to ceiling. How many of them were invaluable treasures? And how many came from the Jewish bookseller?

William stood, agitated, and faced Njata. "Are you saying that the bishop's men expelled Abraham?"

"Not just Abraham, sir. All the Jews."

"So, Petrus Muller stole the books and Abraham's possessions?"

"Yes, Master William. He took everything."

William clasped his hands and then grasped Njata by the shoulders and tugged him to his feet. "Njata," he shouted with triumph, "you have made this beautiful day even brighter. You've given me the way to kill two birds at once. Petrus Muller will rue the day he ever took those books."

Njata, shaking his head in confusion, smiled, and reached

for Meg to steady himself. "I am glad to oblige, Master William, but now I think I need to lie down."

William put an arm around Njata's waist and helped him up to his room where Njata stretched out on the pallet with a long sigh of relief. Meg placed the back of her hand against his cheek. "You are warm, Master Njata, but only from the sun, I think."

After William left, Meg asked, "Master Njata, may I fetch you water, wine, food, anything?

He shook his head.

"Thank you for telling me about your homeland. Perhaps you can tell me more when you are feeling better."

"I would be glad to."

"I, uh, I also want to thank you for helping Gerard, and especially given your distress around sick people." She closed the red curtain and covered him with the red silk cloth. "I have been thinking. Given that Master William is very worried about his friend Robertus, I don't think we need to tell him your secret."

"That is entirely up to you," he said.

"And Gerard doesn't need to know everything either."

"As you wish."

Njata turned over and within a few minutes, Meg heard a rhythmic snuffle. She prayed that he dreamt of happy times on the wide Djoliba River.

Montpellier, May 1327

La Putana was the perfect place for a man who wanted to drink in private. A squat stone building at the end of a dark alley, the tavern had been difficult to find, especially for someone not used to the bewildering labyrinth of narrow streets in the heart of the city. It was also the kind of place where newcomers would be noticed immediately.

As William walked inside and stood near the door waiting for his eyes to adjust to the gloom, the tavern customers raised their heads from their cups and eyed him suspiciously. They looked like regulars, men who made a living with their hands and their backs, hard workers who needed to wash away the daily drudgery before stumbling home.

The only warmth in the tavern came from a feeble fire in the hearth, the only light from a few smoky tallow candles casting narrow pools of yellow across the tables. Four men played a listless game of dice, but most drinkers sat alone. A thick mat of rushes covered the floor but from the looks of it, the rushes hadn't been changed in months. The place stank of soot, rotten food, and vomit. William decided La Putana could use a good scrubbing.

He ordered wine and took a seat on a bench facing both the door and the patrons. He knew better than to turn his back on strangers unless he wanted a clout on the head and his purse strings cut. While he sipped at the wine, he mulled over his plan to confront Petrus Muller. If his plan went well, the Regent Master would have no choice but to change his mind about Meg and perhaps convince the bishop to release Robertus. But first, William needed a witness and participant in the farce he was about to arrange. Hopefully, Sorianus would fit both roles.

William would never forget Meg's crestfallen face when she entered Muller's library after her examination by the masters. Examination? More like intellectual torture. She looked stricken, as if someone aimed a sword directly at her heart. She stumbled into his arms, exhausted, faint, and hopeless. He could tell that it took great presence to keep herself from crying aloud. In fact, he had yet to see her cry, although he was sure he had heard her muffled sobs later that night.

The next morning, he asked her to describe every detail of her examination. Who were the obvious enemies?

Petrus Muller and the Bishop of Maguelone, she responded.

Likewise, who was sympathetic?

She answered immediately: Master Sorianus—he had defended her in the courtyard and was even willing to fight on her behalf.

"I was so astounded, Master William," she said, her eyes wide, "that grown men, men so learned, would be at the brink of fighting over whether to accept a woman in medicine. It was quite shocking."

"Ha!" William said. "You didn't see them actually come to blows, did you? Blustering idiots, all of them. Too cowardly to make a fist."

After that conversation, William made a point to seek out Sorianus. He paid one of Robertus's players to follow Sorianus and to watch his house. Each evening for a week, the man reported to William at sundown with the same message: Master Sorianus left his home shortly after sunset to drink in La Putana. Speculating that Sorianus would be more forthcoming at his favorite tavern with his favorite drink, William gave the man extra coins with an order to alert him when Sorianus next went to the tavern.

That, as it happened, was tonight. The fact that it coincided with Njata's account of the sacking of Abraham's bookshop and home was pure sweet fortune. William wasn't sure what he would ask Sorianus when he met with him. But his instinct told him the man could be an important ally.

The tavern door opened and a short stocky man in a tattered brown tunic walked in. William looked away, dismissing him as a mendicant friar tired from begging at the market, especially as the man was bald with a wreathe of curls near his neckline. However, a second look revealed the friar to be Sorianus, not the master of phisik usually dressed in a plush red robe and red biretta.

Sorianus caught sight of William and yelled, "Hello, my friend. What brings you here?" He called an order to the tavernkeeper, who nodded as if he knew Sorianus's usual fare.

"I would suspect the same thing that brings you here, Master Sorianus." William gestured to the bench opposite him. "A place to drink and think in private."

Sorianus laughed and lifted the earthenware mug from the tavernkeeper's hands. "Or a place to think and drink to oblivion."

"Why the disguise? Or do you not earn enough as a master of phisik and have to go begging in the streets?"

Sorianus chuckled as he sat down. "I'm practicing for the future when I no longer entertain my students and have to beg in the streets." He swallowed a mouthful of wine and wiped his lips on his sleeve. "The truth is, by leaving my medical garb at home, I am free to come and go without being accosted by every man suffering from a boil on his backside or a bug up his nose. Besides, this place reminds me of home." He glanced around the tavern. "My father earned his living as a fuller. We grew up poor, those of us who survived. Our clothes were patched with whatever scraps of felt my father squirreled away. The people here are poor, too. I understand that." He drank the rest of his wine and motioned for more. "So, Master William, meeting you here is no coincidence. What is the *real* reason you've come to The Whore."

"The what?"

"La putana—the whore."

"Ah, a fitting name. But I have come to ask you about Meg."

"I thought as much. She has a sharp mind. I was looking forward to teaching her."

Sorianus related the events of Meg's examination—"rather an interrogation," he said—and described the fight in the courtyard.

"You may not be aware, William, but I would have welcomed her into my classroom. In truth, I do not care whether a woman or a monkey attends my class as long as they pay attention. But my colleagues think otherwise."

Shouts and curses came from the customers playing dice. Two players upended the game board, spilling drinks and game pieces into the laps of the other players, who jumped to their feet with fists raised. Cries of "Whoa there" and "cheater" rang out, along with threats of "daggers" and "run you in." The tavernkeeper ran between them with his arms outstretched and said something to the two who started the fight. He pointed to the door. They staggered away, mumbling and scowling.

Sorianus motioned to William's empty mug. "More?"

William shook his head. He'd have to be hogtied before he drank another drop of the swill the tavernkeeper called wine. He hunched his shoulders and leaned over the table. "I believe we have a way of putting Meg in your classroom."

"Oh, really? Short of divine intervention, what might that be?"

William told Sorianus what he had learned about Muller.

"So, Muller stole the Jew's books and belongings. What of it? Plenty of people stole from the Jews. What does that have to do with Meg?"

"The King of France expelled the Jews, correct?"

"Yes. But that has happened before. The Jews are always being expelled for some trumped-up reason."

"True. But this time the king allowed them to keep their possessions."

"Yes, they could take their possessions with them. So?"

"What happened to their possessions if they left them in Montpellier?"

"If the Jews left empty-handed, their possessions *officially* belonged to the king."

"Abraham's books were very valuable, some priceless. Do you really think he would leave them?" William shook his head at the look of confusion on Sorianus's face. "Think on it. I believe Muller and the bishop knew ahead of time about the expulsion. Is it really a coincidence that Muller visited the bookshop just as the bishop's men arrived? No. They arranged for the bishop's men to raid the bookshop. And they forced Abraham out of his home before he could take anything with him. They stole his personal possessions, his jewels, money, and his books—on Muller's orders."

"Well, that is unfortunate for Abraham, but what of it?"

"Anything Abraham left behind is considered the king's property."

"So?"

"So, do you not understand, Sorianus? Muller, with the

help of the bishop, actually stole property belonging to the king of France. I think the king would be very interested in the plunder that was denied him."

"I see. But what can *you* do about it? Or rather, what can *we* do about that?"

"Probably nothing. But Muller does not know that. Some bluffing on our part may prove valuable."

"And how will anything of this help Meg?"

"I am going to visit Muller tonight. I am inviting you to come as my witness. Stay fast by my side and agree with anything I say, and you may have the good fortune to see Petrus Muller do the unbelievable."

"And what is that?

"Beg."

Sorianus laughed and downed the last of his wine. "For that, I would walk to Paris and back. Let us go."

✳✳✳

As William staggered side by side with Sorianus through the dark streets of Montpellier, he pondered the contradiction which split his heart in two as surely as if someone had taken an axe to it.

Truth was, if someone put him on the rack and threatened him with death if he didn't confess his real opinion, he would have said women should *not* learn the art of phisik. This thought caused him much grief, for he knew how deeply Meg pined for the degree and the license. He knew she had the propensity for learning. Her reading and writing skills were superb. She had a gift for diagnosis. Patients loved her. She didn't flinch when working with cadavers. Her dissection was outstanding—even better than Gerard's. What then was he concerned about?

Gerard.

William could very well jeopardize Gerard's future by

causing an uproar among the phisik masters. He was in direct opposition to tradition and the Church. The latter he could care less about. Tradition, though, would be difficult to overcome.

In addition, his outward pronouncements to the contrary, a small piece of him wanted to keep the world as it was. Women were to act demure. They were to keep themselves properly veiled and look at their feet instead of staring at you boldfaced. They were to stay with their mothers until they were married off in mutual agreement with their parents. They were not to act like free-spirited harlots, engaged in all manner of unseemly behaviors.

With a start, he realized he sounded exactly like Meg's description of the bishop and his sycophants. Yes, he railed against his colleagues who stultified the practice of medicine, who kept it from advancing because they lacked imagination. But a part of him badly wanted the world to turn with endless consistency so that his son's future might not be threatened. Gerard would obtain his degree and license, practice, write books, *ergo* become successful. To do that, he would be competing against the smartest young men in Europe. He shouldn't have to compete against women as well.

But then a memory crept in: Meg seated at the kitchen table well before cockcrow writing Latin words in her wax tablet, her legs tucked under the bench, and the tip of her tongue tapping her upper lip. There were other Megs, he was sure of it. Why should they be married off to strangers who prized *only* their dowry? Why were the ugly girls or the useless old virgins sent to a nunnery to live the rest of their lives in quiet contemplation because their fathers didn't want to feed them? Why shouldn't they be educated and taught to fend for themselves?

His problem, winnowed down to the most obvious, was that he loved both Meg and Gerard and wanted the best for both of them. He let out a heavy breath as Muller's house came into view. Sorianus cast him a sideways glance, which William ignored. When did loving those two young people become so difficult?

At least Sorianus had agreed on their caper without so much as a whimper of protest. "You surprise me, Sorianus," William said. "I thought I would have to argue with you. I even prepared a list of reasons to persuade you to my cause."

Sorianus threw his head back and laughed like a drunken donkey. "My livelihood is always in jeopardy with Muller—that miserable piss-guzzler. But I do not fear him. My students will follow me wherever I go. I've no doubt of that."

"I hope so, Sorianus. Montpellier would suffer if you left, I'm certain of it."

"Perhaps. But one thing for sure. I fear for the school of medicine. Students are flocking to the University of Paris instead. Soon it will surpass us in reputation. We will be the backwater, the swamp mired in old techniques and methods. To change we must bring in forward-thinking masters of vision. We must experiment, question, write. In short, all the things we are *not* doing now. We are allowed to dissect once every two years and even then, we are confined to a pig dissection. We *must* do better. We *must* dissect a human body."

William grabbed Sorianus and encircled the short man in a bear hug. "You have made me very happy. I knew we were birds of a feather."

"Born in the same nest," Sorianus said, grinning.

When they reached Muller's doorway, they were told by a sneering, obsequious servant that the master was not receiving visitors. Without a word, William and Sorianus charged past the astonished man and found the Regent Master sitting by the fire in his library with a hefty book on his lap.

His head snapped up and his hand froze in the act of turning a page. "What are you doing here? You stink of bad wine. And you, Sorianus, why are you dressed as a mendicant friar? Both of you, come back when you're sober."

William ignored him. Instead, he ran his hand along the spines of several books and then turned in a slow circle, admiring the hundreds of manuscripts filling the room from top to bottom. "I am astounded by your library. You have a marvelous collection."

"Yes, I do," said Muller with caution.

"Perhaps you'd like to tell us where the books came from," Sorianus chimed in.

"From many places. I do not remember." Muller frowned and looked first at Sorianus and then at William as if trying to ascertain where the conversation was going. "What business is it of yours?"

"We were wondering," William said, "because we've heard a rumor they were stolen."

Muller jumped to his feet. "What? How dare you accuse me of being a thief. I am a respected professor. Why would I steal books when I can buy them?"

"Indeed," said Sorianus.

Muller laughed. Or rather the sound coming out of his mouth resembled a laugh, but his eyes were troubled. "Both of you are drunk." He gestured to the servant who stepped forward. "Get them out of my house."

William waved his arms, encompassing the vastness of Muller's personal library. "These books belonged to Abraham the Jew. Once Abraham left Montpellier, his books belonged to the King of France. Perhaps I should go directly to the king and tell him how you stole his property?"

Muller's eyes widened. "You actually think that anyone cares what happens to the filthy Jews?"

"You wanted to steal the books before Abraham could take them. What did you think—that a man of your wealth should have anything he wants?"

"You cannot prove it."

William pulled a book from the shelf. "Ah, The Canon of Medicine by Avicenna. I have always wanted this book." He looked at Sorianus. "Perhaps we should do some requisition of our own, Sorianus. Perhaps we should take this to the King of France and describe the hundreds of books still in the hands of the Regent Master of Montpellier."

Muller snatched the book from William and narrowed his eyes. "What do you want?"

"I want you to admit Meg to the school of medicine. And I want the bishop to free Robertus Medicamus."

"What? Have you lost your senses? I have no influence with the Bishop of Maguelone. He is his own man. He has an army of his own and God on his side. As for Meg, the masters do not want her. They've said as much."

"Not true, Muller," Sorianus said. "You forced the decision on us."

"Never. This is ridiculous. You cannot walk in here and threaten me."

William gestured to Sorianus. "There's a very nice book behind you. Grab it and let us go."

"Certainly," Sorianus said.

"Wait." Muller ran to the library door. "Wait. All right. I'll do as you want. Meg may start this summer with Gerard"—he glared at Sorianus—"in *your* class." He turned his scowl to William. "As to Robertus, I will use what little influence I have on the Bishop of Maguelone, but I cannot promise anything."

"I will give you one week," William warned. "If Robertus is not delivered to my doorstep, alive and in one piece, I will be in the king's palace so fast."

"All right. I'll see what I can do. Now get out of my house."

"Oh," said William. "One more thing . . ."

"No! You have enough. Get out." Muller's cheeks were splotched with purple.

"Ah, Muller, Muller. You still do not understand." He glanced at Sorianus and smiled. "There is one more thing. I want Njata Keita to join me. I want him to write and translate my work and to tutor Meg."

"But he's mine."

"You don't own him. He is not your slave. He *works* for you. I want him to work for me."

Muller hesitated.

"Sorianus," William said. "How many books do you think we can carry?"

"Oh, a dozen, maybe more."

With a nod from William, Sorianus yanked books off the shelves. He took as many as he could carry and handed the overload to William.

"Wait. I . . ." Muller jerked the books from William and stacked them on his chair, then he reached for the pile Sorianus was holding against his chest. They engaged in tug-o-war until Muller hissed, "Give them to me." He glowered at William. "All right then. You may hire Njata. Meg may start class with Sorianus. I will talk to the Bishop of Maguelone about freeing Robertus."

"Very good."

"And you will agree not to involve the King of France?"

"Hmm, first, we'll see what the bishop says.

"I've told you—"

"Perhaps the king would like to know that the bishop's men seized Abraham's possessions. I'll wager a check of the bishop's gold and silver chest would prove interesting. Perhaps Njata could identify the plates and cups bearing Abraham's mark."

"When this is over, William, I would advise you to leave Montpellier."

"Are you threatening me?"

"One never knows when a dirk will find its mark between your ribs."

"And I'm sure you'll send someone else to do your dirty work. Your words hold no threat to me, Muller. Remember this, if any harm comes to Gerard or Meg on account of your hatred for me, I will watch you while you sleep and slit your throat from ear to ear. Think of that tonight when you lay your head upon your pillow."

"Get out. And you, Sorianus, your days are numbered at this university."

"Is that a threat or a promise, Muller?

Sorianus and William locked arms and left Muller mumbling over his books like Croesus counting his coins.

Chapter 36

BEHIND THE SCREEN

Montpellier, June 1327

On what promised to be a beautiful Monday morning in early June, William, Meg, and Gerard left shortly after cockcrow to walk to Sorianus's home where Meg and Gerard would begin their first lessons in Montpellier's Schola Medica.

Accompanying them was Master Njata Keita, now in the employ of William of Oxford, master of phisik and surgery. Meg had objected vociferously when William revealed that Njata would accompany her to class. He held up his hand when Meg resisted. "No protesting. This is not a request. It is an order. If you wish to go to university, you will be accompanied by Njata. You will not be welcomed by all the students. There may be trouble."

"But—" Meg said.

"Silence!" William shouted. "Master Njata has been engaged

by me to do his duty. He will accompany you everywhere, including class. No more discussion."

Meg had immediately stomped up the stairs and threw herself on the bed. If Njata was to be attached to her side like a barnacle while she attended medical lectures, she would let William know her opposition by shooting him a look of utter disdain every time he caught her eye. When her silence and her disdain did not appear to affect William in the least, she decided to stay in her room for the rest of the day to punish them all—punish William for not seeing her point of view, punish Gerard for, well, for being able to go anywhere without someone peering over his shoulder, and punish Njata for treating William like he was the Lord Almighty himself. By the end of the day, they would take pity on her and relent.

They did not. In fact, they did not even acknowledge her when she joined them for the evening meal. Instead, William regaled them with his story of rescuing Robertus Medicamus from the bishop's clutches.

"I'm not sure what Petrus Muller promised the Bishop of Maguelone," William said, "but I'm sure it cost him a fine penny to let Robertus go."

"I wish I could have been there," Njata added, whispering a few words in his native language. "Invisible, like the *djinn* of my people, I would have spied upon them and listened when Muller tried to explain his sudden interest in such a man as that magician. And then I would have turned myself into a cat and caused many afflictions on that Muller and bishop, and much havoc in their household."

Meg wanted to ask about the *djinn*, but then she remembered her vow of silence.

William shook his head and sighed. "I'm afraid Muller won't invite Sorianus and me to any soirees at the university."

"I know you are disappointed, Father," Gerard said, and they both chuckled. "But I wish I could have said good-bye . . ."

"Yes, we know. You wish you could have said good-bye to

Serafina, but Robertus had to leave immediately." Robertus and his players had scarpered to Paris as soon as he was freed. A handshake and hug, and a promise to get together again, a promise to write and a quick farewell, and they were gone. "The world is full of young women, my son. I'm sure you will make the acquaintance of many more."

Gerard glanced at Meg, who left the table and flounced up the stairs. William called good night. "We've enjoyed this day of silence, Meg. Quite a relief from your usual endless chattering."

The room filled with laughter. Indeed, Meg could have sworn she heard Njata chuckle.

She stomped harder, hoping to sway them with one last fit of temper but the laughter only increased. She threw herself on the bed with a howl of exasperation.

Master Njata had been fixed to Meg's side ever since. Just as she had predicted, he was like a barnacle at low tide.

Now as they approached Sorianus's home, Meg felt the first tremble of fear. In truth, she didn't mind having Njata accompany her in town while she shopped for market items or took a walk. Still, she hadn't considered the possibility that her fellow students would cause trouble until William mentioned it. But to have Njata sit with her in class? As if she were a little girl?

Sorianus nodded gravely as they approached him. He was standing outside with Petrus Muller and his face was the color of a scarlet rose in full bloom. "You may go to class, Gerard. We will be there shortly."

Muller glowered at Njata Keita who met the Regent Master's fierce gaze with an unblinking stare.

"What is going on, Muller?" William asked.

"I have an additional request, given that this arrangement is likely to upset parents and benefactors."

"One and the same," said Sorianus, rolling his eyes.

Muller ignored him. He stared at Meg. "Here are the rules.

While attending classes, you will enter and exit from the rear door. Once inside, you will be separated from the men by a large wooden screen. You will be hidden for two reasons: our male students will be too distracted by your presence to learn, and you, as the weaker sex, will grow faint at the sight of such appalling illustrations as those found in our masters' medical books."

"Is that necessary, Muller?" William asked. "Njata will accompany her at all times."

"You will sit behind the screen. He will sit with you."

Meg looked to William for help. "But, sir."

Muller lifted a hand to ward off William's comments. "It is better if Meg hides herself, keeps quiet, and learns through listening. A mild hindrance, nothing more. Rest assured, my dear, should you ever tire of attending class, you may ask me to disenroll you and there will be no embarrassment to your name."

"We appreciate your help in this matter, sir," William said. "Meg will be still and silent."

"But," Meg said.

Sorianus raised his voice, apparently more for Muller's benefit than Meg's. "I am sorry you must be hidden, my dear. Apparently, the university does not trust its young men to behave themselves. Perhaps they will faint at the mere sight of such a beautiful young woman."

Meg blushed, knowing that her disfigurement made her anything but beautiful.

"No need for sarcasm, Sorianus," said Muller.

"I was not being sarcastic, Regent. As Meg so skillfully told us at the examination, there is beauty on the surface, and there is beauty below the skin. She has precious little of the former, but volumes of the latter."

Muller's lips curled in a sneer. "Stick to your anatomy lessons, Sorianus. As a philosopher, you are quite the failure."

Sorianus gestured toward a rear entry down the narrow

back alley. "Meg, the other students will enter from the Rue de l'Ecole de Medicine and you and Njata will enter from the alley behind the house approximately one hour early. I will alert the servants to let you in each morning."

Njata cleared his throat and hoisted Meg's books and wax tablets to his chest.

"Well, go in," Muller said. "No need to keep the others waiting."

As Meg opened the back gate to Sorianus's courtyard, she caught William's eye.

"*Bona fortuna, Margareta,*" he whispered and turned away, but not before she saw tears spill onto his cheeks.

The gate slammed behind her and she walked to class with a thudding heart. First, she passed through the kitchen, threading her way between the cook chopping off a chicken's head and a young apprentice pumping the bellows to intensify the fire in the hearth, and then past a housemaid carrying out the night pots.

Sorianus led Meg to a sunny front room—empty except for Gerard— and pointed to two chairs sitting behind a huge wooden screen that blocked the attached classroom.

Sorianus stepped around the screen. Meg listened to the mumbling of sleepy students as they entered the classroom and found a seat next to friends. She imagined Sorianus facing the class. He clapped his hands. The room grew still.

"Students, let us begin," he said.

Chapter 37

Shun Weighty Cares

Montpellier, July 1327

"As you will see here," Master Sorianus intoned, "the heart is the center of the body. It is the center of all thought, feeling, and memory."

Meg could not see the heart. In fact, she could see nothing. She had been in medical lectures at Master Sorianus's house for a month now, entering and exiting by the rear door, taking her seat on a hard upright wooden chair. And always, Njata Keita by her side writing notes on his tablet.

Meg heard Master Sorianus striding about the room, heard him direct the beadle toward a sleeping student followed by a sharp *thwack!* as the beadle's stick made contact with the student's head, but she could only imagine how it looked, for she saw none of it. The huge wooden screen, elaborately carved and in four hinged pieces, blocked her view and kept her hidden from the students and the master.

She heard rustling and knew the students, Gerard among them, were leaning forward for a better view of the book's illustration. They were examining Roger of Wendover's remarkable book *De Mirabilis*. Meg imagined Sorianus pointing to the manuscript, his finger pressing against the human heart, its canals and rivers transporting humors and flooding each organ with the nature of personality.

During the day, she listened carefully and committed each lesson to memory. At night, she, Njata, and Gerard reviewed each lecture by candlelight in Madame Tisserand's weaving room. Gerard tried to re-create the lecture, drawing pictures from memory, showing her what she had missed from her chair behind the infuriating screen, but it wasn't the same.

"At least you needn't fear the beadle's stick," Gerard said one evening in response to her griping. "The man has a fearsome stroke."

"On the contrary, I would gladly take my turn at the stick in exchange for actually seeing a medical book."

Meg returned to the present as Sorianus said, "Here and here," and she realized he was pointing to something in the book. "Where is it now, ah, yes, here you see the heart of a man whose nature was bitter and angry and whose organ shriveled under God's justice. Now, look here, look at the heart of a man who is righteous." Meg pictured the students shifting their attention to the opposite page. "See its fullness, its roundness. Were you to see this heart beating it would astound you with its vigor."

She wanted to take a broadaxe to the hateful screen in front of her and chop it into a thousand pieces. The regent had said it would be a "mild hindrance." Piss and bollocks! How could they expect her to learn when she could not *see*?

"And now gentlemen," Sorianus asked, "does anyone know the *Regimen Sanitatis*?"

There was silence in the classroom, punctuated by an occasional cough. "Come on now, surely you must know of it. It is one of the oldest medical books." Sorianus paused. She heard impatient steps. He was crossing the lecture hall. Sharp taps. He was rapping on the table with his pointer or on some poor student's head. "Come on, gentlemen! There are three-hundred and sixty-two verses in the book. Before you are finished with my class you must memorize all of them." The students groaned and fell silent.

Meg crossed her legs and wiggled her foot. She had read the *Regimen Sanitatis* years ago. Why shouldn't she be able to speak? Njata, reading her thoughts, shook his head and mouthed the word, "No."

Despite the warning look, she was impatient to answer. She sat forward.

"Anyone? The verse for a long life? Shun weighty cares . . ."

She rose. She cleared her throat.

Njata glared at her. "Sit down," he hissed.

Sparks of impatience and anger flew through her. Who was Njata to tell her to stay quiet? The fire flared and was extinguished as she answered her own question. Njata was her tutor and escort. He meant well. And William was paying him for his service. William's anger would know no bounds if she was disobedient.

"As you wish," she whispered. She sat down, her mouth twisted as if she'd just taken a dose of Alice's worst medicine. In whispered words under her breath, she recited the verse that promised a long life if the *Regimen's* rules were followed.

"Shun weighty cares—all anger deem profane.
From heavy suppers and much wine abstain.
Shun idle, noonday slumber, nor delay,
The urgent calls of Nature to obey."

She wallowed in her own glory and smirked at Njata as Sorianus repeated the same verse, word for word, to the students. Almost immediately, a sense of desolation washed over her. She was secluded from her classmates. She was desperate to look at the books. What had begun as an exciting new chapter in her life now made her feel forlorn and pitiful. She longed to be a surgeon and physician like William, not just a village midwife or worse—a lazy good-for-nothing like Madame Petronilla. Yes, she was exasperated by the screen and her isolation from the other students and, yes, truth be told, she wanted to show off a bit to Sorianus, lest he think her a silent numbskull interested in only *playing* at being a student. Fate had propelled her to Montpellier, but William's insistence, endless tutoring for her exam, and arm-twisting of Muller had resulted in the fulfillment of her desire—or the beginning of it, anyway—and she must do her part, screen or not. She must be patient. She must follow the *Regimen Sanitatis*: *Shun weighty cares—all anger deem profane.*

Of course, she thought bitterly, Regent Muller would be happy for her to surrender and disenroll. It would be a validation of his opinion that women were too soft, too delicate, and too weak for the rigors of academics. Besides, if she quit, she would prove to Master William and Gerard, and above all Sorianus, that she was not worthy of their trust. Quit? No! Screen be damned. She was proud and would never give up. Never! Never!

Chapter 38

GERARD'S SISTER

Montpellier, July 1327

Summer in Montpellier brought an intense heat. For Meg, the misty days of her native country existed only as a vague ache under her heart. Occasionally in the early morning hours when she lay in a pool of sweat and wished for a breath of air to find its way through the open shutters, winds from a storm at sea refreshed the dawn and gave her enough relief to doze off before time to rise. It was then that she dreamt of England and the florid green of summer grass or the sweetness of new-mown hay.

Like a rose blossoming overnight, Montpellier's social life burst forth with tournaments, garden parties, and student fetes. Senior students celebrated their final debate and graduation amidst raucous feasting. After that, hardly a day went by without a gathering of some kind—a birthday celebration, wedding festivities, or a drinking party to mourn an unrequited love.

Gerard, so dour and stoic in England, had blossomed with the change of scenery and the fact that Master William was now living in Bologna and not around to observe—Gerard would say *spy on*—his son's behavior. Meg, the secret student, was not invited to any event, but Gerard was invited to all of them, even those held by the senior students. Most nights he stayed out long after the curfew and arrived home the next morning disheveled, having squandered his spending money playing card games and drinking wine at the lodgings of friends. Moreover, Gerard had transformed himself like the alchemist's dream, transmuting the base metal of shyness to the gold of a garrulous and witty student who, while not chasing after *all* the young women in Montpellier, was picking at lovely feminine titbits recommended by his friends. Meg was not among them.

Gerard's body was different as well. He had filled out and grown taller, and his voice had a deeper timbre that made Meg's heart skip when he said her name. As to Gerard's infatuation with Serafina, well, who knew what Serafina had taught him? A lot, Meg reckoned. And none of it good.

With Meg, Gerard was still the same kind and remarkably patient teacher when they reviewed the daily lessons, but somehow, in an unspoken signal, he had heralded a breach, not in their friendship but in his willingness to take their attachment further. Gone were the affections he showed her on the deck of the *Godisgrace* during their sea voyage. The tenderness, the promises, and the possibility of a life together had disappeared like fog banished by the rising summer sun.

Of course, the first-year medical students, known to Meg only by their voices, were oblivious to her existence. She was embarrassed to admit that she, the solitary sparrow, longed to be a part of their social life, to attend the parties Gerard talked about the next morning before he collapsed and slept most of the day.

One morning as Gerard described the latest adventures with his best friend Gunther, he stopped mid-stream and asked, "Why the long face? And the moaning sighs?"

"Don't be a ninny," Meg said. "You're so full of drink you don't even remember last night. And how much money did you lose?"

His broad smile made her heart jump. He dumped a handful of coins on the table. "I didn't lose. I won."

"Then the others must have been drunker than you."

She expected a barbed retort, but instead, he sighed and said, "Look, Meg, I know you would like to attend a gathering of students. You must be weary of staying here all by yourself. But we cannot have them knowing the truth about you. The Regent Master would pull you out of school if your secret is revealed."

"Why do I have to reveal it? I will say I am your sister, here for the summer."

"And then what?"

"What do you mean?"

"Suppose you are spotted at the market in winter?"

"Well, never mind then. Why don't you admit the real reason? You don't want to be seen with me."

"You can hardly say that. I was seen with you all over London. Did it matter? Not a whit."

"Humph. Montpellier is different. Tell the truth. You have no desire to be my chaperone. Not when you and Gunther could be off on your own, getting into all kinds of mischief."

Gerard took another sip of ale. Biding his time, Meg thought, while he came up with a proper answer.

"All right then," he said. "I admit there is truth in what you say. Perhaps you would like to go with me next time. Gunther is having a garden party for classmates at the end of the month. You will be my sister visiting from England. I will be your brother and chaperone."

She looked at him as if she couldn't believe his words. "Are you making me the butt of jest or do you mean it?"

"I mean what I say. I promise. I should have taken you before now. I've been selfish, forgive me."

Meg clasped her hands over her heart as if her deepest wish had been granted. "Thank you, Gerard."

"Just this once."

"I understand. I promise." She attempted a lady-like curtsey and suddenly stopped. "Oh my. I have nothing to wear. How stupid I've been."

"I'll buy some fabric in the market. And I'll pay Madame Tisserand to stitch a costume."

"Oh, Gerard, that is very generous of you. Thank you." She kissed him shyly on the cheek.

"You're welcome. Now let's go to Madame Tisserand's stall and be done with this. My head feels like a donkey kicked me during the night—twice."

✳✳✳

On Saturday evening, a young man opened the door to the house on the Rue de St. Pierre and bellowed, "Gerard, my friend, come in."

Meg recognized his voice immediately. She had heard it many times in class — Gunther, ever the jester and victim of the beadle's stick, but she had never seen his face. Tall, broad-chested, and muscular, Gunther was dressed in a parti-colored tunic of red, yellow, and green. His shoes were the latest style, narrow with long tips adorned by a tuft at the end. Atop his blonde curls he wore a cap of red felt on which were stitched half a dozen bells. He was definitely handsome, Meg decided, and full of life, exactly as Gerard described.

Gunther lifted Meg's hand. "I am Gunther Zorn von Bilstein at your service. And you must be Gerard's sister, Meg. He has told me you are visiting from England. Come in, come in." The bells on his cap tinkled as he bent down to kiss the back

294

of her hand. "Gerard, you did not tell me your sister was so beautiful. You must be a protective brother."

Meg could feel her cheeks grow hot. She glanced at her "brother" who grinned.

Gerard had warned her of Gunther's enthusiasm, but he needn't have bothered. She would have known that booming baritone anywhere, having heard it every day in Master Sorianus's class.

"I know him by his voice," Meg had said as they walked to Gunther's house, "He does not seem to know the answers to the master's questions."

"Sleeping seems to be his preferred way of listening to a lecture," Gerard explained. "When he is not sleeping, he is making mischief. His head is full of knots from the beadle's stick."

Gunther, seemingly no worse for wear from the beadle's vigorous whacks, ushered them forward and ordered a servant to bring them food and drink. "We'll go into the courtyard and await the others." He led them to a garden blooming with vibrant shades of pink, purple, and red, bordered by roses fragrant with the scents of myrrh and cinnamon.

"Look, Gerard," Meg said as Gunther excused himself to greet more guests. "Look at this herb garden."

"Hmm."

"Oh, look at that beautiful rosemary, as tall as my waist, and rue and dittany. Oh, and lavender. How lovely." She ran a hand over the blossoms and breathed in the fragrance. "And look at this. Oh, wouldn't Alice love this," she said as Gerard nudged her elbow and they walked through a small parterre of boxwood in the shape of a miniature labyrinth.

"Yes. I see. Plants. Plants. And more plants. How wonderful," Gerard mumbled, and turned to the courtyard entrance to see who might be coming through.

Nervously Meg pulled at her tunic and brushed a hair from her forehead. Gerard's purchase of fabric for her new costume had been turned into a luscious confection under Madame Tisserand's nimble fingers. She had worked on it all month with a needle and thread in her hand, transforming white silk to a flowing undertunic covered by a pink silk taffeta surcoat edged in tippets at the hem and shoulders. On both silk and taffeta, she had embroidered tiny pink and white roses. Meg was overcome with the beauty of it. Carefully she tried it on and twirled, watching the undertunic swirl about her ankles.

"Lovely," Madame Tisserand said. "And now hair." She wound a gold ribbon through Meg's braids and then placed the braids atop Meg's head, fastening the hair with an antique bone comb she took from a box under her bed. Then she attached a headdress of gauze through which the gold braids shimmered.

"Oh, but shoes." Meg had wriggled her bare toes. "Oh, well, I shall have to make do." She slipped her feet into the well-worn leather slippers Master William bought her after she turned fifteen, and her body seemed to grow in all directions overnight.

She smoothed the soft fabric and fingered an embroidered flower—pink, beautiful, gold braids—*still a silk purse from a sow's ear*, said a small voice in her head. Oh, but it was worth it. Other girls in Montpellier attended parties in beautiful clothing. Why couldn't she for once? Just for once. In the morning, she would put away the dress and shoes. She would return to the conscientious student clothed in sedate gray.

When Meg, dressed in her complete costume, walked down the stairs that afternoon, Gerard's expression caused her to stop mid-stride. He was standing at the bottom of the stairs, his mouth open.

"What is it?" she asked.

"You are . . . you look so . . . different."

She smoothed the taffeta. "Thank you. I feel not quite my usual self."

"I, uh, I realized you had no shoes to wear. I purchased

these with the rest of my winnings." He handed her a pair of pink leather shoes, as soft and buttery, with not a mark on them. They were a perfect fit. "Gerard, I am without words. You have been so generous. I will never be able to repay you."

"You do not have to repay me. Your happiness is all the repayment I need."

"I'll borrow Madame's wooden pattens as protection from the mud and filth. These are too beautiful to soil in the streets."

"You can wear those uncomfortable clogs if you want to, but you'll walk like a stork whose feet are on fire."

She laughed. "So be it then. I'll take them off at Gunther's."

Master Njata, who had agreed to help Madame Tisserand move a heavy load of cloth to her market stall while Gerard accompanied Meg to the party, dropped the fabric he was carrying and bowed before her. "Mistress, I know many languages and you would be called beautiful in all of them."

"Thank you, sir," she said, and immediately was overcome with guilt. As much as she appreciated Njata's concern for her well-being, it would feel good to be on her own without him. She wouldn't be entirely alone, of course. Other girls at the party would be accompanied by their feeble aunts or doting parents, but Meg's chaperone would be her handsome "brother" who had suddenly become the popular guest on everyone's list this summer.

She smiled and head held high, reached for Gerard's forearm. At the top of the stair Madame Tisserand let out a sigh and threw her kisses.

"*Merces*, madame," Meg called in Occitan.

Now, sitting in Gunther's courtyard, she lifted her head to the sky and took a deep breath. So many stars tonight. Were those same stars visible in London? York? St. Michael's Mead? Her beloved Alice would never believe that she was sitting on a marble bench carved with cupids and flanked by a pink and white *rosa mundi*, Alice's favorite flower. She marveled at the extravagance of Gunther's house, such a contrast to Gerard's descriptions of hovel-like student housing where he had gambled and drunk his fill this summer. While their own accommodations at Madame Tisserand's, provided by William's generosity, were lavish compared to other students, Gunther's were fit for a king.

Occasionally one of the guests looked her way as if wondering who Meg was, this stranger in pink with the crippled face. No mingling was necessary, thought Meg, it was enough to sit on the outskirts and watch the dancing, the flirting, the trivial spats that caused fake tears to be spilt, and the apologies and secretive kisses. The colors of cloth, the patterns of brocade, the tinkling of laughter, the glittering torchlight, and especially the irksome looks of parents who hoped for a good match for their daughter, all of it was fodder to her imagination.

Gunther, taking leave of a passel of young women who flirted and chattered like popinjays, spied Meg and walked to the bench.

"May I join you?" he asked.

"Of course," Meg answered.

"Your brother has deserted you." He nodded in the direction of a group of students. Indeed, Gerard had been moving from one conversation to another, as animated as Meg had ever seen him. He approached the knot of young women left on their own by Gunther. Their faces lifted and they twittered in greeting.

"Are you enjoying yourself?" Gunther asked.

"Immensely," she said. "You and my brother have many admirers."

"I have sisters. I know what to say to women."

"Perhaps you only say what you think women want to hear."

"Ha! Gerard told me you speak frankly. No, despite my reputation, my words to women are always true. I do not dissemble. There is too much dishonesty in the world as it is."

"Then you should know play-acting is not in my nature.

Nor am I capable of being coy or flirtatious." She spotted Gerard, seduced by his flock of lovelies. "I mean no disrespect."

"Perhaps you never learned to play in the fields of love," he said.

Meg peeked at him sideways expecting to see a lascivious smirk. Instead his smile was gentle. She thought she saw a sympathetic understanding in his eyes.

"No." She returned his smile. "I had no chance in my childhood. And now, I am far too serious."

"Serious? What have you to be serious about? You are lovely. Obviously intelligent. Young. Soon to be a wife and mother, I'm sure."

"No." She let it stand at that. She was not prepared for a conversation about her future. "And you, Gunther? Will you return to Strasbourg after you earn your degree?"

"My father expects me to."

"I'm curious. Why did you choose to be a doctor of phisik? If you don't mind an impertinent question."

"I do not know, to tell the truth. My older brother, as first born, will inherit the family estate. He has always been the golden son. My tutor encouraged me to seek a profession of the mind and not the sword. But my father disagrees."

"And what does he want?"

"Ach. My father wants me to be a knight. To lead men into battle, rally for the cause—whatever that might be."

"And you?"

"I may look like a fighter, but that is the last thing I want to do."

"Once you've finished medical school, your father may change his mind." *If you finish,* Meg thought.

"Ha. He has never changed his mind about anything. I thought I wanted a life of the mind, but now I think I just want to get away. To have an adventure."

A serving boy brought two beakers of wine and a tray of sugared nuts. Gunther nodded to the boy and offered the tray to Meg. She shook her head. She was far too nervous to eat. But she sipped at the wine, enjoying the warm trail it left in her throat as she swallowed.

"I finished my first four years by the skin of my nose. My father gave me six months to improve but medicine does not seem to be my calling either. He has written the Regent Master for a full account of my school work." He took a sip of wine and added, "Gerard will make a splendid physician, He's a brilliant student."

"If he can stay away from women."

"Spoken like a loyal sister. Let him sow his oats. He'll settle down."

"I thought at one time he would settle down with me. Foolish, I suppose."

"With *you*?"

"Oh." For a moment she had forgotten she was pretending to be Gerard's sister. "Uh. Yes. What I mean is that he has been a good brother. I will miss his company when he marries. I suppose I could run his household if he chooses not to marry, and help him with his patients."

"You? Help with his patients?" Gunther raised his eyebrows and laughed. "Oh, no, medicine is not a suitable job for a woman of intelligence and breeding. Much better to relieve him of the drudgery of household life. My sisters have been trained since childhood in the skills necessary to running a large estate and to taking care of their husbands' needs. I'm sure you could do the same."

"Perhaps."

As minstrels began to play a jolly tune to liven the party, Gunther said, "I asked your brother if I might dance with you this evening, and he gave his permission. Would you care to dance?" He held his hand out, as if to sweep her off her feet.

"Oh, I don't . . ."

"Oh, yes, you do. Come on then," he said, as he lifted her off the bench.

✳✳✳

Later, when Gerard and Meg were walking back to Madame Tisserand's—one of the first nights of summer when Gerard would arrive home before midnight—he asked Meg how she liked the fête.

"Oh, Gerard, it was wonderful. Such beautiful dresses. And lovely music. Delicious food. Oh, and the gardens. Perfume in the air. Thank you so much for taking me."

"I am glad you enjoyed it."

"One thing I do not understand is, how can Gunther afford to have so many parties and to live in that grand house?"

"His father is very wealthy. He purchased the house and servants when Gunther first entered university. He kept the house when Gunther stayed on for medical school." It was an investment, Gerard explained. As well as providing a roof over Gunther's head, the house was a way to trumpet his father's power and wealth. "Gunther says his father has grumbled in the last few letters, especially after he had to pay a fine to get Gunther out of jail."

"Jail?"

"Um, yes. I neglected to tell you—one night I'm afraid we made too much noise, singing some rather bawdy songs, and the neighbors complained. Gunther was arrested and spent a night in jail. His father paid a hefty fine to secure his release."

"I like Gunther."

"I do, too, but why did you give him permission to visit you?"

"I did not," she answered indignantly. "He asked if he might visit me and I told him to ask you first, dear *brother*."

"Well, he wants to come right away. Tomorrow, in fact. What did you do? Bewitch him?"

She laughed. "Hardly. Despite his parties, I think he is lonely. Perhaps he simply wants another friend."

"What can *you* do as his friend that I cannot?"

She smiled primly and cocked an eyebrow. "I'm sure I do not know."

"Well, I do," Gerard said. "And rest assured, I shall be a diligent chaperone."

Chapter 39

DEAR FATHER

Montpellier, September 1327

September saw the beginning of classes for the first term. Meg was dismayed to learn that their morning lecturer would be Master Horlogus, her nemesis from the entrance examination the previous spring.

Horlogus had agreed—reluctantly—to conform to the regent master's orders to allow Meg in class as long as she was hidden by a screen and was silent. The class was held on the Rue de l'Ecole Medicine in the Church of the Immaculate Conception, a modest stone building in the form of a simple rectangle, with no cross-transepts and only one spire. Three leaded glass windows on each side provided light. Benches for the students were installed in the nave, along with a lectern for the master. Meg was to sit in a tiny side niche. Once again, the hated wooden screen was positioned between Meg and the students.

And once again, because of the screen Meg could see nothing.

On the first day of class, Master Horlogus described in his reedy voice their schedule of lectures and his expectations for first-year medical students. Meg sat on the edge of her seat, leaning forward to catch each word. Beside her, Njata took notes.

"As you know, the medical school at Montpellier is renowned for its quality," Horlogus said. "Our physicians are famous the world over. The revered Arnold of Villanova served as regent master recently. The brilliant Guy de Chauliac was a student here. Kings, bishops, even popes have journeyed here to be cured. For that reason, our candidates for the doctor of phisik degree must be honorable, of legitimate descent, and irreproachable character. I expect you gentlemen to act honorably in class, but especially outside the confines of the university, most particularly in town."

The men tittered. Some near Meg even hooted as if they were proud of their brutish behavior. Gerard, during his drunken summer, had confessed the students considered town their personal playground, with no room for honorable intentions.

"In addition," Horlogus said, "persons who are misshapen or repulsively ugly are not allowed to take the degree lest pregnant women see them and bear children with marks corresponding to their deformity."

Was Horlogus talking about her? Was he threatening her? She had thought her place secure in the Schola Medica, but Horlogus seemed intent on causing trouble. She had shown many times that women could bear children without being marked by her presence.

"I will lecture in the morning. A senior student will lecture in the afternoon," Horlogus continued. "Additionally, we will have three special outside lectures this year: the first on the causes and cures of *amor hereos* or lover's malady, the second on witchcraft as a cause of impotence, and the third on corrupt virgins. We will also have three special debates presided over by the masters and senior students. The first is on fever. You are to read *Liber de Febribus* whose author is supposed to be Isaac Judaeus, although I cannot conceive of a Jew writing such a learned piece. The second debate is on consciousness, and third on the nerves. You will be expected to attend every lecture and debate. Absence will be cause for dismissal."

The class groaned. Meg snickered. The days of summer with bawdy rambustious nights and headache-filled mornings would soon be forgotten. Gunther had held his last party just the night before, a party she did not attend as she, in the guise of Gerard's sister, was supposed to be sailing back to England, her summer of gaiety in Montpellier now over and the sobriety of England in her future. Little did Gunther know that she was sitting within yards of him and Gerard.

"If you have not done so," Horlogus said, "you must purchase or borrow your required reading. That includes six books by Galen and one book by Avicenna. In addition, you will be expected to read commentaries from our own masters here."

Meg sighed. How would they ever accomplish so much reading? It was fortunate that Gunther thought her traveling to England as he had despaired of losing her friendship. Throughout the summer he visited two or three times a week on the pretext of being tutored by Gerard.

"He certainly has more of an interest in you than in medicine," Gerard said one day after Gunther left.

She demurred, pleased nonetheless that Gerard had noticed. Usually, she sat in the front room with Gunther and Gerard while they studied. Sometimes she lent a suggestion if Gunther had difficulty with a concept, always being careful not to say, "Do you not remember in Master Sorianus's class?"

Gunther was amazed by her skills in Latin and bodily processes. "Your ability to explain this . . ." He pointed to the book spread before them and its illustration of the heart. "It is amazing. You make it sound so easy, doesn't she, Gerard?"

Gerard grunted.

"I have learned much from Master William and Gerard," she said and lowered her head in what she hoped was an image of humility.

"Humph," Gerard said.

Often after a lesson, she and Gunther strolled to the marketplace or a leafy glade within the city walls, always trailed by Gerard or Njata. Although these outings were enjoyable to Meg, they were taxing as she had to be careful of her speech, careful to play the part of Gerard's little sister. Gunther's questions about her childhood were met with the barest of answers and a quick change of subject. More often than not, they discussed his upbringing as the son of one of the most powerful men in Strasbourg.

Gunther's father was once again badgering his son about returning home, particularly after learning that Gunther was running out of money. One day, as Gunther and Meg sat on the steps of the Church of Notre Dame des Tables after a long stroll through the city, he produced a letter he had written his father.

"I was hoping you would read this," he said to Meg. "I need to know if it is properly respectful."

"Gunther, this is private. Please, I shouldn't."

"I admire you and depend upon your good evaluation of my character, including whether I have responded as a humble son," he said solemnly.

Meg couldn't stop herself. What began as a snort of disdain, changed to howling laughter as she watched Gunther's cheeks grow pink.

"I don't mean to mock you," Meg said, wiping tears away, "but I've never known you to be humble."

He ran a hand through his hair and chuckled. "You're right. Humility is not one of my strong suits, but if I am to stay in Montpellier, I must at least play the part of the dutiful son."

"Well, give it here," she said. "I have to admit that I prefer you as the jolly prankster. Sorianus's class was more amusing because of your comments."

He looked at her in surprise. "My comments? How do you know what I've said in class?"

"Oh, uh," she said, pausing to think of an answer. "Uh, well, Gerard kept me informed every night. I came to know you through his retelling."

"Glad that I could entertain you. Now read this and try not to laugh."

"To my beloved father, greetings from your son," Meg read aloud. "So far, so good."

"I am not amused, Mistress Meg," Gunther said, a look of mock sternness on his face.

"Very well. If you insist." She took a deep breath. "To my beloved father, greetings from your son. I am studying at Montpellier with the utmost diligence, but the matter of money causes me great concern. The city is expensive and I have to provide for many needs. I beg you to send money for buying parchment, ink, a desk, and other things, in sufficient amount that I may finish my studies and return home with honor. Beloved father, I have not a penny, nor can I get any save through you, for all things at the University are so dear. I must have new gowns and furs and decent clothing or I will be damned for a beggar. Wines are expensive as well. I may be compelled to pawn a book to have ready money in my purse. Beloved father, to ease my debts contracted to the tavern, at the baker's, with the professors and the beadles, and to pay my subscriptions to the laundress and the barber, I respectfully ask for your pity and assistance. Through your generosity, I may be able to complete what I have begun. Sending you filial obedience, your devoted son, Gunther."

Meg looked up from the letter to see Gunther smiling with pride. "Could you not send him a shorter letter?" she asked. "One that says, 'Dear Father, Please send money?'"

Gunther frowned. "This is serious business, Meg. My father may force me to leave my studies."

She was suddenly aware that Master Horlogus was droning on about another book to read. She sat up and shook the daydream out of her head.

She heard the sharp crack of a stick on the lectern.

"Now gentleman we begin with the Canon of Avicenna."

Chapter 40

THE WANDERING WOMB

Montpellier, November 1327

Virgins.

It was a topic guaranteed to ensure a full house in the Church of the Immaculate Conception. Students filled chairs, the steps, and every inch of the floor. The senior students, sitting as always in the first row, were singing about an old woman with a farting womb and her ill-tempered husband.

Your womb, old woman, destroys my love. It drowns our moans of pleasure.

Your rod, old man, is too short for my womb. By farts, I will gladly measure.

One of the students made lewd explosive noises, and the nave filled with laughter.

Meg, with Njata by her side, had arrived almost an hour before the lecture so as not to be seen and to take her accustomed seat behind the screen. Behind her, a stained-glass window festooned her secret niche with ribbons of color. Golden saints flanked the Virgin Mary who was tucked into a recess in the wall and was oblivious, Meg hoped, to the sound of farting in a church.

The students were now at the end of term and nearing the Christmas holidays. Meg had acquitted herself well, having passed Horlogus's oral examinations. He seemed non-plussed when she was able to point out each organ and follow their route of function. She owed Gerard and Master Njata gratitude for teaching her at night.

Earlier in the month they had attended the last of the debates, raucous affairs where hooting and cat-calling were encouraged and where the senior students were especially harsh, making snide remarks from the first row, even spitting on the losers. They had debated the issues of fever, consciousness, and nerves.

After the debates, they sat through two torturous lectures where they learned that the cure for lovesickness was a change of scenery and rest and that witches could indeed cause impotence. They were now gathered to listen to the third and final lecture on the subject of detecting corrupt virgins.

"Gentlemen, quiet please. Quiet!" Meg heard Horlogus rap the lectern to get their attention. There was a rustle of feet, a few murmured apologies of "pardon" and a final flutter of robes as students gained their places. "The lecture for today is Virgins: Signs of Pollution. In the course of your long careers as doctors of phisik, you will be asked often whether a young woman is a virgin. This question is usually asked by the father of the bridegroom. He will want to know if his future daughter-in-law is a virgin or if she has been corrupted. He will not want to find out the prospective bride—ostensibly a virgin who will marry his son and produce an heir—is known by half the country."

The room echoed with raucous laughter.

"You laugh today, but let me assure you—if you are unable to detect a virgin, you will be the laughingstock of your patients—especially rich patients who value their reputation as much as their money. In order to ascertain virginity, you must meet with her and observe her carefully. Does she walk with modesty? Is her speech humble? Does she cast her eyes down before men? You will observe her breasts—without staring, if you please. If her breasts point downward, she has been corrupted. This happens when the menses move upwards to the breasts and the added weight causes them to sag."

One of the students in the front row shouted, "When you're drunk, a handful of breast is the same whether up or down."

Meg heard a sharp rap followed by an "ouch!" and knew the beadle had found his target.

Horlogus cleared his throat and continued. "Ahem. Likewise, if a man has intercourse with a woman who says she is a virgin and he has easy entry and his penis is unmarked by sores, the woman is a liar and has been corrupted."

"Master, a well-used spade does not care whether the soil is soft or hard!" a senior student called out.

Horlogus rapped the lectern. "Gentlemen, the next man who speaks out of turn will be reprimanded and shown the door. Is that clear? Now as I was saying, if all else fails, there is one sure way to tell if a virgin has been corrupted and that is an examination of her urine. If it is clear and lucid, sometimes white and sparkling, she is a virgin. A corrupted woman's urine is muddy and the male seed will appear at the bottom of the glass."

Meg shifted in her seat. She had known virgins all her life—indeed, she herself was a virgin—and her urine had never been white and sparkling. The urine of women she had treated varied in color whether the women were corrupted or not. She had never seen muddy urine even in married women unless they were having a bloody flow or had pains in their lower back.

She realized had she not been privy to Master William's clandestine dissections, she would not have known how the body's organs connected one to the other; how the kidneys voided urine, for instance, or the stomach emptied into the intestines. Like Gerard, she wanted to practice both medicine and surgery, to be both *magistra physica* and *magistra chirurgia*. And, of course, she wanted to help women through all phases of their lives, from the young girl having her first menstrual flow to the old woman long past her fertile days dying of a growth in her womb. Perhaps she could even correct notions incorrect to women. She could do all of it, she was sure. The path was long and strewn with obstacles, but she . . .

"I shall explain," Horlogus said. "If you are asked to treat a virgin, but she appears melancholy, or she sighs and mopes about and is loathe to marry, you should investigate thoroughly. She may be experiencing suffocation of the womb. That occurs when the menses are retained and turn poisonous. It could be that the female semen is likewise retained and becomes toxic. The putrefying toxins of the semen and menses cause a cold vapor that rises to the throat and suffocation occurs."

"Master Horlogus?" Meg recognized the voice at once. It was Gerard.

"Yes?"

"Why are virgins so unpredictable? I have noticed that they exhibit peculiar behavior in the days prior to the flow of menses—sweet one moment, a virago the next."

Meg knew exactly who he was describing. Serafina. Poor thick-headed, muddled, besotted Gerard thought Serafina was a virgin. If Meg weren't so furious, she would have laughed out loud and given away her location behind the screen. Serafina was as likely to be a virgin as Meg was the Queen of France, or Queen of England, or Queen of the Cosmos for that matter. But Gerard, having successfully deflowered Serafina—in his own imagination!—now considered himself an expert on women.

"An excellent question," Horlogus said. "It is quite likely

the virgins you have described suffer from a wandering womb. Widows and virgins are most vulnerable to this disorder. The womb, if you remember from your anatomy book, is shaped like a penis and contains seven compartments. We will discuss the wandering womb in more depth next year, but suffice it to say, the womb can move up to the throat, from side to side, and down to the vulva."

Meg looked at Njata. He was making notes. She stood up. Njata glared at her. He hissed, "Sit down. You'll be found out." She sat down. She took a deep breath and exhaled.

"As the venerable Greeks tell us," Horlogus continued, "the womb is altogether erratic, moving by itself hither and thither, sometimes settling near the liver, sometimes pushing against the diaphragm or abdomen. As it moves it causes sighing and moaning. In some horrific cases I have known, it crashes about like a wild animal in its lair. It is insatiable and ferocious."

"What is the treatment, sir?" This from Gunther. Buttering the master? She couldn't believe Gunther was passionate about wandering wombs.

"Marriage and pregnancy. Swiftly."

Meg moved to the edge of her chair. She crossed her legs.

"For a young virgin who is not betrothed, call a midwife," Horlogus continued. "Remember, *you* are doctors of phisik. Midwifery is women's work. It is below you. Just as surgery is below you. Leave surgery and phlebotomy to the barbers. You are professionals who must *never* dirty your hands in a woman's secret places."

"What should we tell the midwife, sir?" Gerard asked.

"Tell her to fumigate the womb. Afterwards, she must rub oil on the genitalia and vulva until the female seed is expelled. While this will work in the short-term, in the long-term, these women need a husband. Remember this: women were created from the rib of man to serve as his helpmeet and companion. Women are the lesser creation. They are weaker. They are promiscuous, lascivious, and lustful. That is why they need a man's rod and his seed to keep them happy within the bounds of marriage. And that, gentlemen, will make your patrons happy."

Meg jumped to her feet. "Master Horlogus!" she called out.

For a moment, there was silence. Not even the scrape of a chair or polite cough pierced the air within the Church of the Immaculate Conception. And then . . .

The room exploded. The men bellowed with indignant outrage. "A woman? A woman?"

Horlogus's fury rose above them all. "You dare speak? You agreed to sit in silence!"

Meg heard rustling and knew that all the men in the room had turned in the direction of the wooden screen. "Yes, sir. But I must speak to correct a misperception."

"Correct?"

Meg was bristling with frustration. Disembodied voices echoed in the church. She pushed against a hinged section of the screen. It moved.

Njata closed his eyes.

She stepped around the screen and out of the side chapel. Her legs trembled. She reminded herself why she must face Horlogus. He was teaching falsehoods.

She faced her classmates. Gerard was looking at the floor. Gunther stared at her dumbfounded, as if she were the Virgin Mary come down from the heavenly choirs.

"My name is Meg of St. Michael's Mead. I am a first-year student."

"What is *she* doing here?" a senior student asked.

Heavy murmuring rolled through the church. Horlogus raised his voice. "I would advise you to keep your voices down. This is a class for studious scholars, not rowdy boys."

"And is *she* a studious scholar?" another senior asked.

"No. But let us hear what she says. If I am not mistaken, she will prove how little she knows. Is it possible, Meg of St. Michael's Mead, that you know more than the ancient Greeks about virgins?"

"Sir, I do not mean to imply that the venerable Greeks were wrong in their approach to women. But I have attended more than thirty births and have helped women with all matters of care, including monthly pains, lack of flow, and infertility."

"Disgusting!" someone shouted. "Do we have to sit here and talk of filthy matters?"

Meg patted the book tucked inside its leather pouch and hanging from her belt. "Sir, I would like to point out that you will find advice about the suffocation of the womb and the menses in Practical Medicine According to Trota."

"Oh, yes, I know of it. From the medical school in Salerno."

"Yes, sir, written by a woman doctor of phisik."

"I doubt that. Nonsense from a wise woman was more likely. But continue."

"According to Trota, the womb is tied to the brain by nerves. The brain must suffer when the womb does. In addition, the womb may move but does not rise to the organs of respiration or fall to the vulva."

A rumble of skepticism passed through the classroom.

Meg persisted. "I beg of you, kind sirs. Listen to me first, before you pummel me with your doubts. The sign of suffocation of the womb is pain on urinating and retention of the menses. I myself have diagnosed a woman ill with this and treated her with a drink of fenugreek and wild celery ground in wine. Within three days, she was cured."

"Sit down!" a senior student screamed at her.

Horlogus shouted, "You put the great Galen or Hippocrates, even Avicenna against an old wise woman?"

She squeezed the little book as if its knowledge could pass through her fingertips and into her mouth. "Why, yes, sir, when it pertains to women's matters. Doctors of phisik leave women's matters to women. As Trota was a woman herself with vast experience in women's care, I would think—"

"You do *not* think," Horlogus snarled. "Like all women you *feel* rather than think."

"But could the Greeks not have been wrong about, about . . ." Horlogus's interruptions were confusing her. She felt as if her tongue were thick, as if it blocked the words from leaving her mouth.

"No. They were superior medical men and were *not* wrong."

"What I am saying, sir," she said, wishing that she could clear her head and make herself understood, "is that without even seeing these women, male doctors write books which order treatment and medicines, and worse, not having beheld a woman's actual organs, as I have seen in cadavers." She caught sight of Gerard who flashed her a warning look and shook his head lest she reveal their experience at dissection. "Uh, as I have seen in books, sir. While I may be a first-year student, I have much actual experience at a woman's bedside. A male doctor of phisik may not have seen a womb. I have, sir, and it is no more shaped like a penis with seven compartments than a chicken is shaped like a butterfly."

Horlogus strode to the step that separated the Lady Chapel from the nave. "You are a liar," he sputtered. "An insolent brazen liar. You shame all women by your presence here."

The lecture on virgins had disintegrated into a debate on her character. She attempted one last argument. "It's simply that, well, how can you teach a lesson about a bird if no one has seen a bird? How can you describe a bird in flight if you have never seen it fly? The same is true of women."

"Are you saying a woman is a bird?" Horlogus asked.

A student stood up and pointed to Meg. "Yes, a thieving magpie."

"A pelican with an ugly beak and a lewd appetite," another student shouted.

"Maybe a woman is not a bird at all. Maybe she is an ass," a first-year called from the back of the room.

Meg was now shouting above the fray. She looked to Horlogus for help but the apoplectic scarlet of his cheeks and his deep scowl showed her he had no intention of coming to her aid. She had been impertinent. He would leave her to suffer the consequences.

She took a breath and continued. "If doctors are to treat women and not just their urine from afar, they must discard the Greeks and look anew at what is standing before them."

The room erupted in howls. The men hurled one insult after another.

"Who are you to interrupt this class and tell us how we are to practice our profession?"

"You corrupt us with your monthly filth."

"You shame women with your immodesty."

"She's probably a corrupt virgin herself. Lift her skirts and spread her legs. Let's have a look."

"I'll wager she's no virgin at all."

Horlogus stepped closer. Phlegm gathered in the corner of his mouth. "Get out. Get out of my classroom and do not come back. You are dismissed from this class and this university."

"But, sir . . ."

"Now! Get out!"

Meg ran behind the screen. She stared at Njata, her face a question mark of pain and bewilderment. "What should we do now?"

"We must flee," he said, as he gathered her books.

There was a rustling in the classroom, a shuffling of feet and a murmur that grew louder until it exploded into multiple voices demanding to know why she had been allowed to speak and indeed why she was in the classroom at all.

"Gentlemen, settle down," shouted Horlogus.

But there would be no settling. Chairs scraped the floor. Voices chose sides as some defended Meg's right to be in class, while others called her a whore—and much worse.

Above the heated debate, Gerard implored the students to be calm. "Give her a chance, gentlemen," he yelled. "She is a gentle maiden and like a sister to me. Please be calm."

"We'll be calm when you keep her at home where she belongs," someone bellowed.

Another voice—the beadle—ordered the students to show respect to the master. "If you don't, you'll feel my stick!"

Suddenly hands pushed at the screen. It tipped forward, banging against Meg's head, and forcing her to her knees. Hot tears filled her eyes.

"Stay still," Njata ordered.

She felt the screen lift away and looked up in time to see it sailing through the air to the rear of the chapel. It fell to the floor with an astounding clatter.

"Are you all right?" Njata asked as he brushed off his hands and gave the hated screen one last look.

"Yes, bruised but not broken." She felt the back of her head where a knot was beginning to rise. "Thank you, Master Njata."

Stunned students and Horlogus froze as if they were statues in a tableau. The men stared open-mouthed, not at Meg, but at the tall, imposing black man beside her. Njata Keita had been tugging at her sleeve but now he pulled himself up to his full height, which, with his turban put him considerably above everyone. He squared his shoulders and fixed his eyes upon them as if he were a lion on the hunt and they were his prey.

"You," he spat, "you whine like little girls. Mistress Meg would put you to shame with her knowledge. She brought me back from the brink of death when I was ill with small pox. Could you have done that? I doubt it. You would have stood over me wringing your hands like a pissing old woman." He pointed to the door. "Go home now and play with your dolls, for you do not belong in this place of learning. And leave this woman alone."

With defiant stares, some of the men backed away. Others appeared to hesitate, as if they were sizing the consequences of testing Njata's courage.

They were discouraged from any further action by Horlogus, who roused himself to order the men out of the church. "The debate is over. Get out." They hesitated. "Out, I say!" Only Gunther and Gerard remained.

"Well, well, well, look who it is. Gerard's little sister," Gunther said.

"She is not my sister," Gerard said.

"Obviously not. I thought you were on your way to England, Meg. It appears you have the uncanny ability to be in two places at once." He grinned. "How is that possible?"

Horlogus stared at the jumble of overturned chairs and scattered books and tablets and then glowered at Meg. "I meant what I said. Do not come back to this university. You have shamed yourself. You do not belong here. I am sure the regent master will agree when he hears of this."

Gerard, as if coming to his senses, added a warning. "You'd better go. They may come back."

Gunther stepped beside her and reached for her elbow. "I will go with you."

As if that were his cue, Njata put his arm across her shoulders, and they guided her out of the church, past a knot of murmuring onlookers. Gunther held her arm tightly, reaching occasionally to adjust Meg's cloak as a chilly wind twisted it 'round her.

"Good riddance!" someone shouted.

Young men no older than Gerard—how could they consider her an enemy? Did they not have sisters or mothers? The words they hurled at her—"grotesque" and "whore"—reverberated in her ears. She had a brief outrageous thought that made her want to laugh. If anyone's womb was wandering today, it was her own. Hysteria was a tell-tale sign or so they said. Well, by God, fumigate her, expel her seed, leech her, cup her, spill her blood, and rip her womb out. Her heart had already been destroyed.

"Do not listen," Njata said. "Ignorance breeds jealousy and fear. They are dumb sheep that follow the flock."

"He's right," Gunther said. "Ignore them."

Their words of support were lost on Meg who walked as if under a spell. She saw nothing. She heard nothing. She was instead transported to another time years ago in St. Michael's Mead when she was barely ten years of age and Alice had taken her under her wing as an apprentice. Alice explained how a healer could be loved and feared at the same time. *They will love you*, Alice said, *and hate you for what they do not understand.*

Still, what could possibly be wrong with sitting in a classroom? How could she threaten the other students by her presence? Yes, her corrupting flow occurred monthly, marking her as a daughter of Eve, but her body's blood had never harmed anyone as far as she could tell. None of William's patients in London were affected by her gender or disfigurement. On the contrary, many of them asked her to return. Some even asked her to return *without* Master William,

As a child, she dreamt of leaving the village. Then as a young woman, she dreamt of a scholarly profession. She was certain that once she lived and worked with learned people, people who read and conversed in Latin, she would be accepted despite her deformity. Indeed, she had hoped to be admired and respected. All those hopes depended on earning a degree as a doctor of phisik, which necessitated finishing university. Now that was over. The regent master would never agree to her return. Master Sorianus might fight for her, but Horlogus would overrule him and the other masters would agree. They would write to Master William and describe her disgraceful behavior. William would return to Montpellier and fetch her, installing her once again as his assistant. Meg would feel his reproach in every unspoken word and sorrowful gaze.

She had called attention to herself, spoken up in defense of women, and look where it got her. Cast out. No better than the pig driver she was destined to be.

Except that she had had a glimpse of a better life, had her head filled with marvelous knowledge, and wild hopes and dreams. Perhaps that was worse. In St. Michael's Mead she knew nothing of the outside world. She had been curious but held no true hope for escaping life in the pigsty. She was doomed to her life and to the mother who hated her. Her mother had blamed her for every bit of bad news, for too much rain or too much drought, for sickness in the family.

"You.'Tis always you," her mother had said.

Alice had saved her. And now she had discovered what the world had to offer. She had apprenticed to the renowned William of Oxford. She had discovered a side of herself she had never known, a woman of skill and patience, a quick study. True, she was not possessed of great wit or flirtatious ways, attributes which would serve her to find a husband. But from what she had seen of men and matrimony, she much preferred a patient's sickbed to the marriage bed.

No, there was no hope for marriage. But there had always been hope for a profession in medicine.

Until today.

Chapter 41

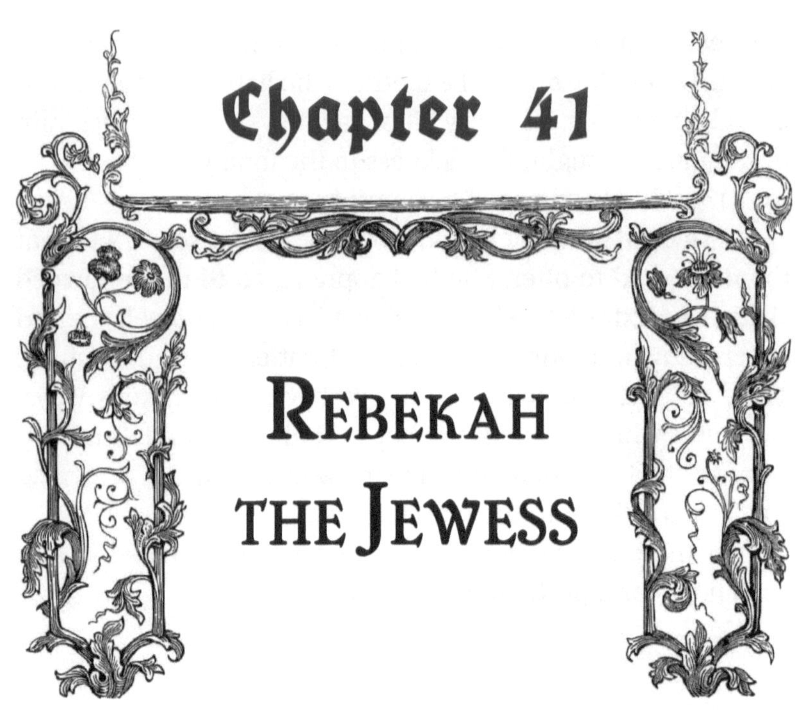

Rebekah the Jewess

Montpellier, November 1327

This was her world now. She could not return to the Schola Medica. She would not return to St. Michael's Mead. Nor did she want to. She missed Alice deeply but . . .

She wondered what Alice would say to her. Probably give her a clout on the head and tell her to come to her senses. *What did you expect, you silly girl? That the hen would hop on your lap and lay an egg in your hands? That the gift would be as easy as that?*

No, not easy. She wasn't that foolish.

And yet, here she was with her clothes and books packed in a leather bag Njata was hoisting to his shoulder. He also carried his own larger bundle of clothes and books—to be truthful, more books than clothes. Arrangements had been made. And so, she was leaving. They were to walk across Montpellier to their new home.

Although Meg understood the usefulness of the new arrangement, she had asked Gerard's opinion, half-hoping that he would object. But he did not.

She wanted him to say: *Please do not go. How could I live without you at my side every day? I love you.*

"Is this what you want?" he asked.

"Master Sorianus thinks it necessary, but I do not, Gerard. I could stay here with you. I don't mind the daily walk. And Njata is always with me."

"It would be difficult to care for patients."

"Of course. I remember London." Oh, so many years ago it seemed when she was so in love with the taciturn boy whose shyness kept him silent. She swallowed and choked back tears. "We lived together and worked together. But, uh, I will miss you and Gunther, of course, and Madame Tisserand."

"Staying with Mistress Rebekah is the most effective plan."

After her dismissal from the university, Meg thought briefly of joining Master William again, but the idea was too painful. Humiliating. When Master Sorianus suggested Rebekah the Jewess as a tutor, Meg agreed but reluctantly. Sorianus wrote to Master William immediately, letting him know of the arrangements. Meg and Njata were to move into Rebekah's home. Meg would be tutored by Njata and Rebekah. Njata would translate books for William and would begin decoding William's Grand Surgery, the book he'd been secretly writing for years.

Now Meg stood in the doorway of Madame Tisserand's cottage and prepared her farewells. She embraced Madame Tisserand, thanking her once again for the beautiful costume she wore to Gunther's fête. Madame Tisserand wiped a tear and waved her hand as if such a beautiful dress was nothing.

Meg kissed Gerard on the cheek, a quick kiss, as sister to brother. His skin, so soft against her lips, smelled of wine and perfume.

"Farewell," he said.

"Farewell, Gerard. Stay true to your studies. Please tell Gunther where I am," she added. "Oh, and perhaps you and he could share a meal with us one day."

Gerard followed her invitation with a brief lift of his hand.

The walk to Rebekah's house took forever. It was difficult to put one foot in front of another with her eyes so filled with tears. Njata walked beside her, silent as usual, but occasionally casting a glance at her and clearing his throat. She felt an odd rupture in her life. That this event, moving to Rebekah's, signified an important new beginning—and an end. A split into two parts: Life with Gerard and Life After.

Rebekah lived only a few minutes from the market, but the house was hidden down twisting lanes only wide enough for two men abreast. "This is the Rue de Juifs, the Jewish Quarter. Or it was," Njata said as they searched for the building Sorianus had described. "Now where?" He stopped and stared at the building on the corner. "Ah, there it is."

Three stories high, the house was a sturdy structure built of stone on the first floor and brick and wood bracing on the upper stories. While the house was larger than most in Montpellier, it was plain on the outside, with an arched understory for storage or a shop, as if befitting a lowly cloth merchant. Only windows of glazed glass overlooking the street hinted at the owner's wealth.

When the door opened, Meg could not help but draw a breath of surprise. The house was far more luxurious inside than out. A Turkey rug of bold red and blue patterns covered the floor. Tapestries of silk embroidery hung on the walls, and the table and chairs were polished to a high shine.

A beautiful woman came forward and bade them enter. "Welcome. Welcome. Come in, please. I am Rebekah. And you must be Meg. It is so good to meet another woman healer."

Meg had certainly seen people of different lands in the market, but never anyone as striking or as beautifully adorned as Rebekah the Jewess. She wore a fine robe of red silk with flowing sleeves over a gauze tunic in a shimmery blue. Although her thick black hair was pulled away from her face, escaping curls wound their way like tendrils on a rose vine through a gold coronet studded with pearls. Coiled around her neck was a necklace of three chains hung with gold coins. The result was stunning, as if she shimmered when she walked.

Rebekah's beauty only served to heighten Meg's ill humor. How could a woman like that deign to get her hands dirty? Not only was she vain and wealthy, but the woman called herself a healer and was probably no better than an old crone doling out herbs.

"And you, Njata"—Rebekah waved to him—"please come in. Master Sorianus has told me about the both of you, although I believe I used to see you, Njata, in the shop of Abraham the Bookseller. Please leave your bags here and I'll have a servant take them to your rooms. I must tell you, I am so pleased you'll be living and studying with me. Life has been dull with just myself for company."

Rebekah led them through a grand hall and into a library overlooking the rear courtyard, bare of any greenery due to the winter's cold. The library was so resplendent in books that Meg could barely catch her breath. Never had she seen so many volumes in a private home, not even in Petrus Muller's library. The books appeared to be in Arabic, Latin, and Greek. She ran her fingers over the bindings, amazed at the treasures found inside such a house.

"We will work in here. I think it is a fitting place for tutorials, wouldn't you agree?" Rebekah asked. "Njata?"

"Yes, oh, yes!" Njata couldn't resist. He raced to the bookshelves and stroked the books as if they were living creatures. "These would put to shame even the caliph's library."

Rebekah smiled. "My father was a master of phisik and a philosopher. He collected manuscripts from all over the world. He was curious about everything pertaining to medicine. And

I think he was well loved by Christian and Jew alike." She motioned toward the hall. "For now, let me show you to your rooms. Why don't you rest and we'll start lessons in one hour."

Despite the promises the books held for her, Meg's spirits flagged as she climbed the stairs to her room. She would no longer be studying by firelight in Madame Tisserand's tiny cottage. No longer leaning over Gerard's shoulder to read his notes and to smell his skin and hair. No longer accidentally touching his fingers as he pointed to a particular word. No longer feeling her heart skip a beat.

Once she closed the door to her room, Meg gave vent to her feelings of loss. Her thirst for knowledge could never be slaked until she read and read, learned from the best, practiced on patients, and later wrote a medical book of her own. But to do that, she needed a teacher, no *many* teachers of the utmost renown. A Jewish healer was not what she had in mind.

She stared out the window at the red-tiled rooftops of Montpellier. Children ran through the streets ducking in and out of doorways, stealing what they could. A tinsmith peddling his wares cursed at them. Women returned from the well carrying pails of water. Some flirted, others hurried to waiting chores in their kitchens. The tinsmith pushed his cart to a stop in front of a housewife who gestured pointedly to a candle holder in her hands. Broken, she shouted. The tinsmith raised his shoulders. Not my work, he seemed to say.

There was a knock at the door, and Rebekah peeked into the room. "May I come in?"

"Yes, of course." Meg wiped away the tears. She knew her cheeks were blotchy and her eyes red, but hoped Rebekah wouldn't notice.

"I am so happy that you and Njata will live here. I haven't had anyone to talk to in so long," Rebekah said.

Meg smiled tightly, fearful that if she uttered any sound, she'd cry again.

Rebekah stood beside her and watched the haggling on the

street below. The tinsmith was now shouting at the housewife.

"He'll get the sorry end of the bargain with that one," Rebekah said. "Most of my patients pay me in coin or services, even eggs or barter, but she has never paid a penny, even when I cured her of a fever last summer. She's tightfisted. See?"

The tinsmith pushed his cart away. The housewife had her hands full of tin candle holders. Meg imagined she hadn't paid so much as a *sous* for her bounty.

"Let's go downstairs," Rebekah suggested. "I've had my cook lay a table of sweets. There's nothing better to heal a broken heart." Rebekah put her arm around Meg's shoulders and squeezed when Meg looked at her in surprise. "Yes, Sorianus told me about your friend Gerard. He suspected more than platonic affection. I've had my heart broken a time or two. I know the signs."

After gorging on dried fruit, sweet pudding, tarts, and miniature marzipan cakes, Meg felt somewhat better. Her stomach, though not her heart, was now full. She joined Njata and Rebekah in the library. When she entered, they were talking about Njata's duties as curator of the library for the Caliph of Grenada.

"Ah, here you are," Rebekah said. "Feeling better?"

"Yes, thank you," Meg answered.

Rebekah pointed to two elaborately carved chairs at the end of the table. "Sit please."

"I want to tell you about myself to assure you of my training," Rebekah said. Her father, she explained, taught at the University of Montpellier medical school until the Jews were expelled from the city. "As women are not allowed in university, I learned at my father's shoulder as girls have always done. You know about that yourself, having learned from Master William." She smiled at Meg as if they shared a secret.

"Yes, mistress. And Master Sorianus spoke highly of you."

"Very kind of him." Rebekah patted her knees. "Now, enough of me. Master Sorianus tells me that you had to stand before the faculty and the bishop before they would allow you to enter the medical school. That was brave of you."

"Thank you," Meg said.

"But your time at university was not a success, I take it."

Meg pursed her lips. "At first, I was thrilled beyond measure to think I might attend class, but the faculty required that I be hidden away from the men. I even entered by a separate entrance. The wooden screen that hid me also prevented me from seeing the books and sometimes, because I was hidden in the corner of the room, I could barely hear. At night I would try to catch up with Master Njata's help, but one can only do so much."

"They expected you to fail, even made it easy for you to do so. And then you dared to speak on your own. Oh, yes, Master Sorianus told me everything. He is fond of you and was greatly saddened when you were expelled."

Meg said nothing. What was there to say? It was done. University was over. Without the degree from the Schola Medica and the license granted by the University of Montpellier and the Bishop of Maguelone, it meant nothing.

"Well, let us begin," Rebekah said as she opened a large book and smoothed the vellum, caressing the letters. "You shall not fail under my roof. I can assure you of that. We will start with Maimonides."

Njata jumped and whispered "Oh!" as if the King of France had just entered the room.

"What is it?" Meg asked.

"My apologies," Njata said. "I was just surprised. I have translated Maimonides. Astonishing cleverness of mind. You will be thrilled to read his work."

"Yes. You're right," Rebekah said. "His philosophy of medicine is based on the conviction that a healthy body is necessary for a healthy soul. Simple. Profound. And true."

Meg saw nothing profound or astonishing in such a concept. Whoever this Maimonides was, he would certainly lack in comparison to a learned English doctor of phisik.

Njata cleared his throat. "May I ask you a question, Mistress Rebekah?"

"You live here by yourself?"

"Yes."

"Your father?"

"Expelled with the other Jews."

"And your mother?"

"Dead. She died when I was twelve years before the Jews were banished the first time. Thankfully, she did not live to see us suffering so. My father and I . . ." She looked over Njata's head as the past played out in her mind's eye. "We left Montpellier thinking we would never return."

Rebekah lifted her head to the sky as the clouds parted and sunshine filled the courtyard. She closed her eyes against the brightness and spoke as if talking to herself. Meg had to lean forward to hear her words. "I have been a terrible daughter. My mother is in the Jewish Cemetery outside the city walls. I should tend her grave, but I've been too frightened to go there alone." She opened her eyes and blinked.

"We would be happy to accompany you," Njata said.

"That is kind of you," Rebekah murmured.

They were about to resume reading when there was a knock at the front door. A servant padded to Rebekah and informed her that a patient needed her.

Rebekah rose, but then turned to Meg. "Come with me, please. You might as well join me in the flesh and blood of medicine."

Meg followed Rebekah into a small antechamber off the front hall. Sitting in the room was a thin young woman cradling a sleeping baby. The woman raised her head. Meg had never seen eyes so vacant. They could have been portals to a bottomless well.

"Tell me, Jehanne, what is wrong today?" Rebekah asked. "Is it the baby? Still crying?"

"No," the woman said dully. "She no longer cries."

"Ah. Well, let us have a look then." Carefully, Rebekah took the swaddled baby out of Jehanne's arms. Meg had observed new mothers whispering, cuddling, kissing, or saying sweet nonsense words to their babies. And unless their babies were extremely sick, they smiled as they handed the baby to a midwife. In fact, a newborn baby invited smiles all around, but not for this mother. She stared at the baby as if it were a strange creature.

"Meg, why don't you hold Fleur? In fact, unwrap her." Rebekah looked at Meg pointedly as if to say, examine her for anything wrong. "I'll take care of Jehanne."

Meg placed the sleeping baby on the table. The child's lethargy was worrying. Most babies squirmed and fussed when examined. This one lay still, eyes closed. Meg pulled at a corner of the swaddling wrap. Immediately, the smell of urine and feces overwhelmed her, and she turned her head to take a breath.

The child was filthy. And desperately thin. Her limbs were stick-like and her abdomen bloated. Her umbilicus was black with crusted scabs through which rivulets of pus escaped. Meg felt for a pulse at the baby's neck. There was a heartbeat, but it was feeble.

Suddenly, Fleur opened her eyes. Placid pools of lapis lazuli stared at Meg. Her thin lips attempted a smile and her fingers curved over Meg's thumb. Meg's heart pounded. She stood mesmerized, as if she could see into the depths of a heavenly soul. And then the baby's eyes closed and her fingers fell away from Meg's hand.

Meg jumped as Rebekah asked a question. "Meg? The baby?"

"Yes, yes. I, uh, she's extremely thin. And needs to be cleaned." She turned her back on the mother who was now dressed only in her chemise. "Her pulse is weak," Meg whispered to Rebekah, "and she appears to be very sick."

"It is called ill thrift. Jehanne has no milk. And the baby is wasting."

"Perhaps her nipples . . ."

"There is nothing wrong with Jehanne's nipples. In fact, there is nothing wrong with her physically, other than the lack of milk."

"What do you mean?"

"I will tell you later."

Jehanne, whose empty eyes and stillness suggested a lack of wits, shrieked and pointed to the opposite wall. "He tells me! He tells me! But I say no, Mistress Rebekah, and still he tells me."

"Who, Jehanne? Who tells you?" Rebekah asked.

"Him." She pointed past Meg to the bare wall. "Him. The Devil!" She clutched Rebekah's arm.

The hairs on the back of Meg's neck prickled. She spun and stared at the wall behind her. A bare wall. There was no one else in the room, certainly no creature from Hell.

"No, Jehanne, listen to me. There is no one there." Rebekah struggled to free herself from Jehanne's grasp. "You have had a difficult time, and now we must try to make your baby better. We'll find a wet nurse. And I'll have Meg here look in on you. She'll bring you some food and take care of Fleur while you rest."

"The Devil wants her. He says I must give him my baby."

"Well, the Devil can't have her. He'll have to take another child. This one belongs to you."

The woman lifted her head. There was a glimmer of something in her recognition of Rebekah, a flicker of understanding, a small sign that she loved this child.

Meg bathed the baby and wrapped her in clean swaddling while Jehanne drank some broth and rested. When Meg placed a clean and sweetly-smelling Fleur in Jehanne's arms, the woman held her baby like a stack of wood crooked in her elbows, her hands hanging limply. Meg took her hands and forced them onto Fleur's body, folding her fingers tighter around the bundle, showing her how to embrace the baby.

"Rest easy," Rebekah said to Jehanne. "Here is a bit of meat and vegetables for tonight." She kissed the baby's forehead and hugged the strangely silent mother, who gave her no acknowledgment. "You will grow to love her. I promise."

As Jehanne walked listlessly away from Rebekah and Meg, she balanced Fleur in the crook of her elbows, her hands hanging limply as if she could not bear to touch the child. Even Njata appeared concerned.

"I would be glad to walk you home," he said to Jehanne. "Perhaps I might hold your baby?"

He looked back at Rebekah who smiled. He reached for Fleur, balancing both the child and the package of food.

Meg was stunned given Njata's confession that he preferred books to medicine, being sickened himself by the sick. Jehanne and her baby must have tugged at his scholar's heart.

After they left, Rebekah said, "Follow me, please." She led Meg into the kitchen and pointed to a bucket of water. "Wash your hands."

Meg held out at her palms. "But my hands are not dirty."

"It is a Jewish rule that we wash our hands after seeing patients. In fact, we wash our hands several times a day. Our teachers say, 'The washing of hands and feet is more effective than any remedy in the world.' To be a healer in my house, you must wash your hands and your feet."

Rebekah lifted the bucket and poured water over Meg's hands as Meg palmed a bar of soap smelling of olive oil and lime.

"Will Fleur live?" Meg asked.

"Perhaps."

"You are not certain?"

"Some women find the burden of a baby to be a burden of the mind. Some lose their wits and their babies suffer."

"She should bathe her baby more often. And feed her. The child was filthy and starving. Perhaps Jehanne is just lazy. And where is her husband?"

Meg thought of her sister Maud who had—how many children did she have by now? Three at last count, but that was years ago. Maud loved them all with equanimity. She doled out equal amounts of smacks and kisses to her dirty-faced brood.

"There is no husband. Like other women who have no way to earn a living, she earns her living by the flat of her back. Is she to be judged because someone whispered fancy words in her ear—a woman who was desperate? I thought you wanted to be a healer, not a judge and jury."

Meg's face grew hot. She felt as if Rebekah had slapped her. "No, Mistress."

"We heal the sick and comfort the dying. We do not judge."

"I apologize. I should have known better. I was thinking of the child and not the mother."

"Life is hard for Jehanne. We should gladden her heart where we can."

"Yes, mistress." Meg dried her hands on a towel and hung it on a hook above the bucket. "May I ask one more question, if you don't mind? Do you see all your patients here?"

"No. I go to the patient's home as well. But some patients, like Jehanne, are more comfortable here."

"Will I be able to help with patients as I did today?"

"That is two questions and, yes, we will see patients together. I learned at my father's side by reading and through patient care. There is not one without the other."

Meg silently agreed. Having served Master William, she knew it was the only way to learn. Books couldn't provide all the knowledge one needed. Indeed, just before Jehanne arrived they had been studying a verse by Maimonides: "*Do not consider it proof because it is written in books. A liar who will deceive with his tongue will not hesitate to do the same with his pen.*"

Meg breathed a sigh of, well, if not quite joy, then relief. Rebekah would allow her to see patients. She would learn at her side. She would read and then practice on the sick. "There is not one without the other," Rebekah had said.

Her dreams of being a doctor of phisik and wearing the long red robe, the uniform of her profession, license in hand from the university masters, was a distant dream. No, not a dream. A delusion. An expectation that could not be achieved owing to the circumstances of her birth. She had been born a female, and even worse, born with a disfigurement that the great masters were convinced would frighten her patients and taint babes in the womb. There was simply not a thing she could do about either problem. Oh, she could dress in men's clothes and pretend to be a man speaking in a deep voice, but without the requisite beard and *membrum virile*, the center of all thought and deed for men, she was destined to stay a girl. And likewise, she had as much hope of changing her disfig-urement, though better now than her horrible pig-like face at birth—at least according to Alice—as Gerard had of growing another head.

So, she would learn under Rebekah, and then apprentice to another sympathetic teacher. She would continue dissections and surgery lessons with William if possible. One day, when she was older, she would write a book about her experiences in medicine and surgery. The book would be her legacy to wom-en everywhere.

She would include only information which pertained to women, like the Trota book William had given her. Her book would also include recipes, beauty instructions, the care of infants, teething, fevers, pains in the womb, the problems of the breast, and so on. Perhaps she would discover the mysteri-ous origin of breast milk, which the ancient Aristotle said was menstrual blood turned white.

While Rebekah and Njata prepared the midday meal, Meg entered the courtyard adjacent to the library. The weather was brisk, the breeze chilly, as it should be in November, but the sun was shining. She had to admit she liked the passing of seasons in Montpellier, so different from her wet, cold-to-the-bone England. She sat on a bench under an arbor of grape vines, bare twisted branches that promised bountiful sweetness to come in the heat of summer.

November in St. Michael's Mead was busy with preparations for winter, and in her case, taking the pigs to the acorn mast in Sir Henry's forest near Alice's cottage. A memory of ice and pigs, chilblains, and scarce food flashed in her mind's eye and an arrow shot of homesickness struck her heart. It had been years since she left St. Michael's Mead. She missed her sister Maud and her many children. Her mother had died years ago. When William received a letter from Father Fitzhugh with the news of her mother's death, he worried that she might be grieving so much she would return home. Grief was not the word she would use, she told him. Sadness, yes. But her mother's senses had flown years before Meg left for France. In truth, her mother was a madwoman. It was hard to love a madwoman.

Her father was still alive in St. Nicholas Leper Hospital in York, as far as she knew. Brother Adolphus wrote to William occasionally with news of her father and the latest gossip. She wrote back to the priest telling him of her classes at the Schola Medica and asking him to read the letter to her father. She didn't tell him she had been banished from the university.

She felt her face flame as she remembered informing Master William at Lady Elisabeth Despenser's terrible birthing that she, Meg, would be the greatest healer in all of Christendom. She had been haughty and cocksure. Knowing William's wrath now, she couldn't believe she had been so foolhardy.

Perhaps by summer Jehanne would have found a husband to take care of her. Perhaps her daughter Fleur would be thriving and growing on Jehanne's milk. By then the courtyard would be redolent with the scents of lavender and roses, figs ripening, and herbs opening to the heat. Insects would fly in and out of the fig tree, chancing a bite of flesh.

She wondered who would present herself at Rebekah's

door tomorrow. Perhaps it would be a woman with a strange malady that she could write about in her medical book.

She smiled to herself, pleased with the thought of leaving a book as a timeless gift to other women. But for now, she needed to meet Rebekah's strict standards. Washing your hands several times a day? Meg wouldn't have any skin left. But if that's what it took to earn a smile and "well done" from Rebekah, she would do it.

On the other hand, earning a smile and "well done" from Master Njata would be difficult. He was a strict teacher, stern and exacting. He translated the Arab books for her, but she had to commit the text to memory and there was so much of it. He was patient, unlike William, but he demanded long hours of work. Still, she had to admit that the Arab practice of medicine was more advanced than the English doctors of phisik or the surgeons, a fact she would never admit to Njata. Now that she was used to his ways, she enjoyed their time together, though she would never admit that, either. At least she could actually see the medical books, unlike her days spent behind the screen, frustrated and angry.

She realized with surprise that the education she would receive from Rebekah and Master Njata was likely far more advanced than the Schola Medica. Perhaps she could incorporate Arab learning in the book she planned to write. And Hebrew learning as well. Perhaps being expelled had been a gift, albeit one that was financed by Master William. His money allowed her to be in a private school of one, where discussions of her sex and disfigurement were never heard.

She rose to join Njata and Rebekah. She was hungry. Her stomach rumbled. She missed William. He was in Bologna now. William, Rebekah, Njata, and don't forget Gerard—her family. They believed in her. They wanted her to win.

For the first time since Master Horlogus banished her from his classroom, Meg felt an inkling of hope in her chest, like the flutter of a small brown bird spreading its wings.

If you enjoyed reading *The Solitary Sparrow,* the first book in *The Margaret Chronicles*, look for the second book, A Pelican in the Wilderness, to be published in late 2024. Meg continues her journey to overcome prejudice and to treat women of the 14th century as a doctor of phisik despite epidemics, war, and the possible loss of the man she loves.

Also, if you enjoyed The Solitary Sparrow, please consider leaving a review online. Reviews are crucial for the success of authors. A review doesn't have to be long – one or two sentences will do. Also important are word-of-mouth recommendations. And thank you. I deeply appreciate it.

About Atmosphere Press

Founded in 2015, Atmosphere Press was built on the principles of Honesty, Transparency, Professionalism, Kindness, and Making Your Book Awesome. As an ethical and author-friendly hybrid press, we stay true to that founding mission today.

If you're a reader, enter our giveaway for a free book here:

SCAN TO ENTER
BOOK GIVEAWAY

If you're a writer, submit your manuscript for consideration here:

SCAN TO SUBMIT
MANUSCRIPT

And always feel free to visit Atmosphere Press and our authors online at atmospherepress.com. See you there soon!

Acknowledgments

The number of people I've encountered over the life of this project would fill a village—a village of fellow writers, interested readers, and civilian reporters whose favorite question was: "Are you finished with that book yet?" Yes, it takes a village—or in my case, a universe.

I used to explain that I worked at glacial speed. Today, with the climate change speeding up the disintegration of glaciers, perhaps I should say I write at a snail's pace. In my case, historical research, meticulous world-building, and OCD-like perfectionism combine to make writing historical fiction a lengthy process. I was advised to follow the "good enough" route, i.e., don't make it the *best* it can be, *just good enough.* I couldn't do it; that's not how I roll. Which explains why my daughters, Amanda and Meredith, grew up with Meg and all the other characters I've kept in my head for years. And why one day I called Meg to dinner instead of Meredith. She understood.

I want to thank my grandmother, a first-grade teacher who taught me to read when I was three and who encouraged my writing. She loved books. One of my best memories is sharing books together and asking, "Are you finished with it yet?" I'm just sorry she didn't live to see my book in print.

To my father, Bill Norwood, and his wife, LaDonna, who gave me the financial wiggle-room I needed to get this book published. Without you, *The Solitary Sparrow* would still be in a drawer.

Cheers to my sister, Mary, and her husband, Frankie, who were positive that publication day would come, and who made it possible through generous gifts. And gratitude to my sister, Judy, who stuck by me, although we had some Jerry Springer moments. Sorry, sis.

My deep thanks to two of my biggest supporters, Lynda Fitzgerald and Kerry Denney, founders of the Atlanta Writers' Collective, who read the first chapters and encouraged me to keep going. To the other members of that group who came and went for ten years, I still keep your suggestions in mind while I do revisions. A special thanks to the "verb lady."

When I first finished *The Solitary Sparrow* and thought I was done at last, a special person helped me see how much better it could be. I met agent Sarah Smith at a conference. We clicked immediately and she agreed to represent me. Sarah tried her best to find a place for *The Solitary Sparrow* but alas, fate was not on our side and she and I had to part ways. Thank you, Sarah, for your constancy, for your willingness to take on a debut author, and for your continued interest. If only every agent could be like you.

To the women in the Women's Fiction Writers Association, particularly the Writing Date and the Hist Fic group, who have served as mentors, cheerleaders, co-commiserators, and all-round pals even though we have never met in person. In addition, my writer friends and book coaches with Author Accelerator have been there for me when I hit bottom. Thanks for picking me up. For Margaret McNellis, Susanne Dunlap, Joan Fernandez, Gabi Coatsworth, Krista White, Stephanie Claypool, Carla Damron, Michelle Montgomery, and others whose smiling faces I see each day and to those who have been beta readers for all the myriad pieces that comprise a book, bless you for taking time to give me your opinions.

To Daphene B., Linda M., Cheryl D., and my other wonderful coaching clients—you have taught me so much about writing. There is truth in the old saying that to teach is to learn. Thank you. I wish you much joy on your writing journey.

To Ray Russell and the members of the Asheville Short

Story Group, your discussions of short story successes and shortcomings have been fun and enlightening. Thank you for supporting me and other writers.

To the ladies of the Guided Autobiography group, Talulah Cartright, Christine Waters, Anne Dillingham, and Donna Hutchins, it's been wonderful to meet again after so many years. Thank you for trusting me with your deepest thoughts and for reminding me that not everything you remember about being a teenager is bad. A special thank you is due to Christine Waters for her generous gift.

I owe a debt to many people I've encountered over the years who knew of my struggles. To members of the Atlanta Writers Group, the Atlanta Writers Conference, former colleagues at my jobs, fellow archaeologists at the York Archaeological Trust, fellow students at the University of York Medieval Archaeology program, the North Carolina Cultural Resources Western North Carolina office (particularly Heather South and Jeff Futch), and old friends, thank you for taking an interest in my passion for the medieval world.

I would be remiss if I didn't mention one particular person, Kathy MacNeill, who has been my best friend since we obsessed over *The Secret Garden* in the sixth grade, sixty-four years ago. We've been there for each other through thick and thin. Thank you for cheering me on. Now, get out there and sell some books for me!

Finally, thank you to everyone on the Atmosphere team, who have treated my book with respect and professionalism. Particular thanks to Kyle McCord, acquisitions director; Alex Kale, my amazing editor; Asata Radcliffe, an extraordinary developmental genius; and Ronaldo Alves, a magical art director. In addition, I would like to acknowledge artist Matthew Fielder, who created the evocative cover that brought the sparrow to life.

I remember reading historical fiction as a young girl and devouring the maps and illustrations included in the books. I really, really, really wanted a map in *The Solitary Sparrow* but wasn't sure it could be done. How could someone draw a place that existed only in my imagination? UK illustrator and artist Alan Gilliland took the challenge. His charming map of St. Micheal's Mead surpassed anything I envisioned. Cheers, Alan.

It is my opinion that a book is not complete without readers. The fact that you have chosen to read this book fills my heart with the deepest gratitude. It's been a long, loooooong journey. There were times when I truly wondered whether I was crazy to keep going. I was giving up nights and weekends for a reward that remained hidden. But I knew that if I didn't finish I would always regret it. Besides, Meg, Alice, Gerard, and William wouldn't let me. They interfered with my dreams, bothered me when I was driving, taking a shower, working at my day job, or running down rabbit holes on the Internet (which sometimes occurred at my day job, but don't tell on me). Writing is a slog and sometimes it's an epiphany. So, I have a message for wanna-be writers. The rules are easy but hard: it takes persistence and determination. And you have to show up to the job—every day.

If I have missed anyone and failed to thank you, please forgive me. I had a lot more memory cells when I started this book.

Life has a way of interfering with writing. At long last, after two marriages, two children, two grandchildren, fourteen jobs, two college degrees, twenty-three moves (one of which was abroad), cancer, other health issues, family issues, and wrinkles, I have finished *The Solitary Sparrow*. Now onward to the end of the series.

About the Author

Photo by Heather South

LORRAINE NORWOOD would love to hop on the Wayback Machine to visit the medieval period in England, as long as she can take a boatload of antibiotics with her. She has participated in archaeological digs in England where her most memorable excavation was a 12th-century cesspit in York. *The Solitary Sparrow* is the first book of her medieval series, *The Margaret Chronicles*. She is at work on the second book, *A Pelican in the Wilderness*, which continues the story of Meg of St. Michael's Mead. Lorraine is a member of the Women's Fiction Writers Association and Author Accelerator. She shares a room of her own with a 13-year-old Lab named Sally who offers writing support in exchange for kisses and food. She lives in the mountains of Western North Carolina. She can be found at www.lorrainenorwood.com where you will find links to social media.